I0615268

Battleborne

Book IV

Dungeon Master

By

Dave Willmarth

Chapter 1

Max stuck his head up from behind the boulder that was sheltering him. Almost immediately, a rock the size of a basketball smashed into the boulder, causing him to duck down again to avoid shrapnel, but not before he got a look at the enemy.

Advancing up the pass below him, a force of about a hundred orcs, with a dozen ogres behind them, were hurling stones and loosing arrows at Max and his fellow War Dogs guild members. Blake had invited him to participate in the raid up into the mountains above their new guild house, on the estate that the gnome had received as dungeon loot.

There were thirty guild members on this raid, including Max, his fellow Battleborne, Dalia, Nessa, and a mixture of dwarves, orcs, gnomes, a couple dworcs, and even Falcon, the human soldier from Westreach.

"Just regular orcs, no red eyes." Max reported through party chat. "Same with the ogres."

"I had no' heard o' red-eyed ogres." Dalia raised an eyebrow at him from behind a different boulder several paces to his left. "Or anythin' but orcs."

"Neither have I. It just seemed worth mentioning." Max grinned at her. "I don't think I'd want to take on a red-eyed berserker ogre."

"That female down there, the one near the back… any chance we could capture her instead of killing her?" Dylan's tone was wistful as he stared down at the advancing ogres. "Maybe she's actually a nice girl, led astray by her tribe."

"Why don't you just trot down there and ask for her number, big sexy." Blake teased.

"C'mon man… at least you've got other gnomes around to hang with. I haven't had any ogre luvins since I left my starter village to find you guys. An ogre has needs, yaknow?"

"Bah! Gnomes? I got my eye on that orc friend of Smitty's wife. The one working the bar at Eats N Treats. She's diggin my vibe." He hopped up on a boulder and shot a couple hip thrusts Dylan's way before a rock that was larger than him whistled past, narrowly missing him as he dodged. He lost his balance and fell, Dylan catching him as both corporals and most of the raid laughed.

"She'd break you in half and take the xp without a second thought, lil dude." Smitty winked at the flustered gnome.

"But what a way to go!" Blake's grin was wide.

"Can gnomes and orcs even… procreate?" Falcon asked. "And what would that look like?" Max couldn't help but grin. The man was loosening up, getting used to their battle banter.

"I'll let you know!" Blake shot him a double thumbs-up, earning more chuckles from the group.

4

"Does this world have cigars? We might need cigars…" Smitty mused. "How long does it take to cook up an orc-gnome bun in the oven? An orgnome? A gnorc?"

"Enough. We've got work to do." Max mock-growled at them before adding, "You ready over there, loverboy?" The ogre rolled his eyes, but nodded. He glanced upward briefly before hefting a large stone and cocking his arm back as if to pitch a fastball down at the advancing force. Instead, he hurled it upward at a pyramid-shaped pile of boulders he'd carefully stacked atop the cliff roughly thirty feet above and ahead of the raid party. The stone flew so fast that Max thought he heard the air whistle around it. It smashed into one of the boulders at the bottom of the pile, dislodging it and starting a massive rockfall.

"Strike!" Smitty punched the ogre in the shoulder as they watched several tons of rock drop down into the narrow pass just in front of the orcs. "Look at em! I think that big one in front just shit himself."

The boulders struck bottom and bounced off the opposite wall before ricocheting down toward the orcs and ogres. Many of the orcs froze, while others had the presence of mind to hide behind outcroppings or press themselves tight against the cliffside in hopes of avoiding becoming orc paste. Roars of anger were mixed with screams of pain as the tightly packed targets were mowed down. Some only suffered glancing blows from bouncing boulders, while others were obliterated by direct hits. One of the lead ogres gamely tried to catch a boulder about half

5

his size, but was knocked off his feet, his chest crushed, one arm broken by the impact.

"Oooh! Ouch!" Dylan sympathized. "His dodgeball kung fu is weak."

"He's down, but he's still holding the rock." Smitty observed. "Does that mean you're out? Or he gets a free shot at you? Been a while since I played dodgeball. What's the ruling, boss?"

Before Max could answer, Dylan snorted. "If he gets back up, I'll give him a free shot."

"Dodgeball?" Falcon asked, watching the carnage below.

"It's a great game! We'll show you when we get back." Smitty stood up straight and fired an arrow at an orc that had its back pressed against the cliffside. The arrow punched through the side of its skull, and it fell limply to the ground. "Hey, watch this guys... bank shot!" He nocked another arrow, took careful aim, and loosed. The arrow sped down the slope, glancing off the stone wall right next to a boulder, ricocheting into the shoulder of an orc that had been peering over top of a stone. The orc was pushed out from behind its cover to be slammed by a passing stone about the size of its head.

"Lucky shot." Blake muttered. "No way you could do that again."

Smitty shrugged. "Don't have to. I can brag about it working the first time."

The orc's shoulder had been broken by the rock, but it wasn't dead. Blake raised a hand and sent a lightning bolt into its face, finishing it off before smirking at the scout. "When you brag, be sure n tell folks you needed me to kill it for you."

Max watched the massacre below, doing his best to get a count of the survivors who were still combat capable. After several long seconds, he called out in party chat. "Alright, maybe forty of them left, including eight ogres. Officers, we're on the big guys. The rest of you, finish off the orcs. Dylan, you take the lead, we'll follow behind."

The ogre tank just grunted as he raised his shield and equipped a massive axe in his other hand. It was the one they had looted from the Westreach dungeon boss roughly a month earlier. Pausing for a moment, he looked around, then moved over next to Max. With a grunt of effort, he kicked the boulder Max had been using for cover, causing it to roll down the hill. Roaring a challenge that echoed off the walls of the pass, he charged down behind the rolling stone. The others took up their weapons and followed behind, except Smitty and Blake, who remained up top where they could shoot over their party members' heads.

The rock picked up speed, and Max thought it might crush a dozen or so more orcs. Until it struck one of the already fallen rocks in its path, and bounced high above even Dylan's head. When it came back down, it crushed three orcs and an already wounded ogre before continuing on its path. Two of the ogres who were still on their feet turned and fled downhill ahead of the boulder.

Dylan ignored the orcs still in his path, bashing any who got too close with his shield as he ran past. With his downhill momentum, he didn't need to use any charge abilities before slamming into the first ogre he reached. His shield rang like a tower bell, and the ogre on the receiving end of the blow was knocked off his feet. Dylan stepped forward and buried his axe deep in its chest.

Max picked a large stone about thirty paces farther down the pass and cast *Boom!* on it just as the two fleeing ogres were approaching. The stone shattered, peppering them with hundreds of sharp shards and causing them both to stumble.

From behind him, Smitty and Blake were punishing another ogre with arrows and ice bolts. Smitty shot it in the face, and when it raised its hands, Blake peppered its oversized belly with ice, the sharp bolts sinking deep into its gut.

The newer, lower leveled guildmembers were spreading out behind the officers, shouting insults and war cries as they battled orcs individually or in pairs. They were all melee fighters, using sword and shield, axe and shield, or twin blades of various types. The orcs were rattled, some of them already injured, and the War Dogs cut them down even though they were outnumbered.

Max shook his head as Nessa appeared behind one of the ogres, leaping onto its back and using both her daggers to slice its throat, nearly beheading it in the process.

Dylan left his axe embedded in the first ogre and produced a boar spear, which he thrust into the side of another ogre, shattering ribs and puncturing a lung before yanking it free. He then spun to his left and hurled the long, heavy spear like it weighed nothing, embedding it in another ogre's throat.

Falcon remained near Dalia, using his shield to protect her while stabbing and slashing at the nearest orcs. He finished off two that had been crushed but not killed, driving his blade into one's heart, then the other's eye. Dalia focused on healing the lower level raiders, as her group had yet to suffer any serious injury. The enemy were mostly between level twenty and thirty, no match for Max's team.

Their only real moment of danger came when Dylan used his shield to deflect a watermelon sized stone thrown by one of the few remaining ogres. He'd correctly angled his shield so that the rock deflected up and away from him, reducing the impact on his shield and shield arm. Unfortunately, that rock knocked loose other rocks high on the cliff, and now Dylan was the one facing a rockslide. As Max warned the others and backed away up the slope, their tank rushed to the base of the cliff. He threw himself to the ground with his back to the wall, pulled his legs up into a fetal position, and set his shield over top of him like a blanket. Both Max and Dalia cast heals on him as dirt, pebbles, and rocks up to the size of cart wheels buried their tank.

Half a dozen dwarves ran toward the rock pile as the dust cleared, while the rest of the raid formed a half-circle perimeter around them. The hardy dwarves lifted and hurled away rocks with ease as they frantically dug their way toward Dylan. Max could see that his health bar was hovering steadily at about thirty percent, but couldn't see him to heal him.

After about a minute, the rocks shifted at one end of the pile, then burst outward as one of the ogre's feet kicked free. Max and Dalia both focused heals on the dusty appendage, then did it again a moment later. They kept the ogre alive while the dwarves extracted him from the rockslide.

Satisfied that his corporal would live, Max surveyed the area of the pass beyond and below their perimeter. A single ogre was limping his way down the hill at the mouth of the pass, retreating alongside a half dozen orcs, none of whom were moving very fast. He considered sending the recruits after them, but decided against it. The enemy was broken, and the lower level guildies had already earned a respectable amount of xp from the battle. Which had been half the purpose of this excursion.

Back on his feet, their tank thanked the dwarves, then turned toward Blake, giving him a pleading look while waving his hand down his body at the thick layer of dust that covered every inch of him. The gnome chuckled, and an ogre-sized spray of water nearly knocked Dylan down the hill a second later. He quickly spun around so that the stream got all of him, then sent the gnome a thumbs-up.

Max watched as Dylan picked his way through the rubble and corpses, searching for the female ogre he'd identified at the start of the fight. He found her a couple minutes later, and cursed quietly. She'd obviously had a run-in with at least one large rock during the landslides, and hadn't survived.

"Sorry, bud." Max approached from behind and gave him a sympathetic pat on the shoulder. "She probably would have just made Princess jealous, anyway."

The ogre shook his head. "We need to visit my starter village, boss. If I don't find some… companionship soon, I'm gonna bust."

Max nodded. "I've actually got that on my list. I want to see if we can recruit them. Lure them to Stormhaven with food, and whatever else might work. Having a whole tribe of ogre tanks to help protect our holdings would be a huge help."

"Get it? Huge help?" Smitty snickered as he looted a nearby corpse. "Cuz they're great big ogres."

Both Dylan and Max rolled their eyes and ignored the scout. They waited while the others looted the remaining bodies, then Max led them all back up the pass and over the top. From there they could see across the foothills to the forest beyond. Barely visible in a clearing near the last hill was Blake's manor, also known as the War Dogs' Den.

Max motioned to Blake, who located the earth mage they'd brought along. Blake had recruited three of them from the Mages' Guild novice class he'd been part of. Over the previous month they'd been constructing walls or paving roads for Max in various locations. Their first project had been constructing high walls near each of the main cavern exits outside Deepcrag.

Now Max motioned to the summit of the pass, talking to the mage. "Just a simple wall that completely blocks the pass, gate in the middle, and a basic tower for scouts and archers. Three stories should be high enough. From there they can see any force coming up the pass from a long way away, and signal us at the manor.

Already familiar with Max's preferences, the mage simply nodded and got to work. Though he'd been included in the raid so that he might share in the experience, he'd been kept out of the fighting specifically so that he'd have the mana to quickly construct the barrier. That was part of the deal they'd made. The mages were being power-leveled by Max's people, either the guild, or Stormhaven war parties, in return for their help in securing the kingdom. Falcon had even taken them, as part of a larger party, through the Westreach dungeon. As payment, they'd improved the walls and structures of the nearby fort that guarded the dungeon.

"This has been fun, but I'm afraid I must return to my duties in the city." Falcon offered Max a hand to shake. The man had finally learned not to bow to Max when they weren't at court.

"Don't forget!" Blake called out as Falcon moved toward his raptor mount, which had been secured to a tree just off the path. "Any of your guys want to join the War Dogs, we're recruiting. They don't all have to be soldiers.

We need hunters, at least one gardener or farmer, probably two. Maybe even a few old timers who just want to stand guard shifts at the Den, polish armor, sharpen swords, and brag about the good old days."

"I'll see what I can do." The human soldier hopped up into his saddle, gave them all a wave, and set his mount trotting down the path.

The recruits all followed on foot, while Max and his party remained with the mage while he worked. Max found a rock to sit on, and pulled out his ever-changing, ever-growing *to-do* list. He nodded, pleased with himself at the number of items he'd already scratched off as completed. Before he could forget, he made a note about sending Dylan back to his home village. Max didn't have the free time to go himself, but he trusted his corporal to get the job done.

In the forty or so days since he and his group had conquered the dungeon and solidified their alliance with the humans of Westreach, Max and his people had been busy. The corporals got together with Smitty's wife, Birona, and started their restaurant, Eats N Treats. They'd chosen a location in Stormhaven city, spent several days working out recipes for both food and drinks, then opened the place up. The menu featured cheeseburgers, grilled cheese sandwiches, tacos, pizza, chili, both hot and mild, breakfast burritos, as well as their closest possible version of milk shakes, candied fruit, and churros for desserts. The food had been instantly popular among citizens and visitors alike, and they were already planning additional locations in Darkholm and Westreach.

Max had placed a portal at the guild house, allowing his guildmates to quickly travel back and forth in case of emergency. There had been a lot of monsters and forest creatures to cull, and the small force of human soldiers that Farstrider had stationed at the manor were happy to be relieved. All of the party members except Max had spent a week wandering the hills and mountain passes, clearing them and harvesting the loot, which they used to recruit additional members. Most of the recruits had day jobs as guards or soldiers in Stormhaven, taking regular shifts at the manor on their days off.

Meanwhile Max took care of kingdom business. He welcomed more than a thousand additional orcs that Or'gral had brought in, defectors from An'zalor's city. About a third of them were warriors, along with some crafters, merchants, and their families. Another thirty or so that wanted to farm had remained back at the Way Station as the others passed through.

Ironhand's promised reinforcements from the other clans had arrived to help Caretaker protect the Heart Chamber. The other clans had sent young but blooded fighters, all of whom promptly requested to become citizens of Stormhaven. They'd dubbed themselves The Heartstone Guard, setting aside their individual clan affiliations in favor of what they saw as a higher calling. Together with Caretaker, they constructed fortifications at the tunnel entrances, as well as in the chamber where Max had encountered the Tuath. That ancient being had made a brief appearance at Max's keep to congratulate him on restoring the heart, (causing quite the fuss as every dwarf that encountered him dropped what they were doing to bow to the Eldest) then disappeared. Redmane had been beside himself at being able to speak with the Tuath during his visit, and had promptly gotten very drunk in celebration.

Twice in the time since the Heart was restored, red-eyed orcs had attacked the cavern. The first group was only a small warband of thirty orcs, who were quickly massacred. The second attack was more serious, with over two hundred orcs pressing the defenders. They had reported to Max the moment the orcs were spotted, and he'd sent reinforcements through the portal. The mutated orcs had fought to the death, taking half a dozen dwarven defenders with them. Caretaker had kept the growing salamander guardian in reserve for both fights, waiting behind the newly constructed walls in case the orcs had broken through. She was growing rapidly, and the dwarves had adopted her as sort of a mascot. Caretaker had to warn them against overfeeding her after they'd looted the corpses of the orc attackers.

Max had several more lessons from Master Oakstone, and was steadily improving his smithing skill. He'd also spent several hours with Dalia and her father, learning new alchemy recipes. The master alchemist had been puttering around, experimenting with the green elemental crystals Dalia had brought back from the dungeon, and claimed he was on the verge of some kind of breakthrough. They'd also been testing one of the vials of the salamander guardian's blood to see how they might put it to use.

Master Erdun had put a significant dent in Stormhaven's supply of platinum and mithril. He'd crafted another hundred communication rings for Max, in bonded groups of five, ten, and twenty. At the same time, he created and discretely sold several sets of five to private clients, who'd paid prices so high that Max actually whistled when Erdun told him about it. The minotaur had become quite wealthy in a very short period of time. Additionally, the latest batch of rings were an improvement over the originals, with a verified range of one hundred and fifty miles, and a second enchantment that made them into dimensional storage devices.

Max had swapped out the rings he'd initially given his group, and gifted the older set to Farstrider. The human kingdom in total was less than a hundred miles across, so they had more than enough range for his needs.

A cousin of Erdun's had arrived and requested that his clan be allowed to join up. But rather than live in or around the Waystation settlement with Erdun's clan, they asked to live in the valley with the dworcs. Master Pickstone immediately agreed, happy to bolster their defenses with fierce minotaur warriors, and Max smiled as he opened a portal to the dworc village, watching all sixty two members of the clan pass through to the cheering of the dworcs. Their addition more than doubled the population in the village after the recent dworc losses. They'd barely settled in before another wave of red-eyed orcs attacked the village. Pickstone called Max for reinforcements, and the two hundred orcs were put down with minimal casualties, and no fatalities.

When Dalia wasn't working with Max, or healing for one of the guild parties, she and her father spent a lot of time out at the ancient battleground, gathering premium herbs and planting more in the mana-rich soil. She was having a difficult time dealing with the loss of Picklet, and more than once she'd traveled to the dworc village to spend time with his father and friends.

Glitterspindle had nearly started a riot one day when he'd activated the portal to Stormhaven keep and stormed through, shouting for 'the tall stupid orc' with a gaggle of nearly a hundred gnomes scurrying along behind him. The guards at the keep had initially thought it was an invasion, and blood was nearly shed before Redmane managed to calm everyone.

Glitterspindle needed additional materials for his ongoing experiments, and hadn't been able to request them because Max had been avoiding the insane little gnome. He'd been meaning to ask Glitterspindle about unlocking Westreach's portal, but somehow hadn't gotten around to it. Redmane saved Max from a stress headache by putting the gnome directly in touch with the quartermaster, and granting him a significant allowance with which to claim materials.

"Ha! Thank you, stupid orc!" the metallic maniac cackled as he made an about-face and stormed back through the portal, knocking over several of his acolytes in the process. "When my Megamagnificent Orcsmasher is completed, I shall try to remember to spare your stupid orc life!"

Max smiled to himself as he recalled Redmane reporting that development a few moments later.

"Max, I fear I might o' made a mistake." The dwarf had a scowl on his face as he entered Max's study.

"That seems unlikely. But tell me what's happened."

"The crazy metal gnome. He just came through the portal with a hundred gnome acolytes, scared the guards. I stopped 'em from attackin, talked to the gnome meself because I know ye don't like to."

"So far, so good." Max grinned at his friend.

"He complained about not havin enough materials, mostly metal, for his projects. Rather than bother ye, and because I know ye wanted him to keep building portal pedestals, I set him on the quartermaster, and ordered he be given more materials each month."

"Okay, good. I would have done the same. The way I'm burning through portal pedestals, we need him to build as many as possible." Max had felt relieved that Redmane took it upon himself to handle the situation. The mines were producing well, and they could afford to redirect some of the refined metals to the gnome.

"Aye, that's what I thought." Redmane nodded his head, but his scowl didn't fade. "Until he mentioned somethin' called his Megamagnificent Orcsmasher." The dwarf tugged at his beard. "Said when it was finished, he'd spare me life."

"Implying that he plans to use it against Stormhaven?" Max leaned forward and put his elbows on his desk. "He swore the oath. Wouldn't an attack against us trigger a penalty?"

"Aye, the gods would likely end his life if he killed a fellow citizen after takin' that oath." Redmane tugged at his beard again, clearly agitated. "That be the problem."

Max took a minute to think about it. "Because if the gods strike him down, we're out one mechamage that can build portals and such. Or if they don't, we might be forced to kill him ourselves." He paused, taking it a step forward. "Either way, if he dies while attacking Stormhaven, as popular as he is among the gnomes, we might have a war on our hands."

Redmane simply nodded, seeming deep in thought.

"It may just be his insanity talking. Did he call you a stupid orc? We know he's got plans to avenge the attack that destroyed his temple and killed his people. Maybe he's planning to attack An'zalor, and not us?"

The dwarf nodded again. "I know ye don't like talkin' to the gnome, but I'm thinkin' it be necessary now. Get him to show ye what he's buildin', and tell ye his plans fer usin' it."

Max had let out a long sigh. "You're probably right. But if he locks me in his basement again, I'm blasting my way out."

*****

Izgren the grey dwarf thief lay flat on a rooftop of one of the surface buildings in Gar'doz. The sky above was cloudy, and the only light came from torches mounted on buildings, or carried by red-eyed orcs as they moved through the settlement. A larger fire was blazing in the main square, but that was three blocks away.

Dawn was approaching, and she'd spent most of the night scouting the orcs' settlement, trying to confirm their numbers, while listening in on their conversations. They spoke orcish, not common, but she'd long ago learned the language as part of her training. Her master had ensured that she was prepared to operate anywhere she was needed, whether that be among dwarves, orcs, humans, or elves.

From what she had been able to gather, these red-eyed orcs were expecting the arrival of someone they referred to as *Master*, or *The One*, in a few days. They spoke his name with reverence and fear, and Izgren thought he was probably a tribal chief or some kind of war chief.

The orcs were gathering food at a frantic pace, sending hunters into the mountains and surrounding forested valleys, as well as underground, to bring in whatever they could. Their chief was bringing an army with him, and the orcs in this settlement would be expected to feed them before they moved on.

They didn't know it yet, but all of the hunting parties that were sent through the underground section of the settlement had perished at the hands of Izgren and her people. More than thirty orcs so far. She expected it wouldn't be much longer before those hunting parties were missed, and others would be sent to find them. A party or two might be written off as having encountered dangerous beasts in the underground, and perished. But five full parties disappearing was going to create some interest.

Which is why her master had instructed her to give the orcs something else to worry about.

She stood and moved to the back side of the roof, unconcerned about being spotted with her stealth ability active. She waited there, watching the alley below until the expected patrol approached. Each of the two orcs carried a sword in one hand. One held a shield on its left arm, with the other carrying a torch, holding it above their heads. As they passed her position, she hopped down off the single story roof, landing quietly behind them and stabbing forward with a poisoned dagger in each hand. Avoiding their chainmail armor, she slashed the backs of their necks, then ducked down as they turned. Both swords flashed over her head as she struck upward, stabbing the orcs in their groins.

The thief winced as both orcs roared at her, having wanted to go unnoticed a bit longer. The fast-acting poison, that normally took down even a full-sized orc in two or three seconds, didn't work as well on these red-eyed mutants. She had to parry a sword strike from one, and dodge a thrust from the other, before both went limp. Quickly sheathing her daggers, she caught the swords that fell from their hands before they could rattle on the stone at their feet. She then grabbed the shield bearer, grunting with the effort of lowering him slowly to the ground so that his shield didn't make a racket either.

When they both perished about ten seconds later, she looted their corpses and moved on, sure that more patrols would turn a corner any second in response to the roar. Hopping up to grab hold of the roof, she pulled herself back up with ease, and paused to listen. No running footsteps, no shouts of alarm.

With a soft sigh of relief, she got a running start and leapt from that roof to the next, then the next, making her way toward the central square. A block short of reaching the bonfire, she stopped on the roof of a large building the orcs were using as a storehouse. After hours of observation earlier that night, she knew that the alley at the back was part of the patrol route of the orcs she'd just killed. She had ten minutes before their route was supposed to bring them in contact with another patrol. At which point they'd be missed, and a search would likely begin.

Dropping into the alley, she used a dagger to unlatch the shutters of a window and climbed through. Inside the large, open room were rows of barrels filled with salted meat, potatoes, and water. Meat hung from the rafters on dozens of hooks, some of it so fresh it hadn't been skinned yet. Leaving the hanging meat alone, she quickly pried open several of the barrels, producing a small vial of liquid to be poured into each one before carefully replacing the lid. When she'd finished with a couple rows of meat barrels, she switched to the water. Each of those got two vials of the greenish liquid.

Unlike the poison on her daggers, this one was slow-acting. The orcs would have plenty of time to eat their fill, even get a good night's sleep, before they began to feel the effects. It was the best way to ensure that as many of them as possible consumed the poisoned food and water. She hoped their chief ate his share and more.

Izgren and her people, the last survivors of Nogroz as far as she knew, planned to claim Gar'doz as their own. They were not inclined to share their new home with these troublesome mutant orcs.

Exiting the window and securing the shutters behind her, she dashed off under the lightening sky, leaving the surface as quickly as she could. Once she'd gotten some sleep, and the orcs completed their feast, her master would form everyone into a raid party that would emerge from the underground to finish off the weakened and dying orcs. A whole army's worth of experience and loot awaited them!

Chapter 2

Queen Anastasia, the Battleborne queen, looked up from the book she was reading as her closest advisor entered her chambers. "What news have you?"

"The battle at the Westreach front rages on, majesty. Losses on both sides continue at a slightly increased pace. My sources tell me that Farstrider has made an alliance with the Battleborne king, Storm, and is discussing a similar alliance with the dwarven clans."

"Storm!" She thumped the table with one hand. "Have you managed to insert anyone into his kingdom?"

The mage smiled. "It wasn't even difficult. He's welcoming all comers, recruiting new citizens as quickly as he can. He requires all citizens to swear an oath, which obviously our people cannot do, but he's allowing visiting merchants to move freely throughout his holdings." He paused, one side of his mouth twitching. "One of my people has even eaten something called a cheeseburger in the palace dining hall."

"Have any of them reported this new king having plans to move against us?"

"Not at all. In fact all reports seem to agree that he is focused on securing and populating his current holdings, and avoiding further expansion for the foreseeable future. His holdings are already quite expansive, both above and below ground."

The queen shook her head, thinking. "I don't like it. Battleborne don't just sit around, picking their noses. He must be planning something." She looked up at the mage. "What about the one we hold in the dungeon? Has he been talking?"

The mage snorted. "He hasn't *stopped* talking since we locked him up! He voluntarily told us on the first day all he knew about King Storm. They apparently knew each other in their previous lives, even served together in some sort of mercenary force. Lagrass claims to be responsible for Storm's death on that world. He also seems quite annoyed at Storm's success on our world." He stopped to clear his throat. "Subsequent... questioning sessions did not alter his claims any. Under duress he has confessed to several murders, thefts, and other misdeeds, here and in his past life."

"He killed Storm?" The queen's eyebrow raised.

"Not directly. He was some sort of intelligence gatherer in that life, and didn't feel Storm gave him the respect he deserved. So he sent Storm and his entire company into an ambush that killed all but one. That one was severely injured, but survived long enough to kill Lagrass for his betrayal."

"So, a traitor in addition to being a murderer, thief, and liar." The queen's fingers tapped a drumbeat on the desk. "Maybe this one can be of use to us."

The mage shook his head. "He is weak of character, devoid of conscience. He's incapable of loyalty, and could not be depended on to do anything but run if released."

"Hmmm… well, continue to question him for now. Maybe we can use his hatred of King Storm to our benefit, at a later date."

"Certainly, majesty. He is currently… recovering from his most recent questioning. We've suppressed his magic, making it so he is unable to escape or to heal himself. It'll take several days for him to recover naturally. Then we shall begin again."

*****

Max, Enoch, and half a dozen Stormhaven guards passed through the portal at the Rest Station, stepping into the lower level of the now improved structure. The room in which the pedestal sat had been enlarged to nearly twice its original size. The narrow stairway to the upper level still remained, as it was a useful chokepoint should the need arise to defend the structure, but on either side the stairs had been smoothed into ramps, so that a wagon might easily be brought up or down.

Up top, the former four-foot high outer wall was still in place, but twenty paces farther out was a new ten foot high wall with ramparts, and a dwarven steel gate. The gate was just wide enough to admit a standard wagon, and should it fall, could be defended by four or five dwarves side by side. There were half a dozen guards atop the wall, all of whom turned to salute Max and company before returning their attention to the chamber around them.

A similar structure, on a smaller scale, was built near each of the cavern's exit tunnels. Three guards manned each of those, keeping watch for spidorcs or other underground denizens. Should an enemy approach, their job was to sound a warning. If the three of them could defeat or repel the intruders, they would. Otherwise they could call for reinforcements, or bar the gate and retreat back to the main fortification. While the cavern itself was not valuable real estate, the portal needed to be defended, and now there was another reason the location needed defending.

That was why Max had traveled there today.

Based on Max and Dalia's feeling that the rest station must have been placed there for a reason, Rockbreaker had sent patrols to thoroughly scout the surrounding area. It had taken them only two days to discover the reason for the rest station's construction.

Down one of the tunnels that Smitty and Dalia had started to explore while baiting spidorcs, the dwarves found a hastily scrawled dwarven rune etched into the floor. The rune directed them to the nearby wall, where they found a well-concealed stone door.

When Enoch led Max to the spot and pointed out the rune, then the doorway, Max saw only the rough stone of the tunnel wall. It wasn't until Enoch activated a hidden switch, by pushing in a section of the wall, that the outline of the door became visible. The dwarf pushed the door inward slightly, then to one side, and it disappeared into the wall on that side like a pocket door. Beyond the opening lay an obviously dwarven-carved tunnel with a perfectly smooth floor and walls, about five of Max's paces wide. It sloped slightly downward, and Max's gift of dark vision showed him it continued on for about fifty paces before turning.

"You say this was a mine? It's awful neat and clean."

"Aye, that be the truth." Enoch stuck his chest out proudly, as if he were the one responsible. "They did right nice work here." He motioned for Max to follow him down, and the guards followed behind. The last in line, an orc, had Max's light globe floating above his head, as he didn't possess any kind of dark vision.

The tunnel curved twice more, and Max imagined it must have been constructed to follow of vein of some kind. Dwarves generally built in straight lines, or graceful spirals, otherwise. After about a five minute walk they reached a wide chamber, also carved from the surrounding stone. Max grinned when the light followed the orc into the room and began to make the back wall of the chamber sparkle with a metallic glint.

"So that's it? I've never seen it in its natural form."

"Aye, me king." Enoch and the other dwarves were all grinning like kids on Christmas morning. "That be a mithril vein!"

Max crossed the room and placed his hand on the wall. The metal felt cold to the touch, and he thought it... buzzed slightly under his fingertips. Though that could have just been his imagination. Enoch stepped up next to him, pressing his forehead to the wall for a moment, eyes closed. After a while, he spoke quietly.

"It be a deep vein. One they followed fer years, by me best guess." He pointed back across the room at a rune carved into the floor just inside the doorway. "That rune tells ye that a Grandmaster were workin' this vein."

"A Grandmaster miner?" Max's eyebrows rose. "Does it say his name?"

"A Grandmaster smith, me king. Though, based on the state o' this place, he were at least a Master miner, as well. Look close at the wall." Max turned back and stared at the wall of stone and mithril in front of him. "D'ya see any pick marks?"

Max had the mining skill himself, but at a very low level. "I don't know. I don't think so?"

"The dwarf that were workin' this vein, whose name be Stouthammer, needed no pick. He pulled the ore from the stone with his bare hands!" Enoch's tone was reverent, and the other dwarves muttered words of respect. "Even among dwarvenkind, that be a rare skill. Those who possess it be honored by their clans. By all clans! After seein' that rune, I asked Redmane to consult the archives. The only Grandmaster Stouthammer he found lived more'n ten thousand years ago."

Max had learned from his time among the dwarves that Masters were deferred to in most things. Whether they were Master smiths, scribes, or weapons Masters, all dwarves paid them respect. Though he hadn't met one, as far as he knew, he imagined a Grandmaster might be more respected than even a king or clan chief.

"So, do we report this to his clan? I assume they'd still claim the rights to it."

Enoch shook his head, the enthusiasm fading for a moment. "Nah. The Stouthammers be no more. Wiped out by the damned greys centuries ago. The clan had a small settlement back the way we came, a day's march past the rest station. The greys killed em all, destroyed all but a few standin' stones." He looked up at Max. "Yer free to claim the mine fer Stormhaven."

Red took that cue to flash a notification up for Max to see. One offering him the option to claim the mine. He quickly selected *Yes*, and read through the congratulatory notification, as well as one awarding him some Sovereign points.

"Alright, Stormhaven has claimed the mine. Can I assume you won't have any trouble finding miners to work it?" He grinned at Enoch, who snorted.

"If ye offer 'em even a one percent share, they'll be lining up fer the chance. But..." His voice faded off, and he shuffled his feet slightly.

"Out with it, Enoch. But what?"

"Ye should only allow Master miners to work this vein, to get the maximum yield. Any lower level miner would be wastin' ore. With iron, or even gold, a wee bit o' waste is acceptable, if lamentable. But with mithril…"

"Every ounce is extremely valuable." Max nodded. "I understand."

The dwarf still looked sheepish. "I took the liberty o' havin Redmane put out a call to Darkholm and the clans. Most o' the Masters will have veins o' their own they be workin. But it might be a few o' the elders that've retired will answer the call."

"How many will we need?" Max eyed the sparkling wall. "Ten, twenty?"

Enoch looked horrified, shaking his head. "Me king! Two would be plenty!" When Max just stared at him with a confused look, he added, "Ye don't want to harvest all o' this in a week! Mithril be of great value, and part o' that value be due to its rarity."

"Ah, gotcha." Max caught on. "Slow and steady. I don't suppose any of you here are Master miners…" His voice trailed off as all the dwarves in the room dropped to one knee.

"Ahem." Max spun around to find Regin standing behind him, waving one hand. "I be a Grandmaster."

Max's mouth opened for a moment before he too took a knee, though he didn't bow his head like the dwarves had. "Regin. It's good to see you again." He smiled at the god, who was already grinning at him.

"And you, Maximilian Storm. Ye been busy since last we talked." He looked aside at Enoch and the dwarves for a moment. "On yer feet, lads. I don't hold with bowin' n scrapin'!"

The dwarves all hopped to their feet as if pulled up by strings.

"Well, you told me to get stronger, and that's what I've been doing." Max spoke as he too got to his feet. He chuckled when Regin shook his head and pointed at the ground.

"Not you, ya lanky mutt. Have a seat before I get a crick in me neck lookin up at ya."

Max obligingly took a seat on the stone floor, crossing his legs. "Better?"

"Much." Regin shook his head. "I told 'em to just go ahead n make ye a dwarf, but they didn't listen to me." He grumbled quietly to himself. "Give'd ye that oversized mutt body n sharp teeth." Regin paced back and forth a couple of times, still shaking his head. Eventually, he stopped and looked Max in the eye. "Right. Not here to waste me valuable time. I've come to nip a wee bit o' yer mithril here. Fer a special project. Ye don't mind, do ye?"

"Of course not." Max waved at the wall. "Anything for you. How much do you need?"

The god in dwarf form snorted, then stepped closer to the wall. He extended his arm, his hand disappearing into the wall. A moment later his second hand followed the first. Enoch and the dwarves gasped as the stone surrounding the metal seemed to just melt away, and Regin was left holding a chunk of metal roughly the size of a basketball. The void left in the wall when he removed it was nearly three times that size, the rock seemingly having just disappeared.

"This'll do nicely." Regin bounced the hunk of metal in his hands as if weighing it. He turned back to Max. "Thank ye, Maximilian." His gaze shifted to Enoch. "Ah, takin a break from yer work on the runes? Been watchin' yer progress. Keep at it!"

Enoch spluttered as if trying to speak, then just bowed his head in acknowledgement. Regin took a look around the room. "So this be the place."

"The place?" Max asked, looking around as well.

"I knew old Stouthammer. I'd even say he were a friend. Wiley old hoarder of secrets! He always had the purest grade mithril, but would never tell me where he got it."

Confused, Max asked, "Regin, you're literally a god. Couldn't you just summon pure mithril out of thin air?"

"O' course! But that takes the fun out o' findin it! Plus, when we use our powers to create things out o' naught, it messes with the natural order. Just a wee bit, most o' the time, but the bits can add up. So we mostly don't do it." As if it were an afterthought, he stuck a hand back into the wall. A moment later he scooped out a large handful of the shining metal and handed it to Max. "This should hold ye till ye get a Master to come harvest the ore."

"Thank you, Regin." Max bowed his head as he accepted the surprisingly lightweight cantaloupe sized chunk of metal. With a growing smile, he nodded toward the much larger chunk that Regin was making disappear. "Special project? Are you building a trap for Fibble the cookie thief?"

"Ha! Not a bad idea." Regin stroked his silvery white beard for a moment, considering. "But what would I do with him when I caught him? Send him off to start his own clan somewhere? The trouble he'd get into might be fun to watch..." His voice drifted off as he grinned at the idea. "Ye've got goblins in yer palace! Maybe I'll send him there!" The dwarven god roared with laughter as if he'd just told an excellent joke. Max and the others laughed along, humoring him though they didn't understand.

"We'd be happy to welcome him." Max offered.

"Aye lad, sure ye would. Fer a day or two... mebbe a week. Then ye'd be cursin' me name fer unleashing that lil pest on ye! No, I'd not do that to ye. It'd be a distraction ye don't deserve." Max just nodded in agreement while the dwarves looked confused.

"Right! Off I go. Things to do!" Regin smiled at Max. "Keep followin' yer heart, Maximilian. Grow yerself and yer kingdom stronger. I have faith in ye!" The dwarf gave a quick half-wave to the group before strolling out the door and disappearing.

Enoch whistled in amazement, wiping his forehead with one hand as he stepped closer to Max. "We just talked to the God o' Crafting hisself!" he reached out a hand to touch the mithril that Max was holding, but pulled it back before making contact. "And he give'd ye this gift!"

Max nodded. "He's actually helped me and my companions quite a bit since we arrived." He looked down at the ball of ore in his hands, noting that Enoch had started to reach for it again, and paused again. The other dwarves were gathering around as well, all of them wide-eyed. "Here, take a look." He made to hand it to Enoch. When the dwarf hesitated again, he asked, "What am I missing?"

The dwarf broke away from staring at the mithril to look up at Max. "Did ye not see?"

Max just raised an eyebrow.

"Regin harvested this for ye. With his own hands." When he saw that Max still didn't understand, he took hold of the ball and raised it to within inches of Max's face. "Take a good look!" Max finally took the hint and *Examined* the metal.

Pure Mithril Ore
Quantity: 2lbs
Rarity: Divine
This mithril was harvested by Regin, one of the Eternals, and gifted to King Maximilian Storm. The touch of an Eternal has greatly increased the natural properties of the ore.

Now it was Max's turn to whistle. "Just... by touching it? And what does the increase mean? Does it make the metal stronger?"

Enoch and the other dwarves chuckled. "Aye, stronger by far. Better able to hold enchantments, to channel spells. Only a Grandmaster could work this metal now, and they'd stomp each other into paste fer the opportunity. Few ever get to work divine metals, and even a Grandmaster might improve his skill with it." He reluctantly handed the metal back to Max, who held it in both hands and stared at it for a while. The other dwarves reached out one at a time, gently touching the metal for a moment as if it were a holy relic. Which Max supposed it had now become. The bored orc standing near the door just grunted.

"Let's get back to Stormhaven, unless there's something else here you want to show me?" Max asked Enoch.

"Ha! I showed ye a brand new mithril mine, ye speak'd to Regin hisself, and yer holdin a ball o' god-touched ore he gifted ye that be almost as large as me own nobblies!" he reached for his crotch and made an exaggerated lifting motion. "What else could I show ye that could compare to any o' that?" Enoch shook his head and took a last look at the void in the wall Regin had left behind, then strode toward the door. Before exiting, he muttered to himself. "Who be this Fibble?"

Max and the others followed, and when they'd exited the mine, Max was about to head back toward the rest station when the orc guard laughed. "King Max." He called out, pointing at the now closed hidden door. When Max turned to look, he rolled his eyes and groaned.

Scratched into the face of the door was a crude representation of his face that matched the one he'd etched into the stone door near Regin's Outpost. The same one that Smitty and many of the Stormhaven citizens had taken to drawing all over the place. Right below it was an equally crude rendering of another face, clearly meant to represent Fibble, the goblin cookie thief. Max pointed at the lower of the two. "That's Fibble."

*****

"So what I hear you saying is that we'll all be getting fancy new mithril armor?" Blake was grinning at Max. The group had gathered at Eats N Treats for an evening meal, and Max had just finished telling them about the mine.

"Well, eventually, yes. As compensation for your previous, and presumably continuing service to Stormhaven, your gracious and most generous king will gift you enough mithril for a chest piece or something. But you'll have to come up with the funds to pay a smith to craft it for you."

"Waaaaiit a minute." Blake held up one finger, then pointed it at Dylan. "That hardly seems fair. A chest piece for me, hell even a whole mithril robe for me, would use up about a tenth of the metal it'd take to make a breastplate for big sexy over there!"

Max nodded. "It's the thought that counts, corporal. And is any price too high to make sure our tank can safely block any and all attacks aimed at our esteemed Lord Blake's august personage? Especially when he jumps the gun with a fireball and draws aggro?"

Blake pretended to consider that for a moment, then leaned back. "I suppose when you put it that way, it's a sound investment." The others laughed as he grinned up at Dylan.

The ogre leaned closer and theatrically whispered loud enough for all to hear. "Just imagine, with you wearing a mithril robe, when we *Gnomerang* your tiny butt at a boss monster, you'll do way more damage on impact."

The gnome eyed the lump of metal Max had set on the table during his tale. "I'd hit even harder if my robe was made of *divine* mithril." He raised one eyebrow, smiling up at Max.

"Not a chance." Max made the metal disappear to the chuckles of those around the table.

"Maybe just a wand then, boss? Imagine how much more powerful my spells would be!"

"Nope." Max reached for his cheeseburger and took a hefty bite. He chewed for a while and swallowed before continuing. "I'm not going to approach a Grandmaster smith and ask him to use what amounts to holy metal for them to craft a tiny gnomey spellshooter."

Blake looked crestfallen. "Size isn't everything, boss."

"Yes it is." Birona, who had just joined them and set a large plate of nachos on the table in front of Dylan, grinned at him. Smitty and Dylan roared with laughter at her perfect timing. Smiling sweetly at Blake, she offered, "If it makes you feel any better, my friend Goselle doesn't seem bothered by your... physical shortcomings."

Blake instantly perked up. "What did she say?" He hopped up to stand on the table and struck a pose, flexing his tiny gnome arms. "Is she warm for my form?"

Birona tapped her chin, searching for the proper words. "I would not say that. It is more that she is... amused enough by your wit to consider spending more time with you."

"I'll take it!" Blake hopped from the table to his chair to the floor before streaking away out the door."

"Where is he going?" Birona asked as he disappeared.

"Presumably to go find your friend." Max offered, shaking his head and smiling at the gnome's enthusiasm.

"But she's in the kitchen." Birona pointed at the door behind the bar that led down a short hall to the kitchen. "She's learning a few of the recipes."

"Don't anyone say a word." Max looked at the group, any one of whom could call the gnome back through party chat.

"Aw that's just mean, boss." Smitty shook his head, staring at the exit door. "I like it!"

Dylan looked at Birona. "Does he actually have a chance with your friend?"

The orcess snorted. "Unlikely. She finds him amusing, and respects his... ambition. Though I suppose stranger things have happened."

Smitty raised his mug. "A toast!" He waited for the others to raise theirs, then called out. "To Blake! And to death by snu snu!"

"Death by snu snu!" Max and Dylan shouted, while the ladies gave them strange looks. They drank anyway, having grown used to not understanding the Battlebornes' homeworld references.

On Max's shoulder, an invisible Red snorted, then whispered. "I got that one!"

"So, what's next, boss?" Dylan asked, a hopeful look on his face.

Max kept his own facial expression impassive. "I thought we'd take a road trip." He watched the ogre's eyes light up. "Head out to the dworc village, then north into the mountains. See if we can locate the One's headquarters. Pickstone tells me it's one huge wilderness up there, so it might take us a month or more to search."

He waited as Dylan's face fell, the disappointed ogre looking down at his massive hands as he crossed them in his lap. "Right, boss. Need to deal with the red-eyed orcs before they overrun the village, or the Heart chamber."

Max looked around the table, then felt bad when he found Smitty, Dalia, and the others were glaring at him. He threw them a wink. "Of course, we can do all that without a tank. I mean, you're really not all that helpful in large battles, corporal. Be a shame not to have Princess, though."

Dylan's eyes shot up, and he completely disregarded the insult. "You mean it, boss? I can go?"

"Never let it be said that I stood in the way of Corporal Big Sexy gettin' some ogre lovins."

"Right on, brother!" Smitty fist-bumped the now beaming ogre. "Want us to go with you?" He indicated Birona and himself. "I can be your wingman!"

Dylan shook his head. "You walk into my village and you might literally be wings. As in wings and drumsticks over the cookfire. I'm good with going on my own." He looked over at Max. "I won't be gone long. With Princess, I can be there in a day or two."

"We'll work out some gifts you can take with you. Some deer and boar meat, fresh fruit, maybe a few dozen pre-cooked pizzas? Whatever you think might work best." He cleared his throat. "I hereby name you Ambassador Big Sexy, plenipotentiary of Stormhaven, representative to all Ogre clans." Max made the sign of the cross in the air in front of him, then dipped a couple fingers into his ale and splashed some on the ogre to make it official.

Dylan's eyes crossed slightly for a moment before he burst out laughing. "I just got a notice asking if I wanted to show the title "Ambassador Big Sexy."

"Oh, man! You totally should!" Smitty leaned forward. "Gimme one, boss! Make it a good one! Like... I know! Smitty the Gnarly One! Or how bout The Earl of Shootyness!"

"No, and no." Max just shook his head and took another bite of delicious cheeseburger.

Chapter 3

Pickstone stood atop the wall, staring northward toward the tree line. "How many d'ya think?"

The orc scout standing behind him shook his head. "It got dark too fast for me to get a good count, but at least three hundred."

The dworc elder nodded once, his heart beating a bit faster. As old as he was, he still enjoyed a good battle. Since the red-eyed orcs started showing up, he'd earned three levels, and was looking forward to another one. "Countin' our new minotaur friends, we've got a hunnert fighters inside the wall. Better call King Max for some help."

The scout nodded and turned toward the guard commander, letting out a piercing two-note whistle. The dwarf waved a hand, then dropped down off the rampart, landing in front of the portal pedestal. Two seconds later the portal was open, and he stepped through.

"How many o' these mutated beasties could there be?" Pickstone muttered to himself. "We've already killed nigh on a thousand of 'em, plus the ones Max told us have been killed tryin fer heart chambers. Still they keep on comin'."

The scout shrugged, thinking the dworc was talking to him. "Mountain orc tribes are usually smaller than tribes like mine that live in forests or cities. Food is harder to find in the mountains. But the one we captured said their chief has gathered many tribes. There could be several thousand more."

A shout of greeting drew his attention, and he saw a line of dwarven guards trotting through the portal below. After fifty or so dwarves came through, a small contingent of a dozen gnomes in mage robes followed, preceding a mixed force of fifty more orcs, dwarves, minotaurs, as well as Max and his companions.

"That evens the odds up a bit!" Pickstone grinned as he waved for Max to join him atop the wall. The catapult crew were getting set up in their designated spots, and a few of the young ones were moving ammunition carts. They were excited to try out their newly improved projectiles. Blake, who had been working alongside them on the experiment, trotted over to check on them.

"Elder Pickstone. I hear you're hosting another party." Max shook the dworc's hand before turning to look toward the forest. "Ah, yes. More red-eyes." He took some time to try and count the enemy. "I see close to five hundred. That includes a column moving up behind the ones who are spread out from there," he pointed to the northwest, then the northeast. "to there." He took a moment to call Rockbreaker via one of the communication rings to order up more reinforcements. The wall gave them an advantage, even over greater numbers, but with his current force they couldn't defend the village without significant casualties.

He looked back at Pickstone. "We were planning a trip north to track these guys starting tomorrow. It's a good thing we didn't run into them in the woods, or one of the passes."

"Their forces be getting' larger with each attack." Pickstone observed, now concerned about the increased size of the army in the forest.

"That would suggest that their main body is moving south. He's breaking his army into smaller forces, which is smart. It makes them easier to feed, and faster moving, and as far as he knows there's no obstacle large enough to resist even the smaller forces. Their orders are probably to capture small settlements like this one to give his main force a resting place as they move southward."

The orc scout, who was still standing behind Pickstone, nodded. "Secure some ground, gather supplies for the main force. That was how An'zalor did it as well."

"A sound tactic, often used where I'm from." Max agreed.

"Well they won't be getting this place to use as an FOB, boss!" Smitty drew his bow, aimed it upward in the general direction of the enemy force, and loosed without bothering to aim. He grinned widely at them when a moment later there was a scream of pain. "Four hundred ninety nine, boss." The orc scout behind Pickstone grunted in approval.

Max shook his head as he observed the orcs nearest the tree line taking a few steps back, deeper into the brush. "You nearly scared them off, corporal." He winked at Smitty.

The walls were six feet higher now, thanks to Blake's earth mage friends, the fully repaired outward facing surface was smooth as glass, and as hard as granite. There were also brand new towers that rose up ten feet higher than the wall on either side of the gate, with more protected firing positions for mages and archers. From those elevated positions they were better able to target any enemies that reached the top of the wall, as well.

The final improvement made to the village came when the dworcs bribed two of the earth mages with kegs of honey mead. The two mages had each spent an entire day using their magic to create slate roof tiles, which the newly adopted minotaurs then installed atop all the buildings. No more thatch roofs that could easily be set alite by orcish fire arrows. This freed up some of the youngsters and elders, who would normally be on the bucket brigade, to run ammunition during battles, or help the healers move the wounded.

Max watched as the approaching column met up with the already arrayed force, then split in two. The new arrivals trotted east and west, moving past their comrades to take up positions on either flank. "They're spreading out more." Max reported aloud and through party chat, which now included all of his party, the dworc elders, and the small unit commanders. "They'll be coming in from the north, east, and west. Probably all at once. Spread your people out accordingly."

In the distance the sound of axes striking wood rang out. "That'll be them makin' a batterin' ram." Pickstone observed.

"Probably ladders, too." Smitty added as he looked down from atop the wall. "Though they're gonna need longer ones than last time."

"We be prepared fer ladders." Pickstone grinned at Smitty. "Them red-eyed freaks won't ever reach the top o' the wall this time!" Smitty believed him. Having farther to climb meant more time exposed on the ladder. Combined with the additional bodies on the wall, the added firepower up on the towers in positions with good angles to hit climbers, Smitty didn't envy the orc attackers.

After a few minutes, Max sent half the defenders down off the wall to grab something to eat and drink. "It sounds like it'll be a while before they're done with the pre-attack crafting." His statement got a few chuckles through party chat. "Let's rotate folks down off the wall so we're as rested as possible when the time comes." He took a minute to generate a village defense quest for everyone present, then sat back to wait.

*****

Dylan walked slowly along a narrow ledge that protruded from a high cliff face. He was getting closer to his home village, and had made good time riding atop Princess. Now he was on foot, having dismissed his giant lizard, who was much too large to walk this path. In fact, Dylan himself was too large to walk it.

"I'll be your freak-a-zoid, come on and wind me up!" he sang quietly to himself, keeping one hand on the cliff face as he tried to distract himself, to keep himself from looking down. The ledge was wide enough for his oversized feet, but his oversized belly and wide shoulders that kept bumping against the stone had him worried about losing his balance and falling a long, long way to the canyon floor below. "How do the other ogres walk this so easily?" he muttered to himself, the song not working to distract him. Worse, it tempted him to execute some awesome robot moves, and the narrow ledge wasn't the place for that.

"Maybe they're just too dumb to think about falling." He mused, focusing on putting one foot in front of the other, still keeping one hand in contact with the stone face. "I mean, they're good people, and all... but there ain't a rocket scientist in the group." He grinned to himself. It had initially been frustrating to him when he'd first arrived on this world. The ogres mostly communicated in grunts, pointing gestures, rude gestures, and two or three word sentences. They were hyper-focused on food, sex, and fighting amongst themselves, so meaningful conversation was nowhere to be found. Still, after a week or so, he'd come to appreciate their simple approach to life. If they couldn't eat it, fight it, or screw it, they had no interest in it. "Not such a bad way to live." He chuckled as he took another step. The end of the ledge was in sight now, only a hundred or so baby ogre steps to go.

Never having been a fan of heights, Dylan was sweating profusely as he tried to keep calm and shuffle along carefully. "Next time I come through here, I'm gonna install grab bars or some shit." He grumbled, wedging his fingers into a crack in the stone to steady himself. "Friggin dwarf-sized road to get to an ogre village."

Dylan had only taken another half dozen steps when an ogre appeared on the path ahead, moving in his direction. "Hey!" he called to the ogre, gently waving the hand that wasn't attached to the wall. "Hey there! Remember me?" The ogre looked up and stared at him a moment, continuing to walk his direction.

"Hey, stop! I'm almost there, and there's only room for one of us on this ledge, buddy." Dylan made a patting motion in the ogre's direction, indicating he should wait on the much wider area he was currently crossing.

The other ogre, whose name Dylan couldn't remember, raised a hand in greeting and smiled, but kept walking. "Great! You do remember me. How bout you stop right there and we catch up a bit when I get there!" Dylan kept making the universal sign for *stop right there*, and the ogre actually mimicked him, patting the air in his direction. While still walking.

"No! Stop!" Dylan let some growl enter his voice. The ogre was approaching the start of the narrow section, and didn't seem to have any plans to halt and wait for Dylan to arrive. "There's not room for me and you both on this path!" The ogre nodded several times, still smiling at Dylan, still moving forward. "Wait!"

He tried to pick up his pace, hoping to somehow reach the end of the ledge before the other ogre, but after just three quick steps he nearly lost his balance and toppled over the edge. "Stop, dammit!" he roared at the interloper. This caused the ogre to stop in his tracks, tilting his head and looking at Dylan, confused by the suddenly hostile tone. He scratched his belly, then his butt, grunting at Dylan in a questioning manner.

"Just hold it right there." Dylan practically scolded the clueless ogre. "Two minutes, and the ledge is all yours. That's right, scratch that butt. Chase that itch. Dig right up in there good and deep." He spoke in a softer tone, just trying to hold the ogre's attention. He knew from experience that using too harsh of a tone would be seen as a challenge, and the last place he wanted to wrestle was on the ledge.

"Hey, I got something for you!" He pulled a cheeseburger wrapped in paper from his inventory and took a couple deep breaths. Muttering, "this is stupid" to himself, he gripped the wall with his right hand as best as he could, then tossed the cheeseburger underhand at the ogre. His aim was off, and it landed about ten feet in front of him. "There you go, check that out." Dylan continued to move as quickly as he dared, letting go of his grip on the wall and shuffling forward again. He held his breath as the ogre stepped forward, then bent down to look at the fallen cheeseburger. Dylan could hear a couple massive inhales as he sniffed at the burger, then reached down and picked it up.

"Yes! That's right, it's food. A little bite-sized snack for you while you stay *right where you are* and let me get off this damned path!" He watched as the ogre grunted in apparent approval of the smell, then bit into the cheeseburger without removing the paper. The result was that the meat and cheese sort of squished out of the paper in every direction. Not seeming to mind the mess, the ogre began to lick burger bits off its fingers before shoving the whole thing, wrapper and all, into his mouth.

"Mmmm. Good." The ogre smiled at Dylan, raising a foot to continue in his direction.

"NO!" Dylan shouted again, but without the growl. He produced another burger and tossed it harder this time, making sure it landed behind the approaching ogre, whose head swiveled up and around, eyes locked on its trajectory. The moment the tasty treat landed, the ogre turned and stomped back the way it had come, quickly retrieving the snack and tossing it whole into his mouth.

"More!" The ogre turned and began to trot toward Dylan, one hand out demanding another treat, grinning widely with bits of paper stuck in its teeth. Before Dylan even had time to produce another burger from his inventory, the big hungry brute was stepping onto the narrow section of the ledge. He moved without a care in the world, one shoulder brushing loose dirt off the cliff face as he plowed forward, licking his lips.

Dylan cursed quietly to himself and stopped where he was, leaning his back against the stone as he tried not to panic. There was now a thousand pounds of unstoppable dumbass steaming toward a head-on collision with him, and he was definitely not an immovable object. A quick glance down at the far away canyon floor just made things worse.

Desperate, he produced his shield and held it in front of him, using it to motion at the ogre. "Go back!"

Seeing the shield, the ogre's grin widened, and he nodded enthusiastically. Pulling his own battered wooden shield from his back, he equipped it and howled with glee, picking up speed as he charged at Dylan.

"What're you doing! Stop that!" Dylan was getting frantic. The ogre was now just half a dozen paces away, and picking up momentum. "No! Get back!" he roared at the ogre, who seemed to take that as a challenge, and roared back.

"We smash!" he shouted and took the last few steps, raising his shield to bash into Dylan's. The corporal winced as the big ogre's momentum forced him to take a single step back with his left foot, the one closest to the edge of the ledge.

"Woooo!" the ogre seemed pleased with the impact. "Good game! Again!" He began to back up, not even looking over his shoulder to pay attention to his footing.

"No! Enough!" Dylan shouted at him, taking a few unsteady steps forward after the retreating overgrown toddler. "We play later!"

Not liking his tone, the ogre scowled at him. "No! We smash now!" He stopped retreating and charged forward toward Dylan again, shield up and ready. Dylan glanced down at the long drop and panicked, shifting so that his back was against the wall, his shield now on his right arm as he crouched down and braced himself.

The ogre's shield struck his, but rather than the concussive impact of the first round, the aggressor's shield skidded off Dylan's, which was angled at about forty five degrees, and the ogre's momentum wasn't stopped dead like before. As Dylan was pressed back against the cliff face by the impact, the surprised ogre flashed Dylan a betrayed look as it tumbled forward over the ledge.

"Whyyyy?" the ogre called out as he fell, not understanding why Dylan had murdered him over a simple game of smash.

Dylan didn't have the heart to watch him fall. He closed his eyes and took several deep breaths. A moment later he felt like he was kicked in the gut when an experience notification popped up.

"I'm sorry, ogre bud. I tried to stop you…" he whispered as he resumed his careful progress toward the end of the ledge. Guilt wracked him as he shuffled toward the safer area. He didn't blame the ogre, really, it probably never occurred to the oversized child that there was any danger. Just as he never suspected that Dylan would fail to hold up his end of the game and let him fall.

There had been times in Dylan's career as a soldier when innocents got hurt. Children. It was never intentional, of course, but it was inevitable, and senseless. They would receive bad intel, and a building they called down an airstrike on wasn't as empty as reported. Or the ordinance from an artillery barrage wasn't one hundred percent accurate. Stray bullets from a firefight claimed a life. That was among the worst, because you had to sit and wait while the investigators figured out whose bullets they were, unsure how to feel until you knew one way or the other. Wanting an answer, but at the same time afraid to hear it. In one instance he had been driving a Humvee, and an enemy combatant had appeared in the street ahead, firing an RPG. Dylan had swerved so hard he'd nearly tipped the vehicle over, and was successful in avoiding the hit. A moment after the hastily aimed projectile sped past his door, it exploded in a building behind them. When the firefight was over, he and his team found a large family of mostly women and children in the rubble.

Their deaths weren't his fault, he knew in his logical mind that was on the asshat who fired the RPG, but to this day he carried a burden of guilt. Survivor's guilt, a case of the 'what if's', call it what you like. More than once he'd wished he'd allowed the vehicle to take the hit, trading his own life for that family's survival. He had asked himself a hundred times if, had he known what would happen, would he have acted differently?

After reaching the wider, safer section of the ledge, he found his legs wouldn't support him. Falling to his butt on the same spot where the first cheeseburger had landed, he bent forward, elbows on his knees, face buried in his hands as his entire body trembled. He did his best to breathe slowly and deeply, to calm his heart and his mind. An image of the ogre's face as he fell joined other images, other faces forever frozen in their final expressions, threatening to overwhelm him. With a groan of anguish, he lay back and stared up at the sky, trying to focus on the clouds drifting serenely overhead.

Tears streamed down his face as his chest heaved and his hands trembled. He clenched them into fists, then pounded the ground next to him, whispering, "I'm sorry." to the ogre and all the other faces.

*****

"Heads up! Incoming!" Smitty shouted from his new position atop one of the towers. The words were immediately followed by the sound of his bowstring snapping, along with dozens of other orcish bows and dwarven crossbows up and down the wall. From inside the towers, fireballs were lobbed into the air alongside ice bolts, arcing across the open area around the wall to land amongst orcs just emerging from the trees. Two dozen or more red-eyed orcs didn't make it ten steps from the tree line under that barrage.

Right behind the lead element that were dashing across the kill zone came teams of orcs shouldering long ladders. Thick, heavy, and hastily built, the long ladders each required three burly orcs to carry them. Others ran alongside, in part to draw fire away from the ladder bearers, in part to take up the burden should one of them fall. They sprinted forward behind the vanguard, shields held in their off hands to try and deflect incoming fire.

Without having to be told, the ranged fighters along the wall focused fire on the ladders. Max watched as an orc at the front of one ladder took an arrow to the face, the ladder sliding off its shoulder as it went down. The sudden jolt when the ladder dug into the soil jerked the other two orcs off their feet, one of them snapping a rung loose with its shoulder. A moment later he heard the clack of a catapult releasing behind him, and he watched a clay bomb arc up over his head. It impacted next to one of the ladder teams, the explosion spraying burning oil over the ladder and half a dozen orcs nearby. The bearers screamed as they dropped the ladder and tried in vain to put out the flames that engulfed them. A second round of what Max was referring to in his head as mortars impacted further to the left, taking out another group. Next to Max, a dworc warrior produced a leather sling and held it open. His partner produced one of their smaller grenade versions of the clay pots, lit the fuse, and placed it in the sling pouch. The first dworc carefully whirled the loaded sling once over his head before loosing it toward the orc line. It was joined by a score of others that peppered the charging force and exploded in a series of eruptions that sounded to Max like microwave popcorn popping. Except for the screaming.

Max noted with pride that the grenades had landed in coordinated clusters that, while each one only took down two or three orcs, forced the others to move to the side to avoid the fire, neatly pushing them into tighter groups. Just a second or two behind the grenades, two more mortar rounds arced over the wall to land at predetermined coordinates marked with stakes painted bright red. Coordinates where the newly herded orcs were clustered. Each of the fiery impacts took out a dozen or more orcs this time, and the grenade teams whooped in celebration.

Max picked a ladder team that was approaching his position and cast *Boom!* on the ladder. The results were less than satisfying. While the ladder did explode right next to the middle bearer, killing the orc instantly, the wooden splinters that spread out from there didn't do as much damage as metal or stone shards would have. Three other orcs stumbled briefly, including the rearmost ladder bearer, but no others went down. He produced his bow and sent an arrow into the lead bearer's chest, dropping him and slowing the ladder's progress enough for a mage to hit it with a fire spell.

Of the two dozen ladders that had emerged from the forest, ten didn't make it to the halfway point. The village defenders were merciless in their massacre of the ladder teams, ignoring the first wave of charging orcs in favor of targeting the ladders. When the leading orcs reached the base of the wall, melee fighters poured buckets of oil on them and dropped torches, turning the base of the wall into an inferno. No boulders were dropped, no spears thrown down at the burning orcs to finish them, the defenders content to let them burn while they refilled their buckets and prepared for the next wave.

"Flanks, report." Max called out via party chat as he looked to his left and right. He could see a bustle of activity atop the walls, but not what was happening below.

"West flank, holdin'. Thirty or so red-eyes down, minor casualties on the wall." Rockbreaker's voice was excited as he gave his report.

"Thirty? Hah! We've killed at least forty on our side." Pickstone reported from the east. "We lost one o' the lads, and a couple others be scratched up a bit. We'll hold."

Max surveyed the tree line, spotting what he was looking for after just a few seconds. A dozen orcs came trotting out into the opening carrying a battering ram. The log was twenty feet long and at least three feet in diameter. The front end had been roughly cut into a dull point, and what looked like a metal chest plate had been beaten into shape to cover the tip of it. Max knew that the orcs would need an hour or more to break open the gate with the makeshift ram, and was tempted to just let them try. But the ram was a symbol, and taking it down would boost morale significantly. So rather than issue an order through party chat, he took a deep breath and roared at the top of his lungs.

"Take down that damned ram!"

The next moment he cast *Boom!* on the metal cladding at the end of the log, grinning as the defenders watched the front of the log, and four orcs, disappear in a mist of blood, metal and wood splinters. The roar of approval that rose up from his people was nearly as intimidating to the red-eyes as the explosion had been. The stunned orcs dropped the log, which rolled to Max's left and crushed the legs of two of the former ram bearers. Rather than bombard the now inert log, his people went back to massacring orcs closer to the wall until another group of orcs had gathered and recovered their ram. The moment they lifted it and took a step forward, a storm of spells and mundane projectiles rained down upon them.

Max drew his sword Storm Reaver and held it aloft and roared "Stormhaven!", more for visual effect than any need to do so, as he activated its enchantment, *Sovereign's Stand*. A quick check showed that all of the defenders, including those at the edges of the flanks, were within range of the enchantment's boost. Every one of them cheered as they felt the ten percent boost in *Strength*, *Constitution*, and health regeneration. At the same time, all of the mutated orcs within five hundred feet of Max took an equal hit to their *Strength* and morale.

Six ladders reached the wall that Max could see, and based on the way his defenders clustered on the flanks, at least one or two had reached their sections as well. Melee fighters gripped swords and axes and stepped forward, while archers and mages tried to clear the climbers from their positions in the towers.

From the tree line, another wave of a hundred or so orcs burst forth, roaring in rage, their red eyes glowing brightly as they sprinted across the kill zone, hurdling or simply stomping on the corpses in their path. The ranged defenders left off their attacks on the climbers and redirected to the oncoming horde, trusting their melee comrades to do their part.

Max decided to test a new ability he'd picked up from a rare dungeon loot scroll. Leaning over the wall a bit, he angled his gaze along its face, taking in two of the nearest ladders and the group of ascending orcs. Taking a deep breath, he activated *Intimidating Shout*, roaring "I am the Chimera King! I will eat your hearts and piss on your corpses!"

Again his defenders cheered, and Max was gratified to see several of the orcs within the one hundred foot range of the spell react by visibly shuddering. A few even lost their grips on the ladders and tumbled back onto their comrades below. One particularly weak-willed orc dropped its heavy axe and simply fled, only to be cut down halfway across the kill zone by a charging orc commander, easily identified by a crimson sash across its chest that matched the three lines tattooed on its face.

Max raised his bow again and put an arrow into the face of that commander, stopping its charge and knocking it flat on its back, never to rise again. He and Smitty had instructed all ranged attackers to immediately take down any higher ranked orcs they spotted. They had learned that within the orc army, fear of the commanders was an even greater motivator than the mutated orcs' bloodlust. Without that threat behind them, the common orc warriors were more likely to retreat when faced with certain doom.

He continued to monitor the tree line for stragglers or officers who were hanging back while his defenders blasted, hacked, and stabbed the attacking horde. More than half of the five hundred Max had counted were already down on the field in front of him, and he expected the situation was similar on the eastern and western flanks. A quick glance over his shoulder to the courtyard below showed Dalia and the healers working on twenty or so wounded, with three covered bodies off to one side.

Grimacing at the loss of even that small number, Max gritted his teeth and turned back to the battle. A pair of red eyes emerged from behind a tree half a dozen paces back from the clearing, and Max loosed an arrow without pausing to take careful aim. Still, the eyes disappeared back behind the tree before the arrow whizzed past to disappear into the night. Frustrated at the miss, growled into party chat. "I think I just spotted their big boss. You guys hold the fort, I'm going after him!"

Before his people could protest, he focused on a spot just past the tree and cast *Jump*! on himself. He was getting used to the dynamics of the spell, and didn't suffer any disorientation when he reappeared, turning quickly to find an oversized orc with its back to Max, still unaware of his presence. Rather than draw his sword and alert the orc, Max leapt up and kicked out, slamming his boot into the back of the orc's head, causing it to impact the tree with a crunch and a spray of blood. The stunned and wounded orc fell limply to the ground as Max drew Storm Reaver and pressed the tip of the blade to its throat. The orc blinked up at him, then growled as it began to come to its senses, spitting out the blood that was leaking into its mouth from its shattered nose and battered face. He *Identified* the orc as it rolled onto its back, wheezing.

Orc Bloodblade
Level 49
Health: 16,230/18,000

This one was unnamed, though it was a higher level than the named bloodblade that had killed Picklet. "Where is your leader? Your war chief?" Max growled back at it, pressing the blade hard enough to pierce the skin, making it clear the orc shouldn't move.

"The One is everywhere!" it glared at him with pure hatred as it answered. "He is coming for you, even now!"

"He won't have to. Tell me where he is, and I'll save him the trouble." Max glanced briefly to the north, letting the orc know he was aware of its leader's general direction. "We'll see if he has the courage to face me himself."

"You are nothing compared to The One!" The orc pushed to rise, then fell back as the blade sank deeper into its skin. It tried to brush the blade away with one hand, but Max pulled it back then parried with enough force to cut deeply into its wrist, making the orc grunt in pain. Max replaced the blade at its throat.

"Last chance. Tell me where your chief is, or I'll drag you back to the village and feed you to the dworcs!" He paused, grinning evilly at the orc, baring his fangs. "Well, not all of you. They'll just fry up your stones, tongue, and eyeballs, then feed the rest of your corpse to their hogs." The orc's eyes widened for a moment before it scowled and spat blood up at him. "I know he's in the mountains to the north. Tell me where, and I'll give you a quick death."

The orc surprised Max then, giving a defiant roar with pure hatred in its eyes before lunging upward and forcing the sword blade deep into its throat and out the back of its neck. The roar ended in a wet gurgle, and the light in its eyes went dead. Max ignored the kill and experience notifications, not even bothering to loot the corpse as he turned back to take in the battle.

Seeing that his people had things well in hand, he began to stalk the forest, looking for more orcs to question.

Chapter 4

Dylan walked into the wide open space at the center of the ogre village. The whole place wasn't very large, an open space at the bottom of a cleft between two mountains. A honeycomb of caves had been hollowed out on either side, and a few rough structures built of stacked stones in the open area. In the center was a large fire pit over which they roasted any large game, and just beyond the pit was a massive stone throne carved directly out of a boulder.

He took a knee in front of that throne, and the ogre chieftain that sat in it, as other ogres gathered around. A few of them grunted his name in welcome as he waited to be acknowledged.

"Dylan." The chieftain growled. "You come back!"

Dylan raised his head and grinned at the chief. The largest and most powerful of the ogres in the village, the chief stood a good fourteen feet tall, and weighed in at easily two thousand pounds. His shoulders were a good two feet wider than Dylan's, and his rounded gut could probably hold an entire cow from Earth.

"Mighty Chief! I bring gifts from my friend, King Max!" Dylan started producing items from his inventory to lay at the ogre's feet. First was an oversized orcish battle axe, the one they'd looted from the orc that took Picklet's head. The moment he set it down, the chief lunged forward and grabbed it.

"Big axe! Sharp!" He tested the blade, creating a deep cut on his thumb before sticking it into his mouth to suck the blood. "Pretty."

Next Dylan pulled out a wooden crate filled with roasted spidorc legs and offered it up. The chief grinned and grabbed one, sticking the entire thing into his maw and crunching happily. Dylan produced a second crate, which the chief graciously passed around to the growing crowd. Dylan continued to produce item after item, each one causing the chief and the gathered ogres to smile and clap their hands in approval. There were three of the oversized carnivorous deer corpses, intact with furs and horns, all the useful bits the ogres could craft with. There were bags of fruit, as well as seeds for various fruit trees that the ogres didn't have in their small orchard. Dylan produced a heavy, sturdily crafted table made by one of the minotaurs, then piled it high with desserts from the Stormhaven bakery, as well as samples of cheeseburgers, tacos, and other items from the guild's restaurant.

While the ogres plowed through the assorted food, he stacked up another twenty orcish axes, smaller than the one gifted to the chief, but still of a size for ogres to wield. He unloaded a pile of hides from the hunters at the Way Station, as well as some basic metal crafting tools like heavy duty needles, skinning knives, and awls to replace the bone versions the ogres had been using. These were quickly snatched up by the village crafters, who thumped Dylan on his back in thanks before grabbing some food and disappearing to their caves or huts.

"King Max good friend!" the chief declared loudly, to which all the other ogres nodded their enthusiastic agreement.

Dylan cleared his throat and stood up, causing the gathered ogres to grow quiet. "King Max is good friend yes. He sends food, supplies, and a warning to his friend the big chief! Orcs with red eyes are moving from the north, killing everyone in their path. King Max sends good weapons to go with the warning, so his friends can protect their village!"

The gathered ogres roared and stomped their feet in a mixture of anger and approval, the combined noise and impacts echoing off the canyon walls and vibrating some loose gravel until it fell into the clearing.

"We have seen red eye orcs!" the chief growled. "They attack flock, six suns ago. They kill three goats, we kill all of them and eat along with goats!" Again the ogres roared, this time with approval as they grinned, a few of them rubbing their bellies to indicate how delicious the orcs had been. Max followed the chief's eyes as he glanced toward a pile of broken orc skulls next to one of the huts. There looked to be about a dozen of them.

Dylan grunted his approval and thumped his chest. "Red eyed orcs attacked King Max and other friends, too. We killed many. As many as the stones." He knew ogres weren't counters, so he grabbed a double handful of dirt from the ground at his feet and tossed them in the air. The chief looked impressed.

"You bring orc meat, too?" he looked hopeful for a moment, until Dylan shook his head.

"We feed orc bodies to our beasts, our mounts, and protectors." He snapped his fingers, remembering. "I will show you my companion. His name is Princess. He is my friend, so no one tries to eat him, yes?" Dylan waited for the chief to consider his request, then nod. He needed to wait for the agreement, because the tribe trying to eat Princess was a real possibility. He moved to the other side of the fire pit, produced the figurine that Erdun had enchanted for him, and summoned Princess. When the massive lizard mount appeared, several of the ogres took a step back and raised weapons before the chief shouted at them.

"This is Princess! Princess, meet Big Chief and my ogre friends." He patted Princess on the side of his neck, beaming at the surprised and suspicious ogres. Seeking to reassure them, he hopped up on the saddle and rode Princess around in a tight circle, smiling and waving at the ogres the whole time. When he hopped down, several ogre children dashed over to pet the giant lizard and ask for rides.

Clearly impressed, the chief looked from Princess to Dylan, who returned to stand in front of the throne. "Princess big! You give?"

Dylan shook his head. "Princess is soul bound to me, great chief. I can not give. But maybe King Max and I can help great chief find a companion of his own."

"How you do this?" The massive ogre leaned forward on his throne, listening intently.

"Well, I learned how to tame Princess. I can teach you. And we can help you find a big lizard like Princess, or some other creature to ride." He paused for a moment, gathering his thoughts.

"King Max is good friend. He wants to help Big Chief and ogre tribe. He invites you to come to his land. Come live with me, King Max, and others, in land with much food like this." He waved at the rapidly dwindling supply on the table, then at the now half-empty crate of spidorc meat next to the throne.

The chief looked at him suspiciously. "Leave our home?" he gestured at the huts and caves, then thumped one arm of the throne. "This good place!"

Dylan shook his head. "More red eye orcs will come. Many, many. Too many for even mighty big chief to kill, even with good weapons from King Max!" Most of the gathered ogres growled at that statement, shaking their heads in denial. Dylan ignored them and continued. "Max offers you better place. Good food, good caves, many friends. King Max fights many battles, against red eye orcs, other orcs, underground monsters, tasty goblins… Great chief and tribe earn much glory, get stronger!"

The chief looked more interested now. "Many fights? Many eats?"

"Many, many!" Dylan grinned up at him. "Plus, armor to help ogres fight better!" He mentally equipped his armor from inventory, causing all the gathered ogres to gasp in wonder.

The chief actually got up from his throne and stepped forward, reaching out to touch Dylan's custom-crafted dragonscale chest piece, then thump a fist on his shield, seeming pleased with the metallic thunk. He nodded his approval before sitting back down, and several of the ogre warriors stepped up to touch the armor as well while the chief considered.

"Dylan mighty warrior, and good friend!" he finally declared. Dylan tried to keep his expression neutral as he pictured the recent demise of one of the village ogres. He couldn't help but think the chief's opinion would be different if he knew about that. "What your friend Max want from ogres?"

"King Max is building a kingdom. Many cities, many villages like this one, but much bigger." Dylan spread his arms wide. "He has many enemies to fight, and needs help from Big Chief and ogre friends. You fight with us, we give you new homes, food, weapons, armor, and many new friends." Behind his back, Dylan crossed his fingers, hoping Max would forgive him for committing to armoring up a few dozen ogres.

Not totally convinced, but clearly interested, the chief leaned back in his throne, tossing another spidorc leg into his mouth and chewing thoughtfully before speaking again. "You stay in village, sleep. We decide with next sun!" He motioned to the remote hut that Dylan had been given to sleep in shortly after his original arrival.

Dylan thumped his chest and smiled up at the oversized ogre. "Chief strong and wise! I stay till next sun."

The ogres cheered, then lit the fire in the pit. Dylan surprised them again with a holdout gift, producing two giant racks of boar ribs and the haunches that went with them. Those were quickly set over the fire to cook as Dylan mingled with the villagers, renewing previous acquaintances and telling stories of the battles he'd fought. Toward the end of the celebration, one particular ogress, the one he'd been canoodling with when he'd received the notification that sent him looking for Max, elbowed him in the ribs before snatching the oversized rib he'd been gnawing on right out of his hand. With a grunt and a look over her shoulder, she waddled her way toward his hut and disappeared inside.

Dylan immediately hopped to his feet and hustled after her, much to the amusement of the other ogres.

*****

As they had done before, Max and his party members donated their share of the loot from the battle to the dworc villagers. The Stormhaven fighters who'd participated as reinforcements kept their share. Along with the shared experience from kills, and the defense quest rewards, it had been a fruitful fight for most of them. All but the five that perished during the battle. Max made sure their families would be taken care of, something Rockbreaker already knew to arrange on his behalf.

"Just heard from Dylan." He informed the others as they helped load orc corpses onto one of several funeral pyres. "He won't have a decision until tomorrow, but he believes the ogre tribe will come down and join us."

"Right on!" Smitty grinned. "Did he find himself a girlfriend, too?"

Max shook his head. "I didn't ask, he didn't tell."

"Oh, right." Smitty nodded, misunderstanding. "I didn't think he swung that way back on Earth, but hey. New world, new body, can't blame him if he wants to experiment."

Max stared at him for a moment. "No, Smitty. That's not what I… you know what, never mind. Let's talk about the trip north. Do we want to wait for Dylan if he's going to be back soon?"

"It would be good to have his shield." Nessa offered. She and the tank had become as close to friends as she was with anyone in the group.

"We don't need him, boss. You can tank." Blake offered. "If finding this One's camp involves any kind of stealth, he'd just slow us down, or have to wait in the car." Though it sounded harsh, Max knew the corporal was just giving his factual assessment of mission requirements. He would have said the same with Dylan standing right next to him. Only with a few insults added in for flavor.

"Are we in a hurry to get up there?" Smitty asked.

Max considered the question for a while. "The sooner we deal with him, the less likely we suffer another attack like this one. Or another raid on the Heart chamber. So while there's no quest clock ticking or anything, we should move to take him down as quickly as possible."

"And if there be too many o' the red-eyed bastards fer us to take on?" Dalia asked. She was especially hostile toward the mutated orcs since the loss of Picklet.

"We withdraw, set a trap like we did near the Den, and lead them into it." He flashed her a grim smile. "And if we don't get them all, we do it again."

"I vote to keep the band together." Smitty offered. "But we don't need to waste the days until the big fella gets back. How 'bout Nessa and I scout our way north? We'll track this bunch back to wherever they came from, and you can follow us when Dylan gets back. Hopefully by then we'll have some better intel, and you'll know what force size and configuration to bring with you." Nessa nodded her agreement with the plan.

"You want to take a few more hunters or rogue types with you?" Max liked the idea, but not the thought of the two of them being out there alone.

"Nah, boss. When exercising great sneakiness, less is more."

Nessa flashed Max a fang-filled smile. "I will keep him from embarrassing you, or getting himself killed and eaten." Max returned the grin as Smitty rolled his eyes behind the panthera.

"Alright, get whatever supplies you need and head out. Stay in contact via your rings. I want to hear from you every four hours, at a minimum. If you get into trouble, run away."

The two of them nodded and headed for the portal, going back to Stormhaven to resupply. Smitty got a few steps before turning back. "Hey, boss? If we find ourselves with a clean shot at their big bad cult leader?"

"No heroics. If you can take him out from a distance and exfil cleanly, it's your call. But the two of you are more valuable to me than any mission objective. If there's any doubt at all, retreat and wait for us."

"Exfil?" Nessa asked.

"I'll explain on the way." Smitty resumed his walk toward the portal with Nessa falling in next to him.

As Max watched them walk away, hoping he wasn't making a mistake, he saw Redmane approaching. He spent a moment wondering why the dwarf hadn't just contacted him via their rings, then decided it didn't matter.

"Me King, a moment?" The dwarf asked when he was within comfortable speaking distance. When Max dropped a final corpse on the pile and walked to meet him, the dwarf stopped and waited.

"A problem?"

"A request." Redmane spoke quietly, surveying the area around them. "One I thought it best to relay in person.

Enoch and Spellslinger be askin' ye to visit their... place o' business."

Instantly curious and excited, Max nodded. "The funeral here will start in a few minutes, then we'll go. Assuming you want to come with me?"

The elder dwarf snorted. "Try n stop me!"

The two of them remained at the village long enough to attend the solemn service for the two villagers who'd been among the battle's fatalities. The others were being taken back to Stormhaven, where a service would be held after their families were notified and given time to attend.

Max found Dalia among the crowd and asked if she wanted to join them. She declined, wanting to remain in the village a while with Pickstone and the dworcs, who had become a sort of extended family for her.

When Max opened the portal and stepped through with Redmane at his side, an honor guard of six dwarven warriors met them. "Greetings, me King." A sergeant stepped forward and started to bow, then paused and simply saluted with fist to chest. Which Max appreciated. "We're to escort ye to yer destination."

"The whole few hundred steps?" Max raised an eyebrow, and the guards looked uncomfortable. "Let me guess, Enoch's orders?"

The sergeant nodded once, still standing at attention. "He said to tell ye it be the principle o' the thing."

Max snorted. Enoch was constantly demanding Max have a proper escort wherever he went. One that befitted his station. Max didn't see the point in arguing right then, or making the dwarves uncomfortable. It was no great sacrifice to let them escort him, though he felt silly as they surrounded him.

They marched as a group to the building Enoch had claimed as an office, the one under which the Runemaster's Guild outpost was hidden. When they reached the front door, the escort peeled off and took up station outside, saving Max from having to determine whether they were in on the secret or not.

Inside, Enoch was waiting impatiently in his office, pacing back and forth and muttering quietly to himself. The moment he saw Max and Redmane, he burst into activity. "King Max! Come! We must get downstairs!" He didn't wait for a return greeting, or a reaction from his king, he simply stormed from the room and headed for the hidden stairs down to the outpost. A few minutes later the trio were crossing the floor of the large chamber created by the Runemaster's Guild. Max couldn't help but glance up at the massive guardian statues stationed along the walls. The battle golems were both terrifying and comforting at the same time.

He'd obligingly followed Enoch in silence on the way down, but was losing patience. "Enoch, what has happened? Have you found something?"

"It be more like somethin' found us." Enoch rounded one of the buildings and halted, pointing toward a statue that stood just a few paces in front of the portal built by the Runemasters.

"That's new. Did you find it in one of the buildings?" Max stared at the statue, and a moment later its description came up, making Enoch's answer moot.

> *Guild Functionary #213*
> *Level ???*
> *Health: ???*

Seeing the look on Max's face, Enoch chuckled. "Aye, that be pretty much how we reacted too. Once the panic and shoutin' quieted down." He nodded toward the portal built into the cavern wall. "That portal opened without warnin', and this functionary fella stepped through, askin fer ye. We told it ye were away, but that ye'd been summoned, and it's just been standin' here ever since." He looked down at his feet briefly. "We thought it'd be better ta bring ye here, than to set this creature loose in Stormhaven."

Max's pulse quickened as the dwarf spoke. Since claiming ownership of the outpost, he'd half expected a wrathful Runemaster's Guild response. If the dwarves' tales of the power of the rune magic were even halfway accurate, and the battle golems suggested that they were, then this guild wielded power that could squash Max and Stormhaven with little effort.

Clearing his throat, he stepped in front of the functionary. "I am King Maximilian Storm. You asked to see me?"

Everyone, including Max, flinched slightly as the thing raised its head, its gemlike eyes glowing with a sapphire luminance.

"Identifying Maximilian Storm, claimant to Guild Outpost 42. Adjusting identification to include Sovereign Class and Title: King of Stormhaven." It paused and tilted its head to one side in a curious gesture. "My records do not include such a kingdom in this region, or in fact in any region. Please clarify."

Glancing at Enoch, and at Spellslinger who had just joined them, Max raised an eyebrow. Enoch shrugged, while Spellslinger made a hand motion that instructed Max to continue.

"Stormhaven is a relatively new kingdom. We conquered the grey dwarf city of Nogroz a few months back, and I was made king. I renamed the kingdom Stormhaven. Since then, we have claimed additional land, including a portion of the abandoned gnome city above."

"Thank you, King Maximilian Storm. I have updated my records. This outpost was dormant for more than a thousand years before you claimed ownership. I would appreciate access to any records pertaining to the history and current status of the region."

"We would uhh... certainly be willing to assist you with that. Though I'm not sure how much information is available. As I mentioned, we found this region mostly abandoned, except for a lich and its undead minions in nearby Deepcrag." Max humored the functionary, still waiting for the other shoe to drop.

"Deepcrag is listed in my records as a neutral trade outpost. You say it is now controlled by a lich?"

"It was. We killed the lich and its minions, and claimed Deepcrag. As well as the goblin city beyond it. Some merchants have claimed the city above, except for the portion that belongs to me, and we are working to repopulate it."

The functionary raised one hand, palm facing outward toward Max. "Please confirm via sworn statement that you have located and eliminated a lich."

Feeling slightly threatened by the change in posture, Max readied himself to dodge any spell the thing might cast at him. "I swear by the gods that I discovered a lich in control of Deepcrag, and destroyed it and its minions." The glow of confirmation swirled around him, and a notification popped up.

Guild Quest 17 completed: Destroy a Lich!
The Runemaster's Guild has issued a standing quest to destroy any lich encountered anywhere in the world. Liches are anathema to life, and a plague upon all who encounter them.
Quest Level: 3; Reward: ??

Before Max could speak, the functionary spoke again. "King Maximilian, you are not a member of the Runemaster's Guild. The standard reward for Quest 17, three rune scrolls, cannot be awarded to you. I shall attempt to determine an alternate reward for your service."

Max saw the dwarves' eyes widen at the mention of the rune scrolls, and he thought Spellslinger actually salivated a little. "Why can the scrolls not be awarded to me?"

"You are not a member of the Runemaster's Guild." the functionary repeated, as if that explained everything. "That is, in fact, the reason for my presence here. The Guild received a notification that this outpost was awarded to you, but we have no record of you being a member."

"Is that a problem?" Max resisted taking a step back from the creature.

"Normally, yes. Such a brazen action would have resulted in your immediate termination." Its eyes blazed brightly for a moment before returning to their normal glow. "However, it seems that due to the extended period of inactivity at this outpost, the extreme reduction in Guild membership, and the fact that the Eternals have deemed you worthy of ownership of the Outpost in question, termination protocols are not appropriate at this time."

"I'm glad to hear that." Max relaxed slightly, though the end of that statement didn't instill a lot of confidence.

"What are your plans for this facility?"

Max shrugged, and was trying to formulate a response when Spellslinger cleared his throat meaningfully. Max nodded for him to proceed.

"I can answer that fer ye." He stepped around so that he stood next to Max in front of the functionary.

"Identifying... Master Mage Spellslinger. Authorized for full access to all facility systems by Claimant Maximilian Storm. Please continue, Master Spellslinger."

"As ye said, this outpost has been abandoned fer a very long time. During that time, the magic o' the Runemasters was lost to our people. The Guild withdrew from the eyes o' the world, and took their knowledge with 'em. We have been studyin' this facility in hopes o' findin' a way to contact the Runemasters."

"For what purpose?"

Spellslinger looked confused for a moment, blinking several times at the functionary. "Fer the purpose o' restoring the lost magic to the world."

There was a slight grinding sound as the functionary shook its head. "There are only six Runemasters known to still be living. All six have gone into seclusion and hibernation, and can not be contacted by any but Guild members. Even then, they have left instruction not to be disturbed except under particular circumstances. Contact is not possible at this time."

The creature's gaze shifted from a disappointed Spellslinger to Max. "I have accessed our records and protocols. As you are the acknowledged owner of Guild Outpost, and a legitimate Sovereign, who has completed an official Guild Quest of level three difficulty, I am authorized to offer you a Novice rank membership in the Runemaster's Guild. Do you accept?"

Max was tempted to jump at the chance, but was still a little suspicious. "What are the requirements of membership? I have a kingdom to run here, so I cannot run off to study at a Runemaster's academy or something."

"Novice rank membership itself has no requirements other than payment of dues, and a commitment to complete any accepted quests to the best of your ability. As well as to complete any Guild-issued missions. Currently, there are no active Guild officers to issue such missions, and the only quests available would be already-issued standing quests like the one you have completed."

"In that case, I accept. Thank you." A moment later the functionary's open palm emitted a burst of golden light that was absorbed into Max's chest, and several notifications appeared.

Congratulations!
You have been accepted as a Novice in the Runemaster's Guild. As a Novice runecaster, you have been granted limited access to Guild facilities, resources, and quests. Complete quests, study, grow stronger, and improve your reputation with the Guild to achieve Apprentice rank.

Guild Quest 17 Completion Reward modified!
Reward received: 2,000,000 exp; 200 platinum coins; three novice rank rune scrolls

Quest Received: Re-establish Outpost 42

As Claimant of Guild Outpost 42, it falls upon you to ensure proper maintenance and readiness of the facility, per Guild regulations. See Sections 11 – 17 of the Manual for details.

Max noticed Enoch practically dancing on his toes behind Spellslinger, his eyes bugging out as if he badly needed to relieve himself. Thinking he knew what the dwarf was after, he grinned inwardly, though he didn't let it show on his face. This seemed like one of those opportunities that the corporals were always blabbering about. In their VR games, if you interacted in a particular way with the proper NPC, you might unlock an epic quest. Taking a deep breath, he addressed the functionary.

"I was not alone when I destroyed the lich. Masters Spellslinger, Redmane, and Enoch assisted, among others. Would it be possible for them to become novices as well, since they helped complete a level three quest?"

"Masters Spellslinger, Redmane, and Enoch are neither Claimants nor Sovereigns, and would be subject to standard Guild application requirements. Applicants must be sponsored by a Guild member in good standing, of Apprentice rank or higher."

"But you said there are no current members active, other than myself. Since they also completed a level three quest, can an exception be made to allow a novice to sponsor their applications? How else can they receive their proper quest rewards? Or has the Guild decided to just completely shut down operations?"

The functionary paused for what seemed like a long time before responding. "My records indicate no instructions to cease Guild operations. However, an exception such as you have requested requires the approval of a Guild officer. I shall send an official query regarding your request." It turned around, and the others all took a step back as the portal on the wall flashed open. The space beyond was dimly lit, and appeared to extend for some distance. There were a few single-story stone buildings, behind which rose a grey stone tower. On either side of the tower entrance stood a battle golem that was at least twice the size of those in Outpost 42. Max thought the place looked similar to his outpost, minus the tower. A moment later the portal deactivated again, without the functionary ever having moved.

"The query has been sent. Pending the outcome, I can grant the non-proprietary portions of the rewards for the quest completions." Max saw all three dwarves blink, then stare into the distance. Each of them received the same experience and platinum that he had, but not the scrolls.

"Should the decision be made to allow you membership, the balance of the quest reward will become available to you." The functionary looked at each of the dwarves as it spoke.

"Thank ye, err... functionary." Spellslinger bowed his head, followed immediately by the other two. Max tried to keep in mind that this creature, whatever it was, probably seemed like some kind of holy relic, maybe even the equivalent of a messenger angel, to them.

"The new quest I received mentioned something about a manual. Where would I find this manual?"

The functionary turned back to him. "Yes, the manual. Normally, a prospective applicant would receive the manual and other study materials at the time of their application, several years before their acceptance as a Novice. One moment, please."

Max barely had time to blink before the creature held out both hands, and a box appeared. "This is a standard applicant's information package. Inside you will find, among other things, the manual you require." It paused for a moment. "As no active members are available to assist you, I have been reassigned to this facility to help guide you."

"Thank you, functionary, your assistance is greatly appreciated." Max paused for a moment. "It's a bit awkward to keep referring to you as functionary. Do you have a name?"

"I have received no designation other than Functionary #213. As Claimant of this facility, you may assign me an alternate designation of your choosing."

Max openly grinned this time, as he heard Smitty's voice in his head. "In that case, Functionary #213, from now on we will refer to you as Funky." All three dwarves glared at him as if he'd committed blasphemy.

The golem, for Max was pretty sure that's what Funky was, bowed its head slightly. "New designation *Funky* has been registered.

"Perfect! Now, we have a quest to deal with." Max opened the box and located the manual, which he handed to Enoch. "Just one second..." He pulled up his quest tab, located the new one, and shared it with the three dwarves. Spellslinger immediately reached for the manual after accepting the quest, then spluttered in frustration as Enoch jerked it away, hugging it to his chest.

Max chuckled at their antics. "This should be interesting." He looked over at the golem. "Welcome to Stormhaven, Funky! Make yourself... comfortable, I guess? Do you need anything while we study the manual? Food, or drink?"

"This facility's mana condensation array is in working order, and is at one hundred percent capacity. I can connect and recharge at need, Novice Maximilian Storm."

"Please, just call me Max."

Chapter 5

After spending most of a day at the outpost with Funky and the dwarven bunch, Max returned to Stormhaven. Redmane reluctantly accompanied him, citing the need to keep the kingdom running smoothly. He made Enoch and Spellslinger swear to provide regular updates, and to summon Max back immediately if Funky got a response on their membership request.

The moment they were back in Max's study, about to address the inevitable and ever-present piles of items to deal with, Red appeared atop the desk. "Ya earned quite a few Sovereign points today."

"Really? For what, specifically?"

"Ya big knob, why d'ya think? First ye personally defended the village, and granted yer people a defense quest that leveled a bunch o' them up. Then ya made contact with a long-lost ancient guild o' runemasters, after stealin' one o' their outposts, and ya didn't get yerself killed for it. Then ya got yerself rewarded a second time *in platinum coins and ancient magic scrolls*, no less, for killin' that lich, and ya wiggled yer way into joinin' the guild!"

"I suspect ye also received a few points for thinking o' the kingdom first before accepting that offer, and fer attempting to get several o' your senior advisors into the guild, as well. Having us rediscover rune magic will vastly improve yer kingdom's power and reputation." Redmane added dryly.

Max thumped his desk, grinning. "Well, who's the awesome and handsome king? I am!"

"Don't let it go to yer head, ya tall lump o' stupid. Ya just got lucky. An hour from now ye'll trip n fall over yer own feet, or somethin equally embarassin' to Master Redmane here, and yer poor unappreciated guide." Red glared at him. Behind her, Redmane struggled not to smile.

"I appreciate you very much, my lovely and fiery-tempered leprechaun goddess." Max smiled down at her. She crossed her arms and intensified her glare, adding suspicion to her expression of contempt.

"See, there ya go! Temptin' fate by callin' me a goddess. Told ya ye'd do something stupid afore long."

"Couldn't help it. I was carried away by the depth of my admiration and appreciation of you." His eyes sparkled as he teased the little redheaded ball of sarcasm and spite that was his spirit guide.

"Bah! Shut it!" Red disappeared without warning.

"It truly has been an amazing day." Redmane spoke quietly, his tone solemn. "Ye made contact with the Runemasters, Max! And did ya get a look at the golem ye named Funky?" The question came with a look of reproach over the choice of name. "It listened and responded like it were alive!"

"Yeah, old Funky is impressive." Max agreed, refusing to be chastened for the name. He couldn't wait to see the look on Smitty's face when he learned about it. "Did you see the size of the battle golems on the other side of the portal?"

"Aye." Redmane nodded. "Taller than our walls here at the keep. I'd not want to be attackin' that place, wherever it was." He shook his head. "I wish ye'd been able to share them scrolls with us."

"Funky was pretty adamant about that. No sharing the rune scrolls with any non-guildmembers. It makes sense, I suppose. If the magic is that powerful, they'd need a way to keep it restricted to those who are trusted to use it."

"Have ya looked at em?" The dwarf's tone was wistful.

"You've literally been right next to me every minute since I received them. You know I haven't looked at them yet." Max teased his closest advisor. "I'll find a secure place this evening and look at them. Without any kind of training, though, they might just look like scribbles to me. Anyway, at least Funky didn't object to you guys looking at the manual, since you're all authorized to access the outpost already." He was about to say more, but Dylan's voice came through one of his rings.

"On the way back, boss. It'll take a few days, as everyone is on foot, and we're driving their livestock and such. The chief is bringing the whole tribe with him. Also, I loaded up fifty storage ring slots with emeralds and other gems, plus a bunch of gold ore they had laying around. You might want to consider claiming their territory for yourself to secure those resources."

"That's amazing, corporal! Well done!"

"One thing, boss. I might have had to promise you'll provide sexy armor for about thirty ogre warriors. I told them it wouldn't be as fancy as mine, but I don't think they'll settle for just leather. Maybe chainmail shirts and shields?"

"I've got Redmane here with me. We'll put in an order through Darkholm right away and get them started. We'll probably need every bit of those gems you're bringing to pay the smiths."

"Totally worth it to have a force of heavily armed and armored ogre shock troops!" Max could picture the look of evil anticipation on his corporal's face. Both his old human face, and the new ogre one, in fact.

"Get them here as fast as you can. We decided to wait on you before we head north. Smitty and Nessa are already out there scouting. Didn't want you to miss out on the chance to kill the big bad orc boss."

"We can be at Darkholm in three or four days, use the portal from there. If you'll give them a heads-up that we're not an invading ogre army, boss?"

"I'll reach out to Ironhand right now. Safe travels, corporal."

Max relayed the news to Redmane. "We'll need to figure out a place for them to live. Dylan said their home is a bunch of caves. Do you think they'd prefer to live on the surface? Or here in Stormhaven?

"Don't ye be thinkin' o putting em up in me outpost!" A dwarf appeared behind Redmane, startling both him and Max for a moment before he was recognized. "I'll get nothin' done with a bunch o' oversized infants bumblin' around!"

Both Max and Redmane hopped to their feet and bowed. "Regin, welcome." Max smiled at the scowling dwarven god. "I hadn't even considered the outpost. But now that you mention it…"

"Ha! It ain't wise to tease an Eternal, young whelp!" The dwarf motioned for them to sit as he took the chair next to Redmane's. "I came to speak to ye about a serious issue."

Max's smile disappeared and he placed his hands on the desk in front of him. "What can we do for you?"

"Ye can adopt a proper respect fer the opportunity ye received today. Respect the power, and the danger, o' the rune magic." Regin's tone was no-nonsense, as was the look on his face. "The runemasters retreated from the world fer damned good reasons. The clan wars, the weapons they unleashed… I'll not allow what happened before to occur again. Dwarvenkind won't survive such. That's the only warnin' I'll be givin' ye."

Max sat back in his chair. Regin had a very good point. He imagined giving the dwarves machine guns, or even nuclear weapons, without the background and context of the destruction they could cause. Looking the god of crafting directly in the eyes, he nodded. "I understand. On my old world we had weapons that could kill tens of thousands, even millions at a time. I'll do all I can to ensure that the knowledge is limited to those with the proper disposition. Though, I gotta say, I think the dwarves learned their lesson the last time."

Redmane nodded at Max before speaking. "Aye, we did." He looked uncomfortable speaking to Regin, but pushed through his hesitation. "We view what happened before as our greatest sin, our greatest shame. The old magic should be used fer good, not fer war."

Regin wasn't convinced. "And when ye need better weapons, better spells to defend yerself against invaders like the red-eyed orcs? What'll ye do with them after? When one clan covets the lands, or the mines, of another?"

When Redmane blushed and lowered his eyes in shame, Max stepped in. "We could require each clan leader to swear an oath not to use the old magic against other dwarves. Except grey dwarves, cuz screw those guys."

Regin nodded. "That'd be a start. Though I'll require that the penalty fer breakin that oath be death. No king or clan leader willin' to use rune magic against their brethren be fit to live." He waited while both Max and Redmane nodded. "Ye'll find, as ye learn more o' the guild rules, that the Runemasters have put a similar law in place after the… previous happennins. Be certain ye follow it, or ye'll be answerin' to me after they're done with ye!"

Max was taken aback by the vehemence of the dwarven god's words. Being directly threatened by an Eternal was not a pleasant experience. His heart raced, and he resisted the urge to hide under his desk.

"I'll swear right here and now to never use the rune magic to attack another dwarven kingdom or clan, unless they're already using it against me and mine."

The light that swirled around him was crimson, and briefly felt as if it were burning his skin. Redmane's eyes widened at the sight of it, even as Regin nodded. "That be a good start, Max. Be sure n pass on me wishes to the others before sharin' what ye learn o' the rune magic." Regin was gone in the next instant, leaving Max and Redmane blinking in surprise, and more than a little intimidated. After taking a moment to recover, Max looked at his advisor.

"I thought you guys were overstating the level of destruction caused by the rune magic." He motioned towards Regin's empty chair. "After that, I believe you. We'll need to be very careful how we handle this going forward. That oath I took, the binding felt… ominous."

Redmane nodded, "I never even heard o' crimson light bindin' an oath, let alone seen it meself."

"Great. I probably just swore myself to eternal damnation if I break the oath, or something." Max took a deep breath. "Or maybe it was just because I swore it directly to a god? I mean, how often does someone get themselves in that situation?"

Redmane chuckled, relaxing a bit. "Ye do seem to constantly find new ways ta get yerself in trouble, Max. But the risks ye take bring great rewards." He paused, thinking. "I believe ye have only good intentions regardin' the rune magic, and I'm thinkin' Regin believed it too, or ye might not be sittin' there still."

Max got up from his chair. "Could you reach out to Ironhand and let him know that Dylan and the ogre tribe are on their way. I'm going to head to my quarters and investigate these rune scrolls." There was a hint of jealousy in Redmane's eyes as he nodded and accompanied Max out of the study. They turned and went their separate ways, the dwarf headed for his own office while Max set off for his private quarters.

Once he'd settled onto one of the sofas in his lounge area, he produced the three scrolls and set them on the coffee table in front of him. His heart rate picked up a bit as he inspected them, looking for some indication of which one he should try first. For all he knew, he was the first being to start studying rune magic in a thousand years or more. A magic so powerful that it nearly wiped out the dwarven race once upon a time. He felt the weight of the responsibility put upon him by Regin, and found himself thinking of J. Robert Oppenheimer and the team on the

Manhattan Project. Most especially his quote from Hindu scripture, which he muttered aloud to himself.

"I am become death, destroyer of worlds."

He shook his head. "Did they know what they were creating as they worked, or were they just focused on the science, on solving the riddle? Did they understand the implications then? Or did it not occur to them until later, when the damage was done?"

Choosing the leftmost scroll at random, he untied the black ribbon around it, and was about to unfurl the scroll when he noticed something. Setting the scroll down, he looked more closely at the ribbon that was draped over his fingers. Stretching it out fully between both hands, he brought it closer to his face and squinted at it. "Well, lookit that." He muttered.

The ribbon itself was embroidered with a series of nine tiny runes stitched in blood red thread that blended in so well with the black fabric that Max had nearly missed it. He ran his thumb over a few of them, feeling a slight itch as he did so. The runes meant nothing to him, yet, but he found himself wondering why someone would go to such trouble for a simple ribbon meant to hold a scroll closed.

Setting the ribbon down, he took up the scroll and unrolled it, only to find more runes he didn't understand. At the top of the page were three large runes written in sapphire ink. Below those the page was filled with hundreds of smaller runes in black ink. Altogether it reminded Max of the first page of a chapter, with the title up top and the text below. "So, are you chapter one, or chapter one hundred twenty three?" He whispered to the scroll. "I'm betting that other novices already knew how to read these runes before joining up and being able to earn these rewards." He paused as another thought occurred to him.

"Maybe these aren't even the magic runes? Maybe this is just really old dwarven script, and the text teaches you the magic, like the scrolls I buy from Josephine. But it's not working because I can't read the text." He set the scroll on the table, used a candle holder and his belt knife as paperweights to hold it open, then set the ribbon on top of the page. Comparing the two sets of runes, he felt that there was a difference between them, but couldn't quite make out what that might be. They were both made of straight lines and sharp angles for the most part, with very few of them having any curves or soft angles. The writing reminded him of old Nordic runes he'd seen a few times, possibly combined with Cyrillic letters. Neither of which he knew anything about, other than to recognize them on sight.

He considered taking them to show Enoch and Spellslinger, who at least were able to read some of the ancient dwarven lettering, like the sign outside the door above the outpost. But he changed his mind when he remembered how explicit Funky had been about not sharing proprietary information with non-guildmembers. He didn't know how those rules were enforced, but he wasn't about to find out.

Staring at the parchment, he unconsciously took up the ribbon and began wrapping it around his thumb. After several seconds, he felt that tingling feeling again, causing him to look down in time to see the runes on the ribbon pulse slightly with a crimson light. The tingling sensation faded with the light, until both were gone.

Intrigued, Max tried to *Examine* the ribbon, but the spell produced nothing but question marks. He then got the same result with the open scroll, and the other two. Whatever the items were, they were either resistant to the magic, or just well above his current abilities.

Max spent a few minutes opening the other two scrolls, examining their ribbons, which were also embroidered with runes, and trying to read the scrolls themselves. The only discovery he made was that all three ribbons held identical runes.

Disappointed, he carefully rolled up each of the scrolls and retied their ribbons around them before returning them to his inventory. Sitting back on the sofa and putting his feet up on the table, he began removing the other items that Funky had given him. He'd left the outpost manual with Spellslinger, but kept the rest of the applicant's kit for himself. Getting comfortable, he picked up the first one, a small, thin book with maybe thirty pages. Excited, but wary, he opened it up and was pleased to see it was written in what he'd come to know as *common*, and he began to read.

*****

Lagrass huddled in the darkest corner of his cell, curled up in a fetal position and rocking back and forth as he whimpered in pain. The term *darkest* was relative, as there was no light source anywhere, other than a single torch placed so far down the corridor outside his cell that it barely registered as light.

His eyes closed, he tried to form an image in his mind of blue skies and puffy clouds drifting by, the feeling of sunlight on his face. Distracted by the pain of his injuries, and the stench of both his own body and the filthy hole in the floor nearby that served as his toilet, he wasn't able to hold the image for more than a few seconds at a time. He reached for it again, needing a focus, something to give his mind a moment of sufficient peace to allow him to cast a spell. He desperately needed healing. The questioners were experts at causing pain without permanent injury, and had practiced their arts on him for hours. When they did slip up and go too far, he was healed just enough to keep him alive and hale enough to allow them to proceed.

Lagrass had told them everything they'd asked about, and a mountain of things they hadn't. He'd answered questions, confessed his sins from murder to theft of bubble gum from a corner store when he was six. He'd told them things about his world that he probably shouldn't have, describing the inner workings of guns, bombs, even his best guess on how steam engines worked. He'd shouted out warnings about bacteria and viruses, eating bad beef or moldy bread, anything he thought might make them stop, then whispered more when he could no longer shout.

He couldn't remember how many days he'd been down there, or how many sessions he'd suffered at the hands of the questioners. After each round, they'd toss him back into his cell and leave him there long enough for his body to heal some. Each time he lay on the cold, filthy floor and try to heal himself, to soothe the physical aches and pains, but could never quite manage it. He couldn't seem to focus long enough to cast the spell.

They brought him a loaf of dark bread and a wooden flask of water twice a day, just enough to keep him from starving or dying of thirst. He learned the hard way to catch both of them as they were pushed through the small, barred window in his cell door. The first time he'd failed to do so, the bread had rolled into the corner by the filth-encrusted toilet hole. He hadn't quite been hungry enough to retrieve it, but he'd been sorely tempted. He'd fought with himself over it for an hour before a rat appeared to drag the bread down into the hole.

There was a tattered, crusted, foul smelling blanket on the floor near the door that he sometimes wrapped himself in when he slept. Exhaustion, both physical and mental, sometimes overcame him after they tossed him back into his hole, and he passed out before reaching for the scant comfort of the blanket.

Still rocking back and forth, his knees folded up to his chest, arms wrapped around them, he tried again to focus. Just one cast of his low level healing spell would make all the difference in the world. It could ease the pain, at least a little. It had been a few hours since his last session, and his natural regeneration was beginning to have a noticeable effect. But that was bad news for Lagrass. Because when his natural regeneration healed him to the point that the pain almost ceased, they'd just drag him out of his cell and start again.

He twitched and screamed when he felt a rat paw at his leg, investigating the smell of fresh blood from a cut that was just beginning to scab over. Lashing out with one fist, he knocked the squealing rat away, sending it crashing into the corner before it retreated into the sewer below. That was another reason focus was so hard to come by. He couldn't sleep for long before one or more rats tried to take a bite out of his wounded flesh.

"What does she want?" He asked the empty darkness for the thousandth time. He'd asked himself, his questioners, the mage that had started this whole mess when he visited the questioning chamber, the various scribes that dutifully wrote down everything he screamed out during his sessions, even the mute and badly disfigured guard that delivered his food and water. No one ever answered him. Some part of what remained of his mind understood that they likely didn't know. Except for the mage.

That bastard knew.

He was the queen's advisor, and had to have some idea what information she wanted from Lagrass. The smile on the old bastard's face as he watched the questioning told Lagrass all he needed to know about that one. He enjoyed watching Lagrass scream, and wasn't going to do anything to shorten the questioning process.

Lagrass shuddered, squeezing his knees more tightly against his chest. For all he knew, he'd already told them all they wanted to know, and the mage was just continuing the sessions for his own perverse entertainment.

Another whimper escaped him as he contemplated an unending procession of questionings and suffering, and a cough that wracked his sore chest muscles and cracked ribs was followed by a gasp of pain. A fine spray of blood spattered his lips, and he felt a wet gurgle as he inhaled. He was sweating as if fevered, and shivering with cold at the same time, and every inch of his body throbbed in pain. He would never leave this place. The pain would never end.

At that moment, he gave up. He'd tried cooperating, but no amount of cooperation stopped, or even slowed, the pain. He didn't have enough left in him to resist, and even if he had, he suspected resistance would only be even more painful. Hearing the shuffling footsteps of the unfortunate creature that brought his bread and water, he waited until they stopped outside his door. Not bothering to get up, he took another ragged, gurgling breath, as deep as he could manage, and spoke.

"Please, just kill me."

*****

Max woke to a frantic knock on the door. Sitting upright, he caught the book that slid off his chest and set it on the coffee table. The knock rang out again, and he wiped his eyes with the heels of his palms before calling out, "Enter."

The door burst open and Teeglin came dashing in. "King Max! Breakfast is ready! Master Redmane asked me to come fetch you." She paused, glancing at the small pile of books and documents on the table. "Oh... were you doing your homework? I hate homework." She grimaced at the pile. "You'd think as king, you could just say you don't want to do yours, and go do something fun, like tell knock knock jokes."

Max grinned at her. "I suppose I could do just that. But this homework is important."

"You mean like... protocols? Master Redmane makes me study protocols every day. Says if I fail to follow one, I might embarrass you at court, or even start a war, like some human king's son has done."

"This is way more important than protocols, my princess." He reached out and tousled her hair, earning him a scowl. "Do you know why Master Redmane sent you to fetch me?"

"He said he tried to reach you through the ring, but that you must be asleep. You've slept in quite a bit, you know? Most people ate breakfast hours ago." She paused to take a breath. "Though I suppose kings can sleep in if they want to, right? And princesses too?" She looked hopefully up at him as he got to his feet.

"Oh, no. Fully grown princesses, maybe. But *our* princess wakes when Master Redmane says she should, and not a minute later." He pretended to scowl back at her, then let it morph into a smile. "I hadn't realized I've slept so long. Lead on, Princess Teeglin! Take me to your master!"

After taking a moment to cross her arms and throw him a pouty look, she turned and rushed back out the door, forcing Max to jog a bit to catch up. He noticed the knowing smirks on the guards' faces as he entered the corridor and passed them by. The little dworc was an unstoppable force of nature, and the entire palace had learned to make allowances.

A few minutes later they arrived at Redmane's office, where he found several platters of breakfast food laid out on the desk and waiting for him. He nodded gratefully to Redmane as the dwarf dismissed Teeglin, sitting down and helping himself to some bacon.

"Good afternoon, Max. Sleep well?" The old dwarf poked at him after he'd stuffed his mouth with bacon and eggs. Max simply nodded, then shrugged. "I take it ye learned whatever was in the scrolls, then." The dwarf looked confused when Max shook his head no this time, struggling to chew and swallow before answering. "But I got a notification in the wee hours o' the mornin' that Stormhaven now has a novice runecaster."

Max finally managed to swallow the food in his mouth, washing it down with several gulps of water. "You got what?"

"It's a part o' me job as chamberlain. When somethin' important happens, like ye claim new territory, or win a battle, do somethin' that earns kingdom points, or ye recruit a noteworthy new citizen, I receive a notification. Havin' a runecaster among us certainly be noteworthy."

"Huh." Max shrugged. "I dunno. I was studying last night…" He set down the forkful of eggs he'd been about to shove into his maw. "I tried to learn the scrolls, but nothing happened. So I started going through the applicant's kit, hoping for something that might help. I was reading, and I fell asleep. Next thing I knew Teeglin was bursting through my door like the palace was on fire." He smiled as the dwarf shook his head, an exasperated look on his face. "Don't worry, she knocked first. More than once."

Max looked to make sure that Teeglin had closed the door when she left, then called out. "Red? You been holding out on me?"

The leprechaun appeared on Redmane's desk, standing between a plate of sausages and a pitcher of juice that was twice her height. "When exactly was I supposed ta show ya yer notifications? Ya were passed out n snorin' until the wee one woke ya, then she was with ya till about one minute ago. I didn't want ya to choke on whatever ya been stuffin' yer ugly face with, now did I?" She waved a hand and a couple notifications popped up.

"Ya didn't fall asleep readin', ya fell unconscious when that book stuffed yer mostly empty noggin full o' useful bits. Ya can now read the ancient dwarven script. As can I, by the way. Like I was born to it." She flashed him a tiny thumbs-up, a gesture she'd learned from him and the corporals.

Ignoring the notifications, since she'd just told him what he needed to know, he pulled a scroll from his inventory. A quick glance at the ribbon as he untied it muted his excitement, as he still couldn't read it. But when he unrolled the scroll, he grinned up at his two companions.

"I can read it now!"

*****

Chapter 6

When Dylan and the ogre chief stepped through the portal, Max, Redmane, and Teeglin were there to greet them. The formalities were swift, Max presenting the chief with a custom created triple cheeseburger the size of a dinner plate with three pounds of meat in it. The chief's roar of delight caused the guards on the wall to jump, and Teeglin to disappear behind Redmane, only to peek out again a moment later, looking sheepish.

As the chief consumed the burger right there and then, the remainder of the tribe filtered through, very nearly filling the keep's courtyard. To Max's surprise, the ogres immediately formed into orderly ranks, and when the last one stepped into place, they shouted in unison.

"That's a fact, Jack!"

Max turned and raised an eyebrow at Dylan, who was doing his best to hold back laughter. "Corporal?"

"I've uh… been working with them on the way here." The ogre corporal confessed.

"Apparently so." Max shook his head, trying not to smile at the obvious movie reference. As soldiers back on Earth, *Stripes* had been one of their favorite movies to watch in their leisure time.

"Don't tell Blake, but I might have also mentioned that the most popular sport in Stormhaven is gnome tossing." Dylan's smile was wide and his eyes filled with mischief. "I want it to be a surprise for him."

Max rolled his eyes at the corporal before he turned and addressed the tribe. "Welcome to Stormhaven! We offer you food, shelter, and friendship!" The roar of approval from the tribe made folks in the neighborhoods outside the keep glance worriedly in that direction and wonder what was going on.

Dylan quickly administered the oath, since Smitty was out on assignment, and the entire tribe was given a tour of Stormhaven city. Max had instructed Dylan to offer them places to stay in any of the kingdom's locations, above ground or below. The tour was in part to show them what was available, but also to let the residents see the ogres and grow comfortable with having them around.

Partway through the tour, the tribe was mobbed by a group of goblin children. After some initial confusion and alarm, Dylan explained that the goblins were friendly, and lifted one of the kids to ride on his shoulder. Within moments the rest of the little goblins also had ogre mounts, and the tour continued.

Being creatures who had lived on the surface, and who enjoyed digging through stone, the tribe were eventually settled near the quarry, not far from Glitterspindle's temple and the mine. Some went to work in the quarry, others were recruited to push heavy carts inside the mine. More than a score of them signed on as guards, taking shifts at various Stormhaven fortifications. A few of the females got together and opened a leatherworking shop at the Way Station. They traded gemstones from their home village for piles of hides that the town's hunters brought in. Initially Max had been concerned that the ogre ladies would be taken advantage of, but Mayor Gro'nag took it upon himself to look out for them. He made it clear that anyone caught overcharging the ogresses for their hides would be dealt with harshly.

*****

"Can you tell how many there are?" Nessa whispered to Smitty from half a step to his left. Both of them were actively using their stealth abilities, but being in the same party, they could still see each other.

Smitty shook his head. "Too many, and they're moving around too much. If I had to guess, maybe a thousand of them so far. More keep streaming in, though."

Nessa nodded silently, agreeing with his rough estimate. After watching another group come marching into the settlement below, she turned back to Smitty. "You should retreat and report in to Max. We're only a couple miles out of range here, so you won't have to go far. I will remain and continue to observe. When you are ready to report, I'll update you."

Smitty gave her a thumbs-up and slowly moved back from the tree he was crouched behind. When he'd backed up enough to be out of sight of the settlement below, he turned and stood upright, then began to make his way down the hill. Five minutes later, when he was reasonably sure he was out of range of any enemy scouts, he broke into a jog.

He and Nessa had backtracked the red-eyed orcs' trail for several days, always heading roughly north. They'd run across, and efficiently eliminated, a few small scouting parties, usually two to four orcs each. Both of them attacked from stealth in those instances, scoring critical and fatal hits on the first two targets each time. Nessa crept up behind the orc scouts and motioned to Smitty before backstabbing an orc in its kidney, then using her other dagger to slit its throat. At the same time, Smitty would shoot one in the back of the head, throat, or heart. Then quickly draw and fire again at others, if there were more than two. That distraction allowed Nessa to get behind a second target and execute another critical sneak attack.

Without exception the orcs were five to ten levels lower than the companions, and worth very little in the way of experience. The loot was decent, though, each of the orcs carrying silver, and even a few gold coins on occasion. Their weapons and armor were mostly common quality, but in good shape. Smitty and Nessa stored them to sell to Max for use in the kingdom's armory.

They'd checked in with Max and the rest of the party twice a day, until they reached a point when their rings no longer worked. Smitty estimated they'd gone about a hundred and ten miles north of Stormhaven City at that point. They stopped there and set up camp before Smitty backtracked, testing the ring over and over until he reestablished the connection. He let Max know that they were passing out of range, and that they'd update him again as soon as they found something.

When the trail finally led to the old settlement, the two of them had spent a full day and night observing the goings-on within the crumbling walls and buildings. Orcs moved about the place day and night, some on patrol, others cooking, drinking, repairing gear, or sparring amongst themselves. They made no attempt to hide their presence, having built several roaring bonfires in a roughly circular pattern within the settlement. They kept those fires going, the columns of smoke clearly announcing their position during daylight hours, and the glow from the high flames acting as a beacon in the dark night.

Smitty backtracked their trail until he reached a familiar stone, one he had childishly marked with the painted version of Max's face that their people had taken to using. Sitting atop the rock, he reached out to Max via his ring.

"Hey, boss. We think we found them."

"Smitty! I was beginning to worry. Report." Max answered immediately, excusing himself and stepping away from the folks he'd been talking to in the keep's courtyard.

"We tracked them to an old settlement in the mountains, just a couple miles north of where I am now. Spent the last twenty four hours watching them, trying to get a count. There are, best guess, a thousand of them there now, but it looks to me like they're just a vanguard force."

"Vanguard? What makes you say that?"

"They've got a forge up and running, with several smiths pounding almost nonstop on armor and weapons. Orc hunters are streaming in constantly with food. More than they need to feed a thousand of them, even if they are big hungry orcs. There are barrels and crates stacked in some of the buildings, and overflowing out into the street. Also, since we arrived, three more groups of fifty to a hundred each have arrived, all from the north."

"So they're preparing for a larger force that's moving south." Max reached the same conclusion as Smitty and Nessa had.

Smitty nodded, then realized that Max couldn't see him. "Totally, boss. We've got a plan to learn more. On my way back I'm gonna shoot a deer or something, then haul it into the camp like I'm one of their hunters."

"You don't have the glowing eyes to fit in, corporal."

"I'll keep my head down, boss. And I only plan to hang around long enough to hear what I can hear while dropping off the meat. Hopefully I'll get some idea what's going on before I have to skedaddle."

"I don't like it. The rest of us aren't there to back you up if something goes wrong." Max started to second-guess the plan, but Smitty cut him off.

"You forget, boss. I spawned as an orc. I speak their language. Nessa and I have killed several of them, and I can put on their gear so I blend in better. I'll be fine.

Besides, if we wait till you guys can get here, the main force might have already arrived."

Max sighed, knowing his scout was correct. "Alright, you do your thing, but be as careful as possible. No heroics. If you get discovered, haul ass." He paused as Smitty made affirmative noises. "I'll start rounding up a group, and we'll head out in a few hours." He spent another couple minutes asking for details on the location and layout of the settlement, and giving Smitty a few instructions, before signing off. Once the attack force transported to the dworc village, they'd be back in range of Smitty and Nessa's rings, and he could update their intel as they moved north. He figured they could make much better time than the two scouts, since they had a destination and didn't need to follow tracks or move in stealth.

First thing he did was call Dylan, Dalia, and Blake back to the keep, then notified Redmane and his General that they needed to organize a strike force. He reached out to Ironhand to let him know they'd be launching an offensive against what he hoped was the main body of the mutant orc cult. The dwarf offered reinforcements, and Max gladly accepted. He also reached out to Caretaker via the ring he'd left with the guardian, to let him and the dwarves that were guarding the Heart know what was happening. If there was another attack there while Max was away, Caretaker would reach out directly to Redmane, who would send help.

Two hours later, Max and his party took the portal to the dworc village, accompanied by a six-hundred strong force of dwarves, orcs, gnomes, minotaurs, kobolds, and ogres. More were being gathered, but Max had brought those he could muster quickly to reinforce the village in the event of an attack there. Rather than march his entire army north and potentially have them waiting in a camp until their target arrived, he left them with the dworcs to get better organized, gather proper supplies, and do a little training to better coordinate the different races and fighting styles amongst them. Specifically, he wanted the dwarves to find a way to work alongside the massive ogres on the front lines. Something Rockbreaker seemed quite enthusiastic about. Max didn't blame him. Having a dozen or so thousand-pound, ten foot tall, heavily armed and armored tanks available to form up behind sounded like a lot of fun.

Leaving the bulk of his force to finalize preparations, Max and his party mounted up and left the village, headed north. Dylan rode Princess, while the rest of the party rode their ja'kang mounts. Pokey led the way, with Princess bringing up the rear. Ten minutes into their ride, Smitty reported in that he'd completed the first of his tasks.

"Found a good spot, boss. It's a narrow pass, not as narrow as the one we used up by the Den, but it should work fine. It's a day's march south of the settlement they're using, in case they leave before you get here."

"Sounds good, thank you corporal." Max replied.

"Bagged myself one of those mutant meat eater deer, and I'm headed into the camp a couple hours after it gets dark. I'll check back after exfil."

"Roger that. Good luck, Smitty."

"Save some for us, little buddy." Dylan added, grinning at the back of Princess's head.

They moved at a trot through the forest as they proceeded north. Pokey and the other ja'kang could have gone faster, but Princess had a little difficulty moving around and through the trees in places. Also, the giant lizard wasn't built for long distance runs, so they paused often to let him catch his breath. At one point Dylan even dismissed him and jogged behind the others through a particularly dense area of forest. With his enchanted *Agility* boots, the ogre kept up surprisingly well, and even urged Max to move a little faster for a while.

By the time they made camp that night, they were a little more than halfway to Smitty and Nessa. Nessa had reported watching Smitty walk into the orc camp successfully, but he hadn't emerged yet. She added that there hadn't been any disturbance to suggest that he'd been caught, which helped ease Max's nerves a bit. As they were talking, she was giving an account of the three additional groups of orcs that had arrived since Smitty's last report, but she paused midsentence, causing Max's gut to clench.

"Nessa, what is it?" He growled through comms.

"I see... there is a grey dwarf in the encampment." She sounded surprised as she said it.

"Could you repeat that?" Max's tone was terse. If the greys had teamed up with the red-eyed orcs, this could be a much bigger fight than he'd prepared for.

"A grey dwarf female in the settlement. She's… she emerged from stealth atop one of the roofs, and is watching the orcs from above. Her weapons are drawn."

"Weapons out, probably not a friendly for the orcs." Dylan observed a moment before Blake offered the same opinion.

"Nessa, keep an eye on her. Smitty, if you can hear me, stay away from the grey dwarf. Nessa, let him know which building, or what general area she's in." Max's spine tingled as he listened to Nessa act as a spotter for Smitty, a feeling he was too familiar with, and not at all fond of.

"I hate complications." He muttered to himself. Already his mind was racing, trying to factor in the implications of a grey dwarf presence. If they were allied with the orcs, that would drastically change the nature of the battle ahead. If they weren't, Max might still find himself battling the greys after finishing off the orcs, likely with his own forces already diminished from the first fight. Though he hated the very thought of it, he used his ring to call Redmane.

"Please put Cavariel on a fast mount, send him through to the dworc village, and have him follow us north. There may be a grey dwarf presence amongst the mutant orcs, and I might need him to speak for us."

"Greys!" Max could hear Redmane spit after saying the word. "Aye, I'll have the elf on his way within the hour."

Max was pacing around their campsite when Smitty's voice came through. "I'm back out, boss. Didn't get a whole lot, except that they are expecting the one they call Master to arrive in the next couple days. They're scrambling, afraid he'll take their heads if they don't have enough food gathered for the main army when it arrives. Didn't even say thank you when I handed them a three hundred pound deer thingy." The sound of mock offense in the corporal's voice made Max smile. "I didn't get a number for how many are on the way, but I got the impression it's a lot."

"Excuse me, Max." Nessa's voice broke in. "The grey dwarf has moved. She lowered herself from the roof into an alley, then in through a window. The building she went into is one of those filled with barrels."

Smitty added, "Those barrels are filled with water, and meat. They're butchering most of the game the hunters bring in, salting it, and filling barrel after barrel."

"Getting ready to move, then." Blake added. "Otherwise they'd just smoke it in big racks of ribs and haunches. I'm guessing they don't have access to storage rings."

"Yes, but move where?" Max mused. "Are they going to continue south toward the dworcs? Or push underground toward the Heart Chamber? Or split and do both?"

Nessa spoke up, breaking the ensuing silence. "Wherever they go, I believe it will be with a smaller force than they expect." There was more silence as everyone waited for her to elaborate. When she didn't after fifteen seconds or so, Max finally asked, "Why do you say that?"

"The grey dwarf. I have been wondering why she would sneak into that building. The best explanations I have been able to think of are… that she's stealing food, or that she's poisoning their food, or water."

Max shuddered, remembering the effects of the grey dwarves' preferred poison from when he'd been stabbed in the first days of their occupation of Stormhaven city. His body had begun to develop a tolerance after the poisoning, but he was far from immune. Others had died that day before the antidote could be administered. Since then, Dalia had insisted that Max and everyone in their party carry a few of the antidote vials. He glanced at her, and she immediately nodded, knowing what he was about to ask. "Aye, me da and a few others made several large batches. Every unit's officers from the rank o' sergeant and higher be carryin' some, as well as every healer."

Dylan looked thoughtful for a moment before speaking up. "Is this an *enemy of my enemy* situation? Can we sit back and watch the greys take out the red-eyes, or vice versa?"

Max shook his head. "That's assuming Nessa is correct, and the grey was poisoning the food or water. If she was just stealing, then maybe we could help the orcs discover her, assuming she comes back. And we have no

116

way of knowing if she's alone down there, or part of a larger force." He scratched his head, thinking. In either case, it wouldn't be a bad thing to use the orcs to eliminate a grey dwarf, or to let her eliminate some of them.

"Alright, Smitty and Nessa, keep eyes on the settlement. One of you sleep while the other watches. We'll get there sometime tomorrow, and get set up. Let us know if there are any more interesting developments."

Something was flitting around in the back of his mind. Some memory that he couldn't quite latch on to as he produced his bedroll from inventory and laid it out. There'd been a mention of a female grey dwarf...

*****

Izgren returned to the building her master was using as his office and residence in the underground section of the settlement. When she found him sitting cross-legged in the center of a room, meditating, he didn't even open his eyes to acknowledge her. "Report, young one."

She smiled slightly at the term, as she was only young compared to him. "More of them continue to arrive. I've poisoned a third batch o' barrels, both food and water." She paused briefly to collect her thoughts. "I'm beginnin' to doubt our plan. Even poisoned, there may be too many fer our remainin' few to dispatch quickly. Even if we use the novices, we be sure to face some healthy fighters before we're through."

The master nodded, still not opening his eyes. "Then we will focus on the leaders, the strongest, you and I. If we can destroy the one they fear and worship, and eliminate a sizeable portion o' the common warriors, perhaps they will break and retreat back to the north."

She nodded once, accepting the wisdom of his advice. "Those who be already here are eatin' fresh meat from the kills the hunters bring in, so none o' the meat I poisoned has been touched, yet."

"Let us hope that continues to be the case." He nodded once again, a gesture that was somehow a clear dismissal. She smiled again at the old man, the closest thing she'd ever had to a father. Though he never expressed it, she knew that he was fond of her, and she loved him deeply. The dismissal was his way of telling her to get some food and rest, in case she needed to go out a fourth time. They had three of their adepts monitoring the settlement, keeping track of new arrivals, watching for more hunting parties entering the underground section her people had claimed for themselves. They'd adopted a more passive approach to hunting parties. They'd moved themselves into the most remote buildings, the ones farthest from the path from the surface, and simply watched the last party pass through. They'd left no evidence of the previous battles, so the red-eyed orcs stomped through the settlement and into the nearby tunnels none the wiser as to the fate of their predecessors.

Though the mutant orcs were now blessed with the ability to see in the darkness of the underground, they were still heavy and noisy when they moved, making them easily avoidable now that her people were wary of them.

Returning to the room she'd claimed for herself, she found several bundles of ingredients waiting on the table near the door. The novices had been sent to gather more ingredients, and had apparently returned with them while she was gone. With a resigned sigh, she set to work preparing and processing the herbs, crushing the crystals, and heating some water in which to mix the ingredients for more poison.

She'd sleep later.

*****

Still meditating in his room, the Master of the Thieves' Guild was smiling faintly to himself, proud of the way his prized pupil was comporting herself. He was imagining her taking over leadership of the guild when he felt a strong presence in the room. One that hadn't been there a moment ago, and that he hadn't felt approaching. Few beings on the continent, above the ground or below, could sneak up on the master thief, and he was instantly wary.

Opening his eyes, he gasped in shock, hopping to his feet before instantly dropping back to his knees and pressing his head to the stone floor, hands open and pressed flat to the stone. "Eldest!"

The tuath stood just inside the doorway, staring down at the prostrate form of the Master Thief, and spoke

in the language of the grey dwarves. "Rise, young one."
He smiled to himself, having observed the old grey dwarf
use the same term on his apprentice only a short while ago.
When the dwarf had sat upright, still on his knees and
staring at the tuath's feet, he hid the smile and continued.

"I bear tidings that should be of interest to you." He
watched the dwarf stiffen, unsure how to act around a being
the dwarves, all dwarves, worshipped. After a brief
moment, he decided to let the unfortunate creature off the
hook. After all, it was not his fault that the fool Nogroz
had cursed his people. "Maximilian Storm, the chimera
who killed your king, seized your city and founded a new
kingdom, has destroyed the lich. Furthermore, he has
cleansed the Heart of the Mountain of the lich's foul
influence, and restored it to its proper home."

At this the Master's eyes widened again, and his
gaze rose briefly to meet that of the tuath. "Truly?" his
surprise was such that he forgot himself for a moment
before once again lowering his gaze.

"You question the veracity of my words?" the Tuath
growled. The impudence of the chimera was one thing – he
was a newly arrived Battleborne with no knowledge of the
world's history or traditions. This elderly dwarf knew
better.

"N-no, Eldest! Of course not! Me deepest
apologies! I were just, surprised at the news. We searched
fer the Heart Stone fer centuries, and even when we found
it, we were not powerful enough to defeat the lich. The
forces we sent simply added to his army o' minions." He

coughed once, embarrassed and ashamed. "It pleases me to hear that the Heart be restored, even if it were done by the mongrel usurper."

The tuath unleashed his aura, putting no small amount of anger into his voice. "That *mongrel* is favored among the Eternals, and by more than one of the Eldest, including myself."

The dwarf's reaction was instantaneous. He flattened himself against the stone once again, a small whimper escaping him as the ancient being's will washed over him. When the tuath once again reined in his aura, the dwarf gasped in relief. When he spoke, his voice was barely above a whisper.

"Apologies again, Eldest. I meant no disrespect to ye, or to the Eternals. I was unaware that the... chimera enjoyed such favor."

The tuath took several breaths before speaking again, during which time the grey dwarf trembled in fear for his mortal existence. When he did speak, his tone was more gentle. "I understand your hatred, young one. It was bred into you, and no fault of your own. The fool Nogroz doomed you and your people, and generations of hatred born of jealousy can not be easy to overcome." He reached down with one hand and gripped the thief's shoulder, pulling him to his feet. "But you would do well to set aside that hatred."

The dwarf gasped, once again looking up at the tuath's face briefly.

"You are sworn to your guild, and the guild's long-held pact is with the crown, is it not?" The tuath waited for the dwarf to nod his head, his eyes once again lowered to study the ground at their feet. "Maximilian Storm now holds that crown. Should you return that which you guard, you might earn forgiveness for past deeds, potentially even achieve eventual peace between the dwarven races."

"The dwarves would never set aside their enmity toward us." The old grey dwarf shook his head, the ring of absolute certainty in his words. "They consider us betrayers, and the blood spilt between us could fill a hollow mountain."

The tuath nodded. "Not on their own, that is true. But the chimera king has created alliances, established an open kingdom that welcomes all races. Should you convince him to accept you, he might aid in your redemption. Assuming, of course, redemption is of interest to you. Perhaps you would rather huddle here in this hollow place, nurse your ancestor's hatred for another hundred generations. Or until your ragtag group of survivors are simply wiped out." His gaze drifted meaningfully upward toward the orcs gathered on the surface.

"I… have never considered redemption a possibility, Eldest." the old dwarf stammered, becoming overwhelmed by the presence of the ancient being and the information it put forth. He truly was pleased that the Heart had been restored, something he and his forebears had tried to accomplish since it had been removed and cursed by the lich. Despite his cursed heritage, he was still a dwarf, and all dwarves were children of the mountains. The restoration of the Heart went a long way toward improving his opinion of the chimera. The favor of the Eternals and the tuath that stood before him factored in, as well. "This all be... hard to take in."

"I've more for you to take in." the Tuath smiled down at him, though he didn't see it with his gaze still lowered. "King Storm is not far from this place, and moving closer. He intends to eliminate the very same orcs that threaten your people. If you were to send an emissary southward up on the surface, or go there yourself..." he raised one eyebrow as he waited for the dwarf to finish the thought.

"Would he not simply execute me on sight?" The dwarf had heard the chimera state his opinion of grey dwarves more than once as he crept about the city in the early days after the battle. He had even ordered the usurper assassinated, and observed more than one attempt from a safe distance.

"You speak common, do you not? I will provide you with a token that should offer you sufficient protection to reach King Storm and state your intentions." The tuath produced a stone disc in the palm of his hand that glowed with a pulsing green light. "You are correct that he despises your people. He suffered a personal loss at your hands when you attacked Darkholm. Whether or not he has achieved the wisdom and maturity to understand the value of forgiveness remains to be seen."

Having the benefit of a centuries-long life of intrigue and political maneuvering, the old master understood at once. This was a test for the chimera as much as it was for him. His thoughts spun into a whirlwind of possibilities, including one that the Eldest or the Eternals might have caused his former king to attack Darkholm in order to set into motion events that would lead to this moment. A scenario that made his gut clench when he considered the number of lives lost, on both sides, to reach this point. He found himself fervently hoping that the Eldest before him was simply taking advantage of a naturally occurring opportunity.

He bowed deeply before speaking. "Eldest, ye honor me with yer presence, and with the challenge ye put before me. I fear I be unworthy o' such a task, but I will attempt it, just the same."

The tuath handed him the stone disk, which continued to pulse as though it had a heart beating within. The moment he touched it, the master thief received a quest, which he immediately accepted, his heart racing at both the difficulty, and the potential rewards. When his eyes refocused from reading the quest, the tuath was nowhere to be seen.

Chapter 7

Max and company passed Smitty's chosen choke point on their way north. It was a reasonably narrow pass with a gradual uphill slope on either side coming from the south. However, from the north there were two steep cliffs on either side, almost as if the hills had calved like an iceberg on that side, making it nearly impossible to climb. This would force a southbound enemy army to gather into the pass, or go several miles the long way around to get through, while Max's northbound force could spread out across the two upper slopes on their side and fire down at the enemy. Max approved.

Marking the location on his map, Max moved on to meet up with Smitty and Nessa. They were less than an hour from their rendezvous point, by Max's estimation, when Smitty reported in.

"Uhh… boss? We have a situation."

The tone of his corporal's voice instantly ramped up Max's stress level. "Has the big boss arrived? Did they make your position?"

"That's a negative on the big boss. And… *somebody* made our position, but it wasn't the orcs." The scout paused long enough that Max was tempted to yell at him to spit it out, whatever it was. "You know that grey dwarf stealthy type that we talked about before? Well, she's here."

"Watch for the poison!" was Max's instant reaction. Followed by curiosity. "What's she doing?"

"Well, she kind of snuck up behind us, then tossed a rock in between us to let us know she's here. Now she's standing with her hands out, staring at us. She doesn't look happy, but she's not attacking." He coughed once as if clearing his throat. "Boss, she coulda killed us both and we'd never have seen it coming."

"Her stealth abilities are quite… impressive." Nessa added in her usual dry tone.

"Is she still armed?" Max growled. "Are there any others around?"

"Affirmative on the weapons. She's got a pair of daggers at her hips. If there are others, I can't see them. Then again, I didn't see her till she wanted us to."

"Alright, see if you can communicate with her. We'll be there ASAP. Keep one eye on her, one eye on the camp. She could be a diversion, or something."

"Roger that boss. Chat with the super sneaky stabby lady murder dwarf. No problemo." There was a long silence as Max urged Pokey to move faster. The landscape had opened up a bit, with fewer trees beyond the pass, so Dylan was back to riding Princess. He and the other mounts increased their pace to match Pokey's.

"Boss, she speaks common. Says she's an officer of the Nogroz Thieves' Guild. Sent by her master to discuss a truce while we deal with the red-eyes."

Max's frown deepened. He'd prefer to be speaking with the thief directly, rather than having Smitty relay info. "Ask her what she was doing in that building." Max waited while Smitty relayed the question, wishing the communications rings could act as a speakerphone. Maybe he'd ask Erdun to work on that feature next. It would come in handy in all sorts of ways.

"She says she was poisoning their food and water barrels, and that was the third building she's hit."

"So we guessed correctly." Blake interjected, then whistled in appreciation. "Three warehouses full of poisoned rations could kill a lot of orcs."

"She's staring at me funny, boss. She doesn't know I'm talkin to you through the ring, so to her it must look like my brain is short circuiting, or I'm just slow."

"Keep her talking. Ask her what she's doing so far from Nogroz. And find out how many she has with her. You know the drill. We're inbound as fast as we can move."

"Roger that." Smitty didn't sound thrilled about dealing with the thief, but orders were orders. He'd get what info he could from the grey dwarf.

Rather than continue to pause for long periods while he spoke to Max, Smitty asked Nessa to relay what the thief was saying. In this manner, while they rushed northward, Max learned that the Thieves' Guild had fled the city a few days after Max and the dwarves conquered it. Days they spent trying to assassinate Max and as many dwarves as possible. They took what remained of their membership and headed out, choosing the abandoned settlement below as their destination. She refused to disclose how many had come with her, which Max understood. He assumed there were a good number of them if they planned to take on thousands of orcs.

After that, things quieted down. Once she learned that Max was on the way, she took a seat and declined to answer more questions until he arrived. She had no way of knowing that he was in on the conversation, and didn't seem to be in the mood to repeat herself to him when he showed up.

The thought that had been worming around in the back of his mind finally struck Max. "Smitty, ask her if she was part of an attempted jailbreak in the city dungeons? The one that killed those guards."

A long minute later, Smitty replied. "Affirmative, boss. She didn't want to answer at first, but she confirms it was her. Said she nearly died trying to rescue her son and the others that were killed during the attempt." He paused to take a breath, and his tone was respectful when he added, "Took some cojones to admit that, boss. Big brass ones."

Max nodded to himself. As a soldier, he understood. "In her situation, we'd have done the same. Only we might have killed a lot more guards. They were prisoners of war, and it was her duty to try. Especially if one of them was her son. We won't hold that against her." He waited as Smitty relayed that response, only as if it were coming from him instead of Max. No point in revealing their comms abilities to a stranger and likely enemy.

"No response, boss. She just nodded and sat down. I think she might be about to… take a nap? Great big giant brass ones this one has, boss."

*****

When Max walked into camp, the grey dwarf had awakened and was getting to her feet. They'd left the mounts at the bottom of the hill and walked up, but neither Max nor Dylan was much good at moving quietly, so she'd heard them coming halfway up the hill.

The dwarf bowed at the waist when Max came to a halt a few paces from her. "King Maximilian Storm, I am Izgren. I come in peace."

Max stared at her for a while, his fists clenched. He felt a significant amount of hostility toward the grey dwarf and all her kind. An image of Thelonia's smiling face came to him, followed by another of her vacant, dead eyes. He closed his own eyes for a moment, gathering his wits. The others all watched quietly, prepared to act if necessary.

"Greetings, Izgren of the Thieves' Guild. What brings you here?"

"My Master sent me. We offer a truce, while we deal with the orc invaders."

Max glanced sideways at Smitty even as he spoke through party chat. "Pretend to whisper a report in my ear so we don't have to go through all the questions again." Smitty snorted, then stepped close to Max with his back to the thief and leaned in close to whisper.

"Glad you're here, boss. This one's got the eyes of a stone killer. Like Donovan, you remember him? That dude had serial killer written all over his face. One time I woke up n caught him staring at me, cleaning his fingernails with his combat knife. Nearly shit myself."

Max had to work hard to keep a smile from his face. Donovan was one of the most loyal, trustworthy, and good-hearted men in his unit. But the guy was a born soldier, and killed without compunction. Smitty was right, though, one look in his eyes sent most people off to find something to do far away from him.

When Smitty stepped back, Max nodded as if in confirmation of a report, then turned his gaze back to Izgren. "You've been poisoning the orcs' food. I take it you planned to sneak in and slit their throats while they are sick?"

She nodded once, a wicked glint in her eyes. "Those that the poison does not take, we will finish."

Max approved. He, Dalia, and Battleaxe had done something very similar to an orc camp once. To Max that seemed like an eternity ago. "We believe there's a large force still coming. Do you have enough people to take them all, even incapacitated?"

She paused briefly, not knowing the word incapacitated, but quickly figured out the meaning.

Shaking her head, she replied, "Likely not. There will be some who don't eat or drink the poison, or who have the strength to resist." She looked Max in the eye, her expression defiant. "This is… not the same poison we used on you and your allies in the city. Not as strong, or fast-acting."

Max nodded. "Makes sense. If they drop dead after the first bite, you wouldn't get as many of them. How long for the poison to take effect?"

She shrugged. "Four hours, maybe six. Hard to say how much each of them will ingest. The delivery method is… crude and imprecise. Some will die, others will only get sick, maybe sleepy."

"That's why you approached us? You don't have enough bodies to get the job done."

She shook her head, looking down at her feet. After a long silence, she took a deep breath and let it out, handing Max the still pulsing token. "My master received a visitor. One of the Eldest. A tuath who informed my master that you were favored of the Eternals, and had received the blessings of himself and another Eldest."

Max nodded. "I know the tuath of whom you speak."

"The Eldest bid my master to seek peace with you." She looked like she wanted to spit after speaking the words. "He said you destroyed the lich that cursed our people, and restored the Heart of the Mountain." Her expression turned to one of curiosity. "Is this true?"

"It is. The lich had taken the Heart as his phylactery. I was able to remove him from it and destroy him, then restore the Heart to its rightful place."

She bowed at the waist, giving him a look of respect. "Then our people owe you a debt. That lich was a plague from which our people may never recover."

Max felt his own hostility fade a bit. He reminded himself that the grey dwarves had been normal dwarves until they were cursed by the actions of Nogroz and the lich. However much they may have embraced their evil lifestyle since then. It was apparent from the respect she showed for the tuath, and for the Heart, that they still retained some sense of dwarven honor.

He found himself thinking of World War II. The Nazis committed horrible crimes, including attempted genocide, torture, human experimentation, and countless other evil acts. But the majority of the German citizens had nothing to do with that. Some even actively worked against the leadership responsible for it. They simply tried to go on about their everyday lives, to live down the shame and stigma after the war.

"What does your master have in mind?" Max tried to keep his voice even, his expression neutral.

"We will work together to eliminate the red-eyed orcs. To kill this One they seem to worship. When they are gone, you leave Gar'doz, this settlement, to us."

The settlement was well outside the lands that Max had claimed for Stormhaven, and he had no interest in further expansion at that time, so what she was asking was easy enough to agree to. But Max had something else in mind. Something his first grey dwarf language translator had found before she was arrested.

"And what are you offering in return?"

She blinked up at him, doing her best to look confused. "We will help you eliminate a threat to your kingdom."

Max shook his head, not buying her act. "You've already delivered the poison. And I'm guessing you only have a few dozen survivors to help you cut throats when the orcs go down. Not enough to do the job, as you've already admitted. I can bring hundreds of fighters to deal with the ones who don't go down so easy. I don't need your few dozen to accomplish a victory here. Give me a reason to not simply sit back and deal with whomever survives your conflict, to clear you and your remaining people from Gar'doz when we're through with the orcs."

She glared up at Max, fury in her eyes as her hands twitched towards the daggers at her waist and she growled, "It would cost you many more lives to remove us from our new home."

Max shook his head again. "I came here to fight the orcs myself, not knowing that you or your poison were here, fully expecting to lose many of my fighters. Many more than you and your thieves could account for after the orcs are done with you. Make it worth my while to help save the lives of your guildmembers and secure your new home."

After a long and tense silence, her shoulders slumped and the heat of her glare faded. "You know of our pact." It wasn't a question.

"Your guild guarded the Nogroz treasury. When we secured the city, we found it empty. Who better to quickly clean out an entire nation's wealth in a short time than a bunch of professional thieves with your very own key to the vault? I assume you brought its contents here with you."

"We secured it." Izgren wasn't willing to disclose the location of the treasury. "I am authorized to grant you one half of the assets once the orcs are eliminated and you depart Gar'doz in peace."

"One half of a treasury that's already mine by right of conquest?" Max flashed her a grin that exposed his fangs. "After we also help save your lives and secure your new home? I don't think so." He paused and rubbed his chin as if thinking things over. "You'll return it all to me, minus ten percent that I'll leave you to help buy food and supplies. That much should feed a few dozen people for many years. I have many thousands of mouths to feed." When she looked about ready to argue, he added, "Your people attacked Darkholm and killed a lot of friends of mine, including one who was dear to me. I have let you live this long because you seem to be potentially useful against the orcs, and because the tuath apparently wants peace between us. I suspect you are only here for those exact same reasons. And while I respect the tuath, I do not worship him as you and the dwarves seem to. Don't tempt me to ignore the Eldest's wishes."

He watched her struggle to remain silent for several heartbeats before she simply nodded once. "I shall pass on your demands to my master. I hope he rejects your offer and chooses to fight you after the orcs have been dealt with."

Max stared down at her. "You're thieves, you could always try and steal the bulk of the treasure back from us later. Though, I don't recommend it."

The discussion was interrupted by the blaring sound of a horn echoing up from the settlement on the other side of the hill from where they stood. Max and company all glanced that way as Nessa and Smitty rushed up the hill to take a look. When he turned back to the dwarf, she was gone. "Shit." Max shook his head, feeling foolish for taking his eyes off of her. He frantically spun around, expecting a backstab at any moment, his eyes attempting to search everywhere at once. When nothing happened for a full minute, he relaxed slightly.

Crouching as low as his frame would allow, he made his way up to join his scouts atop the hill, and look down at the settlement.

His first impression was that it wasn't worth claiming. The ruins were badly damaged and neglected, and would take significant time and resources to repair enough to be habitable. The next thing he noticed was a hint of movement through the trees to the north. He focused on that area in time to see the front line of an orc formation march out from under the trees. Ten wide, the line of long-legged orcs advanced at a quick march, followed by another line, and another. An oversized orc off to the side of the front line raised a horn to its lips and blew another blast, which was quickly answered from somewhere within the settlement.

After the first two hundred emerged from the forest, Max spotted a small contingent of larger orcs in crimson leather armor. They marched in a square, surrounding the largest orc Max had ever seen. He stood easily ten feet tall, with shoulders as wide as Dylan's, arms and legs bulging with muscle. It wore black sleeveless robes with the hood down, revealing a badly scarred face with red eyes that glowed much more brightly than the surrounding orc army's. Its tusks were coated in metal that glinted in the afternoon sunlight. The robes were open at the front, revealing crimson scaled armor from head to toe. As it marched across the open area between the forest and the walls, it let out a roar that echoed through the valley. The answering roar from the surrounding troops, and those already inside the ruins, shook the leaves on the trees, and Max thought he could feel it through his feet.

For the next several minutes, Max watched and counted rows as more than three thousand heavily armed red-eyed orcs followed their leader through the broken down gateway and dispersed through the settlement.

"That's a lot of orcs." Smitty's voice was a whisper even though he was speaking through party chat.

"I hope they're hungry." Blake grinned up at him. "Let's hope they all order the Izgren special for dinner tonight."

Shaking his head, Max scuttled back down the hill and looked around. "We don't have time to go back and set up at the choke point." He picked a spot between two thick roots at the base of a massive ironwood tree that extended up at least a hundred feet, with a trunk that was easily six feet in diameter. "This will have to do. Blake, keep a lookout. Smitty and Nessa, perimeter patrol. The rest of you watch my back." He produced a portal pedestal from his inventory and began the installation ritual.

*****

Izgren activated her stealth ability the moment the horn sounded and the chimera looked away. She immediately stepped behind a tree, immersing herself in its shadow, then transported herself through that shadow to another about fifty paces away. With a quick glance back at the group she'd just left to make sure no one was pursuing, she dashed off toward the entrance to the underground settlement.

As she descended the hill above, she too observed the massive orc leader, and counted the incoming troops without even consciously thinking about it. They were still marching out of the forest by the time she disappeared underground, but she wasn't concerned. Two adepts that she trusted were tasked with keeping track of the enemy numbers and placements, and she would rely on their count. Her job was to report to the master on her meeting with the chimera.

"I take it from the rumbling and roaring that the main body has arrived." She found the master still seated in his chosen room, seemingly unperturbed by the development. "Why must armies always make so much noise? In my humble opinion, they would be much more intimidating if they moved in silence."

She snorted, smiling at the old dwarf. "Then we'd have to work so much harder to track them. I like them better this way."

"What have you learned from King Storm?" he got right down to business.

"He says he can bring several hundred fighters to assist against the orcs. After the battle, he will cede Gar'doz to us." She grimaced before adding, "In return for ninety percent of the treasury."

"And if we refuse this offer?" the old dwarf already knew the answer, but wanted to observe his student as she voiced it.

"He bears a grudge against our people, and would happily eliminate us, or drive us from this place, after the orcs have been defeated."

The master shook his head. "He is not that bloodthirsty. After all, did he not order our people be captured and imprisoned rather than outright killed, even after we attempted to murder him, and did kill several of his people? That is how your son ended up in the city dungeons. I doubt he would dishonor himself by destroying us." He took a breath and considered for a while. "But my doubts are not strong enough to refuse his offer. Even ten percent of the treasury's value, along with a safe place to call home, is more than sufficient for our needs."

She scowled at his words, disliking the compromise. After a moment she offered, "He has no way of accounting for what we give him, or what we keep."

"No, child, he does not. But in all my centuries on this world, I have never broken a bargain once it was made. We will give a true accounting, and hold back no more than agreed. Were our roster still full, I might argue for more. But our meager band of survivors can live comfortably on ten percent, for more than enough time to reestablish ourselves. The value of his assistance, and the lives of our own young ones that it will save, is paramount." His expression changed to a smirk as he held up a hand with a ring on its pinky finger. A ring with the Guild seal on it. "It's not like we have no resources of our own, young one. This new king has no inkling as to the resources we stripped from the city's homes and businesses while his dwarves and kobolds hunted us."

Knowing better than to argue with her elder, she sighed in resignation. "I will prepare the others. The orcs will likely begin feasting soon enough, and we will be ready when they take to their beds." She was turning toward the door when he stopped her with a query.

"Did you see their leader?"

She nodded, turning back to face him. "He is a giant among them, easily three times my height. A shaman, level sixty. He is guarded by an elite force of warriors, all at or near level fifty. He will not be easy to reach."

"He will have magical protections, and wards. Do we leave him to the chimera, then?" the old dwarf smiled at her, flashing a quick wink.

"Ha! You would not pass up such a challenge any more than I would. Let the chimera and his troops provide a distraction when the time comes. We will slit this One's throat and leave his drained corpse for the chimera to find."

"His already looted corpse. In a tent stripped bare of valuables." The master's grin grew wider and he raised one eyebrow. "I assume our bargain for payment to the chimera did not include the spoils of war?"

*****

King Farstrider motioned for Falcon to sit when he entered the study. The soldier didn't bow, simply nodding in acknowledgement of the instruction. "You summoned me, majesty?"

"I'm hearing disturbing rumors from the front, Major. What did you see?"

Falcon blinked for a moment. He still wasn't used to the promotion he'd received as part of his reward for helping to clear the dungeon alongside Max and his party. Along with the promotion, he'd received a significant bonus in gold, and been awarded a small manor house in the city. He'd also been sent to the front lines of the war with the Battleborne queen.

"Enemy troop morale is low, but their numbers are growing. The queen has been emptying her jails, pulling conscripts from quarries and mines, putting them in uniforms and sending them to the front as fodder. They are not well trained, but they fight hard, and they fight dirty, trying to earn the pardons she promised them if they survive a year."

"What sort of numbers are we talking about?" Farstrider leaned forward, setting his elbows on his knees as he studied a map set on a coffee table in front of him. Atop the map sat small stone markers in various colors, meant to represent various unit types of his forces, and the enemy's.

"We're now outnumbered roughly two to one." Falcon's expression was grim. "We are holding, for now, because every one of our soldiers is well trained and disciplined. She's throwing the mob at us, and though they fight with abandon, they are uncoordinated. Her army suffers three casualties for each one of ours, but she doesn't seem to care."

"She'll use the conscripts to wear our troops down, exhaust them, then send trained troops behind them." the king stated. It was an old tactic, one used by tyrants and despots who cared nothing for the lives of their peasants. To them, the lowest classes existed only to serve the needs of the nobles, and should be happy to lay down their lives for their royals.

"Sire, I could lead a small team..." Falcon began, but went silent when the king raised a hand.

"I know you're willing. But we both know that's a suicide mission, and unlike her, I'm not willing to throw away lives. That mage of hers guards her like she's his own child. There are wards throughout the palace that would alert them long before you reached her. The one thing my idiot son did manage to accomplish was observing those wards with his mage vision before they tossed him out on his pampered arse."

Farstrider looked up from the map to see Falcon avoiding his gaze. He could practically hear the man thinking that it was him, and his wife, that had pampered the prince in the first place. A series of decisions that Farstrider whole-heartedly regretted. He'd punished his son, and turned him over to a few trusted friends in hopes of re-educating the boy on the ways of the world before it was time for him to inherit the throne.

"We can't come close to matching her numbers at the front. At least, not for a month, or more." Farstrider had instructed his staff to begin recruiting as many new soldiers as they could. He offered a five gold signing bonus, and a guaranteed pension for those who were wounded or killed in action, and their families. More than a thousand had already volunteered, and were being trained as quickly as possible, but he refused to send them out before they were ready. Proper weapons techniques, formations, even things like proper sanitation and equipment maintenance were vital to the survival of his army, and he would take no short cuts.

He'd informed his nobles that their sons were needed to serve as officers, most of them having had at least some military training as part of their upbringing. Those nobles who had refused were penalized, their taxes increased, their business contracts with the crown promptly cancelled. The noble sons who had answered the call were training alongside their future troops and being tested by his veteran officers to make sure they were well suited to command. In a month's time, he'd be able to field a well-trained, cohesive fighting force.

But he might not have a month.

"Sire, Max has offered more than once to assist us. And we're close to reaching an agreement with Ironhand and the dwarves to join their alliance. Maybe it's time to ask for help."

"King Storm has just taken the bulk of his forces to deal with the threat of the red-eyed orcs north of his lands. A campaign like that, fighting in the mountains, could take months, or years. Even if we asked, I'm not sure he has anyone to send."

"What about their guild? The War Dogs? You could offer them a quest to supplement our forces at the front. There are only a few dozen of them at this point, but every one of them is a trained fighter, and most are higher leveled than all but the officers and long term veterans on the field."

Farstrider rubbed his nose with one hand, a gesture he often made while thinking. Falcon smiled at the gesture, one he'd seen his king make as a very young prince deciding which treat he wanted from the bakery near the palace.

"Yes, I could live with that. I authorize you to offer them a quest. Make the rewards worthwhile, but try not to break the bank?" He smiled at Falcon. With the dungeon cleared, and its monsters back to normal levels, his people were once again benefitting from the spoils pulled from dungeon runs, and their economy was improving accordingly.

Falcon bowed his head in acknowledgement as he got to his feet and headed for the door. "They'd probably fight for just the experience. But I'll throw in a little gold, and some reputation increases, for extra motivation."

Chapter 8

Max lay on his belly atop the rise that looked down upon the settlement. Thousands of orcs cavorted in the streets and alleyways, eating, drinking, and generally behaving like orcs. There were dozens of sparring circles where orcs battled each other singly or in pairs, while others wagered and roared in approval or disappointment. Meat was being roasted over more cookfires than he could count, and he sincerely hoped that all of it was seasoned with Izgren's special sauce.

While poisoning wasn't exactly honorable, Max had been a soldier too long to let that bother him much. His mission was to protect his people, and that required him to overcome this much larger force that outnumbered his own by at least five to one. His kingdom was still in its infancy, and he didn't have the population from which to pull a large fighting force. Nor the funds to pay them for more than a brief period. He vaguely remembered reading somewhere that you needed at least two hundred taxpaying citizens to support each full-time soldier in your army. Though soldiers were *paid* relatively little, the costs of their upkeep, equipment, training, medical care, and transportation added up quickly. Max was nowhere near that ratio, and was having to pay his guards from the loot and other windfalls he'd been able to secure, like the captured grey dwarf bank.

Gathered behind him were a little over eight hundred fighters. A mixture of dwarves, orcs, gnomes, minotaurs, kobolds, goblins, and ogres, he looked down at them with pride. He'd set out to build an open city, and though there had been some resistance, he'd achieved that goal. Now his kingdom was being threatened, and each of the races had stepped up to defend it. Even the goblins, who weren't strong enough to participate in combat, had shown up in support roles, acting as cooks, runners, and laborers for the soldiers.

Unlike when he and his troops had attacked the goblin and hobgoblin forces in their city, this enemy was not weak. Each of the orcs below was of a similar size and strength to Smitty or Max himself, and their levels were in the thirties for the most part. While his own party were all much higher level than the majority of the red-eyed orcs, his soldiers were mostly on par with them. And whatever mutation process the orcs had been subjected to also gave each one of them some sort of berserker ability that made them stronger, faster, and tougher than normal.

Though they were being quiet in hopes of avoiding detection, his troops appeared to be in high spirits. In part because he'd just issued them all a quest to defeat the orc army. One that included a share of the loot, and enough experience, on top of the kill experience, to grant them each a level or three. Max had actually been surprised at how much experience the system had let him assign to the quest, until Red appeared on his shoulder and offered an explanation.

"You're about to send 'em into a battle where they'll be vastly outnumbered, and in some cases out-leveled. And while we be standin' outside your claimed territory, this army has already invaded your lands in both the dworc valley and the Heart chamber, so this battle counts as a defense o' the kingdom against an aggressor."

"Works for me." Max had winked at his leprechaun guide before she disappeared again. Now he looked away from his troops, going back to scouting the force below. Izgren had said her poison would be slow acting, and that they should wait to attack in the early hours of the morning when as many as possible of the enemy would be asleep and afflicted with the poison's effects. It was already past midnight, and the orcs appeared to still be going strong.

He turned to lay on his back, making himself comfortable for the wait. The butterflies in his stomach didn't fade, but that was normal for him. Something he felt before every mission, every battle. In his early years as a soldier, he'd thought the nervous reaction to be a weakness. But over the years he'd realized it was a normal and nearly universal reaction. He'd met few soldiers, and even fewer officers, who never felt such fear. Most of them hadn't survived long, or had recklessly thrown away the lives of their soldiers. So he embraced the feeling, using it as a reminder to go over his plan yet again, searching for any way he might reduce the risk to his troops without reducing the odds of victory.

A few hours later, his contemplation was interrupted when Nessa appeared alongside a young-looking grey dwarf, the two of them emerging from stealth as they climbed to his position. When Max raised an eyebrow at Nessa, she shrugged. "I spotted him coming this way in stealth, and intercepted him. He doesn't speak common."

As if on cue, the thief muttered something quietly at Max, who held up a hand in what he hoped was a universal sign for 'hold on a minute' while he reached out to Cavariel via party chat. A moment later the dark elf translator appeared and, seeing the grey dwarf, offered a query in its language. The thief's face brightened up, and he spoke quickly, the excitement on his face obvious.

The dark elf turned to Max. "He says he brings a message from his master. The poison should be working by now. If we start walking down, move slowly and quietly, the perimeter guards will be eliminated by the time we arrive." As Cavariel spoke, Max watched the thief, who was smiling wickedly, nodding his head and pointing down at the settlement. As if he thought Max still didn't understand, he started to walk over the crest of the hill, motioning for them to follow as he slipped behind a tree and disappeared.

"I can still see him." Nessa spoke quietly. "He's about thirty paces away, waiting for us to follow."

Max nodded once, then used his rings to reach out to all his officers. "This is it, we're moving. Slow and quiet, we want to get as close as possible before they know we're here."

His chest swelled with pride as within a few seconds his entire force turned almost as one and began to hike up the hill. They weren't exactly quiet, as leaves rustled and twigs snapped up and down the line, but Max imagined they were quiet enough to get close to the ruins before being discovered.

When they'd reached the top and started their descent, Max took a moment to activate the enchantments on both Storm Reaver and his Sovereign's Scepter. The scepter's *Inspiration* enchantment increased his troops' already high morale by thirty percent, as well as granting them a twenty five percent boost to their primary stats. Melee fighters would be stronger, casters would be smarter, with larger mana pools and more efficient casts. The sword's *Sovereign's Stand* enchantment gave them all a ten percent boost to *Strength* and *Constitution*, as well as health regeneration. And when he ran down the hill, it would inflict an equal debuff on the orcs' morale and *Strength*. He grinned as he watched the buffs take effect on his people, many of them looking around in confusion for a second before rolling their shoulders or straightening their backs and puffing out their chests a bit.

Reaching out in party chat, he spoke to his group as he descended behind his troops. "Alright, the plan remains the same. If they're mostly down from the poison, we leave the throat slitting to our people and the thieves, and we make straight for the boss. The building he's using is marked on your maps. If the orcs show heavy resistance when we breach the walls, then each of you support your assigned units while we burn them down, then we RV at the boss."

"Roger that." Blake confirmed first, followed by the others.

Dylan, who was walking next to Max, added, "This is a little disappointing, boss. I was hoping to see my ogres hurtling down the hill to smash into the orcs. Not tippytoe down like Fred Flintstone trying to raid the cookie jar."

"I'd pay good gold to see those big fellas actually tippytoe." Blake snarked.

"If some of the orcs are still standing and battle-ready, your ogres will get their chance to rampage." Max gave Dylan a sideways glance. "But I'm hoping they're all down there snoring or doubled over in pain and shitting themselves."

"Ew, boss. Thanks for that visual." Smitty shuddered. "Glad I don't have to get up close in sniffin' range." He patted his bow and grinned at Dylan. Blake, who could also stand way back and cast spells, gave him a thumbs-up.

Just before they reached the mostly crumbled walls of the settlement, Max spotted the corpses of three orc scouts, each with their throats cut and stab marks in their backs. He winced when a heavily armored ogre simply stepped on one of them rather than step over, and the crunch of shattering bones echoed through the night. Surprised, the ogre halted, lifted one foot to examine as if he'd stepped on a dog turd, then shrugged and continued on. Max looked to Dylan, who just shook his head as if to say 'ogres gotta ogre', and there was nothing he could do.

Max's line spread out as they approached the wall, separating into units and moving to half surround the settlement, pushing through from the south, southeast, and southwest at the same time when he gave the order. Each unit had its own assignment. The kobolds would scatter in small groups and focus on slitting throats as quickly and quietly as possible. Gnomes were set on overwatch, hoisted up onto walls and any intact roofs by orcs and ogres, ready to cast AoE spells on any clustered enemies. Dwarves and orcs would enter and clear buildings and tents as quietly as possible, until an organized resistance formed. Then the dwarves would create several shield walls and attempt to seal the enemy in, advancing along with the melee orcs to compress and crush them, while archers and crossbow specialist wreaked havoc from behind the lines. The ogres would be sent in as shock troops against concentrated pockets of resistance. Max knew better than to make any plans for the ogres beyond that, knowing that they'd just rampage on their own no matter what instructions he tried to give. Instead he instructed the casters to keep an eye on them and assist them if they got surrounded and bogged down.

To start with, things went as Max had hoped. His troops approached the wall as quietly as they could, stepping through wide gaps, or through the southern gate, without raising any alarms. They broke into groups and began the slaughter of incapacitated or sleeping orcs wherever they found them – inside ruined buildings, tents, or laying out in the open, clutching their guts and moaning. Even the ogres remained quiet, for them, as they crushed skulls with clubs or separated them from bodies with oversized axes.

Max, who was making his way toward the building where they'd last seen The One, caught brief glimpses of grey dwarves with bloody daggers darting in or out of buildings. He received reports from his unit commanders that they were successfully clearing buildings, or finding the orcs inside already dispatched. It seemed the greys had begun a little early, and were making good progress. Max's improved hearing picked up groans and vomiting nearby, and he took a quick detour into an alley up ahead on his left. There he found half a dozen orcs in the process of violently voiding their guts or bowels. Wasting no time, he used Storm Reaver to finish off each of them with a stab through the chest, or chop of a neck. Only one of them even managed to draw a weapon and attempt to resist.

Two minutes after infiltrating the settlement, his people began to encounter healthy orcs here and there that put up a fight. There was a sudden roar of challenge, and the sound of clashing weapons. Blake reported via party chat that a group of dwarves had encountered a dozen or so orcs that apparently hadn't eaten the poisoned meat. A moment later a lightning strike from the sky cast by one of the gnomes ensured that the entire area was alerted. More roars echoing from various sectors across the settlement erupted, and Max's force, especially the ogres, roared their own challenges.

Max shook his head as he left the alley and resumed his course toward the big boss. He'd known this would happen, and was frankly surprised that it took as long as it did. He only hoped that his people and the greys had managed to eliminate a significant number of orcs in that first two minutes.

"Heads up, boss!" Smitty's voice came through party chat at the same time Max heard a bowstring twang, and the sound of an arrow impacting a skull behind him. He turned to find four red-eyed orcs charging at him from out of a building, a fifth one laying just outside the doorway with an arrow through its head.

Max raised his sword and charged, snarling at the approaching orcs, baring his fangs. Another went down with an arrow in its chest, and Max went to work. The first orc swung a longsword at his head, but was too slow. Max continued forward inside its reach and slammed his shoulder into its chest, knocking it back. His sword shot out and downward, slicing the back of a second orc's knee just as it put its weight on that leg. The knee gave out, and the orc stumbled, abandoning the swing it had been aiming at Max. The third orc, which had been right behind the first, managed to dodge its falling companion and stab at Max with a spear. The point skittered off the dragonscale armor over his ribs, and Max let the orc's momentum bring it closer before he pushed Storm Reaver's point through its open mouth and out the back of its head. Letting go of the sword, he took a step forward and kicked the first orc, the one he'd tackled, in the face as it pushed itself up from the ground. The blow landed hard, and the orc's thick neck snapped, its body going limp.

The last remaining orc, the one with the wounded knee, never made it back to its feet, an arrow from Smitty striking the back of its head and pinning its face to the ground. Max gave the corporal a wave of thanks, retrieved his sword, and continued on. The sounds of battle raging all around him echoed between the buildings. Max winced as he heard a scream of pain that he doubted had been made by an orc. The scream cut off too suddenly to be natural, and he assumed one of his fighters had just perished.

Only a block from his destination, Max paused to fight another orc. This one was larger than most, and wore painted red stripes on its chest that suggested it was some kind of officer, like the one that killed Picklet. He didn't take time to *Identify* it, simply roared his rage at the staggering orc before charging directly at it. The orc was clearly under the influence of the poison, unsteady on its feet but eager to fight. It lunged at Max when he got within range, attempting to stab him with a spike at the end of its battle axe. Max simply turned his body slightly, allowing the spike, and the blade behind it, to scrape across his chest armor. Half a step later he was behind the massive orc, and used Storm Reaver to hamstring first one leg, then the other. When the orc dropped to his knees with a roar of pain, Max stowed his sword in his inventory and wrapped his right arm around the orc's neck from behind. Heaving with all the strength he had, he lifted the monster up a bit, then wrenched his body to the left. When the orc's thick neck didn't immediately snap, and it tried with both clawed hands to loosen Max's grip, he lifted it higher, then twisted both his body and the orc's around and slammed them into the ground, forcing the orc's head down first so that the weight of both their bodies finally snapped its neck. The orc went limp, and Max let go. He spit on its corpse before retrieving his sword.

"That was for Picklet." he growled as he turned away. Focusing on the boss's structure, which looked like it had probably been a warehouse of some kind, he saw Izgren and an elder grey dwarf slip in ahead of him. Increasing his pace, he sprinted toward the door. To his left, a battle between his orcs and the red-eyes spilled out from a side street. His five orcs were outnumbered, facing eight of the enemy, all of them seemingly unaffected by the poison. Altering his course, he drew his sword again and launched himself toward the fight.

The red-eyes didn't see him coming, and he skewered one through the heart from behind even as he landed knee first on the back of another, knocking it down. One of his orcs took immediate advantage of the downed enemy and stomped on its neck, then stabbed it with a sword just to make sure. Surprised by the attack from behind, the other red-eyes turned to stare at Max for a moment. He roared and bared his fangs as he yanked his sword free of his first victim, putting on a show. The brief distraction gave his orcs the time they needed to recover and attack. In seconds, three more of the red-eyes were down, and the rest were being pressed, now outnumbered by Max's fighters. Leaving them to it, he disengaged and raced back toward the warehouse. A roar that literally shook the building from inside told him he might already be too late.

It took just a couple seconds after he passed through the door for his eyes to adjust to the darkened interior. The room still had intact walls and roof, and there were no windows, the only light inside coming from three burning braziers on iron tripod stands set in a rough triangle. The corpses of several scarlet-armored guards lay scattered amidst pools of vomit, and worse, each of their throats sliced wide open.

Off to his left, near the wall on that side, another roar nearly deafened him. He spun in time to see Izgren take a massive fist to her gut and get launched past him to tumble into one of the heavy iron stands, knocking it over. There was a shower of sparks as the brazier hit the ground right by her head, and Max noted that she didn't move, or even flinch, as some of the dislodged coals bounced off her face. Turning back to the fight, Max saw the elder grey appear behind a giant of an orc wearing nothing but leather pants and a harness across its chest. It was easily ten feet tall, with muscles upon muscles over every inch of its body. Each of its sharp tusks was half as long as Max's forearm, and half of its left ear looked as if it had been chewed off.

The grey dwarf leapt upward, surprising Max with his agility, and drove wicked looking twin daggers that visibly dripped with poison into the orc's lower back. Max cast *Identify* as he moved forward and the orc screamed in pain.

The One
Orc Warlord, Elite
Level 60
Health: 27,550/35,000

The red glow in its eyes blazed brightly, and it visibly grew larger as Max gaped at its massive health pool.

Its head struck the ceiling, its shoulders widened even more, and every visible muscle on its body bulged until Max expected its skin to tear open. Blood flowed freely from its eyes, nose, and ears, but Max wasn't sure if that was a result of the poison, or some effect of its enraged state. He took a step forward, raising Storm Reaver and roaring back at the beast to get its attention. But the warlord ignored Max, instead letting itself fall back against the wall in an attempt to crush the dwarf that still hung there.

The elder grey wasn't going to allow that. He ripped his daggers free in a spray of dark blood and poison, falling to the ground and dashing forward between the orc's legs, slicing at both of his inner thighs on the way past. The One screamed in pain and staggered slightly as blood fountained over the fleeing dwarf, who winked at Max as he turned to move behind him, then used his shadow to disappear completely.

Max froze for a moment, sure that the grey assassin intended to break their truce and backstab him. When no attack came, he shook his head and took a deep breath to focus, then took another step toward the orc boss. On the way, he cast *Rot* at The One.

It was still staggering, using its oversized axe as a cane to support itself. But even as Max took another step, he noticed that the slashes on its thighs were already closing, the fountains of blood down to barely a trickle, despite the poison and the decay spell that was in effect. Whatever enraged ability the boss had, it clearly boosted his regeneration quite a bit. And with his massive health pool, Max was afraid this was going to be a long fight.

He lunged forward with Storm Reaver pointed directly at the orc's heart, which at this point was higher than Max's head. The boss somehow managed to bring its axe up to parry the blow, moving the heavy weapon as if it were light as a feather. Max hopped back out of range when it immediately reversed the axe's momentum and swung it at his head.

The One took two unsteady steps forward, roaring once again, causing blood to spray over Max and the still unmoving Izgren on the ground behind him. He started chanting, obviously about to cast a spell of some kind, but Max interrupted it with a quick lightning bolt to its face. Skin scorched and smoking, it raised its axe directly over its head, intending to divide Max right down the middle like split firewood. But the moment it was away from the wall, the old grey dwarf appeared behind it again. This time his leap took him higher, and he drove his two daggers into the orc's shoulders right near its collar bones, hoping to sever vital arteries. Both blades sank partway in, but were slowed and eventually halted by the sheer bulk of corded muscle.

Max cast *Pierce* on his blade and leapt forward as the orc tried to look behind itself at the dwarf on its back, driving Storm Reaver into its chest. He felt the blade scrape against ribs briefly before something snapped and it sank deeper. From the wheezing he heard when the orc growled at him, he assumed he'd punctured a lung. He twisted the sword's blade to do as much damage as possible as he withdrew it, falling on his butt to avoid another home-run swing of the orc's axe that would have cut him in half had it connected. From the ground he cast *Light Dagger* up at the orc's face, doing some damage and momentarily blinding it.

The old dwarf let go of one of his daggers and drew another, reaching around the massive orc's neck and trying to slit it's throat. Either his angle was off, or his strength not up to the task, because the cut was merely superficial. A thin red line appeared across its neck, but it barely bled. A moment later the orc grabbed the arm holding that dagger and yanked, hauling the old dwarf over its head and flinging him down at Max.

Max managed to roll out of the way as the old dwarf slammed into the ground where he'd just been sitting. He winced as he heard bones break, knowing it took an extreme amount of force to break the iron-like bones of a dwarf. The elder grey bounced once, then tumbled to a stop not far from Izgren, leaving Max to face the enraged orc boss on his own.

For a brief moment, Max considered casting *Boom!* at the orc's head and just diving out of the building. But he'd made a truce with the greys, and his conscience wouldn't let him leave them to be shredded by exploding orc bits. As the boss stalked toward him, he closed his eyes and cast *Blind* on the orc, then focused on a spot behind him and cast *Jump!*. Appearing behind the stumbling orc, he spun around, Storm Reaver leading the way, intending to hamstring The One just as he'd done to an orc outside.

Maybe it was because of the recent stealth tactics of the grey dwarves and the multiple backstabs it had suffered, but the boss somehow anticipated Max's move, and spun around himself a split second after Max appeared, blindly swinging the axe. The result was that Storm Reaver sliced across the front of the orc's right leg, doing only superficial damage, while Max grunted in pain from the axe striking his armor above his ribs. It didn't penetrate the dragonscale, but it knocked him aside and drove the breath from his lungs.

He hit the wall near the front door, grunting in pain at the additional impact, and fell to the ground. The massive orc laughed at him as he tried to get to his feet. It mumbled something, and a green glow surrounded its body, closing some of its wounds. Max cast *Zap!* again, but the bolt seemed to be absorbed harmlessly.

"Hahaha! Puny chimera king. I have heard of you. In fact, I hoped to find you and take your head as I moved south. Thank you for saving me the trouble of hunting you down." The One stalked forward, its gait still unsteady from blood loss and the effects of multiple poison injections.

Max was still struggling to get to his feet, watching the axe blade as the orc drew it back over his shoulder, when a roar from outside distracted both of them. The orc's attack faltered slightly, the blade striking Max's hip instead of his neck, driving him back to the ground and biting deep into his hipbone. Max grunted in pain and tried to cast a heal, but found he couldn't concentrate enough to complete the spell. The One barely had time to yank the blade free before the entire wall behind Max shattered. Chunks of stone and an avalanche of dust rained down on Max as he tried to duck and cover, protecting his head with both arms.

A moment later the ogre chieftain stepped on Max, unaware that he was there under the rubble, his weight grinding sharp stone bits into his helpless king. He roared a challenge of his own and swung a spiked stone club that was larger than Max at The One. The surprised orc failed to block the blow, which struck him in the ribs on the same side that Max had stabbed. Several of them broke as its massive body was lifted off the ground and slammed into the same wall he'd tried to crush the dwarf against.

"Puny orc!" The chieftain roared as he followed the boss to the wall. "Me kill stupid orc, Max give much cheeseburgers!" He slammed the club into the side of the orc's head, one of the spikes punching through its skull just behind its ear. The dazed orc fell sideways, and the ogre took another step closer.

Max managed to clear his line of sight through the rubble and dust enough to watch as the ogre swung again and again, hitting The One left and right about the head and body, going full Captain Caveman. Max managed to cast *Drain* on the orc while the chieftain pounded on it, partially healing himself in the process. The ogre continued the barrage long after the orc was dead, until its head was nothing but a deformed mush of bone fragments and brain matter.

"I think you got him." Max half-laughed, half-coughed out a cloud of dust. "Good job, big chief!"

The ogre chieftain turned and grinned at Max, giving the now shrunken corpse one final kick for good measure, at which point his eyes unfocused for a moment to read loot notifications. When he focused again on Max, he rubbed his belly. "I save Max from puny orc! Max owes many good eats!"

"As many as you can eat, great chief!" Max grinned at the happy ogre. He tried to get up, but relaxed and cast a heal on himself when the pain in his side and hip nearly caused him to pass out. Unfortunately, the chief noticed, and promptly stomped over to grab Max and lift him free of the debris. Max managed not to scream as the chief set him on his feet and proceeded to brush the dust off him, his massive ogre hands striking him hard enough to shave off a few more health points each time.

Max quickly held up his hands to stop the abuse, saying "Thank you again, chief." To further distract him, he pulled a dozen skewers of meat out of his inventory and handed them over. "A snack for you."

The chief sniffed at the food and his eyes widened. He licked his lips and grabbed the whole bundle in one fist before plopping down on his butt right there and shoving half of them, sticks and all, into his mouth.

Max, still a little shaky from the pain of his various injuries, cast another heal on himself. After a moment's consideration, he cast a heal each on Izgren and her master, hoping he wouldn't regret it later. The master hadn't attacked Max when he had the chance, so he decided to take that as a sign of good faith.

"Report." He called out through party chat. Blake was the first to answer. "Still some fighting here and there, but I think we've got this won, boss."

Smitty added, "I see half a dozen fights still going, maybe fifty or sixty red-eyes still standing. We're directing reinforcements, and it should be all over in a few minutes."

Nessa chimed in next. "A hundred or so tried to flee to the north in small groups. The grey dwarves were waiting for them, and I have assisted. None have made it through." Despite his pain, Max grinned at the pride in her voice.

He handed the chief another dozen helpings of meat on a stick and patted him on the shoulder, then walked over to check on the grey dwarves. Seeing the master awake but unmoving, he cast another heal on him. The elder thief sat up, his gaze immediately taking in what was left of the orc boss, then moving to Izgren. He said something softly in his language, his tone one of concern, as he moved to kneel next to her.

Max cast another heal on her, then produced a high quality healing potion. Tapping the old dwarf on the shoulder, he offered the potion, which the dwarf took and immediately began to pour down Izgren's throat. "Thank you, King Storm." He spoke common as his gaze met Max's, and he gave a respectful nod.

"We are allies, at least for this fight. From what little I saw, you both fought bravely." Max took a second to cast *Identify* on the old dwarf, but got no results other than question marks.

"I… underestimated the chieftain's strength." The dwarf acknowledged, once again staring at the pulped head of the orc. "We are thieves, not assassins or warriors. Though we train to fight, it is not our first choice." he added by way of explanation. "Had you and your large friend not arrived, the warlord would have made quick work of us."

"You welcome, puny dwarf." the ogre spoke around a mouthful of meat on a stick, giving a friendly wave with his free hand. Max resisted the snort that tried to fight its way free.

"Yes." The dwarf cleared his throat. "Thank you, great chieftain." He bowed his head, getting a wide smile from the ogre in return. "And thank you, King Storm."

"I wish I could say it was my pleasure, but he kicked my ass, too. It hurt." Max shook his head, rubbing his side, then nodded at Izgren. "Is she going to be alright?" He took a knee next to her, looking for any obvious injuries.

"I believe she will be fine. Again, my thanks for the healing magic, and the excellent potion." The thief awkwardly offered the empty vial back to Max.

Outside, the sounds of battle had all but died down. After a brief glance out the door, Max looked at the master thief. "I suppose we should discuss what comes next."

Chapter 9

Max sat near the bonfire that the orcs had built just outside the orc chief's warehouse building. To his left the ogre chief sat with his feet close to the fire, holding out a spear with six pieces of red-eye orc meat skewered on it. This was the second half-dozen that he'd cooked up, in addition to the three dozen helpings of meat on a stick that the ogre had already consumed. Max was idly wondering if the chief's belly would ever be full when his corporals showed up to report.

"Ten dead, nearly everybody else wounded in some way, but healed up now." Blake sat on a stone not far from Max.

Dylan added, "The dead include two of the grey dwarves. Along with two ogres, three orcs, two dwarves, and a gnome that was hit with a stray spear. He was up on a roof, and we didn't find him in time." He shook his head. "Best we can count, roughly a thousand of the orcs hadn't eaten the poisoned food. They fought hard."

"Speaking of the poisoned food, put some people on making sure it's all burned, and the bad water poured out. We don't want our hungry ogre friends to get poisoned." He glanced toward the chief, who was stuffing his face with slightly burnt orc. "Burn the barrels too, in case they're contaminated." Max looked at Smitty, who nodded once and jogged off to take care of it.

Nessa appeared not far away, emerging from Dylan's shadow. "The looting is mostly complete. There are a significant number of bodies we couldn't loot, as they were killed by the grey dwarves. Apparently our truce did not constitute a formal alliance that would allow us to loot their kills, or them to loot ours."

"Damn." Blake looked up at her. "So that would include all the ones that died from the poison, too?"

Nessa nodded. "We have still been able to loot more than half of the corpses, close to three thousand of them."

Max whistled. "That should fill our armory for the next decade or so. Assuming everyone wants to sell their share to Stormhaven."

"Can I get one of those giant axes the orcs used?" Blake asked. When everyone looked at him with questioning faces, he chuckled. "To hang on my wall as a trophy." Max produced one he'd looted from an orc he'd killed on his way to the boss fight and tossed it toward the gnome, who had to scramble out of the way to avoid being crushed. "Thanks, boss. I guess." He grumped as he reached down to touch the weapon and pull it into his inventory.

"I'm a little disappointed that we didn't make it to help you with the boss before he died." Dylan hung his head, a sorrowful look on his face. A second later it changed as a wide grin appeared. "I wanted a chance to toss the gnome at the boss!" He winked at Blake, who flipped him the finger.

"Yes! Toss gnome at puny orc! Fun!" the ogre chieftain eyed Blake and started to get to his feet before both Max and Dylan stopped him. He sat back down, confused, until Dylan distracted him with a still-warm extra-large sausage and mushroom pizza from his own inventory. The easily redirected ogre sat back down, folded the pizza in half, and shoved it whole into his maw.

Shaking her own head at the ogre's manners, or lack thereof, Nessa addressed Max. "Did the grey dwarves honor the bargain? Have they delivered the treasure?"

Both the corporals went silent, unconsciously leaning toward Max as they awaited his reply.

"They have." Max produced a storage ring from his inventory and held it up for them to see. "I only took a quick look, but it has five hundred slots, and all of them are full. Two slots are each filled with nine hundred ninety nine platinum coins, and another is mostly full of platinum bars." He grinned when Dylan whistled and Blake grabbed his chest and fell backward, pretending to have a coronary. "I saw enchanted armor and weapons, scrolls, jewelry, all kinds of stuff. There's a box bigger than Dylan's head filled with loose diamonds." His gaze took in the street in front of them, and the soldiers who were bustling around. "I don't think we'll have trouble paying the troops for a while." He weighed the relief of financial security against the cost in lives for a moment, then tried not to think about it.

"We're leaving this place to the grey dwarves. They've agreed not to operate in Stormhaven territory, and

I've agreed to leave them in peace as long as they honor that. We left the possibility of trade open for further discussion."

"So we like grey dwarves now?" Blake made a face like he'd just sucked on a lemon.

"We *tolerate* this particular branch of the Thieves' Guild." Max clarified. "The master had a chance to backstab me during the boss fight, and didn't. And as Nessa pointed out, they and their poison took out nearly half of this army, while making it easier for us to kill a bunch. They more than held up their end."

Both corporals and Nessa nodded their heads as Dalia came walking over from one of the side streets. She'd been with the rest of the healers, dealing with the wounded, and looked exhausted. Max handed her a couple sticks of meat as she sat down next to him. She thanked him and began eating, the ogre chief jealously watching every mouthful.

Max used party chat to call Smitty. "You might want to message Birona and have her order two or three times the usual supplies for the restaurant. We owe the big chief all he can eat for saving my skin."

Dylan's eyes widened when he heard that, and he quickly added, "Yeah, triple the order for sure." They both looked at the ogre chieftain, who was getting to his feet.

"I go get more meat." He started walking toward the nearest orc corpse, and Dylan hopped up to go with him, to make sure he didn't gather up any that had been poisoned.

Max sent out a general order through his rings for his officers to do the same for the other ogres, and found himself smiling as he wondered if a thousand untainted orc corpses would be enough. Then he wondered if it would even matter, if the poisoned orcs would even give the omnivorous ogres a bellyache.

*****

As agreed, Max left the settlement to the grey dwarves. The bodies had all been looted, including the mostly destroyed orc boss. When Max had looted him, he received nothing but coins, as he hadn't been wearing any of his gear at the time of the fight. The master thief agreed to split the loot they found inside his building, which included more gold that Max gave to the greys, his armor, which went to the ogre chieftain, his axe which Dylan claimed, and a staff that went to Dalia, as none of the thieves had any interest in it. All the loot from his elite guards went to the greys, as they'd been dispatched before Max even arrived.

Between killing thousands of orcs, and the quest rewards, all of the Stormhaven fighters leveled up at least twice. Some of the newer, lower leveled fighters got as many as five levels, and were celebrating accordingly. Max's party members all earned a level or two, with Nessa getting three. Max earned a nice pile of Sovereign points, and a decent amount of experience, though not enough to level him up. The experience for killing The One was split with the greys, who did a great deal of damage before being knocked out of the fight. And of course the credit for the kill went to the ogre chieftain.

Max sent his troops back through the portal to Stormhaven, and was standing near the pedestal with his party, discussing next steps. At the moment, he was trying to decide whether to leave the portal pedestal where it was, or remove it to be used somewhere else.

"If ye be thinkin' o trading with the greys, ye might as well leave it." Dalia's expression revealed what she thought of trading with the murderous cursed dwarves. Unlike Max, they'd been her mortal enemies her entire life, and she wasn't so quick to accept them.

"It's not like the greys, or anyone else, could use it without your permission." Dylan added.

"They're thieves. They could simply steal it." Nessa pointed out. "If for no other reason than to prevent you from using it. In case you change your mind about taking the settlement."

"And it's not on my land, so they could take it, or destroy it, without breaking our agreement." Max nodded.

"We're a good ways from the settlement, boss." Smitty jerked his thumb over his shoulder in the general direction of Gar'doz. "You could claim this land for Stormhaven, then they wouldn't be able to mess with the portal. Or, if they do, you could come back and wipe them out." He sounded hopeful at that prospect.

Max shook his head, grinning ruefully. "The last thing I need is more territory. I can't populate what I already have, and can barely protect it." He was leaning toward taking the pedestal with him.

Red appeared on his shoulder. "What, are ya daft? Ya don't need to protect a bunch o' trees n rocks. If ya claim this land, and all o' the area between here and the dworc's valley, it'll expand yer kingdom enough to level it up again!" She crossed her arms and stomped one tiny foot on his shoulder. "Besides, who's goin to try n take it from ya?" She looked around as if searching for an enemy. "Ya killed the red-eyes, and they likely killed most everyone north o' here on their way down from their home. The greys got more space than they need, and already agreed to leave your territory alone. South o' here is already your land. Ya needn't do anything with the territory, just let it be. Who cares if some beasties or even monsters wander around a bit, or even take up residence? Yer people can farm them for experience."

Max stared at his feisty leprechaun for half a minute, considering. A look around the group got him several smiles or nods of agreement. Blake even put in his two cents. "She's right. We could bring guildies up here to hunt monsters and explore the area, assuming you give them a quest to make it worth their while. Who knows, we might find another mine, or even a dungeon, up here somewhere."

"And if ye want a place to expand, mebbe start a new village, this be a good place." Dalia held out her hands and turned in a circle. "Ye could fortify it, use it to defend against future attacks from the north, in case there be more red-eyes up there."

"Or the thieves bring another grey dwarf clan to live in their settlement." Nessa suggested.

That last bit settled it for Max. The master had bound all the members of the Thieves' Guild in their non-aggression agreement, but he doubted that another clan that settled in Gar'doz would be bound by that.

"Blake, reach out to your earth mage buddies and get them here to construct some walls across this pass. Also a barracks, and a few other generic structures. Offer them a hundred gold each to get it done in the next couple days. You know what we need." The gnome nodded once to acknowledge the order.

Max looked at Red again. "You're sure I can claim this area?"

She shrugged, sitting down on his shoulder. "Won't know unless ya try."

Max closed his eyes and concentrated on his interface. He selected his *Kingdom* tab and scrolled until he found what he was looking for. Focusing on his desire to claim the land under his feet, he was pleased to see his map pop up. On it was a gold star indicating his location, and the map was at least partially filled in between his location and the dworc valley, since he and his group had traveled overland to get there. When he mentally questioned how much of an area he could claim, a huge area became shaded in green. It stretched south to his already claimed valley, north past Gar'doz by several miles, and roughly ten miles east and west.

Not wanting or needing nearly that much space, and having no desire to surround Gar'doz and cut them off from any hunting or grazing lands, he mentally adjusted the northern boundary of the shaded area to just a quarter mile north of his position. He left the eastern and western boundaries where they were, and kept all the area to the south. When he'd settled on that, the system prompted him to confirm that he wanted to claim the territory, and he selected [*Yes*]. After he'd claimed the goblin city, and the land on either side of Deepcrag between its two neighboring cities, Stormhaven had reached level 2. The bonuses to his people and production had been significant, the dwarves had located a mithril vein near where he and Enoch had encountered the rock troll infant, and the kingdom was better off in general. If he could do it again, he would.

Immediately he was hit with notifications, one of which featured text outlined in gold. The first was about the expansion.

Congratulations! You have claimed sufficient additional territory, population, and resources to increase your Kingdom Level by +1!

Next came the gold-outlined notification. It pulsed as he focused on it, and Max felt like fireworks were going off in his mind. A warmth flushed through him, even greater than what he felt when he leveled himself up.

Kingdom Level Up! The Kingdom of Stormhaven is now a Level 3 Kingdom!
Rewards: 5,000 Sovereign Points; 25,000,000 exp; 500,000 gold; Your reputation with allied, friendly, and neutral kingdoms has increased. Your trade relations with allied, friendly, and neutral kingdoms

have improved. The morale of Stormhaven citizens has increased by 5%. Production has increased by 10%.

Level up! You are now a level 43 Sovereign! You have earned 3 free attribute points!

The huge amount of experience, coming right after the battle with the orc army, was enough to get him to level forty three, and more than halfway to forty four! Max waved the notifications away, taking in the satisfied grin on Red's face. "Ye nearly hit the next class level as well!"

"What happened, boss? I felt... something." Dylan rubbed his belly as if that something might be indigestion.

"Stormhaven just leveled up to three. What you're feeling might be the morale boost."

The ogre shook his head. "Nope, I think I'm just hungry." He motioned toward the portal. "I vote we head back to Eats N Treats and get a celebratory meal before the ogre chief cleans the place out."

"The mages will be here in the morning." Blake reported. "Also, I got a message from the Guild house. Falcon stopped by to offer a quest from Farstrider. He is offering gold and good xp for our War Dogs to go fight on his front lines. Apparently the queen has thrown a bunch of conscripts into the fight, and Westreach is having trouble holding out."

Max immediately opened the portal, needing to find out from Redmane if Farstrider had asked Stormhaven for aid. He assumed that Redmane would have contacted him immediately, but wanted to check anyway. As they stepped through the portal, Blake asked, "Boss?"

"Hmmm? Oh, the quest? It's your guild, corporal. Up to you to accept or not. I'm assuming participation will be voluntary?"

"Of course." Blake looked at him like he should know better than to ask. "I'm only asking you because some of the guildies are active duty Stormhaven guards. They might be gone for a while..."

"If they want to go, let them. We'll figure out how to cover for them. We've got enough resources now to hire more if we need to." Max started toward the main doors of the keep. "I need to talk to Redmane for a bit. I'll catch up with the rest of you at the restaurant."

Redmane met him just inside the entrance, already on his way out to meet Max, as was his habit when he was expecting his king. "I hear the battle went well, me king?"

"Yeah, we lost a few fighters, but gained some resources, and more territory, and I assume you heard we leveled up Stormhaven." Make glanced sideways at the dwarf as they strolled toward his study.

"Ha! Aye, I noticed. Well done, Max."

"Farstrider put out a quest for the War Dogs to help in his war effort. Apparently the Battleborne queen has increased her forces. Has he reached out to us for aid?"

"Nay, I've not heard from him." The dwarf shook his head, then began to stroke his beard. "Could be fer the same reason he gave ye before. Bringin' in some mercenaries from the guild is one thing. But bringin' in allied forces from another kingdom would be seen as escalation."

"But if the queen has already escalated, what's he waiting for?" Max was not anxious to get into another fight, especially not before he'd even buried the dead from the last one. But as a rookie king, it bothered him that he didn't understand Farstrider's thinking. "What am I missing?"

Redmane shook his head and shrugged. "I dunno. We could always ask him."

Max shook his head after a moment's thought. "Hold off on that. Instead, send a message to Ironhand, see if I can meet with him in the morning. I'd like to ask his advice."

Knowing Max, the dwarf eyed him with suspicion. "What're ye thinkin'?"

"I'm wondering if there's a way I can help Westreach without joining in the war effort. Like, as an ally, can I make an official visit to the queen and attempt to broker a peace agreement?"

Redmane's eyes widened. "Ye remember she be a Battleborne, yeah?"

Max paused as they reached his desk and he walked around it to take a seat, while Redmane did the same on the other side. "I'm aware, yes. Why?"

"Historically, when Battleborne meet up, at least one o' them doesn't survive the experience."

"I'm not thinking of going there to challenge her. Just to let her know that Farstrider is a friend, one who desires peace, and that there might be some benefit to her if she ceases hostilities."

"What're ye thinkin' o' offerin' her?" Redmane clearly didn't like the idea, but was curious as to what his king was thinking.

"Don't know. Trade agreements? Access to ore from our mines, tasty mushrooms, and crafted goods? The opportunity not to be invaded by a small horde of orcs, dwarves, and ogres?" He grinned at his chamberlain, who was looking horrified. "Don't worry, that last bit was a joke."

Max sobered as Redmane took a deep, calming breath. "Seriously, though. Farstrider once told me that he'd consider sending her his son's head if it meant she'd stop killing his soldiers at the front. That's a man who sincerely desires peace, and is willing to pay dearly for it."

"Be sure ye don't mention that to her. Along with yer invasion joke." The dwarf warned.

"Like I said, I think I'd like Ironhand's advice before I make any kind of decision. I should probably check with Farstrider first, as well. I wouldn't want to work out terms with the queen, then find out he's unwilling to accept them, as unlikely as that might be."

"Aye, I'll arrange a breakfast meeting tomorrow. I suggest ye take him some o' them pancakes with the syrup." Redmane grinned at Max.

"Good idea. I've been meaning to ask him about opening a branch of the restaurant in Darkholm. Might as well take him some samples of the food." Max eyed the inevitable and ever-present three piles of papers on his desk. "Speaking of the restaurant, the others are expecting me there. Want to grab Teeglin and join us?"

"Aye, I'd like that." Redmane got up and walked with Max out of the study. He'd apparently reached out to Teeglin via party chat or a ring, because the little dworcling came rushing down the main corridor at them just as they reached the exit.

"King Max! Welcome back!" She launched herself into his arms, hugging his neck tightly and planting a kiss on his cheek. "I tried to go to the war with you, but they wouldn't let me!" She frowned at Redmane, who chuckled.

"Had to lock the little monster in her room to keep her from sneakin through the portal."

"Bah! How dangerous could it be, fightin' a bunch of stupid orcs! I was there when they attacked our village!"

Max set her down on her feet, then took a knee to be closer to her eye level. "Listen to me, little princess. That battle was terrible. We were outnumbered five to one. Ten of us died, and almost every one of us was injured in some way, including me. I very nearly died." He watched as tears began to form in her eyes, and regretted his gruff tone. "I'll tell you what. We'll begin to teach you to fight here in the keep. That way, when you get bigger and stronger, you can come with us on some adventures. But for now, battles are no place for pretty princess Teeglin. Agreed?"

When she nodded her head, he gathered her into a hug. "Right now it's my job to protect you. When you get big n strong, you can protect me back!" He grinned at her and poked her in the belly with one finger, then began to tickle her until she smiled and squirmed away from him. "Now, we were just headed to Eats N Treats. How would you like a hot n greasy grilled cheese sandwich?"

Teeglin looked thoughtful as she took his hand and they began to walk out of the keep. "Can I have tacos instead? Or a burrito? I really like burritos!"

"You can have whatever you want." Max smiled down at her. A thought struck him just then, and he stopped in his tracks. Bending down again, he leaned close to her ear and whispered, "Want to see something funny?" When she grinned and nodded, he said, "Watch this." and produced the storage ring that the master thief had given him. "Oh, by the way…" He turned to Redmane, who was looking curious about the whispered exchange. "I got this from the grey dwarves. Something they liberated from the city before they left." He stayed on one knee with an arm around Teeglin as they both watched the dwarf examine the ring. When he saw what was inside, his mouth dropped open and his eyes nearly bugged out of his face.

"King Max!" Redmane gasped, and Teeglin giggled. "This be… where'd ye… I dunno how to…" Teeglin giggled some more at the dwarf's obvious shock.

"It's the lost Nogroz treasury. Or, more accurately, ninety percent of the treasury."

"Durin's great hairy stones!" the dwarf exclaimed, earning a shocked gasp from Teeglin, who covered her mouth with both hands before giggling again. Redmane didn't even notice.

"Thought you might appreciate that." Max chuckled at the dwarf who was still perusing the items stored in the ring. His eyes remained wide, and his cheeks were turning red. Max checked to make sure he hadn't forgotten to breathe.

"Just the platinum alone…" Redmane finally refocused on Max. "I'd been wonderin' how ye had the resources to increase the kingdom level again. Figured the loot from the battle musta been above average, or ye stumbled across another gold mine. I had no idea ye'd return with such as this!"

Max shrugged like it was no big deal, getting back to his feet. "When we ran across the grey dwarves, I remembered something that first translator had told us about the relationship between the Thieves' Guild and the crown." He watched Redmane stare at the ring a bit longer, then put it away.

"Ye must tell me the whole story, me King."

"Come on, I'll tell you over dinner. Burritos for everyone!"

*****

The celebration dinner went well. Smitty closed the restaurant to the public for the evening, and had invited all the officers from the battle, as well as the general, the other counselors who were in town, the dworc elders, and the ogre chieftain. They brought in extra help from the palace kitchen staff, and broke open their stock of Firebelly's Finest along with some casks of the dworc honey mead. They began the celebration by raising a toast to the fallen from the battle, and another to all who'd fallen since Stormhaven was born. Max silently toasted the friends and companions he'd lost before then, on this world and the last.

When he got back to his quarters late that night, exhausted from nearly two full days and nights of traveling, fighting, and celebrating, he sat on a sofa and took some time to assign his free attribute points. He considered increasing his strength at first, thinking of how weak he'd felt compared to The One. But the orc had been nearly half again his level, and already gifted with the natural strength of orcs, so he let that idea go. Instead he invested all three free points into one of his lowest stats, *Endurance*. His kingdom was growing quickly, and he had a feeling there would be many more sleepless nights ahead. He couldn't afford to be tired, or dull-minded from lack of sleep, because a missed detail or bad decision could cost lives.

As soon as he confirmed his choice, he felt better. Not fully refreshed, but a little less tired. Despite that feeling, he closed out his stat sheet and headed for bed.

Maximilian Storm	Health: 6,100/6,100
Race: Chimera; Level 43	Mana: 2,900/2,900
Battleborne, Sovereign	16,200,000/25,000,000
Endurance: 38 (48)	Intelligence: 59 (79)
Strength: 66	Wisdom: 59 (80)
Constitution: 73	Dexterity: 34 (35)
Agility: 35 (41)	Luck: 31 (43)

Chapter 10

"Max!" Ironhand stood from his throne and stepped down to greet Max, thumping him on the back and motioning him toward the long table they so often gathered at. Several of the Darkholm elders were already gathered there, eating breakfast. "Congratulations on leveling up yer kingdom, lad!" Ironhand took a seat and motioned for Max to do the same as the elders nodded their agreement and salutations.

"Thank you. None of it would have been possible without your help." Max bowed his head to the dwarven king. "I've actually come to ask for some more of your wisdom today."

Ironhand chuckled. "I'll help ye if I can, lad. What's botherin' ye?"

Max quickly explained the situation between Farstrider and the Battleborne queen, then the quest that the Westreach king had offered the War Dogs. After he further explained his thinking regarding making some kind of formal visit to the queen's court to seek peace, Ironhand and the elders were all nodding along. After a long moment's thought, Ironhand replied.

"It be an honorable desire, Max. Ye'd be putting yerself, and us as yer allies, in a delicate situation. At the moment, though you've allied yerself with Westreach, the war be none o' yer concern. Ye offered assistance, as ye should have, and Farstrider turned ye down. None would look askance at ye fer keepin' yer nose out o' the whole thing." He leaned back in his chair and gazed up at Max, who noticed several of the elders doing the same, a few of them leaning forward in anticipation of his answer.

"This is a test, right? I feel like this is a test." He looked from the elders back to Ironhand, who was now grinning. The dwarf chuckled, then thumped the table with one hand.

"When ye be a king, everything's a test. From the decisions ye make, to the look on yer face when a servant enters with yer dinner. Every little thing ye do has consequences, intended or otherwise."

Max sighed, his shoulders hunching slightly. "I know the war between the two human nations is none of my business. But it's so pointless! As a soldier, I can't… it's hard for me to sit by and watch so many lives wasted over something as stupid as an insult given by a foolish boy."

"Ye know good n well that be only a pretense." Ironhand's tone grew instantly serious. "That woman be ambition incarnate. If the wee lad hadn't offered insult, she'd have found some other excuse. This be about her aims fer expansion, not some silly words."

Max nodded. "Farstrider said as much as well, now that I think about it. Still, I'm inclined to stick my nose in, as you put it. In hopes of establishing peace."

Elder Stonebinder, who'd been critical of Max from the first, snorted loudly. "Battleborne come to this world to conquer! To fight! I've never heard o' any Battleborne ever workin' toward peace. Ye've little chance o' that, young king Max. Not when ye face dealings with another Battleborne. She'll as likely take yer head as listen to yer words."

"Especially that one." Ironhand added. "From all we hear, she's clever as a fox, with a heart o' cold stone. Not known fer showin' mercy. It's said when she killed her husband the king to take his throne, it were a slow and painful death."

Max shifted uncomfortably on the bench. "You think she'd actually attack me? Even if I show up under the flag of truce?"

"Aye." Ironhand nodded. "If ye show up alone. She could take yer head n deny ye were ever there." He paused for a moment, looking at each of the elders in turn, and getting nods from most of them. Except Stonebinder, of course. "But if ye showed up with an army at yer back, she'd have to think carefully before harming ye." The dwarf king's face broke into a wide and wicked grin.

Recognizing that something was afoot, Max raised one eyebrow. "You think I should take my soldiers with me? Won't she just see that as an invasion? Or an escalation?"

Ironhand actually chuckled out loud. "Aye, some o' yer warriors, at least. Along with some o' mine, and some from each o' the allied clans." He paused and nodded at Stonebinder, who was already scowling. "Me cousin's clan holdings border on the queen's lands, a half day's ride from the current battlefront, and nearly a full day's ride from her capitol. We could gather the clans to hold a moot right at that border. Yer human king has requested to join our alliance, and that be as good a place as any fer the clans to discuss it. Fer a human not familiar with our traditions, it might look as if we be considering an invasion!" He slapped the table and laughed aloud, the elders joining in with mischievous twinkles in their eyes.

Max grinned back at them. Once again he found the dwarves to be both clever and loyal allies, and he admired their willingness to participate in shenanigans. He sent up a silent and heartfelt expression of thanks to Regin, who pushed him toward the dwarves when he first arrived on this new world.

"It'd be a two day march from the nearest portal." Ironhand warned. "Ye could bring yer force through Darkholm, and we'll escort ye the rest o' the way. Be sure to invite King Farstrider, and instruct him that it be customary to bring a sizeable honor guard. As well as at least a wagonload o' drink!"

"A large wagon." Stonebinder added. It seemed the dwarf had accepted the inevitable, and was now focused on gaining whatever benefit he could from it. "Feel free to bring along some o' that honey mead ye give'd our king to taste."

Max actually smiled at the grouchy and intractable elder. "I'll bring a wagonload of my own!" Turning back to Ironhand, he asked, "So we gather at the border. How large a contingent do I take across the border with me?"

The dwarf king shook his head. "Ye send a messenger to invite her to join us. We'll see if she's got the courage to come, or whether she sends an underling. Either way, with the obvious presence o' the Westreach King at her border amongst a thousand or so of us, she'll get the point."

"And if she shows up with an army behind her? If she chooses to attack?"

Ironhand and most of the elders snorted. "She'd not dare!" The king slammed both hands on the table, making plates and utensils jump, toppling more than one goblet. "Even if she had not already committed most o' her resources to the battle with Westreach, she has no hope o' defeating even a token force o' dwarves!"

Stonebinder nodded his head, growling. "We'd crush her army and burn her capital in three days. Mebbe two." The other elders thumped their mugs on the table in agreement, sloshing ale everywhere.

Max shook his head in wonder. "Thank you, Majesty. For your support, and for your wisdom." He bowed his head deeply.

"Bah! Been twenty years or more since we got to tweak the noses o' the humans. We've had to settle for takin' advantage o' them in trades, and sellin' em overpriced apprentice level weapons and armor. It'll be fun to make that viper sweat a bit! And we can get some real kingdom business done at the same time." He looked around the table. "If I remember correctly, we've got a couple o' weddings between clan scions already arranged.

We can include those in the celebration! The queen won't know the difference between civilian tents and military. It'll just make our force look that much more intimidatin'!"

*****

Falcon entered his king's study to find him playing chess with the queen. The two of them were masters of the game, and took their matches as seriously as any two knights facing off on a field of battle.

Hesitant to interrupt, he moved over to a nearby sofa and quietly took a seat. His news was important, but not urgent enough to risk interrupting. The queen looked up for a moment and offered him a bright smile before returning her attention to the board. She frowned at her husband, then muttered, "Why would you sacrifice a bishop there? I can see you taking my knight in two more moves, but that can't really be your plan. What are you up to, you craftly old dog?"

"Not so old, my love." The king smiled at her. "Only a year your senior, lest you forget." He paused as her frown deepened, and quickly altered course. "And you're every bit as beautiful today as you were on our wedding day."

"You will not distract me with flattery, dearest. I will discern your plan, and foil it." She glanced up at Falcon for just a second. "While I consider how best to defeat you, let Falcon deliver whatever news has him fidgeting so."

Falcon froze, unaware that he'd been fidgeting. The king laughed, and looked over at him. "Alright, out with it."

"Two bits of news, my lord. First, the War Dogs accepted your quest, with King Max's blessing. They will arrive here in the city tomorrow, and be escorted to the front by our scouts."

Farstrider and the queen both nodded at the good news. She reached out and touched her knight briefly, then removed her hand again, biting her lower lip as she contemplated her move.

Farstrider grinned at the board, then turned his attention to Falcon. "That is good news. And the second bit?"

"We just received a message from King Max. Actually, it's a dual invitation from Stormhaven and Darkholm." He hesitated as both royals forgot about their game and turned their full attention toward him. "It…seems that the dwarves will be holding a moot, attended by all the clans, as well as King Max. The gathering will be held near the bitch queen's border with their closest lands. They plan to discuss our application to join their alliance, among other business, and have invited us to attend." He watched as the two of them exchanged a look. "They suggest we bring a full honor guard, as well as a wagonload of our best wine and spirits."

Falcon held his breath, unsure how his king would take the news. He didn't understand why the dwarves and Max would expect the king to travel so far while fending off an invasion. He relaxed when the queen began to laugh. A moment later, the king grinned at her, then at Falcon.

"Clever dwarves!" He shook his head. "The queen will see me meeting with what I assume will be several hundred dwarves right at the edge of her lands. At a time when she's committed the majority of her forces at our border. She'll have to decide whether to redirect some of those soldiers to deal with the dwarves, or put up a show of force."

The queen nodded. "If she pulls troops back to move toward the dwarves, it'll lessen the burden on our troops for a few days, maybe a week." She flashed a wicked grin at Falcon. "And if you can arrange for the War Dogs to show up at the front at the proper time, it'll complicate her decision greatly." A giggle escaped her lips. "Oh, how I'd love to see the look on her overpainted face!"

Farstrider chuckled at his wife's delight. "Falcon, please accept Max and Ironhand's gracious invitation. Make travel arrangements, and instruct the royal guard to polish their armor. We're going to attend a party with the dwarves!"

*****

"Majesty, I have an urgent message for you, from the pigeon master." The guard, who had just intruded on her meditation, bowed low and presented a tiny bit of rolled parchment with a green ribbon around it, indicating that the message was from one of her spies in Westreach. "He bade me deliver it with all possible haste."

The queen snatched the parchment from his hand and untied the ribbon, quickly reading its necessarily brief message.

King, Queen, royal guard attending dwarven moot.
Dwarves to vote on Westreach alliance.
Prince left under light guard in palace.

Not needing more than a few seconds to consider the implications of the message's content, she crumpled the paper in one fist and growled, "The damned dwarves! Of course they'd stick their noses in my business!" She pounded the fist holding the paper on the arm of her throne once, then again.

Looking down at the guard, she screamed, "Get me the ghost! And the mage! Run!"

The guard, accustomed to his new queen's outbursts, simply spun on one heel and sprinted for the exit, not even taking the time to bow first. The guards had all learned the hard way to obey promptly. The consequences for failure to do so were… harsh.

When her spymaster, widely known by his nickname *the Ghost*, and her royal mage arrived a few minutes later, she'd managed to calm herself a bit, but only a small bit. The dwarves getting involved put her in an untenable situation. While she might muster the strength to conquer a small kingdom such as Westreach, the dwarves were another matter altogether. They were a close-knit bunch of clans, each with de facto kingdoms that operated independently. But when one was threatened, they immediately came together as one nation under their king, Ironhand. Dwarves were fierce fighters, and even more fiercely loyal, and their combined armies outnumbered her entire population at least ten to one.

She tossed the crumpled and now sweaty message to the ghost first. He quickly read it, then handed it off to the mage, his expression not showing the least bit of surprise. She glared at him, leaning forward on her throne. "You knew about this." It wasn't a question.

"I have my own sources in Westreach, my queen. Though it appears your spy's pigeon flies faster than mine. I only just received a similar message moments ago. Though mine included two additional bits of information. First, Farstrider has hired mercenaries to assist him on the battlefront. A new guild called War Dogs. Second, King Storm will also be attending the dwarven moot."

"The Battleborne king!" The mage snarled. "He already allied himself with Westreach, and he'll be pushing the dwarves to involve themselves, to help him seize your throne."

The queen nodded as he spoke, having already been thinking along the same lines herself.

"We must end this before the dwarves have time to muster a force and move against us. I will not withdraw, or surrender! We must force Farstrider to capitulate." She focused on her spymaster. "My spy says the palace is lightly guarded."

"Mine confirms the same. The king took most of his royal guard to put on a show of strength for the dwarves. Shall I proceed?"

The queen simply nodded, and the spymaster bowed deeply before departing. The mage remained standing in front of his queen, patiently waiting. After several minutes of silence, she spoke to herself, barely loudly enough for him to hear.

"I wonder what world he came from."

"Majesty?" The mage took a step closer and cupped his free hand behind his ear to indicate that he hadn't quite heard, though he had.

"The Battleborne king. I wonder what world he came from. He isn't one of those who came with me, according to what you've learned from the wretch Lagrass. He only just arrived after being betrayed and killed. Lagrass has called their world *Earth*, but every inhabited world has earth, so that name is little help. Storm has achieved a position of power as great as mine, or any of my contemporaries. Positions it took us more than a decade to reach." She drummed her fingers on the arm of her throne as she pondered aloud. "What special power, what knowledge did he bring with him to allow this to happen? The wretch said he was a simple soldier. A leader, assuredly, but in a world without magic. He did not bring any of the technology that Lagrass has described, nor do I believe he's had time to reinvent it."

"It is said he is favored by the gods, Majesty. Maybe they have assisted."

"Bah!" She made a dismissive wave in his direction. "All Battleborne are favored by one god or another! It's how we came to be here in the first place. Brought here to fight and die for their amusement! Of the dozen of us that arrived in my time, only half still breathe. Two perished on the first day, before we escaped the trials and went our own ways." She shook her head, remembering. She'd killed a dark elf with her bare hands when the treacherous thief had tried to backstab her. The experience from the kill had leveled her up, and those extra attribute points were what had allowed her to survive the day.

"The gods do assist us in small ways, but operate under a unanimous agreement that limits the extent of that assistance." She watched as the mage nodded in understanding. Between what she'd confided in him herself, and what he'd learned from questioning the Battleborne in the dungeon, he knew well some of the benefits of being Battleborne.

"I need to know more about Maximilian Storm. If we can determine the true name of his original world, it might give us a clue as to what power he might wield. Or what his weaknesses might be."

Again the mage nodded. "Lagrass has reported him to be loyal to a fault. That may be something we can exploit. It is known that he often adventures with a small, close-knit party of non-humans." He sighed. "In the meantime, I shall resume my questioning of the wretch, to see if we can better determine what world they hail from."

"Do it quickly, wizard. Our time grows short. Push him harder. Break his mind, if you must. Get me answers." The queen's flat tone made it clear that she'd tolerate no delays, or failures.

*****

Prince Lucas was bored. His father had confined him to the keep since he returned after the incident with the queen. He'd been barred from attending any court events, as well. His father had said it was to keep from further embarrassing himself, and by extension, the royal family.

Lucas felt bad about what happened, and honestly regretted his outburst upon meeting the queen. But in his opinion, the punishment far outweighed the crime. It had never once entered his mind that people were dying as a consequence of his actions. He shared the view that the queen would have found some other excuse to invade had he not insulted her, and in his mind that absolved him of any responsibility for the ensuing war, and the lives it claimed.

When he'd said as much to his mother, hoping she would intervene with his father on his behalf, the look she'd given him had confused him, as had the tears that streamed down her face before she slapped him hard enough to knock him off his feet. She had departed without further comment, and barely spoken to him since. The next day the first sergeant of the royal guard had come for him, saying that his father had arranged for what the man had called "A proper education."

Lucas had spent nearly every day since with the palace guards. He had been forced to run, train, eat, sleep, and shit with the newest recruits. Peasants, every one of them. They told rough jokes, bragged about their conquests in local bars and brothels, and insulted each other mercilessly as they toiled through the days. Lucas was included in none of that, being the prince and heir to the throne. He was isolated, alone in a crowd of three dozen, all day, every day. When he returned to his chambers each night, he was escorted by two of the royal guard, who posted up outside his door until it was time for him to return to training just before sunrise the next morning.

"No more." He growled to himself. "Tonight I will escape for a bit, have some fun in the city!" He opened an intricately carved wooden box that sat on his writing desk. Several days ago he'd approached the palace apothecary, complaining he was unable to sleep. He blamed it on his sincere regret over the incident with the queen, and the strain of his new training regimen. The woman had given him the box filled with vials of sleeping potion. She'd instructed him to drink half a vial each night before retiring, and warned him against taking any more.

That same night he'd begun offering his guards a snack at night. Nothing fancy, a sandwich, a bowl of stew, some part of the supper delivered to him by the palace kitchen. They would enter his chamber and eat with him one at a time, so as not to leave his door unguarded. Both had initially refused, until he'd pleaded loneliness and asked them not to force him to eat alone, in silence.

Tonight he had requested a large portion of mutton stew. The palace cook made it using an eastern recipe that included spicy peppers. The sleeping potion had an unfortunate tangy and bitter taste, and he needed the spice to hide it. Pouring two full vials into the stew, he called in the first of the guards to join him. As the first guard ate, Lucas spooned another helping into a bowl and took it to the door.

"You should eat this before it gets cold. The grease pools at the top when it cools." He made a disgusted face at the guard as he handed over the bowl. The man hesitated, then accepted the bowl and began to eat it standing at his post. Lucas closed the door and returned to sit with the guard at the dining table. They exchanged bits of news of palace happenings, as normal, until Lucas figured the man had eaten enough of the stew. Standing and clutching his belly, he grimaced at the guard. "I am… unwell. Please excuse me?"

The guard took the hint and returned to his post, taking half a loaf of bread to share with his compatriot outside the door. The minute the door closed behind him, Lucas rushed to change into a set of commoner's clothes he kept in a sack under his bed. A plain white cotton shirt, leather pants and boots, and a wide leather belt with a basic belt knife in a sheath. He completed the outfit with a well-made but worn grey cloak that featured a hood he could use to hide his face when necessary. It was a disguise he'd worn a dozen times during previous adventures in the city.

Dressed for his evening out, he took up position inside the door, leaning his head and pressing one ear to it, listening for the sounds of snoring. He wasn't sure how long it would take, because he had no way to know how much of the potion mixed into the stew they actually consumed. The prince felt a twinge of worry that using two full vials might be dangerous, but the guards were both big and strong, and he felt the odds of doing them harm were small.

He was becoming impatient when he heard a grunt, then a thump. After a second thump a moment later, he was already reaching for the door latch when the entire door slammed into him, knocking him off his feet. When he looked up, he found two men in black leathers looking down at him.

"Look here. The young prince has already obliged us by disguising himself." The nearest and larger of the two spoke. Lucas glanced past them to see that his guards were not just asleep. One had a dagger protruding from his armpit, the other's eye had been stabbed through. His pulse began to race as what was happening became clear to him.

The larger man motioned toward him. "Gag him while I deal with the mess." Without delay, the second man grabbed Lucas and, with surprising strength for his slight build, lifted him bodily from the floor. He shoved the prince into a nearby chair, then produced a leather strap and a dirty looking cloth. He forced the bunched up cloth into Lucas's mouth, producing a bloody dagger and holding it to his throat when he tried to resist. Once the foul-tasting cloth filled his mouth, the man shoved the center part of the strap in behind it, then tied the ends behind his head. While this was happening, the larger man dragged the two guards into the room and off to one side of the door. He then grabbed the linen napkins off the dining table and used them to wipe up the small amount of blood on the corridor floor. Tossing the bloodstained napkins atop the corpses, he quickly checked the corridor, then closed the door.

"It'll be near sunrise before their replacements come to escort him. Unless a servant happens by and notices the guards missing, we should have several hours' head start."

Lucas sat trembling in his chair as the men conferred. The reaction was part fear, and part outrage at being treated so roughly. When the smaller man noticed, he sneered at Lucas, bringing his dagger point to within a quarter inch of the royal eyeball. "Listen, boy. You cooperate, and we won't hurt you. We're just here to escort you to the queen's palace, so she can thank you for your kind words during your last encounter." Both men chuckled when they saw Lucas wince. "If you don't cooperate, well... she'll still pay us half for delivering just your head."

He pulled the dagger back a bit before continuing. "I think we'd both prefer that you be delivered alive. Nod once if you agree."

Lucas nodded, careful not to let the partially withdrawn dagger poke him in the face.

"Right, then. On your feet. We're going to move quickly and quietly. I'll not tie your hands, as that would look unnatural to any who might stumble across us. We're just three friends, headed out for a stroll through the city, yes?"

Again Lucas nodded, the irony not escaping him. These murderous kidnappers were about to help him do exactly as he'd planned to do. He glanced at the two dead guards on his floor as he was walked toward the door. The larger man noticed, and grunted. "They went down much easier than expected. Barely put up a fight. So much for the vaunted fighting skills of the royal guard." The words caused Lucas' gut to clench. The guards hadn't been alert because he'd drugged them, and it cost them their lives.

He was as much their murderer as the two men who now marched him through the darkened corridors of the palace.

They moved quickly, and it wasn't long before they were taking a little-used stairway toward a lower level of the keep. Two minutes later they exited through a thick wooden door with an oversized iron padlock that had clearly been melted with some kind of solvent. The smaller man took a few seconds to replace the damaged lock on the door after closing it. "For appearances sake." He whispered when he caught Lucas watching. "The guards will pass by here in an hour or so. Let's hope for all our sakes they don't look too closely."

Moments later the trio were outside the palace walls, in a park that Lucas remembered having picnics in as a small child. They jogged to a copse of trees in a back corner, where the men had horses waiting. Lucas mounted the horse they shoved him toward after the larger man pulled his hood up to cover his head. "Keep your head down. Can't have any guards recognizing your face, or spotting that gag." Lucas complied, resigned to his fate, and feeling guilty over the deaths he'd caused. The guards weren't exactly friends of his, but they were brave men who served his family with honor, and he'd betrayed them.

By sunrise the three had ridden many miles from the city, and were well on their way out of Westreach.

Inside the palace, two guards arrived at the prince's chambers to find the corridor outside empty. After an urgent knock on the door that went unanswered, they pushed it open, finding their comrades' bodies, and no sign of the prince. A minute later alarms sounded throughout the keep, and soon after bells began to ring throughout the city.

Atop the highest tower of the keep, an elderly man hastily scribbled a message on a strip of parchment before rolling it and inserting it into a tube, which he tied to the leg of a small kestrel hawk. Taking the soft fabric hood off the kestrel's head, he gathered her in both hands and held her closer to his chest. His voice no more than a whisper, he spoke to her. "Go, find our lady queen, sweet girl!" With a quick motion he tossed her out the nearby window, and watched as she took to the air. When she disappeared from sight, he looked down at the bodies scrambling far below, and shook his head with worry.

Chapter 11

Max rode Pokey alongside Farstrider on one of
Westreach's raptor mounts. The creature was glorious
looking, bright white with red eyes that glowed slightly
even in daylight. It was larger than the other raptors Max
had seen, and so well trained that it barely blinked when
Pokey growled at it, then leaned in close to get a good sniff.
Beside Max on the other side rode Ironhand on a massive
battleboar.

Farstrider and his queen, along with their retinue,
had portaled from Westreach to Stormhaven to meet up
with Max and his party. They'd taken the balance of the
day to tour Max's various territories that were accessible by
portal before returning to the keep for a feast of
cheeseburgers, fries, and apple pie. The Battleborne were
all tickled at how much the humans complimented what
was basically junk food from their homeworld.

From there they'd all taken the portal to Darkholm,
then to Stonebinder's clan city, unsurprisingly named
Rockholm. From there a much larger party all exited to the
surface, and were riding toward the spot along the border
with human lands that had been chosen for the moot.

It was a sunny day, with a gentle but constant
breeze that pushed the few clouds in the sky along at a
steady pace. The procession of royals, advisors, and
several hundred guards moved at a leisurely pace as they
chatted and enjoyed the day. There was no rush to get to

the moot, as it would take another day or so for all of the clan representatives and their escorts to arrive.

Max glanced over his shoulder and grinned. Directly behind the three kings rode Farstrider's queen, Redmane, Cavariel, several of Ironhand's elders, Stonebinder and two other clan heads, and a veritable horde of soldiers. His own party were riding amongst his guard force, except Blake, who had accompanied the War Dogs on their quest at the front lines.

Farstrider had brought sixty of his royal guards, while Max had brought a hundred of his guards, a purposeful mixture of dwarves, orcs, gnomes, minotaurs, ogres, kobolds, and even a few goblins. The three ogres he'd brought being too big for mounts, except for Dylan, who had Princess, Ironhand had hooked them each up with a sturdily built chariot pulled by a pair of battleboars. The ogres had been thrilled, and had initially zoomed back and forth behind the rest of the crowd, shouting in delight. Now one rode on their left and right flanks, while the third brought up the rear. He was easily visible over the heads of the rest of the procession when Max looked back.

Ironhand and each of the clan leaders brought a hundred warriors, plus a contingent of family members, prospective brides or grooms, crafters, and support staff. Several merchant caravans would be joining them as well, taking advantage of the gathering of wealthy clan heads and their elite guards. The moot was scheduled to last three days, plenty of time for messengers to reach the human queen's capitol and return.

They were just approaching the hilltop where the actual moot would take place. It wasn't much of a hill, really, only rising up about three stories above the surrounding ground. But its top was wide and reasonably flat, and would offer a nice view of the surrounding area.

Just a few hundred yards from the base of the hill sat a stream that ran wide and deep, which served as the border between human and dwarven lands. Maybe fifty paces from the dwarven bank to the human side. The water was clear and cold, and full of fish, according to Stonebinder.

A few other clans had already arrived and set up tents at the base of the hill. There was a wedge-shaped section roped off and marked for each clan, as well as for Stormhaven and Westreach, the sections completely encircling the hill. Max chuckled when he noticed that some of the clan guards had already set up sparring circles between the hill and the stream, so that any scouts from the queen's forces would first see armed and armored dwarves battling each other. He made a note to send some of his own guards out there once they were settled. Especially the ogres.

Dwarves wearing plain white tabards rode out to meet the procession, each one assigning themselves to a kingdom or clan and leading them to their assigned sectors. Stormhaven had been placed between Westreach and Darkholm in the sections nearest the stream. Redmane took charge of their contingent, barking orders and directing supply movements like an orchestra conductor. In less than an hour Stormhaven's camp was set up. Max's tent, the largest in the group, was set up nearest the base of the hill. Next came Redmane's tent, which also served as the command tent, and two tents for Max's party. Nessa, Dalia, and Teeglin occupied one, while Dylan, Smitty, and Cavariel shared the other. Next came two large cook tents, followed by an open area in which their supply wagons were circled. Finally, row after orderly row of uniformly sized tents for the guards were arranged. Each of the ogres had a tent of their own, while the majority of others slept two to a tent. Except the half dozen goblins who preferred to all crowd into one tent and sleep in a pile.

Max, strictly forbidden by Redmane to take part in setting up the camp, wandered with Ironhand and both Westreach nobles to the top of the hill. There the dwarves had already set up a pavilion with a raised floor and three long tables arranged in a triangle. Two of the tables had benches for the dwarven clan heads and elders, while the third had individual seats for the nobles and their closest advisors.

The four nobles were looking down across the stream at the human lands where a dozen or so riders in military uniforms sat calmly atop their mounts, looking back up at them from a dozen or so yards beyond the far bank. A couple hundred yards further back Max could see a camp with tents already set up. After a moment, Farstrider spoke. "Too many for a standard patrol. As expected, they knew we were coming."

"It's not like we made any secret of it." Max replied. "Our purpose here is to be seen, after all. Should we go down and talk to them?"

Ironhand and both Farstriders shook their heads, and the dwarf spoke. "Nay, let 'em stew a bit. They'll stay put until they're sure our entire force be here, anyway. Then we'll send our message to their queen."

"In more ways than one." Queen Farstrider smiled as she looked down at the sparring grounds, where a hundred or so more fighters of several races were drifting in from the newer encampments. Already it was an impressive looking force, and the fighters were making a point of putting on a show for the observers, and each other.

Max actually laughed aloud as he noticed Redmane himself squaring off against an elder dwarf from another clan, both with shields and swords in hand. His chamberlain did an excellent job of running the everyday operations of Stormhaven. But like any dwarf, he still longed for battle! His laughter was cut short and he grunted in surprise when the two old warriors cut loose and began exchanging blows. The combat moved almost too fast for Max to follow, and the clangs of metal on metal had many of the other combatants pausing to watch the display.

Ironhand snorted. "Aye, those two've been goin at it fer a hunnert years or more. Each claims to be the superior fighter, and they never miss a chance to try n prove their claims." He took a step closer and leaned forward as if to get a better view.

"Who is the other dwarf?" Max asked. "I don't recognize the crest on his shield."

"Ha! Don't let old Redmane hear ye say that! That's his own clan. The other dwarf be his younger brother."

The two dwarves continued to clash, landing blow after blow on each other's shields, impressing Max and everyone else who could see the display. Max was beginning to wonder if they'd ever tire when a high-pitched screech echoed down from the blue sky. Looking up, he saw a small hawk diving directly toward them.

He turned toward it, thinking it was some sort of attack, and had his hand outstretched to cast a spell when the queen let loose a high-pitched whistle and held up her left arm. The little predator flared her wings and slowed quickly, then landed neatly upon the queen's forearm. She gripped tight with her talons, shifting its feet and ruffling her wings a bit before settling down. The queen used one gloved finger to scratch the little hawk's head a bit, speaking softly to her until she closed her eyes and tucked her head under one wing.

"A message from the palace." King Farstrider explained as the queen gently removed the tube tied to the kestrel's leg and handed it to her husband before resuming her petting. Farstrider quickly retrieved and unrolled the scroll, and read it. Max saw his face go pale before he looked up at his wife, who had also noticed. Without a word he handed it to her to read for herself. As she did, he turned to Max and Ironhand.

"That bitch has taken my son."

Behind him, the queen gasped. She turned and approached Max, holding out the arm that supported the kestrel. "Max, would you please?" Confused for a moment, Max finally realized she wanted him to take the hawk. He held up his arm, and the little kestrel obligingly hopped from the queen's arm to his. He felt her talons try to dig into his skin, but they had no hope of penetrating. He held the arm very still as the queen embraced her husband, tears filling her eyes.

"My boy. She'll kill him." She whispered before sobbing into her husband's shoulder.

Ironhand awkwardly cleared his throat, conflicted as to whether or not to interrupt them. He'd apparently decided his input was needed. "If ye'll pardon me sayin' so, I don't think she will. At least, not yet."

Both Farstriders turned to face him, still holding each other. The queen wiped at her tears with the back of her glove as Ironhand continued. "If she wanted him dead, she could've simply killed him without the trouble o' takin' him away. Likely, this be her way o' makin a reply to our lil gatherin' here." The king nodded, but his wife wasn't convinced.

"If she's killed him, or harmed a hair on his head, I'll rip her heart out myself and feed it to my little lady here!" She whistled again, and the kestrel hopped back over to her, this time perched on a shoulder that Max was just noticing was padded with leather, where the other shoulder wasn't."

Red's voice whispered from his shoulder. "They be bonded, the queen and the little lady." Max nodded. He should have guessed from the way the little hawk's expression of rage matched the queen's.

"This changes things a wee bit." Ironhand looked toward the mounted patrol across the stream. "I'm thinkin' we stroll down there and have a word with them lads."

"I'm thinking we slaughter them and send their heads to their queen." Lady Farstrider growled. The kestrel screeched in agreement.

Seeing the rage in her eyes, Max stepped in front of her. "Maybe it's better if I go speak with them alone. In your current frame of mind, you might say or do something… unfortunate." He did his best to sound calm, using a soothing tone.

The queen took a step forward as if to push past him, but her husband restrained her. "He's right, my love. Think of this as a chess game. We can't risk our queen in the opening gambit."

As she calmed a bit, Max smiled, liking the analogy. He was a chess player himself. "Think of me as a knight, or a bishop, sent out to intimidate a few pawns." He waited as she took several deep breaths, then nodded sharply, wrapping one arm around her husband's waist.

"Send them home shaking in their boots, Max. Consequences be damned."

Max looked from her stoney expression to the king, who nodded his agreement. A quick glance at Ironhand showed he was in agreement as well. "Alright. Wish me luck." He began to jog down the hill, keeping his pace steady and his posture upright, knowing the enemy soldiers would be observing him. To make sure, when he reached the bottom he slowed to a walk and let out a loud, piercing whistle in their direction.

Seeing him coming, the fighters on the sparring field went silent, stopping their mock battles and turning to watch him as he passed. Redmane ceased his own battle and hustled over to Max's side, accompanied by his brother. Both dwarves were sweating, but hardly breathing hard after their furious battle.

"What is it, me king?" Redmane muttered just loud enough for Max to hear. Max, on the other hand, spoke loudly enough for everyone. "The bitch queen has taken Prince Farstrider from the palace in Westreach." There were a series of exclamations from the assembled warriors, the loudest and angriest coming from the members of the royal guard. One of them, the unit commander, went sprinting up the hill toward his king and queen, while two others raced toward their encampment.

Max continued to walk at a measured yet determined pace toward the stream, the others falling in behind him in a wide line as he advanced. When he reached the streambank he shouted across. "You over there! Come here! I have a message for your queen!"

The dozen riders shuffled a bit, obviously unsure of what was going on, though clearly aware that something was afoot. Finally, three of the twelve rode forward. They stopped just short of the bank on their side. "Who are you, and what message?"

Max motioned for them to come closer. "I am King Maximilian Storm of Stormhaven. Approach, so that I may relay my message. I'm not in the habit of shouting across streams!"

The lead rider nodded once and spurred his horse forward, followed by his two companions. The horses had to swim at the deepest point of the stream, but only for a moment. Just before they reached the bank, Max held up a hand to stop them. "That's close enough." He waited while their horses steadied themselves in the gravely streambed and settled under their riders.

"What message have you for our Queen?" the lead rider barked at him.

"I have just been informed that she has taken the cowardly action of kidnapping the crown prince of Westreach!" Max growled, still projecting his voice despite having the soldiers draw closer. He wanted the ones who'd stayed behind to hear, in case these three didn't survive the meeting. "Hurry back to her, and tell her to bring the prince here, unharmed, or I will personally slit her throat and toss her body into the sewers!" This time he roared at the three men, who flinched back even as their horses began to shuffle in fear.

"You dare threaten our lady Queen!" The lead soldier, Max guessed he was probably a captain and a noble, bellowed back.

"I dare threaten your bitch queen, you, your men, your families, and anyone standing between me and her palace! I will slaughter every one of you, burn your villages and your cities, feed your corpses to your livestock, then feed your livestock to my soldiers!" He grimaced, realizing he probably took it a little too far with the livestock bit. But behind him, several hundred armored and angry-looking warriors roared their enthusiastic approval, thrusting weapons into the air.

The net effect was better than Max had hoped for. The three men turned their mounts and retreated as quickly as they could. When their horses hooves found purchase again on the other side, the lead noble produced a bow and nocked an arrow, shouting, "You shall pay for your insults, mongrel!" He loosed the arrow, which flew across the stream and hit Max in the chest, but failed to penetrate his dragonscale armor. After a collective gasp of surprise, and seeing the arrow fall harmlessly, the fighters behind Max began to laugh.

For his part, Max bent and retrieved the arrow, then cast *Levitate* on himself, holding his arms out to either side as he rose twenty feet in the air. When he was sure all eyes were on him, he focused on the noble's breastplate and roared, "*BOOM!*"

A second later the noble's horse screamed as its rider mostly disappeared into a pink mist. The riders on either side of him were knocked from their mounts by shrapnel from the noble, both dead before they hit the water. Feeling bad, Max tried to heal the noble's horse, but it was too badly injured. He did manage to heal the other two before they fled up the bank and out of range.

Still hovering, and with his allies cheering behind him, Max motioned for them to quiet down. Addressing the now severely agitated nine riders remaining across the stream, he waved the noble's arrow at them. "That fool just got the smallest taste of what I'm capable of! Two of you, take the others' horses and go fetch your queen! Don't stop, don't even slow down. If she's not here by sunset tomorrow with the prince, unharmed, I will advance and destroy your homes!" He looked down at the bodies as the soldiers began to turn their mounts. "HOLD! One of you come and retrieve this idiot's head before it washes away! Take it to your queen as my warning!" The head and face were badly damaged, the lower jaw completely gone, but if she couldn't recognize the noble from what was left, they could always just tell her who it was.

One of the nervous soldiers rode forward with both hands empty and held up in the air. He hopped off his horse, stepped down into the creek, making a disgusted face as he retrieved the severed head from the mud by its hair, then retreated. Max watched them all return to the camp, then was distracted as one of the ogres splashed into the stream. He strode across, grabbed hold of what was left of the dead horse, threw it over his shoulder, and waded back. The other two ogres took the horse from him and helped him climb back up the bank before the three of them set off to find a cookfire.

Redmane nodded his approval up at Max before turning and shouting for the gathered soldiers to get on about their business. Max waited until he saw two men on horseback, leading two more horses each, take off in what he presumed was the direction of their capitol. Turning in midair, he moved himself through the air back to the top of the hill.

"Damn, Max." Ironhand greeted him with a rueful smile as his feet set down on the grass.

"Agreed." Farstrider gave him a nod of respect. "Thank you for that."

"And you were worried that I would do something unfortunate?" The queen smiled at him. "You killed a noble, Max. That won't make you many friends in the queen's court."

"He tried to kill me first." Max shrugged, holding up the arrow. "I was just better at it than he was." He heard Red snort on his shoulder, but didn't turn his head to acknowledge her.

*****

All of the clan elders had arrived by the end of that day, so they began the moot just after sunrise the following morning. Max and the human nobles, having never participated in a moot, sat back and observed as the dwarves performed the formalities of the gathering. Introductions were made, oaths of fealty to Ironhand were renewed, a ritual song was sung. When Ironhand began singing, he was alone for the first verse. The elders joined in on the second, and Max's heart swelled when, at the beginning of the third, every dwarf in all the encampments joined in from below, stomping their feet in rhythm. The entire hill trembled beneath him, and a quick glance showed that the Farstriders were just as enthralled.

The dwarves then got straight to business. King Farstrider was asked to stand and make his case for membership in the alliance. His speech was short, but eloquent. He spoke of promoting peace between the nations, giving Max much of the credit for his thinking in that direction. He spoke of trade, of access to a deep water port via his city's portal, and of mutual support in times of need. When he was through, a few elders asked him questions, mostly to gauge his sense of honor. The entire process took maybe ten minutes. The clan elders voted by raising their mugs, and were nearly unanimous in their support of Westreach's application. Stonebinder being the sole holdout.

Ironhand stood, meaning everyone else did as well, and formally welcomed the Farstriders and Westreach into the alliance. Factors were called forth and retired to one of the tents to work out the details and record the agreement in writing.

The dwarves then settled into internal business. Grievances between clans were aired and argued loudly, several times resulting in physical tussles inside the triangle of tables. Reports were made of recent windfalls, or setbacks, among the clans. More than one clan had been subject to attacks by the red-eyed orcs, so Ironhand bade Max to stand and report on his victory over The One and his army of several thousand. To which the elders cheered and thumped their mugs on the tables in approval. They were much less enthusiastic when he described his truce with the grey dwarf Thieves' Guild, muttering amongst themselves and throwing glares of contempt and suspicion at Max. That is, until Ironhand stepped in.

"Ye all know o' Max's actions during the battle o' Nogroz. Not one o' ye here has personally killed more o' the damned greys than Max has. Against all o' yer advice, and me own, he made Stormhaven a kingdom open to all races, *except the greys*. Don't ye doubt his hatred fer them!" He paused and gave Max a nod of respect. "If he saw fit to call a truce with the guild, I trust that he had good reason." He motioned for Max to continue.

"I had two good reasons. First, the poison they used killed nearly three thousand of the mutant orcs, and weakened another two thousand enough that we could slaughter them. Instead of facing a force of six thousand that would have overwhelmed us, we faced roughly a thousand healthy warriors, and were victorious." He paused, a smile starting to form as some of the elders nodded their heads. "The second reason was that, as part of the truce, they returned to me ninety percent of the Nogroz king's treasury, which they had seized and hauled away during the battle."

There was a period of surprised silence as many of the elders looked toward Redmane, who grinned and nodded his head. The silence was broken by a roar of laughter from Stonebinder, then more as others joined in, and more approving mug-thumping. Before it faded, Redmane stood and spoke up. "The victory also allowed me king to claim much o' the land south o' Gar'doz, raising Stormhaven to a level three kingdom!"

The glares and grumblings ceased after that, though Max imagined his stock with most of the elders had still gone down a bit. Even after his display of the day before, which they'd all made a point of congratulating him on. He added, "The grey dwarf elder told me he'd been visited by the same Tuath we met beneath Stormhaven. It was the Eldest that suggested he make a truce with us." The entire pavilion went silent for a moment, then the elders began to mutter amongst themselves. Max figured few of the dwarves would second guess the revered Tuath.

Before retaking his seat, Max offered a warning. "Though we destroyed their leader and their army, there may still be some of the red-eyes in the mountains. So keep a watchful eye out. If you discover more, I will commit myself and a hundred fighters to assist in prosecuting any further aggressions." The dwarves chuckled at his phrasing as he sat back down.

The subject turned to proposed marriage agreements, dowries, and the relative qualities and shortcomings of the candidates. These discussions were quite frank and businesslike, and included everything from physical attractiveness (or the lack thereof) to earning potential, cooking skills, ancestral reproductive rates, and with which clan the newlyweds would reside. The prospective spouses were placed together within the triangle during these discussions, and Max felt bad for them on more than one occasion. Queen Farstrider blushed or covered her mouth in astonishment more than once. As brutal as the discussions were, the dwarves all seemed to take it in stride, and by noon the agreements had all been hashed out, seemingly to everyone's satisfaction.

The wedding ceremonies were held all at once, ten pairs of brides and grooms standing before King Ironhand in the pavilion. Gathered close by were their parents and clan elders, and the entire hilltop was covered with observers and well-wishers. The ceremony was short and sweet, mostly involving binding life oaths between the brides and grooms. When it was over, the newlyweds kissed, some of them for the first time, and the crowd cheered.

They separated back into their various clan groups and descended the hill to begin the celebrations. All around the hill dwarves raised toasts and danced, until they got sleepy, napped, and rallied for a second round!

Max and the other royals joined in, making their way around the base of the hill, congratulating and toasting each couple and their clans. They gifted each couple a few gold coins, and offered blessings for prosperity and many offspring, which the dwarves seemed to regard as much more important than the gold.

Max kept glancing across the stream when it was in view, looking for a procession from the queen's city. Seeing nothing as the sun progressed across the sky, it became harder and harder to maintain a celebratory composure. He noted the human royals fretting as well, concerned for their son. Overnight their anger had faded and concern had grown that Max's actions might have resulted in retaliatory harm to the prince. Neither of them had voiced it, but Max could see it in their eyes.

Just before the sun dropped below the horizon, a group of twenty riders raced past the scout camp and halted at the stream. This time Max was accompanied by the other royals as he approached the water's edge. The riders all dismounted and took a knee, an officer in front speaking loudly to be heard across the water after bowing in respect. He was an elder man, in his late fifties, but had the look of a veteran. His armor was functional, not decorative, and extremely well made.

"King Storm, I am Lord Everett Hastings. My lady Queen sends her greetings." He paused for a moment, raising his head to look across at Max, who interrupted him, putting some growl in his voice.

"The sun is setting, and I do not see your queen among you. Does she doubt my resolve?"

"She does not, Majesty, nor do I. Her caravan approaches even as we speak, but will not arrive for some few hours yet." He motioned to the group behind him. "My men and I have ridden ahead to ask that you hold your wrath and speak with my Queen in the morning." He motioned for his soldiers to stand. Max noticed that about half of them also appeared to be nobles, and every one of them held themselves like veteran soldiers. After a brief pause, Lord Hastings added, "Failing that, my men and I have volunteered to face your wrath and offer honorable combat, that you might be satisfied until her arrival." Not one of the soldiers, nor the leader, flinched in the slightest, or shuffled their weight. They stood strong and firm, and Max found that he was a little bit proud of them.

Not bothering to check with his fellow sovereigns, Max offered the group a sincere nod of respect, saying, "Combat will not be necessary, Lord Hastings. My compliments to you and your men for your courage and loyalty." The entire group bowed their heads in acknowledgement, then saluted in unison with fists to chests.

Max did glance over his shoulder this time, taking in the ongoing celebrations. Turning back to Hastings, he called out. "We've just had several weddings over here, and I expect the celebrations will extend well into the night. I offer you and your men safe conduct if you would like to join us and unwind after what I'm sure was a long and taxing ride."

Hastings' eyebrows shot up in surprise before he recovered himself. After a short consideration, he bowed at the waist. "We accept your majesties' generous offer with our most sincere thanks." The others bowed as well before mounting up and crossing the stream. They immediately dismounted again on the dwarves' side, and bowed again to the gathered nobles.

They suffered another small shock a moment later when six liveried goblins came racing over to take the reins of their mounts and lead them away. A concern look from several of the group got Max chuckling. "Don't worry. They won't eat your horses. They're in my service, and will take good care of your mounts."

A few of the group still looked toward their retreating mounts, but Max could tell it was more out of the ingrained habit of taking care of them personally, than any fear for their mounts' lives. "Of course, we won't be offended if any of you feel the need to see to your mounts yourselves." Four of them, two of them nobles, sagged slightly with relief and, after another quick bow, jogged off after the goblins.

Hastings just chuckled and walked toward Max and the others. "Old soldiers become set in their ways, as I'm sure you know, Majesty."

Max just nodded before introducing Hastings formally to Ironhand and the Farstriders. The remaining fighters offered proper respect to each, thanking them for their hospitality. Hastings bowed most deeply to the Farstriders. "Majesties, as a father myself, I would ease your worries a bit and assure you that the crown prince was alive and unharmed when we left the procession around midday."

The king and queen nodded their thanks, remaining stoic in the presence of the enemy. Max found himself thinking that the queen had chosen her envoys well, rather than just throwing fodder into a potential meat grinder.

Not wanting to force the soldiers' presence on the human royals, Max invited them to his section, where tables of food and drink had been set up, and were being constantly replenished. Once the visitors had had a chance to eat and drink, and had stopped flinching any time an orc or ogre passed close by, Max motioned for Hastings to join him. The noble promptly gave his men some muttered instruction, then got to his feet and followed Max into his tent.

"Majesty, how may I serve?" The lord bowed yet again, clearly still a little nervous.

"You can start by relaxing. You're under my protection here, and despite my threats from yesterday, I have no desire to harm you. Or to rampage across your lands, for that matter. Though I will do so if necessary." He frowned at the noble to accentuate his point.

"I saw the torches of my Queen's caravan in the distance just before stepping in here, Majesty. She will be prepared to meet with you by morning." Max nodded, having seen the torches long before that with his elven vision. It was part of the reason he had called the noble over. "I'm going to do something that, as a soldier, and most especially as a king, I should not do. I'm going to explain something to you." He watched as the noble took in that information, and saw that he understood.

"I arranged this moot in order to draw your queen here for a peaceful discussion. To encourage her to accept peace with Westreach. As a former soldier, I'm inclined to despise her for wasting so many lives in a meaningless skirmish. If she was determined to conquer Westreach, she should have gone ahead with it, instead of playing at this extended and wasteful border fight." He paused again as Hastings nodded, the look on his face expressing his mutual distaste for the tactic, though he did not express it.

"However, the despicable tactic of kidnapping and threatening the prince, killing his guards in the process, and the subsequent attack on my person by the idiot whose head I sent back, forced me to take a more... aggressive posture."

"I understand, Majesty." Hastings nodded. "I might add, in confidence, that the man you rightfully executed was the son of a minor noble, one of my Queen's more... ardent supporters. Neither father nor son are well liked by many of us at court, and would not be widely grieved over."

Max took a moment to stare at the noble, wishing he'd brought Ironhand or Redmane in with him for this discussion. He wasn't sure, but he thought the man had just expressed a hint of rebellion. When he raised one questioning eyebrow, Hastings nodded almost imperceptibly.

"Well, that is good to hear, Lord Hastings. While I have found you to be a man of honor, and a worthy noble, that little shit was both foolish and annoying." He grinned at the soldier, who did his best to suppress a grin of his own as they shared a moment of disdain for unfit officers.

"I'm sure now that your queen is near, you and your men will want to return and report. I'm equally sure she'll be glad to see you alive and unharmed. I will have a tent set up near the stream, and invite you to return with your lady queen for breakfast."

Hastings bowed deeply at the waist and remained that way for longer than was necessary before returning to an upright position. "Thank you, Majesty. I shall indeed return and report." His expression made it clear he would pass on the information Max intended. "I hope to see you again at breakfast." Hastings retreated quickly, not turning his back on Max until he reached the tent flap, then called his men together and departed.

Chapter 12

As Hastings had promised, the human queen had arrived during the night. Dawn's light revealed a much larger encampment where the smaller one had sat across the stream. From atop the hill, Max watched soldiers and servants bustle about, guessing there had to be three hundred people in the camp now. Off in the distance his improved vision noted a dust cloud, likely reinforcements the queen had moved from the front line with Westreach.

Max found himself wondering if the War Dogs had reached the front, and if so, whether they had taken advantage of the reduced enemy force. Which then had him speculating whether the queen had heard of the War Dog's attack, and how she viewed it in light of his current proximity and recent aggression.

"So many factors to consider when you're in charge." He shook his head. On his shoulder, Red commiserated.

"Aye, there be no end to it, either. Every word, every deed, ya have to think not just about what ya say or do, but how others will take it. Sometimes those others are people ya don't even know." She put her hands on her hips and tapped one foot in annoyance. "Then there be the one's who'll take everythin' as a slight against them, whether ya meant it as such, or not."

Max blinked a few times, looking over at his tiny but fiery guide. Her words were strangely insightful. As if she'd been in such situations herself. A few seemingly random comments she'd made since joining him started to make more sense.

"Red, before you became my guide... were you by any chance a noble? A leader among your people?"

"What?" The leprechaun froze mid-tap, her gaze snapping up to meet his. "O'course not! Shaddup, ya big lump o' stupid. Me past be none o' your affair!" Now her arms were crossed and her lips pressed together as she glared at him.

Max raised both hands in surrender. "Okay, okay, no need to bite my head off. I was just asking. Your advice just now, it just sounded like..."

"Extremely good advice! O' course it was! I'm meant to guide ya, after all, aren't I?" She stuck her tongue out at him, hands back on her hips now. "And here's some more advice! Ya should head on down to the stream, because it looks to me like miss high n mighty herself be leavin' her camp."

Max's head snapped toward the stream, and the camp beyond, where sure enough a small force of soldiers in shiny armor were forming up as an escort. He couldn't see the queen, but if they were making ready, she wouldn't be far behind. When Max looked back to his shoulder as he started back down the hill, Red was gone.

He used his rings to alert both Ironhand and Farstrider that the queen's arrival was imminent, and increased his pace slightly, half-jogging down the hill. By the time he reached the tent that had been prepared for the meeting, he could see the other royals making their way, with small honor guards accompanying them. Max cursed quietly to himself. He hadn't thought to arrange such a thing, and as far as he knew none of his Stormhaven guards even had matching armor. Rather than have Redmane assemble a ragtag force that would look foolish next to the pristine and well-geared escorts of the others, he decided to invite his companions to look foolish instead. With a grin, he called out in party chat for Redmane, the corporals, Dalia, and Nessa to join him at the tent.

It was more of a pavilion, really. Large enough that a hundred or more people could take shelter from the rain under it. As long as none of them were ogres, of course. Ironhand's dwarves had constructed a wooden floor underneath the tent, and placed the same three tables from atop the hill inside. At the moment, the sides of the tents were all rolled up and fastened, allowing sunlight and a pleasant breeze to pass through.

Behind the large tent, a smaller one housed a mobile kitchen that was busily preparing breakfast. The side facing the large tent was down, as apparently it was somehow improper for royals to see their meals being prepared, but the other three sides were open to allow that same breeze to cool the chef and staff. Max grinned as he watched them prepare. He'd made a point the night before of insisting that at least a few of the goblins help serve the meal, just to see the queen's reaction.

Ironhand and the Farstriders arrived just as the queen's escort was nearing the stream. They joined Max in standing near the bank on their side, their retinues arranged behind them, on either side of the pavilion. At Max's request, his companions moved to stand directly behind him and his allies.

As they watched patiently, the queen's escort produced a small boat and lowered it into the stream, both ends secured by rope to nearby mounts. Maybe ten feet long, and half that wide, the boat had a shallow draft, much like a bass boat Max had owned at one time. Half a dozen riders spurred their mounts forward, one of them holding the rope attached to the boat's prow. As they moved forward, the queen stepped confidently into the boat, along with three men – one in decorative plate armor, another in black leather that screamed rogue or assassin to Max, and the last obviously a mage of some kind in tailored robes, holding a long staff with a crystal mounted at the top. Once all three were situated, more riders moved into the stream, and the lead riders began to pull the boat gently and carefully across. A final rider, holding the stern rope, followed at a distance and kept the rope taught so that the boat didn't drift.

The crossing went more smoothly than Max had expected. He'd half hoped that the boat would shift violently and dump the queen into the water. But it barely bobbed in the gentle current. It moved so smoothly, in fact, that Max suspected the mage was using magic to steady them through the crossing.

The queen didn't so much as look up at them until she was helped by the heavily armored man up the bank on the dwarven side of the stream. At which point she motioned for the boat to return, then flashed a wide smile at the Farstriders, ignoring both Max and Ironhand.

"Your majesties." She inclined her head just a fraction of inch. "Lovely morning for breakfast with one's contemporaries, is it not?" Her smile was wide, and so false that Max wondered if she'd practiced it to look that way.

"Where is my son, bitch? You were to bring him with you." Queen Farstrider growled, causing her husband to blink in surprise, while Ironhand guffawed.

Pretending not to have heard the insult, the queen waved one hand over her shoulder carelessly. "Oh, he'll be along shortly. I've sent the boat back for him, so he doesn't get damp in the crossing." She then turned to Max. "I've brought along a surprise for King Storm, as well." Her attention immediately shifted back to the Farstriders. "Shall we take our seats and begin breakfast? I find that the… unexpected journey here has left me quite famished!"

Without waiting for confirmation, she strolled right past Max and the others, making her way toward the pavilion, her escort moving right behind her. Smitty and Dylan each took a step to the side, creating a gap between them for the visitor to pass through. She moved inside and promptly took a seat at the head of the table, a position that should have been Ironhand's as the hosting royal. When the others looked to him, he just chuckled and shrugged, moving to follow.

When the kings and queens had all settled into seats, and their chosen few had taken up positions behind them, Ironhand let out a piercing whistle that let the chef know to begin serving. Since the queen had elected to forego introductions, or pretty much all normal protocol, the dwarf had decided to roll with it.

Max kept his expression neutral as he waited for the goblin servers to approach the queen. Since she had taken the head of the table, they would be approaching from behind her.

"King Storm. May I call you Max?" She didn't wait for a reply. "Max, I must congratulate you on your sudden rise to power." She flashed the false smile again. "Being a Battleborne, and new to this world, I'm not surprised that you're unfamiliar with our customs." She waited to see his reaction at being publicly outed, but he kept his poker face in place. "For instance, it's very bad form to kill one's emissaries, threaten to murder everyone within reach, and demand another Sovereign attend you on short notice in some gods-forsaken wilderness." Her tone was sweet, but the look in her eyes was filled with pure malice.

Max noted two things as she spoke. First, the goblins were approaching, wide smiles of pride on their faces as they carried platters of food. Second, the boat was returning across the stream, bearing two figures in oversized cloaks whose faces he couldn't see. Not that it would matter just then, as he'd never seen the crown prince of Westreach before.

"As you say, *majesty*." He put as much sarcasm into the title as he could manage. "I am new to this world, and though my chamberlain has made a heroic effort to educate me, I'm afraid I'm still a simple soldier at heart. One who, when your noble bounced an arrow off my chest in a foolish attempt at regicide, reacted as a soldier instinctively would." He paused, looking at the armored gentleman behind her. "I can demonstrate for you, if you have another noble you're not too fond of." His smile was just as fake as hers, except his displayed his fangs.

He had to give her credit, she didn't even blink. "That will not be necessary. The message you sent, and the messenger who brought it, were quite descriptive."

Just then the goblins arrived, one of them appearing next to her elbow. Max allowed himself to grin openly as she jumped slightly, even as her escort all took a half step forward in alarm. When the goblin simply raised a plate of food and placed it in front of her, they all relaxed. Though she did make a disgusted face at first the goblin, then the food, pushing the plate forward to make it clear she had no intention of partaking.

Max, on the other hand, thanked the goblin that served him, then took a moment to make a show of sniffing the food and rubbing his belly. "My compliments to the chef, King Ironhand. This smells delicious!"

Ironhand chuckled as he nodded in acknowledgement, grabbing a fork and digging in, as if to say if he was going to be ignored, he'd happily take the opportunity to fill his belly. The two Farstriders, who'd been glaring daggers the entire time at the queen, took a moment to offer their compliments as well. As Max cut and raised a bite of sausage to his mouth, he noted that the boat had arrived. He took a moment to chew and swallow as the queen stared, then spoke.

"I had intended a much more polite invitation, as I hope your messenger also informed you. As I said, I am a career soldier, and it pains me to see the lives of common soldiers thrown away over a pointless border skirmish. My hope was to bring you here to discuss a mutually acceptable resolution to your differences with Westreach, and end the bloodshed."

She frowned at him in what he suspected she considered a pretty pout. "The crown prince offered me grievous insult, in my own court, in front of most of my nobles." She looked toward the Farstriders. "One would think a prince and heir would be better schooled in etiquette, as well as diplomacy."

Max leaned forward between them, drawing her gaze to him before the other royals could respond. "He offered an unfortunate and thoughtless, but relatively minor, insult. Which you chose to use as an excuse to take action against Westreach. Your nobles aren't here, Majesty, and everyone in this tent knows the truth of things. No need to put on a show."

"Oh, but I do so enjoy a good show. As a matter of fact..." She waved toward the stream, where one of the cloaked figures was walking toward them, the other being carried horizontally on a litter. When Queen Farstrider saw the litter, she gasped, her eyes widening as she gripped her husband's hand tightly. Clearly she feared her son was hurt. A moment later, her fears were allayed.

"Here he is, your son and heir, unharmed, as King Storm so forcefully demanded." As she spoke, the prince pulled back the hood, his gaze locked on his parents, who visibly fought the urge to jump to their feet and embrace him.

"Mother, father, I am sorry to have worried you." He bowed his head, looking ashamed. Neither of his parents spoke, just ran their eyes over him as if searching for wounds. "I am quite well. The queen has been a gracious host, despite my previous behavior toward her." The last bit sounded a little rehearsed to Max.

"You see? He's perfectly fine." The queen cooed at them, motioning for the litter to be brought closer. "On my world, noble hostages, and most especially royal hostages, are much too valuable to mistreat." She looked away from the prince to fix her gaze on Max. "What world are you from, King Storm?"

Since she'd already outed him to everyone present, he saw no harm in answering. "I am from Earth. A world without magic, or many of the races you see arrayed behind me."

"This Earth of yours, is it a harsh place?" She didn't wait for him to respond before continuing. "My birthworld was harsh. A cold world, with a dying sun. Each year our winters lasted longer, and our summers grew shorter. Until it came to pass that the land only thawed enough to grow crops for just a few months during the warmest season.

Food was scarce, and land in the temperate zones was priceless. As a result, our people fought constantly, and without mercy, over the dwindling resources."

"Guess that's meant to explain why she's such a bitch." Dylan muttered under his breath to Smitty. The queen's eyes blazed, and she pointed at Dylan, obviously having heard him. The ogre froze, embarrassed, as she shouted.

"General, take that thing's head!" The grizzled armored gentleman took a step forward, his hand going to his sword as he glared up at the ogre, who was raising his empty hands in a patting motion. Both Ironhand and Max shot to their feet, Ironhand beating Max to the punch as he roared in a commanding voice.

"Ye'll not be touchin' any o' me guests here!" He slammed a fist on the table to emphasize his words, cracking the wood and making all the plates and goblets jump. Around the pavilion, every allied soldier drew a weapon and stared at the queen's escort.

No fool, the man withdrew his hand from his hilt and leaned forward to speak quietly in his queen's ear. Her eyes still blazed with anger, but she nodded curtly. Behind her the mage pointed his staff at Dylan and shouted, "Who are you, that you dare to insult my Queen!?"

Dylan, seeing that he was in no danger, and not much caring about offering further offense, replied in the deepest voice he could manage, faking a southern accent. "They call me... tater salad."

Next to him, Smitty smothered laughter, while Max bit his lips to keep from smiling at the joke.

Confused, the mage stared hard at Dylan for a moment, then his eyes widened in surprise. He glanced at the rest of Max's party, then stepped forward and leaned down, whispering urgently into the queen's ear. Her own eyes flicked between the corporals, surprise evident in her expression for a moment, before she shook her head slightly. He stepped back to his original position and simply frowned at Dylan. The ogre did his best to look innocent, making it even harder for his fellow Earthlings to stifle their laughter.

Max quickly changed the subject. "Hostages were often held on my world, as well. Though sometimes they were not well treated. As I'm sure it was on your world, the killing of hostages might result in severe repercussions, or even all out warfare." He watched the prince take a seat next to his mother as he spoke to the queen. "I'm glad you saw fit to treat the prince well."

"Yes, I have recently made it a point to study your world, King Max. Which brings me to the gift I've brought you. I'm afraid it's a little… worse for wear. But I'm betting you will appreciate it regardless!" She motioned toward the men who were now standing on either side of the litter. Two of them took hold of the cloak that covered the figure that was now standing upright, with assistance from two other men. When they yanked the cloak free, Max heard queen Farstrider gasp, along with Dalia and Nessa behind him. Both corporals and Redmane cursed under their breath, as did Ironhand and the dwarves behind him.

Max's own mouth dropped in surprise, then snapped shut as disgust washed over him at what he beheld. Standing atop the litter, with a soldier holding each arm to steady him, was a man. A man who'd been impaled on a long metal spike, the pointed end of which sprouted up from his shoulder, while the base touched the ground between his feet, acting as a sort of third leg. Dried blood, and worse, soaked the entire length of the spike, as well as the man's clothing. Someone had clearly healed the man after the impalement, as no new blood escaped him, and Max thought it extremely unlikely he'd have survived more than a minute or two, otherwise.

Confused, Max looked from the man to the queen, and back. While she appeared to be quite pleased with herself, the man's eyes held the blank look of someone who's mind had suffered too much, and had retreated to some inner place. His mouth hung open, and Max thought he heard a soft moan of pain as he breathed out. He was about to ask the queen what the hell was going on, when behind him Smitty cursed.

"Oh, shit. That's Lagrass."

Max's eyes widened and he quickly cast *Identify*, seeing the man's name for the first time. It was indeed Lagrass. The man who'd betrayed his unit and gotten them all killed.

"Ah, I see you recognize my little gift. An old friend of yours, is he not? Well, I suppose not, after what he told us he did. An old comrade in arms, then." Her smile was predatory, and completely sincere this time.

Max took another moment to stare at the one man he'd come to hate more than any other, on either world. He'd dreamed many times of killing Lagrass himself, in a multitude of ways. But none of them compared to what he'd clearly suffered at the hands of the queen. He scowled as he imagined the pain of having a six-inch wide spike driven up through his rectum, through his body, and out his shoulder. And of being kept alive in such a condition.

Seeing him scowl, the queen feigned surprise. "You do like my gift to you? I thought, as one who'd been so horribly wronged by him, you might appreciate his pain. And the opportunity to extend it, or end it, as you see fit!" She beamed at Max, then at Queen Farstrider as she noted the tears running down the woman's face. Next to her, her husband was shaking his head in disbelief, while the prince, who'd already known, kept his eyes down.

"Was this meant to ingratiate you to me?" Max jerked a thumb at Lagrass, who was moaning more audibly now, drool running unnoticed down his chin. "Or to shock me?"

"Why not both?" The queen responded. "I have learned quite a bit about you, your past, and your world, from… questioning your comrade here." Her smirk made it clear what that questioning entailed. "Though he failed to inform me that there were other Battleborne here from your world." Her gaze flitted back to the corporals for a moment. "I must say, this is most unexpected."

Max shook his head, tearing his gaze away from Lagrass. "He died after we did. And I assume he was reborn here in a human kingdom. So he wouldn't have known about the others. Neither did I, until they found me."

Shaking his head, he got to his feet and walked around the table to where Lagrass was still being supported by two soldiers. Drawing his dagger from the sheath on his belt, he stared into the man's eyes for a second. "You were a real piece of shit, Lagrass." He whispered. Seeing no recognition or response of any kind, he quickly drove the dagger up under the man's chin, piercing his brain and ending his second existence. Wiping the dagger on a mostly clean section of the man's sleeve, he sheathed it and returned to his seat. On the way, he got nods of approval from his corporals, as well as Redmane and the two kings at the table.

"Enough of the games, Majesty." The look he gave the queen made it clear he meant business. "I summoned you here to achieve peace. I haven't been able to go about it the way I had planned, but as they say, no battle plan survives contact with the enemy."

She nodded at that, speaking before he could continue. "I quite like that."

Ignoring her, he glanced at Ironhand, then Farstrider. Both of them nodded.

"Here is what will happen. Here and now, at this table, you will agree to withdraw your troops from your border with Westreach. You will sign peace accords, which King and Queen Farstrider will negotiate in good faith. Once that is done, you will be given the opportunity to further enter into trade agreements with Stormhaven, and the dwarven clans." He paused and took a sip of water to calm himself a bit before continuing. "If you conduct yourself in good faith for a period to be determined here, probably many years, you may be allowed to join the alliance that currently includes the dwarven kingdom, my own, and Westreach. By that time, I hope that it will have grown to include other nations as well."

The queen had stiffened while he'd been speaking, her expression cold and calculating. When Max finished, she leaned forward, placing her elbows on the table. "And if I should refuse?"

Max shook his head. "Then I will destroy you. I don't care how harsh your homeworld was. The shit you've pulled here is inexcusable. You've thrown hundreds, if not thousands of peasants into a meat grinder to satisfy your own desire for expansion. You kidnapped the prince and, I suspect, would have killed him had I not intervened. Not to mention this sick shit right here." He waved at Lagrass, who had been lowered to lay facedown on the litter. His voice dropped into a growl. "Which speaks to a deep mental instability that I'm not sure should be allowed to remain in a position of power."

He held up a hand when she opened her mouth to reply. "If you're about to deny that I could destroy you, don't bother. My kingdom is small, my resources limited. But I would have the support of Westreach, and the entirety of Ironhand's dwarven kingdom. Should we choose to do so, we could sweep across your entire kingdom and scour the land clean in a week."

The queen stared at him, rage in her eyes, as she contemplated her response. Farstrider took the opportunity to add his opinion. "Personally, I hope you refuse." He smirked at her when she shifted her attention to him. "You have spies in my city. I'm sure they've told you that we have a working portal. A brand new one, separate from the one that was locked down due to its connection to your own. I'm sure you are also aware that Max here installed our new portal." He paused and waited for her nod. She had indeed been given that information.

"Now, imagine that, as we advance across your lands, Max installs a portal at each town, each city we take. Portals that will allow us to instantly advance additional troops and supplies to the front lines, while yours will need to travel by horse and by cart." He smiled when he saw the realization in her eyes. "Max isn't kidding when he says we can be knocking at your palace doors in a week."

Grinning from ear to ear, Ironhand added, "Never owned a palace above ground. I'm sure our lads can rebuild quick enough, if we be careful how much o' yers we knock down, and don't be startin' too many fires. I'm bettin' the view from the towers be lovely."

Max spared a moment to turn his head slightly and wink at Ironhand out of the queen's sight. Turning back to her, he took a deep breath. "I would be completely justified in sacking your kingdom after your noble tried to assassinate me. My friends and fellow royals have agreed to support me in the event I find myself at war. Look around the table, majesty. Do you see any sympathy or hesitation in these faces?" He watched her gaze move from royal to royal.

"Now, as I said. If you agree to cease hostilities, we will negotiate in good faith. You are the bad actor here, but we will set that aside and treat you fairly. Or you can choose to fight, and throw away all you've achieved. As I said before, I hate to see the blood of innocents spilled for nothing but the pride of those in power. So I hope you'll see reason. Take a moment to think it over." He reached for his water glass and took another sip.

Redmane spoke from behind him through party chat. "Well done, me king." The others were right behind him with various comments of support or congratulations.

The queen got up from her chair, turning her back on the table for a moment as she looked to her advisors. Seeing defeat in their eyes, she turned and leaned on the back of her chair, glaring at Max.

"As I said, my birthworld did not suffer weaklings. I fought almost from the day I could walk, every day until the day I died defending one of my people's farming villages." She paused for a moment, her head tilting as if something had just occurred to her. "Ironically, whether my people won that battle, or lost, my corpse will have been fed to the pigs in that village. We could afford to waste nothing. We are a practical people." She sighed. "Which means I know when it would be fruitless to fight. Even should we manage to hold out and defend against

242

your aggression, there would not be enough of my kingdom left to me to be worthwhile."

"Glad to hear it." Max thumped the table, and everyone else relaxed. "Have a seat, your highness, and let us begin the process of securing peace between our nations."

Chapter 13

"It never occurred to me that there might be Battleborne here that didn't come from Earth. Though, I suppose it should have." Max shook his head. He was sitting near the fire outside his tent, his party gathered around him, along with Redmane and Cavariel. It was a conversation he'd normally only have in private, but the bitch queen had outed him to so many people at breakfast, there was no hope of keeping his secret now.

His fellow royals had made her pay for that, and her various other sins, by negotiating terms that would leave her kingdom much worse off than before she attacked Westreach. While the cessation of hostilities did allow for her portal to be unlocked, along with Westreach's original portal, if she or her merchants wanted to use it to access any of their kingdoms, they would be paying onerous fees. The same if they wanted to cross into any of the allied territories overland, or enter at their ports. Max had a feeling that many of her merchants, and maybe her nobles, would be deserting her rather than beggar themselves by remaining in her kingdom.

"I wonder how many Battleborne there are?" Smitty asked aloud, though he was clearly talking to himself. "Also, tater salad? Really, dude?" He grinned up at Dylan, who was sitting on the ground next to him.

The big ogre shrugged. "Seemed like a good idea at the time."

Cavariel, ignoring their off-world humor, attempted to answer Smitty's question. "It is known that the queen arrived on this world with a group of Battleborne. Exactly how many arrived is not known, as apparently several of them were promptly murdered." He shook his head. "As far as the Mage's Guild knows, there are five remaining from that group, including the queen." Cavariel didn't mention that just a few days earlier there had been six, until Max and the ogre chieftain killed the orc Battleborne known as The One. He hadn't known this fact when he accompanied Max to the battle at Gar'doz. It wasn't until he reported in to the Archmagus after the battle that the connection was made. By then, he wasn't sure that Max would believe he hadn't known, so he simply kept his mouth shut. It bothered his conscience a bit, but it was one of many things in his long life that weighed on him. Shaking off that train of thought, he continued. "Educated guesses based on bits and pieces gleaned from the other Battleborne suggest there were a dozen." He looked at Max. "Clearly this time the gods sent at least five of you, though not all together. It's possible that more came along when you did, and we simply haven't heard of them yet."

"But you keep track of the queen's group?" Max was curious now, and wondering if Cavariel hadn't just been sent to do translation work. He doubted the Archmagus would have tried to convince Blake to spy on him, but Cavariel might. Or maybe it was the earth mages Blake had recruited from the Guild.

Cavariel chuckled. "Battleborne have a way of... how do you Earthers say it? Making waves?" He waited for Max to nod. "Not all of them have managed to secure their own kingdoms as you have, but all have grown into beings of power. They often don't advertise the fact that they're Battleborne, but any sufficiently leveled individual, or those with extremely high perception skills, can identify them on sight."

Max nodded. Ironhand had recognized him immediately. Or one of his elders had, and informed him. And apparently the queen, or more likely her wizard, based on their earlier meeting, had recognized Lagrass. The dragon they'd run across in the underground, as well as the Tuath, the Archmagus, and Caretaker, had all been able to tell, as well.

"Well, our secret's out now. I suppose that will change how others see us, and interact with us." Max shook his head.

"Indeed. Some will seek you out, hoping to gain your favor, as you are likely to grow in power. Others will fear you, *because* you are likely to grow in power. Of those, at least a few are sure to try and eliminate you before you grow much stronger and become a threat to them."

"The other Battleborne." Dylan concluded. It wasn't a question.

"They would seem the most likely." Cavariel agreed. "Nearly every mention of Battleborne in the histories I have read, both from the Mage's Guild and from my own people's libraries, record them as being hostile toward each other. More than one war was fought between them. A few of the victorious were good leaders and well respected. Most were tyrants."

"The boss was a tyrant long before he came to this world and stole himself a crown." Dylan smirked at Max. "For instance, he once cancelled Taco & Tequila Tuesday because we were deploying the next morning, and he didn't want to smell the farts on the plane. I mean, we had a constitutional right to go full taco, and he violated it!"

Several of the gathered group looked to Smitty to see if he'd agree, but the orc just shrugged. "Don't remember that, so it must have been before my time. But for the record I'm totally pro-taco!"

The group chuckled at that. All of them had eaten tacos at the group's restaurant, and enjoyed them just as much as the corporals did.

"So we'll have to watch out for the Battleborne who have been here longer." Max brought them back to their discussion. "And maybe newly arrived ones like us."

"Speaking of ones like us," Smitty held up a finger. "If a dozen came in the previous group, do you suppose more of our guys got here, and just haven't found us yet?"

"Or aren't interested in finding us and serving under Max the tyrant." Dylan winked at Max, who missed it, as he was already focused on Cavariel.

"Have you, or the guild, heard of more who arrived when we did?" He paused for a second, then added, "Are there others who've been here longer than the queen and her group?"

The dark elf shook his head. "I am not aware of any other recent arrivals. As for older Battleborne, the last I know of, before her group, arrived more than a hundred years previous. He was a crafter, uninterested in ruling, or amassing power. Last I heard he had earned a small fortune selling his crafted goods, then disappeared into a vast forest on the far side of the continent to further study his craft. He may still be alive, but I doubt he is a threat to you." Cavariel, in fact, knew that the crafter was alive, and precisely where he was. Or at least, where he'd been two years ago. But he'd given his word to that Battleborne not to disclose either fact to anyone. He was speaking the truth, though, when he said the elf was no threat. He was focused on mastering several crafting professions.

Max leaned back in the hunk of dragon vertebrae he was using as a chair. It had been a long day of debate and negotiation. He'd killed Lagrass, an act about which he wasn't sure how he felt. They'd completed their negotiations with the queen, had the documents drawn up and executed, then sent her on her way.

Her general had left within moments of her acquiescence. Max had watched him cross the stream on a horse and gallop toward the approaching forces. An hour later those forces had been moving back toward the queen's city, minus several riders that headed toward the border with Westreach.

Max had reached out to Blake and the War Dogs at the front line via communication ring. They reported that they had participated in two battles, and been reasonably successful. When he informed them of the peace agreement, they promised to pass it on to the Westreach commander when they went to turn in their quest.

The Farstriders were anxious to get back to Westreach, and would be leaving first thing in the morning. Max offered to escort them, but the king reminded him that since Westreach was now part of the alliance with the dwarves, they could portal home directly from Rockholm. Their royal guards were more than enough to defend them against any dangers they might encounter in the dwarven lands on the way there.

Nessa had quietly suggested that their party make a stealth visit to the queen's city, or a nearby town, and set up a hidden portal they could use in case she misbehaved. Max liked that idea a great deal, but shelved it for a later date. Besides, he didn't really need to be stealthy. He could simply make an official state visit, then slip away and install a pedestal somewhere. He'd given Redmane instructions to have one of their factors purchase a few properties in her city, and he'd choose from among those when the time came.

"So what's next, boss?" Smitty asked, using a dagger to clean under his thick, claw-like fingernails.

"Well, I've got a lot of work to do in Stormhaven, at least for the next week or more. We've got people to recruit, cities and settlements to fill. Between the trip up to Gar'doz, and this one, Redmane and I are a bit behind on housekeeping." The dwarf grunted in agreement. Max knew that his always reliable advisor was keeping in touch with palace staff via one of his rings, but there were always stacks of things that needed his and Max's direct input.

When he saw the disappointed looks on the faces of everyone but Smitty, who would be perfectly content to lounge around his quarters in the palace with his new bride, Max shrugged. "You guys could always go hunt critters in the mountains above Blake Manor. Or check on the fortification the earth mages are building near Gar'doz, maybe see what kind of monsters are lurking around that area."

"We could run the Westreach dungeon." Dalia suggested. "It be back to normal levels, accordin' to the queen." Max smiled at her. She and her father wanted more of the life crystals from the tree creatures in the dungeon to use in their alchemy.

"You certainly could." He wasn't worried about them going without him if the monsters had returned to manageable levels. One of the hard lessons he'd learned over the years was that he couldn't be in the fight with his troops all the time. Sometimes he had to let them fend for themselves.

"The dwarves will likely be celebrating for a few more days." He smiled as he took in the ongoing parties in the nearby encampments. "But we might as well head home in the morning."

*****

Balerin looked at his companion, who's head was cocked to one side, listening. "I didn't hear anything. What did it sound like?"

Slagle shook his head. "I'm not sure. I thought I heard something moving through the trees. Something big. But it has either stopped, or I just heard a falling branch."

The two earth mages, who'd been hired by Blake on behalf of Stormhaven, stood atop the rampart of a newly constructed wall. The two of them had worked together on several fortifications for King Max now, and had developed a sort of shorthand that allowed them to work quickly and smoothly. This job entailed constructing a walled outpost with several buildings around a portal pedestal.

Slagle glanced at the pedestal, which now sat just inside the gateway opening in the wall beneath them. The gate hadn't been installed yet. They'd been told to leave that to the dwarves, as usual. Those dwarves were out harvesting a massive ironwood tree at the moment, planning to bring it back to shape into the gate. This being an outpost, the opening was just wide enough for a full-sized wagon to pass through with little room to spare on either side.

The other three walls had been constructed, each thirty feet high and three feet thick. The outer faces were smooth as glass, being formed with magic rather than mortar. Inside, there was a set of stairs leading up to the top of the wall, and a walkway that ran the whole circumference. Their next objective was to construct a tower in the northeast corner, tall enough to allow lookouts to spot any incoming threats at a distance.

Another loud crack and the sound of something heavy falling caught both of their attention. The two mages turned toward the north, where the settlement known as Gar'doz was situated a ways off. Whatever was coming, it was coming from that direction.

"You're right." Balerin elbowed his companion. "Whatever it is, it's big. Should I alert the dwarves?" When Slagle nodded that he should, the mage raised one arm and sent a small but bright fireball streaming high into the sky. He aimed it so that it would fall in roughly the direction the dwarves had headed to harvest their tree. Based on the next crashing sound he heard, though, Balerin thought that whatever was approaching was already closer than the dwarves.

Slagle seemed to be thinking the same thing. "We've warned them, if they haven't heard it for themselves. Let's see what it is. When it enters the cleared ground, if it's something we can't fight, we retreat through the portal." He made for the stairs. "I'll go open it, you keep an eye out."

Balerin nodded, his gaze locked on the forest north of their little outpost. If whatever it was that approached them, knocking down trees in the process, had waited just another day... the outpost would have been manned with a contingent of fighters. Then he and his partner wouldn't have to worry about it.

Checking his mana level, he produced one of the potions that Dalia had gifted them. They'd just about drained their mana raising the wall he stood on, and the potion immediately replenished half of his reserve. A second later, his level ticked up again. It would continue to do so for another half a minute, bringing him up to full. Assuming he didn't use any mana before then. He smiled at the empty vial in his hand before putting it away. Purchasing such a high quality potion from the Mages' Guild shop would have cost him ten gold coins, maybe more. Dalia had given each of them a dozen, and told them to see her for more if they ran out.

This was only the second one he'd consumed, and he was only doing it because of the potential threat. Normally he and Slagle would simply rest a while, eat a snack, and chat a bit until their mana was fully restored. Sometimes they played cards, or swapped tall tales with the dwarves to pass the time. Both mages were truly enjoying their time in Stormhaven, and the work they were doing. They'd been included in several quests, and had been taken out with hunting parties to help them gain some experience. They had already discussed more than once asking to become permanent citizens. The magus in charge of their department at the Guild had already informed them that it was allowed, simply hinting that they might be asked to report on their activities on behalf of King Max. Another crash jarred him from his musing and his eyes snapped to where he could see a tree canopy swaying in the distance.

Down on the ground, Slagle activated the portal. Seeing Stormhaven keep's courtyard on the other side, and a pair of dwarven guards walking past, he jumped up and down and waved his arms. Luckily, the activation of the portal had drawn their attention. When they looked his direction, the mage waved for them to step through. Both dwarves obligingly did as he requested. The moment they set foot in the outpost, he blurted out. "Thank you for coming. Something big is approaching! The dwarves that were here with us are out in the forest. We don't know yet what it is, but-" he paused as the sound of splintering wood and a falling tree echoed between the walls around them.

One of the dwarves nodded. "Aye, it sounds big alright. King Max be away at the moot, but we'll sound the alarm." The two dwarves nodded at each other, one retreating back through the portal, the other running with Slagle back up onto the wall. Without speaking, Balerin pointed to where more trees were shifting as something large pushed against them. Whatever it was, it was only a half mile or so away.

"It's not moving straight at us." Balerin reported in a whisper.

"Well, that be a good thing." The dwarf grinned at him. All dwarves enjoyed a good fight, but something large enough to knock down the massive trees of this forest was nothing to take lightly.

Balerin shook his head. "Maybe not. I think it's heading toward the gate crew. They were going to chop down an ironwood tree. Maybe it was attracted to the noise they're making?" When he saw the look on the dwarf's face, he added, "We sent up a flare as soon as we heard the thing coming."

The dwarf nodded, staring out toward where Balerin had just pointed. "Send another. Send it right at whatever beastie be out there. Better we get its attention and face it from atop these walls than fer me kin to have to fight it in the woods."

Balerin nodded and, after taking a moment to observe the path of shaking trees, sent a second fireball soaring into the sky. Larger this time, and aimed into the path of the creature. At the same time, the dwarf put two fingers in his mouth and let loose a piercing whistle that echoed through the forest.

Whether in response to the fireball, or the whistle, something in the forest let out a roar that shook the trees, and caused the wall under their feet to vibrate.

Looking down at the wide open gateway, the guard pointed. "Can ye do somethin' about that?"

"Aye, we can." Slagle nodded. "Narrow it so that it's just wide enough for a dwarf to squeeze through?"

The dwarf grinned. "Aye, that'd work." The two mages took a knee and placed their hands on the wall. A moment later a block of stone began to rise from the ground inside the gate opening below them. The dwarf nodded as it filled in most of the space, leaving only a narrow gap to one side, about three feet wide and five feet high. "Ye do good work." He gave them a nod of respect, followed by a grin. "Another fifty years or so, ye'll be almost as good as dwarves when it comes to workin' stone!" He slapped Slagle on the shoulder, causing the human mage to stumble slightly.

The three of them turned back to the north and watched the forest shake as whatever it was moved directly at them now. Behind them, Rockbreaker stepped through the portal and jogged up the stairs, a stream of heavily armed and armored guards following behind.

The creature roared again, causing everyone to pause for a moment. A few of the guards cursed, recognizing the sound. Rockbreaker was one of them. He reached the top and stood next to the others. "Mountain troll." He practically spat the words. He turned to shout orders down to his troops, but one of his lieutenants had also recognized the sound, and waved as he stepped through the portal back to the keep. They were going to need special equipment for this fight.

"Mountain troll?" Slagle repeated. "How do you know?"

"Fought one before." Rockbreaker grunted. "Up in the mountains. We were hunting grey dwarves, not so far from here, actually. Stumbled on its lair. A huge hole in the side o' the mountain. Smelled so bad it made me eyes water. Thirty dwarves entered that cave, only nineteen survived."

All eyes went back to the forest. The creature was approaching the tree line now, and would soon be visible. Dwarves, orcs, and a few minotaurs joined them atop the wall, more still emerging from the portal. Rockbreaker took in the layout of the outpost, then nodded in approval. After a glance at the portal, then at the stairs, he asked the mages, "Can you two smooth the stairs into a ramp? I'm expecting a few heavy ballistae in a moment."

"We can do better than that." Balerin offered. "Place them at the base of the wall where you want them, and we'll lift them up. Instant weapon platform."

Grinning happily, Rockbreaker pointed to three spots along the north-facing wall. "There, there, and there." The two mages instantly got to work. By the time more guards came through the portal pushing ballistae on wheels, there were three stone platforms on the ground waiting for them. Rockbreaker shouted at the three crews and pointed, and the dwarves quickly shoved their weapons into place. While they were working, he quickly accessed his interface and created a defense quest, sending it out to every citizen in the area.

The two mages closed their eyes, taking sitting positions atop the wall. One by one the ballistae, their crews, and the small ammunition carts they'd brought along were lifted atop the stone platforms, which became stone columns. When the first one reached the level of the top of the wall, the mages moved on to the next, while the crews readied their weapons for battle.

Rockbreaker silently blessed Max for hiring the mages, as they'd been instrumental in fortifying a number of Stonehaven's holdings. Rockbreaker himself had supervised the construction of the keeps at the two entrances of the Deepcrag cavern, and had given the two humans a hard time, yelling at them every chance he'd gotten. Now he found he regretted hazing them so enthusiastically.

"Well done lads!" He thumped them each on a shoulder, his way of apologizing. They both grinned at the rare praise. The dwarf might have said more, but at that moment, their foe emerged from the forest.

The trees in that area were, on average, over a hundred feet tall, with trunks several feet wide. Deeper in the forest, they grew nearly twice that size. Balerin had expected that something that could rattle or even topple such trees would be strong, and large.

He didn't expect the mountain troll to be *that* large.

The creature roared again as it stepped free of the trees, sighting the newly constructed walls, and the tiny defenders atop it. If Balerin had to guess, the monster was taller than the thirty foot wall, with shoulders half as wide as it was tall. It had almost no neck to speak of, its bulbous head sitting low on its shoulders. Each arm was thicker than the surrounding tree trunks, and its legs bulged with muscle. Each foot sank deep into the forest floor as it trod toward them, leaving tracks deep enough for a man to fall into if he wasn't careful. When its jet black eyes focused on him, Balerin trembled with fear.

"Thank Durin, it be one o' the smaller ones." Rockbreaker breathed a sigh of relief, and a small cheer went up among the dwarves.

"S-smaller? What?" Balerin blinked at the dwarf. "Are we looking at the same monster?"

Rockbreaker chuckled. "The one I tell'd ye about? It were half again as large as this one. Was all I could do to reach up n poke it's ankle. I never even broke its skin." He smiled at the two shocked humans, as well as a few nearby orcs who were listening intently. They too were seeing a mountain troll for the first time. "Only way we killed it was old Puckerface blinded it with magic, boiled its eyes. It tripped and fell while stumblin' around. Crushed a few o' me friends. Then some lads with axes managed to make a wee cut on its neck, and we spent the rest o' the fight tryin' not to get crushed while it bled out.

"I thought trolls healed quickly." One of the orcs asked.

Rockbreaker shook his head, then pointed toward the approaching behemoth. "Not those. Different kind o' troll. Their skin be mostly stone. They chew on rocks, suck the minerals out o' them, which strengthens their bones n makes their skin tough. Ye could hack with a sword fer an hour n not make more'n a scratch." He pointed to the ballistae. "These lovely things can punch right through, though!"

The dwarf leading the nearest crew added, "They be strong, but slow and clumsy. Easy to hit!" As if to demonstrate, he pulled the lever that released the six-foot long steel bolt with a wickedly barbed tip. The projectile whistled through the air, plunging itself into the mountain troll's shoulder. "Bah! Missed the heart!" the dwarf cursed quietly as his crew reloaded. A process which required two of them to wind a winch that pulled back a steel cable while a third grabbed a new bolt to slide into place.

The troll barely seemed to notice the impact. It's ponderous steps slowed slightly, and it looked down at the bolt stuck in its flesh. With a confused grunt, it grabbed hold of the shaft and yanked it free, roaring in pain as the barbed head ripped a significant chunk of flesh free on its way out. Glaring at the wall, the troll hurled the bloody bolt in their direction. It flew sideways, slamming into the wall near the gate with a loud clang.

Turning to its left, the monster strode over to a nearby tree and took hold of its lowest branch, which was itself a good two feet thick, or more. Bending down and grabbing it with both hands, it flexed the bulging muscles of its arms and easily ripped the branch free. Holding the base with one hand, it circled it with the other, then pulled. All the smaller branches were quickly stripped free, along with much of the bark, as the stone-hard skin scraped along its length. When the troll turned back to them, it carried a twenty-foot long log as a club. As tall as it was, it could easily sweep the fighters from the top of the wall, or smash them to paste.

The other two ballistae fired almost simultaneously while the first crew reloaded. One bolt struck the troll in the gut, punching through the skin and sinking deeply. The other struck its sternum and, while it made a nasty gouge in its flesh, failed to penetrate the bone. It bounced off, but did manage to stagger the troll slightly from the impact.

Another roar shook the walls and caused more than one defender to have to consciously control their bladders. Spittle flew from its wide open mouth, mixed with bits of flesh and bone from its last meal.

The troll stomped forward again, now only about fifty of its paces from the wall. The first crew leader shouted "Tethers!" at the other two crews. Slagle poked Balerin with an elbow to get his attention, then pointed to the weapon's rigging. The dwarves of the first crew had already attached a rope through a hole in the butt end of the ballista bolt. The rope was only an inch or so wide, and both men shook their heads. Slagle looked over at Rockbreaker. "What're they going to do with that? The brute could snap that rope without even thinking about it."

Rockbreaker shook his head, impatiently eyeing the weapon, then the approaching troll. "Not that rope. There be mithril wire woven into it, and it be enchanted. Ye cannot cut or break it, except with magic."

Just as he finished speaking, the crew leader pulled the trigger. They had adjusted the aim of the weapon, and the bolt flew much lower this time, embedding itself in the troll's leg just above its knee. To the surprise of both mages, the other end of the rope wasn't attached to anything, and it flew off the wall just a second after the bolt, a large metal ball tied to it. As they watched, the heavy ball flew past the monster until the rope went taught. At which point it jerked to the side and began to spin toward its opposite leg.

Balerin caught on first. "It's a bolo! Well, sort of. Half a bolo? You're trying to trap its legs!" As Rockbreaker nodded, the other two crews fired, one hitting each leg. The three ropes haphazardly wrapped around the trolls legs, the last one getting a lucky swing that wrapped it fully twice around its ankles. Ignoring the annoying ropes, the troll tried to take another step forward. But as its back foot came closer to its front, the weight of the flying balls pulled the ropes tighter. There was a creak of straining rope versus muscle, and the muscle lost! The troll, unable to finish its step forward, overbalanced. It let go of its new club as it threw both hands out to catch itself as it fell facedown.

"Quickly now!" The crew leader roared as all three ballistae were reloading. He fired his weapon two seconds later, and Slagle cheered as the bolt slammed down to penetrate the back of the troll's hand, pinning it to the ground. He was about to ask what was next when familiar-looking dwarves rushed from the forest and began hacking at the troll's neck with axes. Three of them were using oversized battleaxes, while the other three employed the specialized woodsman's axes they'd been using to cut down the ironwood tree.

After just a few swings, the dwarves had to retreat as the troll first tried to stand, then gave up and simply rolled toward them in hopes of crushing the annoying little morsels.

Rockbreaker eyed the two mages. "Think ye can help with this?" He whistled loudly, and the dwarves that had been about to charge back in stopped abruptly, then quicky retreated as they looked up at him.

"We could... build a wall in front of him, but I don't see how that-" Slagle was cut off as Balerin shouted.

"We need mud! Soften the ground under him so he can't roll around." He practically shoved his friend down as he put his own hand to the stone of the wall and closed his eyes. "Start under his torso." Slagle nodded and mimicked Balerin's actions. Rockbreaker watched as the two of them concentrated, and the frustrated troll roared, thrashing about, trying to free its legs. The dwarf saw sweat break out on the mages' foreheads, and they began to breathe a bit harder from the effort they were expending. He saw another bolt fly downward and impact the trolls skull, scratching a bloody line in its flesh before bouncing off, the tip bent.

"Come on, lads!" he encouraged them. He eyed the dwarves on the ground, who were poised to charge back in, watching him for the signal. Turning back to the troll, he let out an excited shout of joy as he saw the ground under the troll liquify, its body starting to sink. It thrashed even harder, trying to roll onto its side, but it simply sank too fast, and couldn't get a purchase in the mud.

In less than ten heartbeats, its legs, backside, and one arm were sunk deep into the mud. The arm was buried from above the elbow down. "Reverse it!" Rockbreaker called out. Both mages opened their eyes to stare at him for a moment, until they understood what he meant. Grinning, they went back to work.

The process was faster this time. Liquifying a solid took a lot of effort and energy, but returning it to its natural state was much easier. The mud quickly dried up under and around the struggling giant. Then they took it a step further and hardened the entire area.

Now mostly immobilized, half its body sealed in a massive block of stone, the troll used its free hand to pound on the ground around it, trying to break the stone. After the third blow, small cracks began to form, and it growled with pleasure. It knew as well as the defenders did that it could eventually break free.

Rockbreaker whistled again, and the lumberjack crew rushed forward, axes already raised. At the same time, a flood of guards pushed through the small remaining gate opening and ran to join them. From atop the wall, the three crews shot more bolts at the monster, aiming mostly for its face, hoping to blind it with a lucky shot.

The two mages leaned forward over the rampart, watching the swarm of guards attack the trapped monster. One unfortunate orc was snatched up in its free hand and crushed into pulp that oozed between its fingers. A dwarf was pounded into the dirt as its elbow came down. It reached out and grabbed the makeshift club it had created, and Rockbreaker roared a warning to those on the ground. "Ware the damned log!"

Unable to see most of its attackers, who were tight up against its neck and shoulders hacking away with axes, the troll flailed the log around. Most of the fighters managed to drop below the swings, or otherwise avoid them. But a lucky shot swept three orcs and a dwarf off their feet, knocking them into the air far enough to disappear into the forest. Balerin winced, sure that their bodies were broken, hoping that they were dead before they hit the ground. He watched, shaking his head as a healer sprinted out the gate in the direction they had flown, thinking they were probably too late.

The dwarves cheered as blood fountained from the troll's neck where several of them had been hacking for all they were worth. The cheering stopped abruptly when the troll once again dropped its log and slapped a hand to the wound, crushing a dwarf that failed to get out of the way against its neck from the waist up. They could see his legs twitching angrily for a while, until they slowed, then stopped.

Blood flowed freely from the wound under the troll's hand, forming an ever-widening pool on the ground. Three dwarves who'd dodged the hand produced spears and ran forward, jabbing them at the hand and wrist, trying to free their companion in case he still lived. A ballista bolt slammed into its open mouth, pinning its tongue down and making it squeal in pain. It removed its hand from its neck to pull the bolt from its mouth, and more dwarves rushed in to grab the one that had been trapped. They quickly dragged him away toward the gate, one of them pouring a health potion down his throat as they moved. Rockbreaker and the mages took that as a good sign. They wouldn't have wasted a potion if he were dead.

With the neck exposed again, the spearwielders thrust their weapons deep into the open cut, then used their entire bodies to lever the shafts back and forth, up and down, doing as much internal damage with the sharp ends as they could. One of them backed up, then with a running start, drove his spear so deep that only about a foot of the shaft was still visible. He must have hit something vital, because the troll went stiff for a moment, then began to twitch.

Rockbreaker called all the melee fighters back to a safe distance, but allowed the ballistae to keep firing, which they did with enthusiasm. All the defenders cheered with each hit as the dying troll twitched and groaned, its free hand not flailing about, still holding the bolt it had yanked free of its tongue. It took several minutes for the trapped giant to bleed out. When it was reduced to weak spasms, the dwarves with spears ran back in and got back to work, hastening its end. When they all received experience notifications, and most of them leveled up, they cheered loud and long. Rockbreaker put a hand on each mage's shoulder. "Drinks be on me when we get back, lads. Without yer help, we'd have lost many more to that beastie."

More healers ran out toward the forest, while others helped gather up the bodies of the dead. Rockbreaker sent someone through the portal, and a few minutes later a large group appeared, trotting directly out to begin work harvesting the giant. As he walked the mages down off the wall, Rockbreaker explained. "Every bit o' that beastie be useful. His skin will make excellent armor, his bones can be shaped into weapons. His flesh and blood can be rendered down into potion ingredients that give terrific boosts to *Strength* and *Constitution*." Leaning close, he whispered, "It be said that if ye drink the blood raw, it'll give ye permanent boosts to them attributes. But none that I know of has been willin' to try it!"

He laughed as the two humans shuddered at the idea. "Alright lads, finish what work ye have left to do here, and I'll buy ye them drinks back at home!"

Chapter 14

Max was sitting in his study, having just finished going over the day's business with Redmane, and expressing his appreciation for Teeglin's latest knock-knock joke before the dwarf led her away to make grilled cheese sandwiches. He was settling down in his most comfortable chair to begin studying the ancient runes he was trying to master when corporals Dylan and Blake burst into his study. The big ogre spoke first.

"Boss, you gotta settle this for us!" He paused for a second until Max looked up, one eyebrow raised. "You know that song *Ring of Fire*, by Johnny Cash, right?" When Max nodded, because of course he did, everyone knew that song, Dylan continued, pointing a meaty finger down at the gnome next to him. "This sick bastard is claimin' that the lyrics are about..." He shook his head in disgust. "I can't even say it."

Blake smirked up at him. "C'mon man... burning ring of fire? It burns burns burns? He's talking about having sex and catching an STD!" The gnome turned his head just far enough to throw Max a wink that Dylan couldn't see. Max immediately went stone-faced, looking from one corporal to the other as Dylan took a deep breath.

"The man in black *most certainly did not* write a song about catching the damn clap!" He huffed, starting to pace as he flung out his arms in frustration. "That is a sweet love song, about the passion between him and the love of his life!" Now both Blake and Max were grinning.

Dylan had made them listen to that, and other country songs, more times than they could count. Even getting helo pilots to play them during transport when he could. While neither had anything against country music, listening to *anything* that often could start to grate on a guy.

Dylan stopped moving and spun to face Max. "Tell him, boss!"

Though Max was anxious to get back to his runes, this opportunity was hard to pass up. "Hmmm... you know, I never considered that. I mean, there is *a lot* of burning going on in that song..." He put a finger to his chin, pretending to think it over.

"Boss! How can you... there's no way..." Dylan growled and stomped toward the door. He was almost out the door when Max burst out laughing. A half step later Blake joined in, bending over and slapping his tiny gnome knee as he giggled like a small child. Dylan paused and turned in the doorway. "Oh, screw you guys!" He glared at both of them before disappearing.

Blake saluted Max and took off after him. "Wait! The boss agreed with me! You owe me a pizza!"

Max grinned to himself, giving a bemused shake of his head as he listened to the two of them retreat down the corridor, Blake still poking at his large buddy, the ogre growling back at him. As the sounds faded, he looked down at the scroll he'd laid out in front of him. He was reaching for a glass of water when his improved hearing picked up a faint sound that registered as wrong somewhere in the back of his brain. The faintest sound of an intake of breath, directly behind him. His soldier's instincts sent a chill up his spine. Still, he paused for an instant, thinking maybe Teeglin had snuck in while he was distracted. One of the guys had taught her how to play 'guess who', and she'd already snuck up behind Max while he was sitting, putting her tiny hands over his eyes and trying to fool him with a deep voice, more than once.

That pause was a mistake.

From behind him, a hand gripped his forehead and yanked his head back against the chair, while a second hand placed a dagger at his neck. Pressure was applied, but his thick skin resisted for a second. There was a grunt of surprise near his ear, but Max ignored it. Even as the assassin pressed harder on the dagger, and his hide began to split, Max grabbed hold of the arm holding the dagger and yanked with all his adrenaline-fueled strength.

The knife was pulled away from his flesh, having barely made a scratch. Max saw a thin layer of his blood on the edge of the blade as it came into view, held by a dusky-skinned hand with long, delicate fingers. He roared in anger as he pushed to his feet and bent at the waist, still pulling on the arm. A second later the body that belonged to that arm was lifted over his shoulder to smash onto the table in front of him.

It was a dark elf, dressed from head to toe in dark grey leather that resembled Nessa's favored attire. It grunted again when it impacted the table, trying to roll away from Max, who continued to maintain a vise grip on its wrist. "Guards! Assassin in the palace! Max roared at the top of his lungs, making the dark elf flinch. He reached to grab hold of the assassin's face with his other hand, but the surprisingly strong and agile elf managed to spin away on his back, leaving Max grasping at air. It kicked him in the face with both feet, and nearly caused him to let go.

Using his rings, he sent out a general alarm as he grappled with the dark elf. "Assassin in the palace! Lock everything down!" He growled at the dark elf, tightening his grip until he heard bones crack, and it gasped in pain. Max's vision began to grow red, and he yanked the now broken wrist toward himself, exposing his fangs as he prepared to sink them into the assassin's neck.

Pain flared in his lower back as a dagger sank deep into his flesh. Max took a staggering step forward from the force of the blow, roaring in pain this time as the dagger was yanked free, then slammed into him again. He let go of the first assassin, turning his head to look over his shoulder to see a second dark elf, a cruel smile on its lips as it removed the blade and reinserted it yet again. Max felt his legs start to wobble. Three critical hits in a matter of seconds had dropped his health by half, and a bleed debuff icon was flashing in his interface.

Max spun clumsily to face the second assassin. He'd been wearing casual attire, rather than his armor, not feeling the need for protection in his own keep. That had obviously been a mistake. Even as the dark elf drove the bloody dagger toward his gut, Max mentally equipped his dragonscale armor from his inventory. The dark elf's blade impacted less than a second after the armor appeared, skittering harmlessly off the scale. A second blow struck his back at almost the same time, both assassins surprised by the appearance of the armor.

Two dwarven guards burst through the open study door as Max grabbed hold of assassin number two. His right hand wrapped around the dark elf's neck, claws digging into the leather armor, while his left hand grabbed hold of the arm holding the dagger. Max roared in its face, spittle mixed with a little blood spraying it liberally.

Blood? He must have hit a lung, or a kidney. Max thought as he quickly cast a heal on himself. He held the dark elf's knife hand immobile while he squeezed harder with his right hand, his sharp fingernails now starting to penetrate the leather armor and dig into flesh. The elf squirmed, punching him in the face with its free hand, kicking at him with both legs as he lifted it off the ground.

"Me king!" One of the dwarves shouted as both guards rushed the first assassin, who quickly dove behind Max's desk. It activated some kind of stealth ability as soon as it was out of sight, and when the dwarves rounded the desk, they'd lost track of it.

"Watch your backs!" Max shouted, stepping forward and slamming the dark elf he held into the wall behind it. The blow stunned the assassin, its eyes unfocused and its body going limp. Max tossed it to the dwarves, who let it hit the ground, then proceeded to stomp on it. "Keep it alive!" Max shouted before they could crush its skull. He had questions.

More guards appeared in the doorway, an orc and a gnome this time. The gnome was a caster, wearing the standard mages' robes, but held a long dagger in one small fist, and looked like he knew how to use it. The orc carried an axe on its back, but held a short spear in both hands as its wide shoulders filled most of the doorway.

"Dark elf!" Max growled in their direction. "It's stealthed. Close that door!"

As the orc reached for the door handle to pull it shut, the gnome let out a cry of pain. He was knocked back into the corridor, a dagger appearing in his chest very near his heart. The assassin with the broken wrist appeared above him before dashing off down the corridor. The surprised orc bellowed in rage and took off after it, shouting for more guards.

Max cast another heal on himself as he rushed to the fallen gnome. He was relieved to see that the guard was still breathing, if barely. He cast a quick heal, waited a moment for the gnome's health to recover a bit, then yanked the blade free and cast a second heal on him. The guard groaned in pain as his eyes rolled up into his head and he passed out.

Dropping the blade into his inventory, he used his ring to call Redmane. "Two dark elves, that I saw. We've got one here in the study. The other ran toward the kitchen."

"Aye, we be chasin' it now." The dwarf replied. Max checked the gnome's pulse, nodding in relief when he found it strong and steady.

"Behind ye, me king!" One of the dwarves in the study shouted. Max didn't have time to turn before a heavy blow landed on the back of his head. Had he been human, that might have been the end of him. But his combined troll and stonetalon heritage left him with bones that were extremely hard to break. Still, the blow knocked him forward to sprawl across the gnome's body. He pushed with his knees and rolled as he fell, trying not to crush the diminutive guard. When his back hit the corridor floor, he saw another grey-clad dark elf standing over him, a dagger in one hand, a wicked looking flanged mace in the other. One of the sharp edges of the mace had some skin, blood, and several of his white hairs tangled in it.

Between the blood loss and the blow to the head, Max was dizzy. The mace might not have cracked his skull, but the impact had rattled his brain around inside it pretty well. Holding his head with one hand, he tried to cast *Zap!* at the assassin, but the spell failed. The assassin, seeming surprised Max still lived, stepped toward him, raising the mace for a finishing blow. Before its foot touched the floor, a flying hand axe struck the elf in the back, the blade sinking deep, knocking it down next to Max.

Still unable to focus enough to cast the spell, Max did have enough to raise a leg and slam his heel down into the assassin's face. The force of the blow caved in its cheekbone and shattered its jaw with a satisfying crunch. Max grinned, baring his fangs, as he allowed himself to fall back and stare up at the arched ceiling of the corridor.

As he lay there trying to gather his wits, Blake and Dylan arrived, followed quickly by Dalia, who started casting heals as she ran toward them. The corporals took in the two prone dark elves with quick glances, and Blake asked, "How many?"

"One more, that I saw. Could be others." Max grunted, already feeling better from Dalia's ministrations. He pointed down the corridor. "Third one went that way, guard chasing it."

The dwarf that had thrown the axe dropped to a knee next to Max, concern on his face. "I'm sorry, me king!" He turned and spat on the dead elf on the floor. "We shoulda see'd it sooner."

Max shook his head, wincing in pain. "It was stealthed. Nothing you could have done." He patted the guard on the shoulder. "Don't sweat it. Help your partner secure the other one." The dwarf nodded once and rushed back into the study. Max grinned as he saw the dwarf deliver what he thought was a discreet kick to its ribs before rolling it over and binding its wrists behind its back. When that was accomplished, his partner plopped down to sit on the elf's back none too gently.

Redmane came jogging up, a worried look on his face. Max resisted the urge to nod at the dwarf, instead saying, "Report."

"Everything be locked down, as ye ordered."

Shortly after taking control of Stormhaven, when the grey dwarves were still attacking random guards from stealth with their poisoned blades, Max had instituted a lockdown procedure. One that they had further tweaked as improvements were made in the palace. He'd had his corporals help Redmane run half a dozen drills over the intervening weeks, making sure new arrivals knew what to do.

If everything had gone as planned, every door in the palace was now closed and locked. Staff and non-combatants were secured in whatever room they were closest to, while guards and anyone able to fight were spreading out, securing the common spaces, and beginning to search each room carefully. Outside the keep, the bailey gate would have been closed, as well as the city's outer gate, and Max could hear the horns sounding the alert for everyone in town to get inside and lock their doors.

Redmane continued. "We be chasin' the one that ran from here, and we found two injured guards in the stables. Both poisoned." The dwarf grimaced. "Healers be seein' to em."

"Is this an invasion?" Max asked, sitting up now that his head had stopped spinning. "Or just an attempt to kill me?"

Redmane shook his head. "Dunno fer sure, yet. But it looks like ye be the target, Max."

"Good." Max held a hand out to Dylan, who easily pulled him to his feet. He would rather they were coming for him alone, and not killing his citizens en masse. Nodding at the elf with the dwarf on its back, he instructed Redmane. "Secure that one the same way you did the translator thief. Put him in the cell that suppresses magic, too. Just in case. Triple the guard down there, and warn them he might have stealthy friends."

The old dwarf nodded and started barking orders.

"Who do ye think sent 'em?" Dalia looked up at Max, then answered her own question. "That bitch queen."

Max shook his head. "I don't think so. We've only been back a day. Unless she sent them before we even met…"

Dylan glared at the dark elf being marched past them. "I'm happy to question this little shit, boss. We'll find out soon enough!"

"No, you won't." Cavariel spoke as he approached from down the corridor. When they all turned to look at him, he added, "That one probably doesn't know who sent them. Even if he did, he won't be able to tell you." He looked down at the dead elf at Max's feet. "They're Shadow Walkers. A guild of assassins. Each of them swears a binding oath to die before disclosing the guild's secrets. Questioning that one will only cause him pain, and his eventual death, without gaining you any useful information."

"Sounds okay to me." Dylan growled down at the translator. Blake grunted in agreement, while Dalia just looked worried.

Rubbing the back of his head, Max simply replied, "We'll see."

"Max! Be ye still alive?" Ironhand's voice came through one of his rings. "What's this about assassins?"

Confused for a second, Max answered. "I'm fine. How did you…" He paused, remembering that he'd sent an alert through his rings. He hadn't taken the time to specify which rings. "I'm sorry. I didn't mean to call out to you."

He heard Ironhand chuckle. "I'm glad ye be alright, Max." A moment later, he got similar comments via his rings from Farstrider, Erdun, and Elder Pickstone in the dworc village. Feeling embarrassed, he apologized again. "Sorry to have concerned you all. In the heat of the moment I just…" Shaking his head he blushed. "Guess these rings will take some getting used to."

"No apology be needed." Ironhand spoke first. "If ye need assistance, we be here."

Max nodded, despite knowing that the others couldn't see him. "I think we have it under control. One assassin is dead, another captured. A third is being hunted." An alarm went off just as he finished speaking. "Sounds like the third one just set off one of the wards." Among the improvements that Redmane had paid Spellslinger and his people to install along with the mage lights was a series of wards throughout the keep that could be activated during lockdown. Anyone not oathsworn to Max and Stormhaven that passed through a ward would set it off. Right now, guards would be swarming toward the one that just activated.

Max looked at Redmane. "Tell them to try and capture the assassin if possible, but not to risk their lives."

Redmane just stared at him, and Max realized the dwarf would have already given that order. "Ah, right." He offered a rueful smile.

Blake brought them back to the important question before them. "Could they have been sent by one of the other Battleborne?"

Cavariel looked thoughtful for a moment. "I doubt that any of the others are aware that you're Battleborne. Until very recently, that is. Unless… do we know how long ago the queen learned your secret? She might have passed on that information to one or more of the others, if they're on speaking terms."

"Who else knew?" Blake looked at Max.

"Ironhand and some of the dwarven elders. But they'd never share my secret. The Archmagus knows. King Farstrider and his inner circle." Max shrugged. "I'm not sure who else. All of you, Smitty's wife… Picklet might have told his father, or other dworcs."

"So we're not gonna narrow down the candidate list that way." Blake scratched his head. "And soon enough everyone will know. With the queen's portal unlocked, her people will already be spreading the word far and wide. Also, maybe it has nothing to do with you being Battleborne. They could have been hired by An'zalor the orc, or some other enemy you've made."

Max looked at Cavariel. "You're familiar with this assassin's guild?"

"I have… had some dealings with them over the years." The dark elf confirmed.

"Can they be bought off? Can I offer them more than whoever is paying them to kill me? Or at least pay them to tell me who it is?"

The elf shook his head. "Strict confidence is a basic tenet of their code. If clients couldn't trust their discretion, they wouldn't last long. As for outbidding your apparent enemy, that won't work either. For the same reason. At least, I've never heard of anyone buying out their own contract. Or heard of anyone trying, for that matter. The guild is an ancient organization, their rules well known. I doubt it would occur to anyone to try."

Max had a sinking feeling in his gut. "So… what? They just keep coming until they kill me?" Cavariel offered a grim nod.

"That is the way of it. Though…" He paused to consider for a moment. "If the client misled them in some way, or purposely understated the difficulty of the contract, it is possible the guild will cancel it themselves. Or up the price to reflect the difficulty. If the client can't pay the higher price, you may be saved."

Max growled in frustration. "How large an organization is this guild? And where are they located?" He disliked the idea of waiting around for more assassins. Not just because it would feel like an axe hanging over his head, but because more of his people could be hurt when the killers came for him. If the guild couldn't be bought off, maybe they could be eliminated altogether.

Cavariel's eyes widened as he realized what Max had in mind. "I have no firsthand knowledge, but I would guess that they're a small organization. A few hundred members? Few can afford to pay their prices, so their business is limited." He shook his head. "But every one of them is a trained killer, m'lord. Specializing in stealth, observation, and ambush. They use poison, enchanted weapons, traps, any dirty trick that might give them an advantage. And it is unlikely that they'd all be gathered in one place for you to attack. Were you to destroy every Shadow Walker in their headquarters, there might still be a hundred scattered elsewhere that would come after you."

"But you do know where their base is?" Dylan growled down at the elf.

"I do." Cavariel confirmed, not liking the direction of the discussion.

Max nodded once. "Then when we've found the other one, and questioned whichever live ones we have, we'll send them back to their guild to deliver a message."

Cavariel audibly gulped, taking a moment to wet his lips before asking, "What kind of message."

Blake grinned up at him. "You might want to leave that to us."

*****

Max sat behind his desk, drumming his fingers on one arm of the chair as he waited. They'd set up the room to prepare for the interrogation. Several mage lights had been brought in and placed along the walls, banishing shadows from the corners. An oiled canvas tarp had been placed on the floor in front of his desk, a simple wooden chair set in the middle of it. Manacles were attached to both arms and legs of the chair to keep the assassin from fading into stealth, or struggling too much. Max had instructed that an array of nasty looking blades, hooks, saws, and mallets be placed on his desk for the elf to stare at.

Not wanting his people to witness what he was about to do, the only people in the room were Max and his corporals, along with Redmane, and Cavariel who had asked to attend. Since the elf was oathbound, and the only one familiar with the assassin's guild, Max had allowed it. But only after requiring Cavariel to swear not to reveal what happened.

A group of six dwarves marched the prisoner into the room, forced him into the chair, and quickly bound his limbs using the manacles. After taking a moment to make sure they were secure, they bowed to Max and left the room, closing the door and taking up station outside.

Max wasted no time, addressing the bound assassin who was sneering at him. "Your two friends are dead. You saw one die. We caught the other trying to escape the keep. He forced us to kill him rather than surrender." That was a lie, the third one had been captured, but Max had kept them separated. He waited a moment, but the assassin didn't react. Reaching out across his desk, he carefully picked up a very thin, long-bladed skinning knife, and began to use it to clean under his claw-like fingernails. "We're going to ask you some questions. Refusing to answer will not go well for you." Max did his best to imitate an insane laugh, making it much too loud on purpose. Again there was no reaction from the dark elf.

Max started off easy. "You are a Shadow Walker, yes?"

The assassin stared, the sneer never leaving his face. Behind him, Dylan smacked the back of his head, knocking it forward so that his chin bumped on his chest. "Answer him!" The assassin simply raised his head again, and continued to sneer at Max.

Max decided to cut to the chase, not inclined to waste a lot of time on the interrogation. "You tried to kill me. For that, your life is forfeit. Which I'm sure you already knew. The thing is, there's dying, then there's dying." He looked around the room for any squeamish faces. "I understand that you've probably sworn certain oaths of silence, but I don't care. You're going to die very soon, one way or the other. If you answer me, and the gods enforce your oath and stop your heart, that's a much faster and more merciful death than I have planned for you."

Max stood up, baring his fangs as he leaned across his desk and pointed at the tarp beneath the assassin's chair. "This is to keep from ruining my carpet as I remove your fingers one by one, then your toes. I will cut you, remove bits of you, and heal you as I go. You won't bleed to death, so there's no escaping that way." He lowered his voice to a growl. "I will make it last as long as it takes. Days. Weeks. How tough are you?"

The sneer had disappeared while he was speaking, and the elf had struggled briefly against his bonds. Still, he did not speak.

Cavariel, obviously nervous, stepped forward as Max had previously instructed. "I know your history, and your oaths. Save yourself the horror of what my king has planned for you. Simply disclose who ordered his death, and let the gods take you." Beads of sweat had formed on his forehead, and he wrung his hands together as he spoke. The translator sincerely wanted to avoid the torture session.

For emphasis, Max picked up a hooked blade in his free hand, keeping the skinning knife in his other, and walked around his desk to take up a position behind the assassin. He saw the dark elf fidget a bit, clearly resisting the urge to turn and look over his shoulder.

"Now, in a moment we will officially begin. Cavariel here will ask you a question. You will answer, or you will suffer." Max took a deep breath. "I've never dissected a live dark elf before. Are your hearts strong? Will yours hold out? Do you have a family history of insanity?"

Closing his eyes, Max brought up a spell he'd obtained a while back, but never used. It had been awarded to him when his *Drain* spell had killed an orc during his early days on this world. He didn't feel good about what he planned to do, but didn't feel particularly bad about it either, considering the circumstances.

Motioning for Cavariel to proceed without opening his eyes, Max cast *Mind's Eye* on the assassin in front of him.

"Who hired the Shadow Walkers to kill King Storm?" Cavariel asked, his gaze flicking to Max and the two blades in his hands. Max hadn't told him about the spell, needing his reactions to the stressful situation to be sincere.

Almost immediately, Max began to see brief flashes of the assassin's memories. The first several were so rapid and brief that Max had a hard time following them. Each one featured the moment of a victim's death. After several dozen of them, there was an image of his comrade's face being crushed by Max, then one of his other companions running away. Another image appeared, Max cleaning his fingernails, an evil smile on his face. He was pretty sure that was wrong, as he hadn't smiled like that until later, but this was how the dark elf remembered their discussion. He made a mental note that memories he saw going forward may not be fully accurate.

Max growled behind the assassin, shuffling his feet slightly to increase his stress. The assassin remained silent, but another memory emerged. The assassin was standing in an austere, barely lit chamber. In front of him was a white-haired dark elf with wrinkles at the corners of his eyes, indicating great age. The elder spoke in a soft voice. "You are to eliminate King Maximilian Storm of

Stormhaven, formerly the grey dwarf kingdom known as Nogroz."

Next to him, out of sight, another elf spoke, presumably one of the three who'd tried to kill Max. "Does the client require a trophy?"

The elder shook his head. "His death is sufficient. The client asked only that it happen quickly." The memory faded, along with the spell, and Max let out the breath he'd been holding.

Spell level up! Your Mind's Eye spell is now Level 2!

Opening his eyes, he saw Cavariel staring nervously at him, his gaze shifting to the blades he held, obviously expecting Max to begin cutting since the assassin hadn't spoken. To keep both dark elves on their toes, Max moved the skinning knife so that it was just a few inches in front of the shadow walker's nose. "I was tempted to start with your ears, but I need you to be able to hear our questions. And your own screams." He moved the blade so that it was touching the elf's forehead just in front of his hairline. "On my world, in the old days, warriors would collect the scalps of defeated enemies. Often taking those scalps while their foes lay bleeding, but still alive. Do they do that here?" He asked the elf while he put a little pressure on the blade, pressing it into his skin but not breaking it. "I got partially scalped in a recent battle with some orcs. It was nasty. Big flap of my skin hanging off the side of my head, blood everywhere. It tried to heal it myself, but..." He let his voice trail off as he cast *Mind's Eye* again.

This time he was shown a memory of a portal. He recognized it as the portal near Deepcrag just before the elf stepped through it into the courtyard of the keep in Stormhaven. The assassins had followed a supply wagon that had come through, one belonging to a family that had taken up residence there.

"Have you ever met a stonetalon?" Max pulled the knife away for a moment, opening his eyes. "I'm assuming you have, since you have undoubtedly spent time in the underground." He saw Cavariel nod in agreement. The translator looked relieved that Max hadn't started cutting. "I only ask, because stonetalons have a few special skills. They hunt in the dark, so their hearing and sense of smell are vastly improved over yours. For example, we have a stonetalon here in the palace, and were able to use that excellent sense of smell to backtrack you and your comrades' path. A path that went back through the portal here to Deepcrag."

He saw the assassin's body stiffen, and smiled. He was making progress.

"I'm thinking that killing you and sending you in pieces back to your guild won't be enough of a deterrent." He saw Cavariel's eyes widen at this, his face growing pale, for a dark elf. "I think I'll just backtrack your trail all the way to wherever you came from, and take an army with me. How many of your fellow assassins will I find there to kill? Do you have families? Will I find them there, as well?" He closed his eyes and cast the spell again.

An image of a cavern appeared. It was pitch dark, but the dark elf's night vision made it easy enough to see a stone fortress rising up from the cavern floor. Looking down from above, he could see dozens of dark elves moving about inside the walls. That image was replaced by one of a beautiful female dark elf. She was dressed as an assassin as well, but was smiling and flirting with the one whose memory this was. Max felt a little dirty as she leaned in to deliver a kiss before the memory faded again.

The assassin remained silent. Max took the hooked knife in his right hand, sending the skinning knife into his inventory. Pushing the elf forward in his seat, he hooked the blade on the top of the dark leather armor, right at the base of his skull. "I think I'll start by removing the skin on your back. Lots of room to work, no major arteries, but lots of nerve endings." He ripped the blade downward, and it sliced open the armor from his neck down to his tailbone, but left the skin underneath undamaged. The elf let out a small grunt at this.

Max could practically hear the elf's heart racing as the sweaty skin under his armor began to dry in the open air, and he cast the spell again while motioning with the knife for Cavariel to ask again.

"Who contracted with your guild for King Storm's death?"

Max found himself back in the elder's chamber, where the old elf was just motioning for his underlings to leave. "Make haste, and do not return until the job is done." Max got a brief view of the stone floor as his subject bowed to the elder, then turned and exited along with the others. Almost as soon as the door closed behind them, his subject asked, "How long will it take to reach this new kingdom?"

The one Max recognized as the first to die in his study replied. "A day, maybe two. He has a portal, and has declared his city open to all races. We can simply pose as merchants and stroll right in." the assassin chuckled. "Which is good, as I'm sure the Master charged the client extra for haste."

"Who do you think the client is?" the third assassin spoke quietly, glancing over his shoulder at the closed door behind them.

The deceased assassin shrugged. "Don't know. But I've only seen two visitors in the last week. One was a grey dwarf, the other an orc."

Max opened his eyes again as the spell faded, and he got another notification that it had leveled up. He sighed, then used party chat to send a message to Dalia, who was waiting outside. Two seconds later, she burst through the door. "Me king! There be an urgent matter!"

Max grinned at her from behind the assassin, who was tense, his spine stiff as a board. "I'm busy here." He growled, placing the knife against the dark elf's shoulder blade. "You should go, you don't want to see what's about to happen here."

Dalia, who hadn't been told anything except when and how to burst in, took in the scene, and a horrified look spread across her face. She gulped once, then took a deep breath and followed Max's instructions. "There be an attack at the Way Station!" She started toward the door and beckoned for him to follow with a wave of her hand. "Yer people need ye!"

Max pretended to think it over for a moment, then tossed the blade past the assassin so that it landed among the others on the table. "Fine. We aren't getting anywhere, anyway." He started toward the door, stopping at the last moment and turning toward Cavariel. "Slit this fool's throat, cut him up into manageable pieces, put his parts in the box with the other two. Make sure the heads are on top. Then send it back to that fortress of theirs." He watched the dark elf's eyes widen as he walked out and slammed the door behind him. In party chat he added, "Let him sweat a bit, then throw him back in his cell."

Chapter 15

The second interrogation went about the same. Dalia was clearly upset by the potential torture of the dark elves, despite them being assassins, so Max clued her in on his *Mind's Eye* spell. When she realized what he was doing, she laughed aloud, mostly out of relief, and actually hugged him. She gladly participated in the second round, playing her part to perfection.

Cavariel, on the other hand, was not told. The translator was confused by the first interrogation, but took heart in the fact that Max hadn't actually hurt the bound assassin. Even more confusing was the circumstance under which Max had ended it. There clearly hadn't been an attack on the Way Station, so Max was up to something. Cavariel just didn't know what. Watching the second one being strapped to the chair, he feared Max's lack of success the first time did not bode well for this one.

As a result, the translator's nervous demeanor and rapidly shifting gaze made his part in the little drama even more convincing. He actually pleaded with the assassin to answer the questions, and his hands twitched when Max picked up the blades before moving behind the dark elf.

The main difference was in the information Max got. Both the assassins' stories were consistent, but this one had actually seen the two visitors to the guild's fortress. The first had been a well-dressed grey dwarf. By the quality of his attire, Max guessed he was a merchant, or a noble. The second was a large, battle-scarred orc in chainmail armor who stomped his way through the gate and up the path into the inner keep without stopping, or even acknowledging any of the dark elves he passed. When he passed through the main door, the oversized axe on his back scraped the top of the door frame. Max noticed that both had been carrying ornately carved boxes that appeared to be made of bone, or ivory. He was tempted to ask the second assassin the significance of this commonality, but couldn't think of a way to do so without revealing that he'd seen their memories. He couldn't even claim the other dark elf had told him, because that one hadn't seen the visitors.

When he'd sent the second prisoner back to his cell, Max sat behind his desk, thinking. The others took seats in the various chairs around the room, which was silent for a solid minute before Cavariel cleared this throat. When Max looked up at him, he hesitated, then spoke. "Your majesty, I… do not understand."

Realizing that he'd still not explained to the translator what was going on, Max chuckled. "What I'm about to tell you is another of the things you must never disclose to anyone outside this room." When the dark elf nodded his agreement, Max smiled at him. "They were never in any real danger. I have a spell that allows me to see their memories. Your questions, and my threats, were simply meant to get them thinking about their contract, their client, to trigger the memories I needed to see."

Cavariel took a moment to digest that information, thinking back over the two sessions. Now Max's odd behavior made much more sense. But the inevitable question arose. "Majesty, did you not trust me to keep this secret from the assassins? Was it because I am also a dark elf?"

Max shook his head. "I trust you, Cavariel. You have proven yourself more than once. I didn't tell you simply because I don't know how good an actor you are. Your reactions were a key part of our little show, and I needed them to be as convincing as possible."

"Ah, yes. I understand." the elf let out a long exhale of relief. "My compliments on your clever ruse and forethought, majesty." The smile he gave Max was weak, and obviously not sincere.

"If it makes you feel any better, there is no one I trust on this world more than Dalia, and she was unaware as well, at least during the first session, for the same reason. You being left out of the loop was truly no reflection of my faith in you. On the contrary, the fact that you were included at all should speak to how much you are trusted." Max watched as the elf visibly relaxed a bit more.

"Thank you, majesty. That does indeed help." He bowed from his sitting position.

Max filled in the group on what he'd seen, relaying only the facts, without any suppositions or opinion. Blake was the first to speak up when he was done.

"So an orc, and not a red-eyed orc. Possibly sent by An'zalor? Would the war chief stoop to hiring assassins?"

Max shook his head. "I wouldn't have thought so. He's more of a send an army to crush me kind of guy. In fact he's already tried that. He just didn't send enough guys."

"The grey dwarf, mebbe one o' them thieves?" Dalia asked, a scowl on her face. She still had a hard time with the fact that Max had let those greys go in peace.

Again, Max expressed doubts. "I don't know how far the guild keep is from Gar'doz, but I doubt it. Unless they sent their representative before the battle with The One. Also, none of the thieves, even their boss, dressed fancy like the one I saw."

"The bank." Redmane muttered, mostly to himself.

"What was that?" Max turned to him, as did the others. He was sitting in one of the chairs facing Max's desk.

"I be thinkin' it might o' been one o' the bankers. From here in the city. When ye claimed the bank, ye claimed a significant amount o' wealth they'd left behind. Might be that the bankers be wantin' revenge." He paused for a moment, still thinking it through. "Or they be plannin' to retake the city, and hoped that takin' yer life would make that easier."

"Great, so there might be a grey dwarf invasion soon." Dylan scratched his face thoughtfully. "Are there a lot of grey dwarves left?"

Dalia nodded emphatically. "Oh, aye. They be spread out in clans, just like me own people. Last I heard, there be five grey cities. Well, four now." She smiled at Max. "But they fight amongst themselves nearly as often as they fight us. So if they be plannin' to attack us, it'll likely be a single clan, mebbe two."

"Didn't they use several clans to attack Darkholm back when we first met?" Max tried to remember what he'd heard back then. It had been a busy time, filled with loss, anger, and almost nonstop battle.

Dalia half-smiled at him. "Aye, at least two clans, mebbe three. But, and I mean no offense here, Max… Darkholm be a much larger, more powerful kingdom. A long-time foe. I doubt the greys would think they'll need more'n one clan to defeat ye and yer small army."

Max snorted, and the corporals all laughed aloud. Dylan grinned at the dwarf. "Damn, Dalia. Didn't anyone ever tell you it's not the size of the boat, it's the motion of the ocean?"

She looked confused for a moment, until she saw the looks on their faces and realized what the ogre meant. Blushing, she shot him the single-finger salute that they'd taught her.

After a much needed laugh, Max nodded her way. "No offense taken, and I see your point. So, for now, let's go with master Redmane's theory that the greys hired the assassins. We'll also have to assume that more Shadow Walkers will come for me. And I suppose we'll need to expect an attack from a significant force of grey dwarves as well." Max sighed, frustrated. Being a sovereign seemed to mean he faced a never-ending string of crises and threats to the people he was supposed to protect.

"Alright, first… everybody put the word out. Everywhere you can. We need people. Offer them good money to become guards or soldiers, free housing for crafters and support, tax breaks for merchants, whatever we need to do to bring in more people. I've got too much territory to defend with the forces we have." He held up a hand when Blake opened his mouth to speak. "I know, the portals let us bring in reinforcements quickly, and we have allies to call on. But I can't keep calling Ironhand and the others for help every other week. We need to beef up our own army, our own resource production, and trade." He waited as the others all nodded.

"Don't hold back. Recruit from anywhere you can without angering our allies. That includes dwarven clans, goblin tribes, kobolds, Mages' Guild, Westreach, more orc defectors from An'zalor's city, even from the queen's territory. Speaking of that, Redmane, I'd like to get a message to that Lord Hastings guy. He seemed solid enough, and was no fan of the queen. Maybe we can recruit him, and some of his disenfranchised friends."

The others started to get to their feet, headed out to follow his orders, when Cavariel asked, "And what of the Shadow Walkers?"

Everyone paused, wanting to hear the answer to that question.

Max drummed his fingers on the desk for a moment, considering. "Is there *any* chance that, if I let them go to carry a message back to their guild, they won't just return and try again?"

Cavariel shook his head. "Sadly, no."

"What if I had them take an oath not to attack me or mine ever again?"

Again, a head shake. "They could take no such oath. Their existing oaths to execute their guild's orders without fail would prevent it." He paused for a second. "You might secure an oath that those two individual will not harm any of your citizens, excluding you, for whom they already have a contract. But nothing that would prevent others from coming, or those two from trying to take your head again."

The drumming stopped, and Max leaned forward, elbows on the desk. "Then I can't let them live. Unless, would they serve any purpose as hostages? Do they provide any leverage with the guild if I hold them here? Like, *leave me alone or I kill your guys*?"

"They have failed their mission. Worse, they were captured alive. They are less than worthless now, in the eyes of their guild."

"Do we need to put them on suicide watch?" Blake asked the translator, who looked at him in confusion for a moment.

"If you mean are they likely to take their own lives in shame, they might try. Once they are convinced that they cannot escape and make another attempt on your life, sire."

"So, to summarize, I can't let them go. I can hold them here, but they'd just be a drain on resources and likely to try and hurt someone in order to escape and try to kill me. Their guild is going to keep trying to kill me no matter what I do with them." He looked down at his hands, which were now clasped on his desk. "Do they have any value at all? Can we sell them to a guild enemy, or something?"

Cavariel seemed to brighten at that question. "They might have… some value. Were you willing to spend more time… err, mining their memories. If you could identify some of their targets, and the client who paid for their deaths, you might sell that information to the target's family or clan. Many would pay well for the opportunity to take proper vengeance for those deaths."

Max thought about it for a while, then shook his head. "That sounds like it would take a lot of time, and based on what I've seen so far, getting solid information on clients is a long shot. I don't have enough time to handle what's already on my plate."

Max made a decision. "Dylan, go ask Erdun to make me a storage item with two slots." He looked over at Blake. "Kill them quickly. Chop them into bits along with the third one, put them in a box. Heads on top. We'll put that in the storage item, along with a note from me to the guild boss, and Cavariel can send it back to them." The others nodded their agreement, including Dalia. While she objected to torturing the assassins, she agreed that a quick death was the best they deserved. As for what happened after, that didn't matter as long as she didn't have to do the butchering.

"Can you make it three slots, boss?" Blake asked, a wicked grin on his face. "I just had an idea I'd like to try. It'll take a little experimenting, but if it works…" He gave them his best evil villain laugh. "Muahaha!"

*****

"Majesty." The Ghost bowed deeply at the waist, standing a few paces in front of his queen's throne. "My sources tell me that Shadow Walkers made an unsuccessful attempt on King Storm's life two days ago."

"Shadow Walkers? And they failed?" She huffed in frustration, pounding one arm of the throne with her fist. "I suppose I should not be surprised." She smiled then, realizing the inevitability of Max's situation. "Hopefully the next attempt will succeed. That would solve several problems for me."

"You still believe he and the other Battleborne have designs on your throne." It was a statement, not a question.

"Not immediate ones, no. Had they wished it, they could have killed me and advanced with that army of theirs the day we met." She leaned back in the oversized chair. "No, for now Max and his alliance are content to wait and see if I behave. They'll trade with us, in some limited fashion, and go on about their business until some future situation requires action." She raised an eyebrow at her spymaster. "I fully intend to create that situation. But I will do so in my own time, when I'm properly prepared.

We shall bide our time, play nice, gather resources and information, then make our move."

"The fool has declared his kingdom to be open to everyone. We could insert a small army into his city without him knowing."

The queen stared down at him. "I was told that he requires an oath of loyalty before accepting any new citizen."

"There are ways around that. To begin with, we ask to establish a formal embassy in their city. We can fill it with 'staff' that should be allowed to avoid the oath and remain our citizens in the employ of the ambassador. Then we do the same with a trade emissary, and their staff."

"You're talking about a few dozen people. A hundred, at most." the queen observed.

"A small group of well-trained individuals can cause a lot of trouble behind enemy lines, given proper preparation, and with the right timing." His smile was wide, and wicked.

Returning the smile with an evil one of her own, the queen agreed. "Make that happen. Whatever resources you need. The boy that Max killed, whatshisname. Offer his father the opportunity to serve as our ambassador. It can't hurt to have someone with a grudge against Max lead our mission there. In fact, have him attend me, and I'll even offer him a quest…"

*****

In a dimly lit corridor, deep inside Shadow Keep, an apprentice knocked on the Grandmaster's door. When the door clicked, then opened on its own, the nervous apprentice bowed deeply, keeping his eyes on the floor near the master's feet as he shuffled forward. "Grandmaster, a messenger arrived a short time ago, bearing this. They said it is from King Storm, and is to be delivered directly to you."

"So our brethren failed in their mission. And the chimera king has learned they were ours." The elder frowned in disappointment. The three he had sent were far from his best, but should have been more than sufficient to accomplish the removal of a fledgling king. He looked at the youngling, who held out a small box that barely covered the palm of his hand. The apprentice was sweating, and appeared to want to say something, but had his lips pressed tight together.

The elder elf growled quietly. "Out with it, youngling, before I remove your too-silent tongue."

"G-grandmaster, the m-messenger. When he delivered the package, he said something. He… he called King Storm the Battleborne king."

"Battleborne!" the elder snatched up the box so fast that the apprentice didn't even see it happen. He simply felt a slight breeze on his sweaty palm, and the box was gone. "What else?"

"Nothing, Grandmaster. Nothing else." The apprentice lowered his hand to his side, then bowed again. "He was quite nervous, and fled the moment I accepted the message."

"Send someone after him, immediately! I wish to ask him more about this Battleborne king." The growled order sent the apprentice fleeing from the room, barely pausing to pull the door closed behind him. The elder set the small box on a nearby polished marble table, staring thoughtfully down at it. When he *Examined* it, he found a simple description.

> **Dimensional Storage Device**
> **Quality: Uncommon**
> **Capacity: 3**

After quickly confirming that the box was not trapped in any way, he took it to hand again, and pulled open the inventory. The first slot gave him a start when he saw that it contained the butchered remains of his underlings. He immediately began to pace, snarling. "Impudent whelp! He dares insult me, insult the Shadow Walkers in this manner?!"

He raged around his office for a few moments, cursing quietly to himself, describing all the ways in which he would ensure the target would suffer. He even considered returning the fee for the job to the client, when another thought struck him. "Battleborne! The client failed to inform us of Storm's true status. Had I known he was Battleborne, I'd have sent more experienced operatives, and not wasted these three." He looked down at the box again. "We shall be discussing that with the client very soon." The threat in his voice would have made the recently departed apprentice shit himself.

Looking into the box again, he saw that the second slot contained a piece of parchment. He willed it from the box to the table without touching it. More than one of his targets had died from touching poison-treated parchment. When the folded note fluttered down onto the table, he used a pair of throwing daggers to push it open and pin it to the table. His anger only increased as he read its contents.

> *To the big boss of the Shadow Walkers, whatever your title is.*
>
> *You sent three of your assassins to kill me. It didn't go well for them. I understand this is just a contract for you, and nothing personal. But it is very personal to me. Any additional assassins sent my way will be returned to you in the same manner. In hopes of avoiding further unfortunate interactions with your guild, I have included a small gift with this message.*
>
> *-King Maximilian Storm, of Stormhaven.*

His temper flaring, his temples throbbing as rage caused his blood pressure to rise, the elder elf inspected the third slot. The item appeared to be a small silvery orb of some kind, roughly the size of an apple. In fact, it looked like it might even be mithril. Attached to its surface were at least half a dozen sparkling diamonds. The old elf's brain automatically estimated its value to be at least a few thousand gold. "Fool! Idiot! Does he not know that we cannot be bribed? Such a bauble will not save his insolent hide!"

Once again assuming the item would be coated with poison, or potentially trapped with a hidden blade, he caused it to transfer directly onto the marble table. He immediately cast *Examine* on the orb as it began to roll across the table.

He never saw the results.

Less than two seconds after emerging from the storage device, the small orb exploded. Sharp bits of metal, stone from the table, and even the embedded diamonds shredded the elder's robe and flesh even as he was knocked back against a wall by the force of the blast. His health dropped to ten percent, and after slumping to the floor, he saw that he was suffering from both bleed and poison debuffs.

He pulled a high-grade health potion from his own inventory and uncorked it with blood-soaked fingers as his health continued to tick downward from the debuffs. He barely managed to keep hold of it as he tilted the vial and downed the potion. Almost immediately the bleeding debuff faded, but the poison remained. He heard the sound of pounding feet and shouts of alarm in the corridor outside as he wiped his hand on what was left of his robes.

Reaching into his inventory again, he produced a general poison cure potion and downed that as well, his hand slightly steadier as the healing potion took effect. His health bar had gone up to about one quarter, but as he checked it, he saw it tick back down. Despite the excellent quality of the cure potion, the poison debuff had not gone away.

His door burst open and several underlings entered the room, eyes wide as they took in the destruction wrought by the explosion. It took a few seconds before one of them located the fallen elder against the wall, and rushed over. "Grandmaster! What has happened?"

"Healer! Call the healer!" the old elf croaked, pushing the underling away and leaving a smear of blood on their armor. "Now! I've been poisoned!"

*****

Max and his party were sitting at their usual table at Eats N Treats when Cavariel came through the front door and approached. Max motioned for him to grab a free chair from a nearby table and join them.

"We're having Taco Tuesday, Cavariel. Good timing."

"Sounds delicious, sire." The dark elf smiled across the table at him. "I bring tidings from an old contact of mine."

The table went silent. Everyone there knew which contact he spoke of. Not their identity, but the purpose of their interaction. "Good news, or bad?" Max set down his taco and waited, holding his breath.

"It seems the Grandmaster of the Shadow Walkers has retired,.. quite abruptly." Cavariel grinned at them as the table erupted with cheers, startling the other patrons in the room.

"I told you it would work!" Blake stood up on his chair and puffed out his chest. "I'm a friggin genius!"

Max didn't disagree. When Blake had initially described his idea to them, Max had little faith in it. But after several hours of very careful experimentation and tweaking of the plan, they'd thought they had an effective delivery method for their message.

Max spent most of that time working out a way to modify his *Boom!* spell to build in a short delay. The most he'd been able to manage was three seconds, but as it turned out, that had been enough. Working to modify it had also raised his spell level by three points. Redmane had commissioned the orb from Master Erdun, who had crafted it with glee when told what they intended to use it for. He'd even suggested the modification of a hollow core filled with the grey dwarf poison. This had the added benefit of using less of the expensive mithril.

Cavariel was of the opinion that a guild of assassins would certainly be familiar with the grey dwarf poison, and have the cure on hand. But Max didn't care. "At the very least, it should put a few moments of fear into them. I don't imagine they're used to being afraid. Maybe THAT will convince them to stay away."

When the carefully composed note was written, designed to make it seem as if Max was offering a bribe, and stored in the device with the bodies, Max had cleared the room. Dalia was outside with the proper cure potion in case something went wrong. While Max's most recent attempt at delaying the spell trigger had been a success, several of his earlier efforts had failed. He'd tested his troll regeneration quite a bit in the process.

With the expensive orb in his hand, he had extended it so that it was nearly touching the storage box. After licking his lips nervously, he cast *Boom!* on the orb then instantly willed it into the inventory. The second it left his hand, he dove to the floor behind his desk. When it didn't explode, he stuck his head up, then laughed at his own antics. Blake had counted on the fact that items sent into storage seemed to be frozen in time. Warm food stayed warm. Wet items remained wet when you pulled them back out, even months later. If the detonation delay from his spell could be frozen in time, only to resume when the item was removed...

"You can come in!" He shouted, and the door flew open. Dylan came in first, his shield raised, the others peeking out from behind him. Just for fun, Max pounded the top of his desk hard enough to make the items on it jump, screamed at the top of his lungs and fell to the floor. Dylan flinched, ducking down behind his shield as several of the others dove backward and to either side of the corridor beyond the door. Laughing as he got up, Max called out. "It's okay, I think. If it was going to blow, it should have by now." After shooting him some dirty looks, insults, and various rude gestures, the others entered.

"No way, it actually worked?" Smitty stepped out from behind the ogre and approached the table where the little box sat. "That is one expensive little grenade!"

Max didn't even blink. The cost of the mithril, and the diamonds, were absolutely worth it if their trap worked as planned. He'd chosen those materials because they were the hardest he knew of, and he hoped the shards would penetrate armor and flesh better than iron or steel. Plus he needed to entice the assassin master to take the thing out of storage to look at. While he didn't expect to actually kill someone that was high enough level, and tough enough, to be the head of an assassin's guild, he'd wanted to do as much damage as possible.

As the cheers died down around the table at Eats N Treats, Max raised a glass and waited for the others to do the same. "To early retirement!" The others laughed and they all clinked glasses before drinking.

After a few minutes of self-congratulation and celebration, the table grew quiet. They all knew that the death of the assassin boss was probably a pyrrhic victory. Cavariel had warned them as they prepared their response that killing the Grandmaster would force the Shadow Walkers to respond with an extreme amount of violence, to maintain their reputation, if nothing else. Pretty much exactly as Max had done.

Max and company had not been deterred by the warning. They were not ones to sit back, do nothing, and passively wait for their deaths. If the Shadow Walkers were going to come anyway, Max figured they might as well score some hits before then. He had decided to hope for the best, and had sent a second note to be delivered a day after the first.

To the new assassin boss. Leave us alone, or I'll destroy you and your entire guild, the same way I just destroyed your predecessor.

-King Maximilian Storm, of Stormhaven

He was counting on fear of the unknown to bluff the guild into backing off. If he was lucky, the old assassin would have removed the note before the orb, and done so alone. In which case, the note, the orb, and the elf would have been destroyed. If the new boss couldn't figure out how exactly Max had killed his master, that might worry them enough to make them cautious.

"How long before they are likely to respond?" Max asked Cavariel.

"Assuming the new Grandmaster steps in immediately, a few days, I would think. Longer if they need to summon the assassins they plan to send from somewhere else. This delay is likely, as they'll want to send more experienced operatives this time, and those aren't likely to be sitting around the guild lounge playing cards. The delay will be much longer if they don't try to use the portals again, and travel here by foot."

Max grinned. They had brought Master Spellslinger and his assistants back to install another upgrade. This time it was a ward across the surface of each portal, and each physical gate. It was keyed to the citizen's oath, and further designed to interrupt stealth abilities. Guards at each location would be stopping and inspecting anyone who activated the ward. It would slow the progress of merchants coming through for trade, but had a high probability of exposing stealthed assassins trying to sneak in to murder him.

Max had taken to wearing his armor all the time now, except when sleeping. Redmane had insisted that he have a full-time escort of four guards everywhere he went. The dwarf had even tried to station them in his bedroom as he slept, but that was where Max had drawn the line. Instead they were stationed in his sitting room, just outside the closed door of his bedroom, and he agreed to allow them to sweep the room before he went to sleep. As there were no other doors or windows to that room, Redmane had capitulated.

Max was still annoyed by the constant company - even now, his four guards stood near the door of the restaurant, two outside, two inside, ever vigilant, but he understood the necessity.

Max raised another toast. "To things that go boom in the night!"

The others grinned and raised their mugs again, the three corporals shouting, "Boom!" in unison as they slammed the mugs down on the table, sloshing ale everywhere.

Chapter 16

Max stood next to Ironhand atop a wide stairway, positioned between two thick stone columns, both of which were partially carved with dwarven runes and scenes of crafting. Behind them, Enoch, Spellslinger, Redmane, Cavariel, and his party members were clustered with a couple dozen clan elders and dwarven Masters, including Oakstone and Steelbender.

At the bottom of the stairs nearly a thousand citizens and visiting crafters, the entire population of Stormhaven's section of the Dara Seans settlement had gathered, minus a few guards manning the walls. This was a big deal.

They were opening the first of the new temples to Regin.

After the dwarven god of crafting had visited them and explained the significance of the strange square silver coins Max had found, Max and Ironhand had both vowed to construct temples where they could be put to proper use again. Max had decided that since they'd previously been used along the ancient abandoned trade route, that was where he'd construct his first temple. And since he already had a massive rebuilding effort underway in the gnome city, he took advantage of the crafters being there. With the funds from the recovered grey dwarf treasury, and the twenty thousand gold that Ironhand had paid for a thousand of the coins, he could afford to pay them easily enough.

When they'd heard about the project, every dwarf in the settlement had volunteered to help. Max had sent the gnome and elf earth mages he'd recruited from the Mages' Guild, but the dwarves shooed them away, considering it their right and duty to construct the temple themselves. Max hadn't minded, as there were plenty of other jobs for the guild mages to do. He sent them to the goblin city instead, to increase the height and strength of the perimeter wall there.

The dwarves had worked tirelessly, day and night. First Enoch chose a location next to his office, the building that sat atop the Runemaster's outpost. He'd already expanded into the building to the right, building a wing between them and creating visible space for Spellslinger, Redmane, and others to sleep while visiting the outpost. There was even a fancy suite for when Ironhand chose to visit, with space for his honor guard as well. This was mostly for appearances' sake, as they didn't want to have to explain why so many dwarves went into Enoch's office and stayed there for days on end without leaving. In reality they slept down in the outpost.

Now he'd demolished several buildings on the opposite side to make room for the temple. The dwarves began by digging out two underground levels, then began construction of the temple proper. The portal operated almost nonstop, bringing in the sparkly stone from the quarry near Glitterspindle's temple, as well as other supplies from Stormhaven and Darkholm.

Enoch and Spellslinger had taken a couple days off from their work in the outpost to explore Deepcrag, where they located one of the old temples to Regin. Enoch practically spat on the ground when he found it. "Bah! This were built by humans! No sense o' grandeur!" Not satisfied with the small, understated structure, they'd had an architect draw out its floorplan, then vastly expand it for the new temple. The layout was the same, just on a larger scale. The structure was two stories tall, with wide front doors that arched up to twice Max's height. Four thick columns supported a portico that extended the entire width of the building. Scaffolds still stood along the front wall, and around the columns, where dwarven crafters were still carving images of tribute to Regin and the crafting profession in general. Spellslinger had installed mage lights on either side of the doors, as well as up underneath the portico, so that the stairs and the street in front of the temple were lit with a soft glow.

The basic construction was now complete, though the aesthetic touches were still underway, as evidenced by the partially carved stone. The very first carving that had been completed was above the stairs on the front face of the portico, a six foot high image of Regin's face in profile, much like the ones on the coins. Regin himself had appeared as it was being finished, much to the delight of everyone nearby. As they all dropped to a knee and bowed their heads, the god had snorted at the likeness, shaken his head, and disappeared again. Several of the witnesses claimed to have seen the slightest hint of a tear in his eye before he vanished.

Max had elected to hold a grand opening ceremony as soon as possible, wanting to express his sincere gratitude to Regin for all that he'd done to help Max and his companions.

"Thank you all for coming!" He grinned at the crowd standing five steps down, opening his arms wide. "And thank you for your dedication and hard work in constructing this beautiful temple!" He waited as the crowd cheered, as did the dwarves gathered behind him. Max took a deep breath, and pushed on. "As I'm sure you've all heard by now, I am a Battleborne. When I first arrived on this world, not so long ago, I was clueless and all but naked, lost and alone. Regin took pity on me, gifting me with clothes, armor, weapons, and supplies. He gave me a purpose in the form of a quest, and nudged me toward Darkholm, where I found so many friends!" He turned and motioned toward Ironhand and the dwarves behind him, then expanded the motion to indicate the crowd.

"From that day till this one, Regin has blessed me with his guidance and support! This temple is one small way of expressing my gratitude!" He paused again for the cheers of the crowd. When it died down a bit, he grinned wickedly. "Regin has often said he's not one for bowing and scraping, or expressions of respect he hasn't earned. I know how he feels!" There were a few laughs from those behind him. "But if I have to put up with it, so does he!" He dropped to one knee as he spoke, as did a chuckling Ironhand next to him, which naturally caused everyone in front of and behind them to do the same before Max continued, laying it on thick.

"Oh wise, handsome, and powerful Regin… we dedicate this temple to you! Constructed by hand, with love and respect in our hearts as each stone was placed!" Max lowered his head and hid a small grin as he pictured the look Regin likely had on his face. "This temple shall forever be a place where the troubled may seek peace, the frustrated may seek inspiration!" There was a quiet cheer at that. "Where those who need it may seek solace, or guidance!" He raised his head, then nodded to Ironhand, who stood next to him, obviously smothering a grin of his own. Max produced a small chest from his inventory and held it up for the crowd to see. He then set it at his feet and opened it, taking a small handful of the silver tokens and holding them out in his open palm.

"In times long past, crafters created these as a sort of tribute. Citizens would bring them to temples like this one and offer them as tribute, as a sort of prayer to Regin. Today we restore that tradition!" The cheer was much louder this time. "All of you here have contributed in some way to this day. Whether you placed stones in the foundation, carved images into them, provided supplies, fed those who were doing the work, or watched over them while they labored. So please, come forward and receive a coin, then step inside and look around. Offer tribute if you feel so inclined, or hold on to your coin if you like. They are simply a physical symbol, a manifestation of our regard for Regin in all his glory. You can certainly express your admiration and thanks without them."

From somewhere near the back of the crowd, a small voice called out, "Gnomes rule!"

Max motioned toward the dwarves at the front of the crowd, who promptly climbed the stairs. Max and

Ironhand scooped up more coins from the chest, and handed them out. Max smiled at everyone as he pressed a coin into their hand, a lighthearted warmth spreading through him. As the last of the crowd accepted their coin and passed by him, the warmth intensified. A white light enveloped him, causing Ironhand and several others to turn back in surprise, and a notification popped into view, filled with light and golden lettering.

Congratulations!
New Title received!
Due to your heartfelt expressions of gratitude and respect, as well as your construction of a temple, and your efforts to restore ancient traditions of worship, you have earned the Title: Paladin of Regin, Dwarven God of Crafting!

As Max finished reading, a shocked expression on his face, an invisible Red started giggling from atop his shoulder. Max and everyone else started slightly as much louder laughter echoed through the temple and the city streets. "Bwahaha!" Max recognized it as Regin's laughter a second before the god's voice whispered in his ear. "That'll teach ye not to poke at the gods!"

Ironhand, obviously having heard Regin's words, burst out laughing as Max groaned. Holding his belly, he bent over double, then straightened back up and wiped tears from his eyes, snorting as he saw the look on Max's face again. After a few deep breaths, he clapped a hand on Max's back. "Ye did ask fer it, Max" the dwarven king grinned up at him. "C'mon, let's go inside."

The two kings were the last to enter the temple, where they found everyone silent and staring wide-eyed at Max. The stone interior of the temple sparkled, more of Spellslinger's mage lights reflecting off the glittery stone, as well as the water in a fountain that burbled near the back of the temple in place of an altar. Some of the crowd had already tossed their coins into the fountain, while others had paused with their hands extended, interrupted by the light display outside the doors. Ironhand couldn't help but laugh again before stepping aside and waving at a still dumbfounded Max, shouting. "I give ye Maximilian Storm! Battleborne, King o' Stormhaven, and now Paladin o' the Light!"

The temple erupted with a combination of cheers and laughter that echoed throughout the stone interior, growing louder as it bounced back and forth. The loudest laughter came from the three corporals who stood just to one side of the door. A moment later the entire structure began to glow faintly. As the sounds of the echoes increased, the light grew brighter. The crowd went silent as the light spread, swirling through each of them before it faded, along with the echoes. Every set of eyes went blank as they all received notifications.

You have received the blessing: Regin's Regard!
Crafting production and quality increased by 5%!
Health regeneration increased 10%; +1 to all Attributes;

The silence was broken by whispers and murmurs of surprise that quickly grew to loud exclamations and joyous laughter as the crowd embraced the blessing. Max shook his head, looking up at the ceiling as if he'd find Regin up there somewhere.

Ironhand thumped him on the back again. "Congratulations, Max!" His eyes sparkled with mischief as he grinned up at the chimera.

Coming to his senses, Max grumped at his friend and fellow sovereign. "Laugh now, my friend. Isn't your own temple in Darkholm just about complete?"

The dwarf's eyes widened briefly, then Ironhand's expression became thoughtful. "Ye think Regin will make me a Paladin too?"

"I certainly hope so!" It was Max's turn to flash a mischievous grin. He was slightly disappointed when the dwarf didn't appear to be at all displeased by the idea.

*****

"What does it mean, being a Paladin?" Max asked no one in particular. He looked around at the others seated at the long table. After spending a short time celebrating with the exuberant crowd in the temple, he had quietly retired to the underground Outpost. His party, along with Ironhand, Redmane, Spellslinger, and Enoch had eventually all joined him. The corporals had all taken multiple stabs at him, while the dwarves sat back and enjoyed the ribbing.

"It means many things." Spellslinger was the first to speak, leaning forward with his arms on the table. "First, it means ye should have access to a few spells o' the divine variety. There be a wide range o' those. Some be extra effective at healing or protection, others be focused on doin extra damage to undead and other creatures o' the dark." Max nodded, about to pull up his interface when the dwarf continued.

"It also means Regin hisself may give ye quests from time to time." The dwarf paused, raising one eyebrow. "Though that be nothin' new fer you."

"That doesn't sound so bad." Max tapped his thumbs on the table as he considered. "Do I need to lead prayers, or… I don't know… recruit more followers, like a priest?"

"It couldn't hurt." The old mage winked at him. "But no, I doubt Regin would expect such from ye. If he does, he'll let ye know."

"Besides," Ironhand added, "Ye already be recruitin' more followers, just by reviving the use o' the tribute coins, and providin' new temples fer folks to visit."

"Build it, and they will come." Dylan whispered loudly enough for all to hear, earning a glare from Max, and snickers from Smitty and Blake. Ironhand simply nodded as if the ogre had imparted some wisdom.

"Speaking of that, let me know when you're opening your temple. I want to be there when you get the same treatment." Max looked sideways at Ironhand.

"Aye, o' course yer invited." The dwarf still didn't seem concerned about being made a Paladin, further frustrating Max, who wanted some payback.

With a sigh, he changed the subject. "Alright, how are we doing on the quest that Funky gave us?" He looked at Enoch and Spellslinger, smiling as Smitty snorted at the name Max had given the golem.

"Nearly there." Enoch replied.

The old mage next to him nodded in agreement. "We read through the outpost manual, and from what we've learned, this place was left in close to full readiness when it were abandoned. In fact, most o' what we need to do fer the quest now is because we made use o' some o' the resources before we knew better. We'll have it restored to the way we found it right quick."

"How are ye doin with learnin' the runes?" Enoch asked.

Max shrugged. "I'm... not sure? I read what I guess is a sort of primer that came with the rest of the initiate's package. It was written in common, and it taught me to read the ancient dwarven runes, the language the three scrolls were written in. After that, I apparently became an official novice, and was able to read the scrolls. But when I did, there were no notifications or anything that suggested I picked up a new rune magic skill or anything." Max suspected this was one of those things that, as someone new to the world, he lacked background knowledge that everyone else had basically from birth.

Spellslinger leaned closer. "Did the scrolls disappear after ye read em?"

"Nope. Neither did the silk ties that bound them, which have runes embroidered into them as well." All three of the elder dwarves at the table sighed. Max could almost feel them itching to get their hands on the primer and the scrolls. None of them seemed to have any advice to offer, though.

"Different magic, different rules?" Blake suggested.

Grunting in agreement, Max asked, "Still no word from Funky on an ETA for a response on your membership requests?"

"ETA?" Enoch raised an eyebrow.

"Sorry. Estimated time of arrival." Max explained the Earth term.

"I've asked him twice now, but he does no' answer." The dwarf frowned. "Mebbe if you ask, as a guild member?"

"I'll do that as soon as we're done here." Max agreed. "I'd like to ask him about the scrolls, as well." He looked around the table. "Anything else we need to discuss here before I go take care of that?"

Ironhand cleared his throat. "Is it true, what I hear'd? Did ye assassinate the Grandmaster o' the Shadow Walkers, Max?"

Max leaned back and took a deep breath, holding it for a moment before letting it out. "It's true. Someone hired them to kill me. Their attempt failed, and I've been told repeatedly that they'll just send more. That I can't stop them with bribery, or get them to disclose who hired them so I can take care of things myself." He shrugged as Ironhand nodded in agreement. "So I figured I have nothing to lose. I'm hoping that a little extreme aggression will make them reconsider. Or at least make them raise the price of the contract so high that it beggars whomever hired them."

The dwarven king shook his head. "Ye don't do things the way ye should, Max. But it seems to work fer ye!" His smile was mostly sad, as if he knew he was speaking to a dead man. "This time, though. Ye've poked the bees' nest Max. They'll send their best after ye, and likely they'll have orders to make it hurt. It'll be public, and bloody, to help mend the damage ye've done to their reputation."

Frustrated, Max growled. "Dead is dead. The moment they accepted the contract to kill me, my options were limited. Sit back and accept my fate, or take the fight to them."

"Maybe it's time to send them another message." Blake suggested. "Second verse, same as the first?"

Max had already been considering just that. He'd ordered two more orbs from Erdun, which should be ready any day now. After taking a second to confirm who was sitting at the table, and what secrets they all should be privy to, he turned to Ironhand. "We killed the first one using what amounts to a mithril grenade filled with the grey dwarf poison." He went on to describe the design, and the trigger method, then told them all what was written in the note. When he was done, he asked, "What're the odds the new boss would fall for the same trick?"

Spellslinger laughed out loud and thumped the table as Ironhand stroked his beard thoughtfully. "Me guess is that depends on what evidence they found. There would be mithril bits scattered everywhere. And they be experts at poison, so it seems likely they'd have identified what ye used. Especially if the Grandmaster survived the explosion long enough to die o' the poison."

"Maybe we send something completely different?" Dylan suggested. "Instead of a mithril orb grenade, we send an iron box grenade? Or a dagger with a hollow hilt full of poison?"

That tickled a memory in the back of Max's mind. He'd looted a pair of daggers at one point somewhere. Ones designed to hold poison. A quick search of his inventory located them, and he pulled them out to set on the table. The moment he did, Nessa leaned forward with interest. "Something like these?"

Nessa shook her head. "Those are beautiful, but they have small reservoirs for the poison. They're meant to inject small doses of lethal poison. If you're going to explode them and spray the poison in every direction, you'll need more than they can hold."

Max smiled down the table at her. "You just want them for yourself, don't you?"

"I do, yes." She actually returned his smile with a rare one of her own. "But my assessment is also accurate."

Max slid the weapons down the table toward her, and she deftly retrieved them, lifting one to make a closer inspection.

Spellslinger asked, "How long between removal from storage and the explosion?"

"One second, maybe two." Max looked a little sheepish. "The longest delay I've managed so far is three seconds, and it takes one to store the item after I cast the spell. So two seconds at the most. Probably."

The old mage nodded. "Then hide yer metal ball inside somethin' larger. Somethin' the new master won't suspect."

"Like… what?" Blake raised an eyebrow. "Wait for the next assassination attempt, and send it stuffed inside a severed assassin's head?"

"Ooh. I like that!" Smitty gave him a thumbs-up.

Ironhand shook his head. "Were I to get such a thing delivered to me, I'd not remove the head. I'd just pass it on to someone fer burial. Ye'd likely end up killin' some low level novice instead o' the master."

Max wracked his brain, trying to think of something that the new assassin boss would be tempted by, without suspicion. That train of thought led him to the possibility of not having it delivered as a message, but instead having someone sneak it into his chambers and just leave it somewhere he might notice and open it. Which got him wondering if it was even possible to sneak into his quarters, and who might be qualified to accomplish that task. Which is when lightning struck!

"Is there... a competing assassin organization?" He looked at Ironhand, who nodded.

"Aye. The Shadow Walkers be the largest, but there be others."

A smile spread across Max's face. "So what if we hire one of the others to plant a small storage box on the new master's desk? He sees it, opens it, boom!"

"Boss!" Blake's eyes widened, and he climbed up on the table in his excitement, walking toward Max. "If we're going to do that, why not pull a Capetown special?"

Max blinked at the gnome a few times, his thoughts racing. Their assignment in Capetown had been to take out an entire terror cell. They'd accomplished it by infiltrating a warehouse and planting a couple dozen explosives, then waiting until most of them were inside. After roasting them inside, and dropping the building on their heads, they'd cleaned up the few stragglers in less than a day.

Noticing the questioning looks from the dwarves, Max explained. "He means if we're going to have someone sneak inside, why not have them leave a bunch of explosive gifts all over their castle, or whatever. Kill a bunch of them all at once. Maybe use simple steel, filled with flammable oil instead of poison."

Dylan, who had been thinking during the explanation, asked, "Could that even work? I mean, after the first one or two were opened, wouldn't the others avoid opening suspicious boxes, or whatever?"

Max's momentary excitement waned. The corporal had a good point. "Still might work on just the boss." He muttered.

Smitty, who had been staring out one of the building's narrow windows, muttered mostly to himself. "Too bad we can't fit one of those guardian golems in a storage device. It could flatten the whole assassin castle all by itself."

"Way to go right to the nuclear option." Dylan chuckled, even as Max shook his head.

"We're just starting to learn about rune magic, and to establish relations with the guild. This magic is supposed to be used to help people, not take on a bunch of assassins to save my neck." The dwarves all nodded their approval.

"For now, can you put me in touch with one of the other assassin guilds? I want to at least explore the possibility of hiring them, see what might be possible."

Ironhand was nodding his head, but before he could speak, Blake butted in. "Why not just hire your girlfriend the grey dwarf. She's got stealth skills."

The look Max sent him was one he'd rarely received in the entire time they'd served together. The gnome instantly pressed his lips together and hunched his shoulders, bowing his head in acknowledgement of the line he'd crossed.

*****

When Max stepped through the portal into Stormhaven, he found Or'gral waiting for him. Standing behind his orc captain were half a dozen hulking orcs he didn't recognize. Three of them were older orcs with grey streaks through their hair, their skin showing a multitude of battle scars. The others were warriors in their prime. When Max raised an eyebrow, Or'gral wasted no time explaining.

"King Storm, may I present the leaders of the Bearclaw clan." He motioned toward the group, who all bowed their heads respectfully, if not deeply. "You may remember that one of the ten clans who occupied the city chose to abandon it when An'zalor became war chief?" He waited for Max to nod. "That was the Bearclaws. I sent word to them before I brought my people here, and they have answered the call. They are willing to consider joining us, if you have time to speak with them."

Max nodded, keeping his expression neutral. "If you vouch for them, then I will make time." He looked past Or'gral to the three veterans. "I was just about to eat something. Please, join me." He led the way into the keep, then to his private conference room, which featured a long table and chairs sized to fit him and his orc guests. After calling for Redmane to join him, he took a seat at the end of the table. When Or'gral had taken a seat at his left, leaving the chair at his right empty for Redmane to occupy, Max produced a dozen sticks of meat and handed them to Or'gral, who passed two to each of the orcs. They each took a curious sniff before smiling or nodding and taking a bite. Or'gral grabbed plates from a side table, along with mugs and a pitcher of water, and passed those around as well. By the time that was done, Redmane appeared and took his seat. Max produced more sticks for Redmane, Or'gral, and himself.

"These are delicious, King Storm." One of the older orcs, the one closest to Or'gral, complimented him.

"My favorite travel food." Max grinned. "I keep a few dozen of them on me at all times." He was about to tell them about the vendor in Darkholm, when one of the younger orcs interrupted.

"Is it true you fought in the arena trials, and won?"

Max stared at the orc for a moment, trying to decide if he'd intended to be rude. When he saw nothing but curiosity in the warrior's eyes, he nodded. "That is true. I went to see An'zalor on a diplomatic mission. Rather than honor my status as a king and a diplomat, he tossed my companions and I into a cell and forced us to fight in the arena. We were victorious in all four fights, though I lost a good friend in the final battle."

"Their second battle of the day." Or'gral growled at the young warrior. "The coward An'zalor defied the gods' rules for the sacred trials, forcing King Max and company to fight twice on the third day, and pushing the arena master to pit them against what should have been unbeatable foes." He went on to describe how the arena master had tried to force them into a fifth fight on orders from An'zalor himself, and how Max had cornered An'zalor into admitting defeat.

"Ha! I would have paid much to see this happen!" the elder orc thumped the table with one hand. "To see that honorless dog made to bow before the clans!"

"I take it you're not a fan." Max half-smirked at the orc.

"I fought alongside him when he was a green recruit, both of us under Or'gral's command. An'zalor was bigger, and stronger, than the others his age. During sparring sessions, he would purposely injure his opponents. In battle, rather than quickly kill an enemy and move on to the next, he would toy with them, kill them slowly and as painfully as possible, even while his comrades perished nearby for lack of support. He sees honor only in self-glorification." Or'gral nodded in agreement of the assessment.

"So when he took over, you left." Max skipped ahead.

"It would have been a stain on our own honor to fight for him." Another of the older orcs spoke. "We tried to convince the other clans to leave with us, but too many had grown comfortable within the city walls."

"How long ago was this? And where did you go?"

The first elder answered this time. "It has been… nearly three years. We chose a valley four days' ride from the city, and set up camp there. An'zalor sent a war party to punish what he considered disloyalty. We defeated them, but knew it was unwise to remain there to await another attack. So we moved north into the mountains between the dwarf kingdom and the sea."

"So, not far from the dworc's valley." Max speculated, picturing a map of the region in his head.

"That is correct. Our scouts discovered the dworcs as we moved, but we left them alone and continued further west."

"And do you wish to remain in the mountains?" Max asked. "I recently absorbed the dworcs and their valley into my kingdom. I could do the same for you."

All six orcs shook their heads. "We found shelter in the mountains, but they are not our home. Or'gral says you took some of An'zalor's northern lands from him as your prize. We would like to live there." The orc leaned forward and growled. "And when the time comes, we would help you take the honorless dog's head!"

Max resisted the urge to high-five his visitor. "How many of you are there?" Max asked, then was distracted for a moment when Or'gral chuckled and leaned back in his chair, folding his hands together atop his belly.

"We are just over four thousand, King Storm. Fifteen hundred warriors. The rest are farmers, crafters, merchants, and our families. Though, if necessary, all but the very youngest and oldest can fight!"

Max let out an appreciative whistle, causing Or'gral to chuckle again. Four thousand new citizens were just what the doctor ordered! Looking over at Or'gral and Redmane, Max smiled. "It looks like we're going to have to expand the Way Station wall again."

Chapter 17

Max walked into the main dining hall in search of breakfast. He was surprised to find Smitty and Blake sitting with the six Bearclaws, along with another half dozen dwarf and orc guards.

"And that's when an arrow hit King Max right in the ass!" Smitty produced an arrow from his inventory and mimed sticking it in his right butt cheek. The others chuckled at his antics, and his story. "He yanked it out right away, and we all pretended we didn't notice, but-"

"But obviously you did." Max finished for him, causing the corporal and most of the others to cringe when they saw who was speaking.

"Uh, hiya boss! We were just talking about the run through the Westreach dungeon!" Smitty offered a half-hearted wave and repentant grin.

"So I gathered." Max motioned for everyone who'd started to rise to sit back down. "What's for breakfast?" he nodded a greeting at the Bearclaws, who all bowed their heads in return.

"I think Smitty just dished up a big helping of shutchomouth." Blake elbowed the scout in the ribs with a wide grin on his face.

Max shrugged. "I'm just glad that arrow hit where it did. A few inches closer to center, it would have been a whole other experience." He waited for a second until the others caught on and started to laugh. Relieved, Smitty dug into his breakfast with gusto, shoveling scrambled eggs into his mouth.

Addressing the leader of the Bearclaws, Max asked, "Are you ready to meet up with your people today?"

The orc nodded. "They should be nearing the Brightwood battlefield any time now." During their first meeting they had informed Max that the entire clan was already on the move, heading toward the mine where Or'gral had instructed them to find him. Rather than have them march for another day or more, Max offered to take six of them through the Outpost portal to meet up with their clan, then take them all through that same portal to the temple.

When he warned that it would take some time to absorb four thousand new residents at the Way Station or the mine, he'd offered them temporary housing in Stormhaven or Deepcrag. They had respectfully declined, assuring him that the clan would be perfectly comfortable camping outside the walls until accommodations could be built.

Or'gral had already explained to them before they met Max about Stormhaven being an open kingdom, and the Bearclaws had no issue with that. The elder suspected there might be some initial friction from the youngest warriors, but promised to keep them under control.

So after breakfast Max and Or'gral escorted the orcs to the portal. Their mounts were waiting for them, having been cared for overnight by the stable boys. Max activated the portal to the Outpost, and they all stepped through.

Once out of the tunnel, they rode at a trot down to the overgrown ancient road, then headed west. It was less than an hour before they ran across the long caravan of carts, ja'kang, and orcs on foot that was the rest of the Bearclaw clan.

Their leaders called them together, having them gather around Max to be introduced. Many of them called out to Or'gral, recognizing their old war chief's commander. When they had all settled down, he called out loudly enough for all to hear, and introduced Max.

Wanting to be seen and heard by all, Max produced his dragon bone seat and stood atop it, holding up one hand in greeting. He welcomed them all, gave them a brief history of Stormhaven, assured them that as citizens they'd be free to pursue whatever profession or career they chose, and made it clear that all of them would be required to live and work peacefully alongside dwarves, goblins, and the other races. "If any of you feel you cannot accept this, speak up now. Once you take the oath, you'll be bound to it." he called out, then waited for several seconds for someone to speak up. When no one did, he added, "Again, welcome to Stormhaven!" He stepped down, and allowed Smitty to step up in his place to administer the oath. Half an hour later his population had grown by forty three hundred citizens, and they were marching at a sedate but steady pace back to the Outpost.

By nightfall the Bearclaw clan had been settled. Nearly two hundred of them had elected to remain at the mine, while the rest proceeded to the Way Station. Gro'nag found temporary accommodations inside the town for nearly a hundred of the eldest, many of whom were old friends of his, and families with several very young children. The rest quickly set up tents and huts that they had packed along with them from the mountains. Gro'nag had put them just inside the forest that bordered the farmlands outside the wall, a short hike from the Minotaur encampment. The thick canopy offered decent shelter from the elements, and the creek provided plenty of fresh water, as well as fish. Having been warned the night before, the residents of the Way Station had welcomed the new arrivals with open arms. Hunters brought in fresh game, cords of firewood had been stacked around their campsite, even the local children had helped prepare for them by clearing the area of small stones and sticks that might poke through tents or bedrolls.

Max had Redmane send people to Darkholm and Westreach to clean out several bakeries, food vendors, and a big chunk of Firebelly's stock to present to the clan as welcome gifts.

As he walked among the newly settled families, offering greetings and well wishes, he was surprised to see Elder Pickstone among them. He was sitting on a log, speaking to two orcs that looked to be roughly his age. When he saw Max, Pickstone waved him over, standing to introduce the orcs.

"King Max! These be Do'lig and "Ba'dor." Max smiled at the orcs, who bowed their heads slightly. "They be brewers!" the dworc's smile stretched from ear to ear. "We've been talkin' about expanding our honey mead production."

Immediately interested, Max pulled out his dragonbone chair and sat, motioning for them to do the same. "What are you thinking?"

Pickstone launched into an enthusiastic reply. "Y'know the minotaurs ye brought us, they been buildin' like a whirlwind! New homes been going up, old ones repaired. When they saw the state o' the brewery, they offered to build a new one, at least twice the size! It ain't built yet, but it will be soon."

Max nodded. The minotaurs had also been a big reason for the rapid growth of the Way Station, so he wasn't surprised. More than fifty of them had moved into the dworc village. As he pictured the old brewery, which he'd toured on his first visit to the village, and tried to picture a larger one, a question occurred to him.

"What about the honey? Can you even harvest enough to increase your production?"

"Ha!" Pickstone hopped up off the log and stomped around a bit, beaming and waving his arms. "Aye, o' course we can!" When he realized he was yelling, he took a deep breath and sat back down. "Ye know lady Dalia has been spendin' a good bit o' time with us since… well, you know." He waited as Max gave a sympathetic nod.

"Well, bein a druid, she went n charmed the queen bee, she did! Brought her and the whole hive from the base o' the mountain where they been since we found 'em, all the way back to the village!"

"She did what?" Max's mouth hung open, his eyes wide as he pictured Dalia walking down the dirt trail where they'd first met the dworcs, a swarm of giant bees buzzing behind her.

"Ye hear'd me! She and the big fella, Dylan, got to talkin' bout beekeepin'. He told her he knew how to build boxes fer the bees to live in. They loaded up three wagons with three great big boxes each, took two more empty ones, and headed on out to the hive. By dark, they come rollin' back to the village with them boxes filled to the brim with them big bees, with even more a-sleepin on top! Even better, the two empty wagons were piled high with honeycombs!"

Max chuckled at the elder's enthusiasm, picturing the scene in his mind.

"Anyhow, with old Cantankerous gone, she figured it'd be safe to move the hive close to the village. She set up them boxes in a copse o' trees just outside the wall. Now, instead o' spendin' two days travelin back n forth n harvestin' the honey, we can just take a lil stroll out the gate!"

"That's amazing!" Max's own enthusiasm reflected Pickstones, as well as the two orcs'. "But how does that solve your production issue? Will the bees produce enough honey to double your production?"

The dworc shook his head. "Not right away, no. But lady Dalia be sayin' that another queen or two will be born soon. She'll be takin' them and startin' another hive for each one somewhere in the valley. The minotaurs already built the boxes for 'em!"

"Wonderful!" Max chuckled, relaxing and enjoying the moment. Looking at the two orcs, he asked, "And where do you two fellows figure into this?"

The larger of the two orcs replied, "We're not just brewers, we're distillers. Elder Pickstone here mentioned some failed attempts by one of the dworcs to create honey brandy. We believe that, with a little experimentation, we can make that happen."

Max immediately leaned forward, placing his elbows on his knees and whispered. "What do you need in terms of resources?" When the surprised orc stammered a bit, he laughed. "Consider my assistance a shameless bribe. I want to buy your first few dozen bottles, to ensure I get at least a few before old Spellslinger buys up your entire supply!" Pickstone guffawed as the two orcs just looked confused. He quickly explained to them who Spellslinger was, and his legendary fondness for spirits. Eventually the orcs smiled and nodded at Max.

"If you are serious about assistance, we can compose a list of items we'll need."

"Do that! I'll get our merchants on it right away." Max didn't hesitate. "If you can manage to create honey brandy, I predict you three will quickly become some of my wealthiest citizens!" He made a show of glancing over both shoulders before whispering. "Just keep it quiet for now. That crafty old dwarf has eyes and ears everywhere!"

Max stayed for the welcome celebration, eventually retiring to the suite reserved for him at the inn-slash-municipal building. He'd tried to get Gro'nag to use it for one of the larger Bearclaw families, but the mayor wouldn't hear of it.

When the birdsong woke him just as the morning sun was rising, he shared breakfast with the town council. They gave him a brief report on the town's status, finances, and a few small issues that had cropped up. Just a few disputes between merchants, and one drunken fight between an orc and a dwarf. They assured him it was a simple disagreement over who could chop down a tree faster, and not a racial issue. They spent a little time discussing the next expansion, which was now necessary to accommodate four thousand new residents. The engineers from the mine already had a new diagram to show Max, unrolling it on the table after they cleared away the breakfast dishes. It showed another wall, encircling the existing one about five hundred feet out.

"We'll need to clear the forest farther out, and it'll eat up a bit o' the farmland here, and here." The dwarf pointed to two areas that cut off corners of existing farmer's fields. When Max opened his mouth to ask about that, the dwarf raised a hand. "We warned 'em they might have to relocate if the town expanded. But don't ye worry. The wall won't be finished till well after harvest time, and we'll make sure they have help tillin' new fields farther out fer the next plantin' season."

Max pulled up his interface map, then zoomed out until he could see the town and the land around it. "That's fine, for now. But we can't keep displacing the farmers every time the town grows." He studied the map a minute. Most of the farms were set up to the south and east of the town, with just one on the north side. "How about we set aside this land here." He pointed outside the northern section of wall on the diagram. "We can design future expansions to push northward. The town won't be a pretty wheel shape anymore, but I think that's okay, don't you?"

The engineer clearly wasn't happy about having an oblong-shaped town, but didn't argue. Instead he ran his finger along the space inside the new wall. "With this much additional space all the way around, plus the space we ain't yet filled inside the current wall, we can easily house another ten thousand, plus shops, streets, parks, and such."

Max took another look. The perimeter wall was already nearly a mile long. With a little quick and dirty math in his head , he estimated that another five hundred feet of space, all the way around, would give them at least sixty more acres of land between the walls. While that didn't sound like a lot in terms of a human city, it was sufficient space for a great deal of growth.

As Max was nodding in approval, the dwarf who ran the quarry asked, "Don't suppose ye got any more o' them big ogres ta help us quarry all the stone fer this wall? They be naturals at it!"

Max laughed aloud. "Ha! There are dozens of them. I'll tell you a little secret. You can bribe them with food. A lot of food. Pay them a fair wage in gold on top of that, teach them to use the gold to buy more food, and you could probably have your own little army of ogre masons."

An hour or so later, as Max trotted out the gate atop Pokey, he was surprised and pleased to see that a team of dwarves, orcs, and minotaurs were already staking out the location of the new wall and digging the first foundation trenches. He'd volunteered all three of his guild earth mages to help, and the engineer had accepted, but only wanted their help in securing and smoothing the stone once it was brought in from the quarry. The dwarves took well-deserved pride in their construction methods.

Upon arriving at the mine, Max took a little time to look around. They showed him the newly completed secret tunnel that let out the back of the mine just a few hundred yards from the temple. From the outside, even knowing where it was, Max couldn't see the exit door once it had been closed. He heaped praise on the crews that had done the work, and offered a bonus of ten gold to each and every one of them. When the mine foreman offered to let them just take it in raw ore, Redmane loudly cleared his throat somewhere behind Max.

"Thank you, but it's easier for us to account for the expenditures if we pay them in actual coin." Max resisted the urge to roll his eyes as he spoke. His chamberlain was right, as usual.

They took a bit of time to observe the gaggle of gnomes and dwarves that followed Glitterspindle around the temple like ducklings, furiously scribbling notes and asking questions as the insane inventor went about his business. Max was tempted to ask him about the scary-sounding invention he'd spoken to Redmane about, but opted not to interrupt whatever was going on. He noted that the temple now had a roof covering the entire structure, which had been expanded a bit to accommodate the influx of new acolytes, as Glitterspindle dubbed them, when he wasn't calling them all stupid orcs.

He smiled to himself as he activated the portal back to Stormhaven. Every one of his holdings, even the goblin city, were growing at a rapid pace. He still needed to find more citizens to occupy those spaces, but he felt a strong sense of pride in what his people had accomplished.

He'd put his trust in competent, motivated, hardworking people, who had taken the opportunity and authority he'd given them, and run with it. The results proved his trust had been well-placed.

*****

Morning brought an event he'd been looking forward to. He was sitting on his throne, his party and a multitude of interested citizens gathered in clusters, chatting as they awaited the arrival of the guest of honor.

After a brief knock on the door, and a shouted announcement that was just for show, a tiny and obviously nervous goblin named Drig was escorted into the room by two guards. Behind him walked Brilon the butcher, a serious look on his face. The goblin's eyes darted back and forth, from the guards on either side of him, to the gathered citizens, then up to the imposing figure of Max on his throne.

Max leaned forward as the now trembling goblin approached. He almost felt sorry for the little guy, as the last time he'd been in this room, he'd been on trial for theft, after nearly being executed for a crime he didn't commit.

When the guards came to an abrupt halt, the distracted Drig kept walking for a couple steps, until he found himself alone and facing the imposing king just a few paces in front of him. "Eep!" the little guy squeaked before retreating to stand by the guards.

Biting his lip, Max called out, his voice silencing everyone in the room. "Why has the goblin Drig been brought before me this day?" The goblin's eyes rolled up in his head, and Max worried he would pass out. One of the guards put a steadying hand on his shoulder.

Behind Drig, Brilon replied. "At my request, King Max. I seek your approval to enter young Drig here into an official apprenticeship!"

Max smiled down at the goblin, who hadn't yet processed his boss's words. When the gathered citizens began to clap, he blinked several times. A moment later, as if his mind finally caught up with his ears, he looked over his shoulder at the butcher. "What? Drig... be 'prentice?"

Max spoke as the butcher smiled down at Drig. "Drig, is it your wish to be apprenticed under Brilon the butcher?"

The goblin spun his head back around and looked sheepishly up at Max. Unable to speak, he simply nodded his head vigorously, his oversized ears flapping. The crowd chuckled good-naturedly.

"And do you believe you are capable of doing a proper job?"

This time the goblin found his words. Still nodding, he squeaked out, "Yes, big king!"

"Then I hereby declare you, Drig, to be an official butcher's apprentice!" Max smiled at the little goblin, whose body was still vibrating, and held out a rolled parchment tied with a bright red ribbon. The goblin hustled forward and, reaching way above his head, accepted the scroll. He bobbed his head a few times at the king, then quickly retreated and ran back to stand next to Brilon. The crowd cheered, making Drig jump again. After a moment he smiled and waved at them. Half a dozen goblins who worked as palace staff jumped up and down and cheered wildly.

"Drig, you are the first of the goblins in my kingdom to earn an apprenticeship. For your hard work and dedication, I award you five gold coins." Max gently tossed a tiny sack of gold to the goblin, who failed to catch it before it bonked him on the forehead and fell to the floor. He quickly stooped to pick it up, hugging it to his chest.

"Thank you, big king!" his smile was wide now.

"No, thank you, Drig. You have helped to prove that my faith in goblinkind was justified. You and the other members of Ugnok's tribe have made me proud." He pointed to a framed drawing mounted on the wall to his left. "And thank your little one for the wonderful letter."

Drig's eyes followed Max's pointing finger. His eyes widened when he saw the stick figure drawing his child had made for the king when Max had set him free during his trial. The little goblin processed Max's words, then nodded emphatically yet again. "Yes! I tell little one, big king! I tell!"

The smile stayed on Max's face as the butcher guided the flustered goblin back out of the throne room, clutching his scroll and bag of gold. Next to Max, Teeglin leaned in close and whispered, "That was very nice of you, King Max." Standing behind her, Redmane grunted his agreement, trying to force a smile from his own face. Despite his initial frustration with Max for bringing the goblins to Stormhaven, he'd grown quite fond of the little rascals.

As Max rose from his throne to depart, his gaze was caught by the only other display in the throne room. Set high on the wall to his right were the five swamp hydra heads. Redmane had more than lived up to his promise, having them preserved and mounted in an uneven pattern on the wall. Below each of them, an artist had painted very realistic looking long necks, each of them winding down to connect with a life-sized body. Every muscle, every scale and claw seemed so lifelike that Max had seen several people recoil when they first saw the beast on the wall.

He took a moment to *Examine* it. As he'd seen when he first killed the hydra, having its heads mounted where citizens, allies, and enemies alike might observe it provided solid boosts to his kingdom. Plus five percent to Morale, and Diplomacy, plus increased Intimidation of enemies and Inspiration of citizens who saw it. Significant enough benefits that he almost wished the ogre chief hadn't so completely crushed The One's head. Mounted atop his walls, it might have provided similar benefits. As gruesome as the practice was, at least to his Earth sensibilities, anything that provided such a benefit to his people had to be considered.

Max snorted as he pictured a time some years down the road where his throne room and keep walls were adorned with dozens of heads or other trophies, like his uncle's hunting cabin. Everywhere you looked there were mounted deer heads, boar, bear, fish, a stuffed bobcat, even a few stuffed hawks hanging on strings from the rafters.

He just hoped the hydra heads didn't start to smell at some point.

*****

The balance of Max's day was spent crafting. He had another lesson with Master Oakstone first. The smith was waiting for him at the forge they'd built for him in the palace. Max was actually early for their appointment, but

Oakstone had arrived earlier. When he saw Max, he smiled and stood, waving toward another dwarf that Max hadn't seen until he stepped further inside. The obviously much older dwarf had stark white hair and beard, with deeply wrinkled skin that looked more like stone than flesh.

"King Max! It be me honor to introduce ye to me great grandsire, Grandmaster Smith Oakstone." Max's eyes widened as he turned to face the Grandmaster, bowing his head with respect. The old dwarf did the same.

"Pleasure to meet ye, King Storm. The young lad here's told me much about ye."

"The pleasure is mine, Grandmaster Oakstone. Welcome to Stormhaven! And please, call me Max." Max felt slightly giddy. He'd never met a grandmaster, other than Regin, he supposed. They were the most honored among dwarves, possibly even above Ironhand himself. "Are you the one who used to craft the stone dragon scale armor?"

The old dwarf shook his head once, then resumed looking around the forge. "That were me boy. Gifted he were. Often worked with his eyes shut, feelin' his way through the work with his fingers." He paused for a moment and looked at Max. "It were right kind o' ye to gift them scales to me grandson, Max." He went back to examining the space around them. "If ye keep learnin' at the pace ye have been, we'll be needin' to improve this place a bit."

Max looked around. While the smithy that Oakstone had built for him wasn't fancy, it seemed more than adequate to him.

Oakstone the younger laughed. "What he means is that if he's to be workin' here, he'll be needin' a big fancy forge worthy o' his presence." He winked at Max, who was immediately confused.

"Working... here? I'm honored, Grandmaster, but confused. Why would you want to work here?"

Now it was the old dwarf's turn to look confused. His gaze went from Max to his grandson, and back. "Did ye not call fer a Grandmaster?"

Everything clicked for Max at that point, and he smiled. "Indeed I did! Though I didn't expect you to want to work at my forge. While exploring some of our territory, we discovered a partially mined mithril vein that had apparently belonged to a Grandmaster Stouthammer. One of my advisors, Enoch, recommended we invite another Grandmaster to properly mine the vein, so as not to waste any of the precious metal. He said that at your level you don't need to use a pick or any tools, you just harvest the mithril with your bare hands. I didn't believe him, until Regin showed up and grabbed a couple chunks right out of the stone."

Now the elder dwarf's focus was fully on Max. "Ye met Regin, and he pulled some mithril from the stone?!" He took a step closer to Max, tilting his head to look up and meet his eyes.

"Yes." Max produced the small lump that Regin had given him. "He pulled out a much larger piece for himself, maybe twenty times this much. Then he pulled this handful for me."

Both dwarves gasped as they *Examined* the rough ball of mithril. The Grandmaster held out a shaking hand, and Max obligingly set the metal on his weathered and calloused palm.

"It be divine grade." Oakstone the younger whispered. "Never thought I'd see this in me lifetime, Max. And a god just… handed it to ye?"

Max resisted the urge to shrug. "Well, I mean… I had just claimed the mine, and I did let him take a large amount of valuable ore for himself." He smiled at the two dwarves, who just shook their heads.

Grandmaster Oakstone looked up from the metal n frowned at him. "Ye shouldn't mock him, lad. Nothin good'll come of it."

"Tell me about it. I teased him a little bit when I was dedicating his temple the other day, and as punishment he made me his Paladin. He laughed so loud the entire city heard him." Now both dwarves were staring up at him again. "What?"

"Ye be a Paladin?" the elder asked. His eyes unfocused as he used *Identify* on Max. Nodding his head, he muttered. "Sure enough."

"And a Battleborne, in case that particular secret hasn't reached you yet."

"Ah, well… that'd explain some things." The elder looked at his grandson, who nodded in confirmation. Master Oakstone had known his status since his second day in Darkholm.

"Alright, that settles it! If the god o' craftin' has a habit o' just poppin' in wherever ye be, than I'll be stayin' here fer a bit." He looked at his grandson. "I'll not work a metal forge, though. We'll be needin' a block o' dragonstone. Got some projects to finish in me own forge, first. I'll complete those, retrieve me tools and return here in a week. Mebbe ten days. I'll take care o' the shaping, and the carving, meself. Have this hovel torn down, and more space cleared. Double this size." Master Oakstone made some notes, smiling at both his grandfather and Max.

When he was sure the Grandmaster was done speaking, Max took the opportunity to ask, "Dragonstone?"

Oakstone the younger clarified. "Aye, black shiny stone, holds enchantments better'n any other stone, except gems. Ye been to Steelbender's forge, yes?"

Max remembered the magically charged forge quite well. "Obsidian! Yes, I have seen it. His forge felt like it was filled with power."

"As does mine." The elder dwarf smirked at him. "Only mine be bigger! And three hunnert years older. It were me da's before I took over, built by his da when he were but a wee lad." He jerked his thumb toward Max's mentor. "This one'll inherit it when I'm gone back to the stone."

Oakstone the younger had a wistful expression on his face. "They say the stone o' that forge were heated by a dragon."

"Oh! Like an obsidian dragon? I met one of those. Thought he was going to eat me at first."

The dwarves went silent as Max recalled his meeting with Lysbane. When he snapped out of it, he found both dwarves glaring at him. The Grandmaster let out a loud huff. "Ye battled an obsidian dragon, and lived?"

"Oh, no. We didn't battle. He growled a lot, and threatened my party and I, but..." Max paused, not wanting to out Red by explaining the prank she and Lysbane pulled. "It turned out he was more interested in company than a light snack. He'd been asleep for what sounded like a very long time. He even spent some time cooking with us, sharing recipes. Then he opened a portal and took off to some valley filled with oversized herd animals to fill his belly."

The dwarves just continued to stare at him, and he was beginning to feel uncomfortable. As if they were angry with him for some reason he didn't understand. Another thought occurred to him. "Also, Lysbane, that's the obsidian dragon's name, was a cousin of the stone dragon that all those scales came from. I didn't learn his name, I'm afraid. That might be part of why he didn't kill us. He smelled the other dragon on me, and I told him about his cousin's death. I also agreed to try and retrieve the stone dragon's head from An'zalor's city."

The Grandmaster took a deep breath, then asked in an accusing tone, "Why didn't ye ask the stone dragon's name?"

Max opened his mouth to answer, then paused, then said, "I don't..." His voice trailed off as both dwarves burst out laughing.

"Bwahaha! I be pullin' yer chain, boy!" The Grandmaster was laughing so hard he had to wipe tears from his eyes with his sleeve. "If one o' the Eldest reared up in front o' me in a cave somewhere, I'd likely soil me britches! No chance I'd have the stones to chitchat about family trees, or swap recipes." He patted Max on the arm. "If so many o' the amazin' things ye telled me today weren't true, I'd think ye were lyin' bout the dragon."

Max, slightly relieved that the dwarves weren't sore at him for some reason, but also slightly offended by the implication that he might be lying, produced the dragon stone he'd found inside the stone dragon's ribs so long ago. "I only asked because this is called a dragon stone, and I thought this was what you meant before."

The laughter immediately died away as both dwarves *Examined* the stone before Oakstone the younger just threw up his hands and started walking away. "That's it! Can't take no more today." He stomped out of the smithy and disappeared around a corner. His grandfather, however, was already reaching a tentative hand toward the smoky grey gemstone.

"Ye know what this be, boy?" Grandmaster Oakstone's fingers gently touched the stone, causing it to wobble slightly in Max's hand. He quickly gripped it with his other hand as well, steadying it before he dropped it.

"I believe it's the heartstone of the stone dragon that was killed at the battle of Brightwood. I harvested this along with the scales, and some pieces of bone."

"Aye, that be true enough." the elder dwarf agreed. He asked with his eyes if he could hold the stone, swapping it out for the mithril he'd been holding. The dwarf cupped the melon sized gem in both hands, bobbing it up and down slightly, taking measure of its weight. After a long moment during which Max just patiently waited for him to speak, he cleared his throat.

"Ye spoke about the magic ye felt in young Steelbender's forge." Max smiled slightly at Steelbender being called young, and nodded.

"With this stone, were ya to bind it to the forge I aim to build ye, the power it would hold could be… ten times that o' his forge. Three times that o' me own!" He handed the gem back to Max and began to stomp back and forth, one hand clenched behind his back, the other stroking his snow white beard. "The enchantments ye could build! Can ye imagine?!" He turned and glared up at Max, who shook his head.

"I actually know very little about enchanting, and I'm still a novice when it comes to smithing, so I'm afraid that no, I can't imagine."

Oakstone shook his head. "Dragons be one o' the first races. As old as the world itself, or very nearly so.

Beings o' pure magic that can create worlds o' their own once they've grown strong enough." Max nodded, remembering the way Lysbane had transformed the cave around them. It hadn't been illusion, as they'd sat on the chairs, felt the heat of the cookfire, and eaten the meals they'd cooked.

"This be a dragon's heart. Not the one that pumped the blood through its physical body, but it's *true heart*, the core that controlled its magic!" The look of ecstasy on the old dwarf's face was making Max realize how important the stone might be. He knew it had value, but was just beginning to understand how much.

The chimera and the dwarf just sort of stared at each other for a bit, the dwarf awaiting a reaction, Max unsure how to react. He was saved by the huffing of Oakstone the younger as he stomped back into the smithy.

His mentor glared at him, asking, "Anything else? Ye gonna pull a diamond the size o' me head outta yer arse next?"

Despite the tension in the room, Max laughed at the mock outrage. A moment later, the Grandmaster began to laugh as well, and eventually Oakstone the younger broke down and chuckled. Feeling a bit less nervous, Max clarified. "So you're saying we could somehow bind this heart to the obsidian you use to build the forge? And it'll make the enchantments worked into weapons much stronger?"

"Stronger, aye. But more'n that. Better quality enchantments." Grandmaster Oakstone tapped his chin.

"Ye know the sharpness enchantment, yeah?" Max nodded. "Now imagine one that makes the blade so sharp it'll cut stone, metal, even the air itself. Or a flame enchantment that produces white hot flames instead o' the standard orange, or red. If I were ta bind that stone to me own forge tomorrow, then craft an inscribed mithril blade, it might be the mightiest blade crafted anywhere on the continent in thousands o' years!"

Oakstone the younger chuckled. "And if he forged the blade from that divine mithril…"

"Ha! I'd become the most legendary Grandmaster in history!" he grew quiet for a moment before adding, "Exceptin' Regin hisself, o' course." The smile returned to his face as he looked up at Max. "Right! So here be me offer. I'll mine old Stouthammer's mine fer ye, keepin' twenty percent o' the metal to use or sell as I see fit. Another ten percent I'll use ta craft items o' yer choosin' for ye. The rest be yours. We'll build ye a decent dragonstone forge, I'll pay fer the materials, o'course, and I'll work here fer a time, rather than travel back n forth to me home. Ye'll provide me a room in the keep, food, and a reasonable supply of ale." He held out a hand for Max to shake.

Max paused for a moment, one concern keeping him from immediately accepting. "When you say dragonstone, you mean the obsidian, right? Because I'm not sure I can commit to binding the stone dragon's heart to the forge." He held up a hand to keep the dwarf from responding. "It's just that Lysbane mentioned the stone dragon's mate and offspring, and returning his head to them. I don't know if they'll expect me to return the heart, as well."

Grandmaster Oakstone opened his mouth, closed it, then opened it again. "Aye, lad. Just the obsidian, as ye call it. Fer now. Do yer best to keep hold o' that heart, though. It be more valuable than ye know."

Max knew he should haggle over the mithril percentages, but he simply shook the old dwarf's hand. "In that case, we have an agreement!"

Both dwarves beamed as golden light wrapped around Max and the elder. As the elder dwarf began to depart, anxious to get started, Max asked, "What exactly is a *reasonable* amount of ale?"

Chapter 18

Max spent the next two hours with Master Oakstone, learning to better forge dwarven steel. He was learning at a rapid pace, but still didn't quite have the hang of it. Oakstone watched patiently as he heated the metal, worked it, then reheated it. Occasionally he'd provide a bit of advice here and there, but he was clearly waiting for Max to figure something out on his own.

Max didn't mind a bit. He enjoyed working at the forge. The physical exercise loosened up muscles, and he found he could let his mind drift a bit while he was working. Not too much, or he'd make a misstep. Let the metal cool too much, or hit it too hard and deform it.

By the end of the session, he finished a simple dwarven steel sword. It looked good, but he wasn't confident in its strength. An itch somewhere in the back of his mind warned him that there was a flaw deep inside. Apparently, Oakstone agreed. When Max showed him the blade, he took the hilt in hand, got up from his stool without a word, and slammed the flat of the blade on the anvil. There was loud tinging sound as the blade snapped just above the ricasso,

"Ye knew that was gonna happen, didn't ye?" Oakstone turned to regard Max, finding no surprise on his face.

"I... suspected. I felt something. Not sure how to explain it."

Oakstone nodded. "Good. Ye be learnin. Next time ye get that feelin', follow it." Before Max could ask what he meant by that, the dwarf tossed the hilt into the scrap pile and departed. Max bent and retrieved the broken blade and added that to the pile as well, before removing his leather apron and cleaning up. When everything was back in its proper place, he headed for the palace's alchemy lab. Dalia had mentioned that she and her father had made an interesting discovery, and he was curious to see what it was.

Both of them were hard at work when he stepped through the door. He arrived just in time to see a green glow briefly light up the workbench in front of them, though he couldn't see what caused it. A moment later the two of them grinned widely at each other.

"Something must have gone right." Max called out as he crossed the room. "When I saw the glow, I thought there might be an explosion."

"Ha! There has been more than one." Dalia rolled her eyes at her father as he spoke. "But not today, Max. Today, we have very nearly perfected a new formula, I be thinkin'."

Even more curious, Max stepped up next to him and peered at what was set on the bench. "Perfected what?"

The master alchemist held up a vial of liquid so bright green that it appeared to glow softly. "We've decided to call it a panacea potion." The pride in his eyes was obvious. "The first one o' these that didn't explode earned me two skill levels in Alchemy!" He beamed at Max.

"I got six!" Dalia stuck her tongue out at her father, making Max laugh.

"If I remember it right, panacea means it fixes everything?" He asked Dalia, one eyebrow raised.

"Well, not everything." She admitted with a shrug. "But it'll cure poison, negate venom, give ye a two thousand point health boost, restore two hundred points o' stamina, and remove every kind o' negative status we've tested so far. Blindness, deafness, muteness, fear, and regeneration reduction curses!"

"Wow!" Max was truly impressed. His thoughts swirled with visions of every one of his people carrying a couple of these potions. He knew they'd been experimenting with the green concentrated life crystals he and Dalia had pulled from the Westreach dungeon. "Is this all because of the crystals?"

"Aye, in part." Dalia nudged her father, indicating he should explain.

"Well, we started out usin' em to create better health potions. If ye distill em' down carefully, and mix em with common ingredients, they increase the healin' effects by a lil more than fifty percent."

Dalia interrupted him. "That be what we think the alchemists in Westreach been usin' 'em fer." Her father glared at her, and she covered her mouth with one hand.

"As I were sayin… next we mixed em with the high quality ingredients from the battleground. As expected, the increase was much greater. The best o' the lot from that batch instantly heals fer three thousand points! Plus another thousand over one minute." Max's eyes bugged out. Both dwarves chuckled before he continued. "That were impressive enough to have us wantin' to dive into that dungeon every day fer more crystals."

Dalia shook her head. "I told him it won't be the same. The tree monsters we killed that day were higher level than they'd be now. Falcon says the tree beasties be in the low twenties now, which be normal. We'd have to keep everyone out o' the dungeon fer months to let 'em level up again. Still, even a supply o' lower level crystals would be a boon."

Max was nodding along as she spoke, agreeing with her argument. But they hadn't explained the other effects. "How did you get from three thousand points to the panacea?"

Dalia's father grinned. "Troll blood!" He held up a vial of thick black liquid. "It were Dalia's idea. When we mixed just a few drops into the potion before distillin' the crystal, it actually lowered the amount o' health the end result restored. But the natural regenerative abilities, and the poison resistances o' trolls changed somethin' important in the mixture's properties."

Max started to open his mouth, but Dalia spoke first. "We've a very limited supply o' both the crystals and the troll blood." A wicked smile began to grow on her face, and Max knew what was coming. "If ye be willin'… ye could help us with part o' that."

"I thought my troll blood was too diluted." He flashed her a mock scowl.

"Aye, it is." She stuck her tongue out at him this time. "But we figure it'd still be worth experimentin' with."

Her father, clearly worried that Max might take offense to the insult, quickly added, "Even if we get a lesser version o' the panacea, their value could no' be overstated."

Max patted the dwarf on the shoulder. "No worries, I'm more than willing to help." He reached out and grabbed an empty vial from a rack near the back of the workbench. Using his sharp thumbnail, he sliced open a fingertip, then squeezed a dozen or so drops of blood into the vial before the wound healed. It took him six more punctures before he filled the vial.

Handing it over, he offered, "Maybe the properties of my other bloodlines will add something."

"Aye, mebbe." Dalia agreed. "We'll let ye know."

"What, I don't get to stay and watch?" Max stuck out his bottom lip, making his best pouty face.

"Oh! O'course ye can." Dalia replied, already distracted. "I just figger'd ye were busy with king stuff."

Max pulled over a stool and took a seat on the other side of her father. "If you got six skill points from this, I'll probably get at least ten!" He grinned at them both, and they got to work.

Three hours later, Max had actually earned a dozen skill points in alchemy. It had required that he help prepare ingredients, mix one of the potions on his own using the normal troll blood, as well as one using his own blood, after watching Dalia and her father work. Still, that was an enormous boost for a single day's work, and he was quite pleased with himself by the time they broke for supper.

As it turned out, using his blood did reduce the health benefit by about a third. However, perhaps due to his elven and human heritage, his blood added a ten percent increase to mana regeneration, which the troll blood formula did not. The cures and debuff removals appeared to remain the same, but Dalia's father wanted to do some extensive testing to make sure.

Max kept the ones he'd made with the normal troll blood, as well as two of those he'd made with his own blood. Neither were as high quality as Dalia's father had brewed, but they'd work well enough for him. Before Dalia would turn them loose, she demanded two more vials of his blood, which he gladly donated.

"We're also gonna try mixin' in some o' the guardian's blood that I gathered." Dalia explained. "Ye probably shouldn't be here fer that, though. With the magma skin ability she had..."

Max finished for her. "There might be explosions." He'd had the same concern when he'd received that ability as part of her blessing. While he was probably safe, there was no point in risking it. If they managed to make it work without explosions, he could always come back and try it himself.

As they left the lab, closing and locking the door behind them, Max asked, "What value would you place on the panacea potions?" When both dwarves gave him a blank look, he added, "I mean, value in gold. If you were to sell it."

"Ah." Dalia's father considered it for a moment as they walked toward the dining hall. "Fer a potion that'll do all that the panacea does? I'd charge fifty gold each, and could probably get more." He smiled at Max. "The ones with yer own blood, that also regenerate mana, would sell fer nearly as much. The lower health boost be offset by the mana boost."

A question occurred to Max, and he just blurted it out. "Are you going to teach the formula to others? Are there… patents here?" He was thinking that new potion formulas were probably rare, and being able to sell the formula exclusively might earn some serious gold.

Dalia nodded. "Aye, there be patents. Though in this case, as rare as the ingredients be, we'll likely keep the formula to ourselves." When Max looked confused, her father explained.

"Alchemists be a competitive bunch. If we publish a patent, Masters and Grandmasters will be buyin' the formula fer sure. They'll want to see if they might improve it. But if fifty other alchemists be tryin' to buy up all the crystals from the dungeon, or our high quality ingredients…"

Max finished for him. "Either the price for the crystals would go way up, or we'd be unable to even get them, or maybe both." He nodded in understanding. "Not worth the quick cash you'd earn from selling the patented formula." He found himself facing a similar issue to the one he'd had with Erdun and his communication rings.

"How about this. You guys make as many as you can with the materials we have. Stormhaven will purchase them from you for… let's say thirty gold each. We'll keep them to ourselves, use them to save our people during battles or quests. I'll give you my share of the crystals from the dungeon at no cost, and donate more of my blood as needed. When our current supply is gone, I'll give some folks, maybe the War Dogs, quests to run the dungeon and get us more crystals. Plus put a bounty on troll blood. I'll also ask Redmane to quietly have someone research possible other sources." He held a hand out to Dalia's father to shake.

"Aye, that be fair." The dwarf shook his hand. "I've already made a good bit o' gold from the high quality health potions alone."

"Great!" Max shook Dalia's hand as well. "Do you need any assistance from me? Should we… make an expedition out to Brightwood and plant more herbs n stuff?"

Dalia shook her head. "Already been out there to do just that twice. Planted more than two hundred seeds and cuttings from the rare growths out there. In a year, we'll have a steady supply from mature plants. I'll keep plantin' a few more each time I go out there to harvest."

Max nodded, not saying anything. She'd gone out there in part to distract herself from her grief over Picklet's death. He didn't want to turn the focus to her sorrow.

"Just tell me when you need more of my blood. Or… I have a bunch of vials of the guardian's blood if those turn out to be useful." The two dwarves simply nodded as they all turned to enter the dining hall, where most of the rest of their party were already eating.

*****

Max had just gotten to sleep that night when he was abruptly awakened by an alarm. Before he'd even managed to scramble out of his bed, the door burst open and the guards from the other room rushed in. "One of the wards has been activated!" A large orc practically shouted at him. "You must remain here until we apprehend the intruders, sire!"

Max sat back and let out an aggrieved sigh. As much as he wanted to help take down the assassins that had invaded his home, he knew there was no point in arguing. The guards had instructions from Redmane to physically restrain him if necessary. Failure to do so would involve stiff punishment. Of course, as the king, Max could always override his chamberlain's orders, but that would cause other complications that he didn't want.

Max could hear the sound of pounding boots and shouts of alarm somewhere in the palace, but not well enough to pinpoint a location. Six more guards appeared in his sitting room as the orc and his dwarf partners shut and barred his bedroom door, with two of them on the inside. They immediately put their backs to the door and began scanning the room for stealthed assassins.

Blake's voice came through party chat a couple minutes later. "At least three Shadow Walkers, boss. Two were stunned by the wards, the third managed to resist the stun, but was spotted before he was able to stealth again. Guards put a couple crossbow bolts in him, but he's still alive. All three are in custody, and we're searching for more."

Just as he was completing his report, another ward went off. "Shit. Guess there's at least one more, boss." Blake added unnecessarily.

"Seems like you pissed them off." Dylan added dryly, making Max snort. Which in turn made his guards jump, as they weren't in on the conversation.

"Sorry, getting a report in party chat." Max explained, then updated them as well. All of his guards were familiar with the spell now, as they'd begun using it while on duty. Which was one of the reasons they'd been able to subdue the first three assassins so quickly. Between the spell, and liberal distribution of the lower grade communication rings, his guards and soldiers had access to what was effectively a real time radio network. There were still a few bugs, and limitations, but they were making it work.

A third ward went off, followed immediately by a scream that echoed down the corridor outside Max's chambers. He got to his feet and began pacing, frustrated at being trapped and unable to join the hunt. His people were out there risking their lives against Shadow Walkers who were trying to get to him specifically, and it wasn't in his nature to stand by and let them.

"That was much closer." He commented to his hyper-vigilant guards. They'd already made that determination on their own, but it made him feel better to say it.

"Three more Shadow Walkers fought to the death, boss, and another is in custody. If they are working in threes, which they definitely seem to be, then we're hunting two more. They're getting better at bypassing the wards." Blake's tone was grim.

There was more shouting, and this time Max could tell it was right outside his chambers. The outer door was struck hard, a scream coming half a second later, one that ended abruptly. Max wasn't the type to pray, but he found himself most earnestly hoping his people weren't the ones screaming in pain out there.

"Talk to me, dammit!" He growled into party chat. He heard with his ears the familiar sound of Dylan shouting a taunt out in the corridor before Blake reported through party chat.

"The other two made it to your door. One just lost his head, but he took a guard with him. Two more guards down, but alive. Dylan's been poisoned, but he's still on his feet, squeezing the assassin's head like a pimple."

"Don't kill him. Lock up all the ones you've captured. We're going to have a little talk before they die." Max roared the command out loud as well as in party chat. It was faster than Blake trying to repeat it to the guards who weren't in their party.

Nessa's voice came through party chat next. "The wards are being reset, and Spellslinger just came through the portal. He and his mages are sweeping the corridors. Smitty and I are in stealth, looking for more, along with half a dozen other scouts."

Max let out a frustrated growl, which apparently also went out through party chat. Smitty answered, "Relax, boss. We got this. Don't throw an embolism or anything."

"You mean aneurysm." Blake corrected him.

"What? No I don't. Embolism! You know, when part of your brain explodes."

"That's an aneurysm, bud. If we had web access I'd pull up Webster's and-"

"FOCUS!" Max roared at them through party chat, creating an instant silence. He knew they were just trying to reduce his stress level, but if someone got hurt while they were screwing around, he'd have a hard time forgiving them.

Max endured another twenty minutes of pacing and growling to himself before Redmane called for everyone to stand down. His guards allowed him to leave his bedroom, but only as far as the sitting room, where Redmane, Spellslinger, and the corporals met up with him. Blake gave the report.

"Nine of them total. Five dead, four captured. They've been put in suppression cells. All of them were over level forty, the highest was level fifty one. He's one of the prisoners." The gnome paused to clear his throat. "We lost two guards. Eight more were injured, but are recovering."

"How did they get through the wards?" Max asked Spellslinger, trying his best to keep an even tone and not sound accusatory.

"We be investigatin'." The dwarf didn't sound any happier than Max. "So far, it seems they used the simplest method. They sent a group to set off the first one, then followed 'em through right quick. Second group set off the next one, and so on." He looked up at Dylan. "A couple o' the cowardly arses had high enough constitution to shrug off the stuns n keep goin.'"

Max held his breath for a moment, then let it out slowly. When he was feeling more composed, he offered old puckerface the best smile he could manage. "Can I assume you'll be taking steps to counteract that?"

"Aye, it be already happenin'." The old dwarf coughed once. "I'll be needin' yer permission to set some deadly wards instead o' just stuns."

Max started to shake his head. They'd discussed this before, and he had declined the killing wards, not wanting to accidentally murder a visitor. But now that the Shadow Walkers had penetrated the stun wards, and two of his guards had paid with their lives… "Go ahead. But try to limit them if you can. Like, at my doorway, my study, places where non-citizen visitors aren't likely to roam uninvited."

Spellslinger looked vaguely insulted, but simply nodded and left the room. Max should have known the old mage would have thought of that, wards were one of his specialties after all. With a sigh of resignation, he made a mental note to send a bottle of Firebelly's as an apology.

Maybe two.

*****

Max was about to head down to the dungeon level where the assassins were being held, planning to interrogate them much as he had the previous two, when he was distracted by a call from Redmane. They had visitors in the courtyard.

Turning around and walking out the front doors of the keep, he was surprised to find Archmagus Eldilon, along with the dark elf female translator that had tried to steal from him, and a gnome whom, based on her robes and staff, he assumed was also a mage.

371

"Archmagus! Welcome back to Stormhaven. Was I… expecting you?" He glanced at Redmane, who shook his head.

"You were not. My apologies if this is a bad time."

"No, of course not. Please forgive my rudeness. We're just a little out of sorts. Nine Shadow Walkers just tried to assassinate me."

The eyes of the three visitors widened, and the gnome's mouth dropped open in surprise. "Nine?" She asked. "You must have made them very angry."

Max shrugged. "After the first time they tried to kill me, I might have murdered their Grandmaster."

"Ha!" Eldilon's burst of laughter surprised his companions again. "You don't do things in half measures, do you Max?" Shaking his head, he motioned toward the dark elf and gnome. "Asliane here has been tried, her punishment administered. She has expressed a desire to accept your offer of citizenship, if you're still willing to have her."

Max shifted his gaze to the dark elf, who was staring at the ground, her shackled hands clasped tightly in front of her. "Have they… taken away your magic? I'm sorry, I don't know the proper term."

The shake of her head was barely perceptible, her voice hardly more than a whisper when she replied, "They have not. Yet."

Eldilon cleared his throat. "Though her crimes against you and the Guild merit such an action, your willingness to show mercy has… inspired me. I thought to leave that decision up to you, should you choose to accept her request. Your options are to have her mana core broken, which would prevent her from casting all but the most basic of spells, and even those would cause great pain. Or we can suppress her core for a given period. Or leave her fully capable."

He paused as he watched the expression on Max's face. "In any of those cases, we recommend you bind her with extensive and carefully composed oaths." He pulled out a scroll and handed it to Max. "We took the liberty of providing examples."

Max took the scroll and opened it, reading through a series of quite intimidating oaths. "These are… impressive." He handed the scroll to Redmane, who started reading as Max addressed the elf. "Have you seen these? And if so, are you willing to abide by them?"

"I have." She nodded, her voice holding more confidence as she straightened her back and looked at Max. "Though, if you take away my magic, several of them become unnecessary." She let out a ragged breath, her shoulders shuddering slightly. "If you allow me to serve you, I will abide by them."

Max pretended to consider for a moment as he checked with Redmane via party chat. "If we let her keep magic, will those properly bind her?"

"I'll be needin a bit more time ta read, but aye, I believe so."

"What type of mage are you? What is your specialty?" Max asked, curious. The answer wouldn't impact his decision any.

"My class is Scholar. I specialize in ancient languages, civilizations, and artifacts. As for my magic... I have learned a wide range of useful spells in the last two thousand years."

Max pulled one of the square silver coins from his inventory and flicked it to the elf. "Can you tell me what that is?"

She barely glanced at it before nodding. "Commemorative coin from the period just after Regin's ascent to Eternal status. That's his face. They were often left at temples along with a prayer."

Max nodded. "A custom I've just begun to reinstitute here." He motioned toward the coin. "You keep that. Maybe offer it up to Regin as thanks." Looking at the Archmagus, he added, "If she's willing to serve, and be bound by the oaths so that she can do no harm to me or mine, I'm inclined to let her keep her magic. For two reasons. First, I can't imagine not having access to my own magic. The thought of it makes my spine crawl. And second, she'll obviously be more useful to Stormhaven with her magic intact."

As Eldilon nodded, the elf dropped to one knee. "I thank you, King Storm. You have shown more mercy and generosity than I would ever have expected. I pledge myself to your service, regardless of the oaths." When she looked up, he motioned for her to stand.

"I accept your service, Asliane the scholar. But you're still swearing the oaths." He grinned at her, causing Eldilon and the gnome to chuckle.

Eldilon cleared his throat. "I'll remove the suppressive shackles once she's been oathbound." He then motioned toward the gnome. "On a much lighter note, Mage Lightsprocket is here in regards to your request for someone with knowledge of dungeon cores." The tiny gnome smiled and bowed at the waist.

"Honored to meet you, King Storm."

"And I you, mage Lightsprocket." Max's heartrate picked up a bit. They'd been searching for someone who could help him make proper use of the dungeon core he'd been awarded by the Westreach dungeon's final boss. "We're very happy to have you here."

Again Eldilon cleared his throat, gaining Max's attention. "In light of your recent disclosure regarding the Shadow Walkers, I have concerns about my mage's safety."

Max raised an eyebrow. "Are you saying you're unwilling to loan her to us as agreed?"

Eldilon held up his hands, patting the air in front of him. "No, no. Not at all. I'm simply asking that you agree to keep her safe. From assassins, at least."

Max nodded. He couldn't blame the Archmagus for looking out for his people. "I would do that, regardless." He smiled at the gnome. "The assassins so far have been pretty focused on my head alone. As long as you don't get in their way, I doubt you'll be in any danger. But just in case, we'll put you in chambers far away from mine, and I'll have a couple guards assigned to you at all times." He looked at the dark elf next to her. "In fact... Asliane, do you have stealth abilities?"

"I *am* a dark elf, sire." Her lips twitched, threatening to reveal a smile.

"Wonderful! Then your first assignment will be to accompany Lightsprocket here as she goes about her day, keeping watch for stealthy stabby types. If any of the wards go off, you're to secure her in the nearest lockable room." The elf nodded her agreement, and the gnome smiled. Max looked at Eldilon. "Will that ease your concerns."

The Archmagus chuckled. "I am a battlemage of some skill, and I myself might hesitate to take on Asliane in single combat. Her protection is more than adequate."

"In that case, please come inside, all of you. We can have breakfast in my study and discuss a little business." He motioned toward the doors, then waited while the Archmagus moved to walk beside him.

Five minutes later they were all comfortably seated on the sofas and chairs in his study. Redmane had ordered food for all of them, and Max did his best to make them comfortable. Almost as soon as he was seated, Eldilon asked, "I must admit to being curious, Max. Though I conquered my share of dungeons as a young mage, I've never sought out or actually seen a dungeon core. Might I take a look at it?"

"Of course." Max produced the core from his inventory, setting it gently on the table between them. Everyone else in the room, including Redmane who'd already seen it once, leaned toward it to get a closer look. He quickly relayed the highlights of their discovery of the secret compartment in the dungeon, and their eventual award of the core after the final boss fight. Then he described the scene the boss had shared with him of the half-elf child's birth, its mother's death, and its conversion into the core.

"Fascinating!" The Archmagus beamed at him. "I've never heard of such a thing."

Lightsprocket nodded briefly. "In general, dungeon cores form when high concentrations of mana are compressed over a long period of time. Then the gem is awakened by some event, usually catastrophic. A large number of deaths in its immediate vicinity, for example. There are legends of sentient beings being reincarnated as dungeon cores, though they are rare, and unconfirmed. But never have I heard of anything like this. A living infant being converted directly into a core inside an active dungeon by its core's avatar!" She practically hopped in her seat. "I cannot *wait* to study it!"

Max smiled at her. A quick knock on the door was followed by three carts worth of breakfast being wheeled in by smiling goblins. He waited until everyone was served some food and the goblins had departed before responding. "You are, of course, welcome to study it. But please do so quickly. We're anxious to plant... to... activate? To use the core to create a dungeon for our people to train in."

"Oh! Certainly, King Storm. Most of my studies would occur after the core is in place. I'll want to interview it, study the formation and growth of its dungeon." She paused for a moment. "I'd also like to visit the Westreach dungeon and attempt to interview its core regarding this one's creation. If that is something that can be duplicated..." She pressed her lips together and shot a guilty glance at the Archmagus.

Laughing, Max finished for her. "Then the Mages' Guild could corner the market on newly created dungeon cores?"

Eldilon sighed, shaking his head. "Yes, that would be our hope, now that we've heard the core's origins. I suppose this means we'll owe you yet another favor, Max?"

Redmane snorted and replied before Max even opened his mouth. "Aye, quite a large one, methinks."

Chapter 19

The following morning, right after breakfast, Max gathered his party in his study, along with Redmane, Asliane, and Lightsprocket.

"So tell us, what do we need to do in order to create a dungeon, lady mage?" He asked the gnome, who was sitting between Blake and Dalia on a sofa.

"Well, the first thing to consider is where you wish to place it." She smiled up at him. "Ideally, you'd place it in an area of high mana concentration. The more mana it has access to, the faster it will grow, and the more powerful it may become." She waited for Max to nod, which he did, along with everyone else. That, at least, was easy enough to understand.

"Next, you'll want it to have access to a variety of… samples." She looked slightly uncomfortable, her hands fidgeting in her lap.

"You mean, creatures to use as dungeon monsters. The way the Westreach dungeon used wolves and bears and such."

"That is correct. Though, creatures implies only local wildlife. A new dungeon doesn't have to be limited to such samples." She looked even less comfortable now.

"Like orcs." Smitty observed. "At some point orcs must have wandered into Westreach dungeon and died, allowing the dungeon to copy them."

The gnome mage nodded, smiling. "Not that I'm suggesting you feed sentient beings to your new dungeon, mind you. I want to make that very clear."

"As long as it's not friggin giant spiders." Smitty shuddered.

Max, seeing an easy opportunity to mess with his corporal, shook his head. "I don't know. I mean, having a constant, renewable source of spidorc or rock spider legs sounds like a good idea to me."

To his disappointment, Smitty unexpectedly agreed. "Good point, boss. Hadn't considered the dungeon as a source of tasty treats. We could add spidorc meat to the menu at Eats N Treats."

Lightsprocket straightened her posture for a moment, clearly struck by Smitty's words. "That's a very good point. You have, as far as I know, a unique opportunity here!" She began to rub her hands together. "You can basically design your dungeon. Feed it samples that you consider most desirable. Some, like spidorcs, for what you might harvest from them. Others that might help your people train up a particular attribute. Like... fire elementals to help everyone increase their resistances to that particular element." She looked confused as Max shuddered, and everyone else began to shake their heads.

"Okay, not fire, then. But you get the idea."

Right away, Dalia spoke up. "We need to feed it some o' them tree creatures, Max!" Max was already nodding his head, having thought the same thing. A continuing supply of the crystals needed to create the panacea potions would be of great benefit.

Nessa's contribution quieted the room. "We could feed it the Shadow Walkers. To help train our people to better detect and defeat stealthed enemies." When everyone just stared at her, she shrugged. "What? You must kill them anyway, yes? Unless you wish to keep them in captivity for the rest of their lives, which might be a thousand years or more. Why not benefit from their deaths?"

"She's got a point, boss." Blake observed. "Though I'm not thrilled about fighting assassins over and over in the dungeon, it does seem to be a part of our new reality until we deal with the Shadow Walkers for good."

"There are other potentially useful opportunities, as well. Dungeons harvest surrounding resources as they grow. In part for raw material used in creating their structures and rewards. If they come across gold as they hollow out their structure, for example, then they can duplicate that gold as a reward."

Redmane's eyes bugged out for a moment. "So yer sayin if we were ta feed the wee dungeon some diamonds, or mithril, as it grows, it'd offer them back as loot?"

"Precisely!" Lightsprocket beamed at him. "There is no guarantee, of course. But the likelihood is high. There have been cases where dungeons formed in areas distinctly lacking in valuable natural resources, other than mana, of course. But after consuming things like gold coins and useful potions held by adventurers who perished inside them, they reproduced those coins and potions as loot. Dungeons observe those who enter them, learning as they grow, and some learn faster than others. Some reproduce epic arms and armor that they absorb from their kills. I have even read very old accounts of one that learned to reproduce dimensional storage items." She tapped her chin for a moment. "This is another area in which I hope you have a unique opportunity. If this core retains the potential intelligence of the infant that formed it, and has the ability to learn as that infant might have..."

There was a long silence as everyone considered her words. Eventually Dylan asked, "Are you saying we might be able to communicate with the dungeon? To educate it?"

"Communicate, almost certainly. I'm told you communicated with the Westreach dungeon boss, did you not?"

Max nodded. "Mostly after we killed him. Before that it was all shouted threats. But after he died, his... I guess you could call it his ghost? His ghost spoke to us, and showed me the vision of the baby's birth and conversion into a core. He also expressed a desire that we tell tales about him, which I guess means he has knowledge of the outside world. And he stated that he hoped to have a rematch."

The gnome's expression was pleased. "Likely that dungeon core absorbed an orc with an exceptionally strong personality or will, and used it to learn. In that case, the dungeon has had hundreds, if not a thousand or more years to develop. This core, if my guess is correct, has the potential to learn much faster. Just as a newborn humanoid learns quickly over its first ten or twenty years of life."

"Ten or twenty years?" Dylan sounded disappointed. "It'll take that long for it to grow?"

Lightsprocket laughed. "Dungeons don't just spring from the earth fully formed. They need to grow just like everything else, and continue to grow as long as they exist." She scanned the party's faces, seeing more disappointed looks. "To be clear, it will take many years to reach the size and levels of the Westreach dungeon, for example. Older dungeons have been reported to have twenty or more levels, each one so large that it might take days to complete. There is a dungeon near one of the elven cities that regularly takes experienced parties a month to clear."

She laughed when Dylan's mouth dropped open. "That is not to say this one won't be useful in the beginning. At first it may be just a single level, or even just a few chambers. Not much of a challenge to any but the lowest level individuals. But I'm sure you have some of those here, yes?" When Max nodded, thinking of Teeglin and the goblins specifically, she added, "And it may begin producing useful items as loot almost immediately, if on a small scale. Again, the more mana it has access to, and the more materials, the faster it will grow."

Max, slightly disappointed by her description of its likely initial stages, was still excited about the possibilities. Feeding his new dungeon things like mithril, even epic level weapons that could be reproduced, had his mind whirling. His pulse quickened even more at her next statement.

"There is another possibility that I have been speculating about since you told me of the vision you received." When she saw that she had Max's full attention, as well as that of the rest of the room, she grinned widely. "We do not know how long the infant core resided within the Westreach dungeon. It is possible that it has been able to observe years, even centuries of the dungeon's activities. Or even that the... let's call him the parent core... has been instructing your infant core the entire time."

Now Max had even more questions than he'd had when the meeting started. While he was trying to organize his thoughts, Dylan asked a question that snagged his attention. "Mage Lightsprocket... when a dungeon creates loot, we can remove it and use it, or sell it, outside the dungeon. And according to King Farstrider, their dungeon has erupted in the past, with the creatures from inside emerging to attack the city. So clearly dungeon creatures can exist out in the world." He paused, and she nodded. "What I'm wondering is, if we fed the dungeon a petramander like Princess, my giant lizard mount, could we tame the ones it creates and turn them into mounts for my fellow ogres?" He held up the figurine he used to summon Princess. "Store them in figurines like this, and bring them out?"

The gnome tilted her head slightly, considering. "I am not sure that's ever been tried." she speculated. "Certainly dungeon creatures have been captured in summoning stones before. Summoners then release them to attack enemies at some later date, or even in other levels of the dungeon. And those with mind control abilities have dominated dungeon denizens and compelled them to fight alongside them. I have even heard of necromancers building up forces of reanimated dungeon beasts to fight alongside them as they cleared a dungeon. But I can't recall anyone having attempted to bond with dungeon monsters and use them as mounts, or long term companions. It would be an interesting experiment!"

She clapped her hands together and hopped up on her feet atop the sofa. "Most interesting indeed! You must let me accompany you when you attempt this. I could write an entire study…" Her voice faded away as she realized she was rambling. Clearing her throat as she sat back down, she concluded, "Yes, this core presents many exciting possibilities."

Smiling at the gnome's infectious excitement, Max got back down to more immediate and practical questions. "Alright, so maybe we place the dungeon near Glitterspindle's temple? We know there's a mana spring there. As well as a mine filled with silver, gold, and other valuable resources nearby."

Blake shook his head. "But if An'zalor managed to retake that territory, you'd be giving him a dungeon along with it."

Dalia put in her two cents next. "Ye remember our talk about mana springs after ye took ownership o' the temple? I told ye that most dwarven cities be built over mana springs, or at least areas o' high mana concentration."

She stared at Max as he nodded. Then she stared some more. Eventually the light bulb went off in his head.

"This was a dwarven city!" He looked down at the ground, as if peering through the stone to find a mana spring.

Lightsprocket giggled. "Yes. The mana concentration here is higher than normal. Not as high as it is at the Mages' Guild headquarters, but significantly more dense than normal."

Max frowned. As did Blake. "I hadn't noticed that."

The gnome looked a little sheepish. "Uhm... no offense, King Max, but you're still a low level magic user. As your skill and sensitivity to mana grows, you'll be able to sense subtle differences in the mana density around you. At very high levels, like the Archmagus or Asliane here, you might actually begin to feel uncomfortable in low density areas. I've heard the sensation described as if the air is slightly too thin to breathe properly."

The entire group turned their gazes to the dark elf, who nodded. "At higher levels, we cast much more powerful spells that require significant mana resources. In areas of low mana density, more of the mana required has to come from our own cores. At the same time, there may not be enough ambient mana for our natural regeneration rates to be maintained. It is... an uncomfortable feeling." She produced an item from her inventory and held it up. "If I know I'm venturing into a low mana zone, I carry several mana storage items." Max and the others *Examined* the item she held.

Mana Crystal
Item Quality: Epic
Storage capacity: 120,000/120,000mp

Blake let out a whistle of appreciation. "I could cast a lot of spells with a hundred and twenty thousand mana.

She favored him with a slightly condescending smile. "While I, were I in combat for example, would burn through the mana in this crystal in half a minute."

Blake nodded. While attending the academy he'd seen demonstrations from high level mages. The spells they could cast were this world's equivalent of weapons of mass destruction. He'd seen one mage call down a meteor storm that covered the area of a football stadium. Another, a druid, had caused an entire forest to spring up in a matter of minutes, complete with trees that looked to be decades old. The Archmagus had used a wand to fire a beam of white light that burned through a ten foot thick slab of stone during his opening day welcome speech.

"Any chance we could feed the dungeon one of those crystals?" He joked with the dark elf. To his surprise, she nodded.

"I have a much smaller one I might be willing to contribute, in return for the right to harvest three more from the dungeon in return."

"Deal!" Blake shouted, pumping a fist in the air, before remembering himself and turning to Max. "Uh, I mean, I recommend you accept the lady's offer, boss."

Laughing at the outburst, Max did just that. "After careful consideration, and on the recommendation of my excitable corporal, I accept your generous offer, Asliane." Even Nessa and the reserved dark elf chuckled at that.

"So we could place the dungeon somewhere here in the city." Dylan mused. "But then if for some reason the dungeon spews monsters, they would already be inside the walls. Then again, if we put it outside the walls, that'll make it harder to protect, and control access."

"That's right." Smitty agreed. "If we design this dungeon so that the loot is super valuable, everyone will be wanting to run it. We could charge big moolah for access!"

"That is the case for many of the larger, more profitable dungeons. And those that are higher level, as well. High level adventurers find it difficult to earn sufficient experience to continue leveling. A dungeon controlled by my birth city, with monsters above level one hundred average, costs each adventurer two hundred gold to enter. The loot they bring out is mainly crafting ingredients – herbs, hides, bones, and such. Often worth less than the entry fee they paid. But the experience they gain is worth much more to them."

Max thought it over. "Obviously it'd be a long time before our dungeon reached those levels..."

"Probably a thousand years, at least." Lightsprocket interrupted. "Unless of course you let it grow without clearing it for a few years."

Max continued his line of thought. "But if the loot is valuable enough, like the dungeon occasionally drops a few ounces of mithril, we could charge something like ten gold per ticket. With one group per day running through, that would pay a bunch of the city's guard salaries."

"That would depend on a few factors." The gnome corrected him. "First, if your core creates an instanced dungeon, more than one group may be able to enter at the same time. On the other hand, if the dungeon is not instanced, and its regeneration rate is low, it may take anywhere from several hours to several weeks for it to reset and allow entry to the next group."

"That totally makes sense." Smitty nodded at her, and she held up a finger.

"If an adventurer, or a whole party, perishes inside the dungeon, it will obviously regenerate faster. That rate increases further if those adventurers are carrying a large quantity of resources." She turned to the dark elf. "Your mana crystal there would make a tasty snack for all but the largest dungeons. Also if, as the group battles through the dungeon, they expend large quantities of mana in the form of cast spells, the dungeon absorbs that mana and regenerates more quickly. If the adventurers did not kill many monsters before perishing, and little regeneration is necessary, it may either store the resources it garners from them, or put the energy toward growth."

"Boss, I gotta say, this is friggin *amazing!*" Dylan gushed. "Getting to help design and create a custom dungeon? I mean, come on!" His smile was wide as he reached out to Smitty for a fist bump, which the scout happily obliged. "I can't wait to be able to run it!"

"I agree completely!" Lightsprocket was back on her feet again. "I am most fortunate to be here to assist in this endeavor. The opportunity to study and learn from this infant core is once in a lifetime."

"I have an idea." Max got everyone's attention. "Deep below the keep, partway down to… the thing that's down there, is the chamber where we met the tuath."

Lightsprocket gasped. "You've met an Eldest?!"

"We have. Long story." Max didn't want to get sidetracked, or discuss the Heart chamber, so he moved on. "We already have fortifications below that, and could have the dwarves install a heavy door or similar fortification above. That way we have control over entry, and a way to contain any monster outbreaks."

Redmane was already shaking his head. "Find a different location, sire." In party chat he warned, "That be too close to the Heart Chamber. And ye don't need every adventurer wantin' access to the dungeon creepin' through the bowels o' the palace. Also, we'll need to be providin' easy access to healin' fer those who come out wounded."

"Ah, good point." Max replied aloud, seeing the curious look the mage was giving them. "Somewhere outside the city then. A place we can defend easily."

"Or inside the city, but easily blockaded." Redmane countered.

"Space is limited inside the city." Max reasoned aloud. "But we have three talented earth mages who could quickly build a new wall, an extension outside of our existing wall, inside which we could place the dungeon portal, as well as a guard barracks, and healing station, and I suppose a small inn and tavern, like Westreach has. Adventurers we're not willing to let inside the city could wait their turn in there."

Blake added, "Maybe also a crown-sponsored merchant to purchase the loot and sell supplies, same as Farstrider does. No point in passing up the chance to make money off of tired and overburdened dungeon runners. Or those who are both excited and unprepared, who need supplies before going in."

Dalia agreed with a wicked smile. "It'd be a good place to sell overpriced potions."

"Heh. That sounds about right." Max thumped the table. "Alright, first step, I'll pick a spot outside the wall, and ask Mage Lightsprocket and Asliane to confirm the mana density there. Blake, round up your earth mage buddies and bring them here in the morning. In the meantime, Master Redmane, Dylan, Dalia, design us an outpost for them to build. And ask the engineers to get to work on a gate strong enough to keep out hostile adventurers or invaders, and keep in rampaging dungeon monsters."

He paused, thinking. "Let's do this right. I'm as excited about creating a dungeon as the rest of you, but we don't need to rush things."

As the others hopped up to pursue their assignments, he asked Redmane to remain behind. "I have a few things I'd like you to consider." he began as the dwarf retook his seat. "First, what do you think of letting Teeglin, and maybe some of the other kids, as well as the low level goblins, run through the baby dungeon?"

"Aye, that be a good idea, Max. She's gained several levels, along with all o' the dworc children, from being there when the village was defended. Enough so that she'd likely survive anything a new dungeon might throw at her."

"Great, let's think about how best to make that happen. I promised to help make her stronger, and this might be an excellent way to start. As well as a way for her and the others to earn some money from loot." Max was feeling better about that idea. "Also, I plan to place the dungeon outpost up against the cavern wall, literally up against our existing walls. So our defenders can move from our own wall to that one and shoot down at any monsters that escape. But I think it's also a good idea to have a dwarf-made secret door or tunnel that leads from the city to the outpost, just in case."

"Aye, we can manage that." Redmane got to his feet. "There be several vacant buildings near the wall, still. Once ye've placed the dungeon portal, I'll get me clan started workin'." He got halfway to the door before he stopped and turned back. "Ye understand why I said the Tuath's chamber be a bad choice?"

Max nodded. "I do. Both reasons. Thanks for pointing them out. As always, I'm glad you're here to shoot down my stupid ideas." The dwarf snorted, gave a half-wave, and departed.

*****

Though Max hadn't been to the area outside Stormhaven's wall since the day before the battle for the city, he'd spent most of the day out there, moving back and forth and shooting grey dwarves off the top of the wall. Or fighting a running battle with the groups they sent after him.

Now he stood near a set of boulders he'd taken shelter behind that day, thinking back over the battle. Next to him stood Lightsprocket, Asliane, Dylan, and Redmane, all of them patiently watching him. When he realized this, he coughed. "Sorry guys, just remembering the fighting I did out here. I was thinking… it was easy for me to sit this far out and pick off the greys with my bow. They didn't have any way to hit me back. Their crossbows didn't reach, and there were no bigger weapons that might have helped. We should address that."

"Ballistae atop the walls." Dylan agreed. "Maybe some magical mines? Are those a thing?"

"Magical mines?" Asliane asked.

393

"Oh, sorry. A term from… our homeland." Dylan clarified. "Explosive charges buried under the ground, set off when someone steps on them. Like… traps."

"They would need to be remote activated." Max muttered mostly to himself. "So the hunters and mushroom farmers don't accidentally set one off."

"That is certainly possible." Asliane confirmed.

"A project for another day." Max turned and began walking to his left, toward the spot where the wall merged with the cavern stone. "I was thinking over there. We could build an extension from the existing wall, have it curve around in a similar arc, and attach the other end to the cavern wall."

"So like a bubble pushing out from the current wall." Dylan nodded. "Good. Same height n everything?"

"Same everything. With a smaller gate, though. No point in having a massive opening. Maybe just wide enough for a supply cart to fit through. If we have to, we can always use a crane system to lift supplies up inside the city, pass them over the wall, and lower them into the outpost the same way."

Dylan smirked at him. "Or just toss a storage ring over. You're still thinkin' like you're at home, boss."

Max resisted the urge to facepalm. "Right. Let's make the door just wide enough for Princess to walk through, then." He grinned at Dylan. "Smaller doors set in thick stone are harder to break open."

When they arrived at his chosen spot, the gnome and the dark elf confirmed that the higher density mana from the spring below the city extended that far.

"Then this is the spot." Max officially declared. "As soon as the outpost is constructed and secure, we'll place the core and see what happens!" He looked around at the faint smiles and nods he got, and cursed to himself. "I should have made a bigger deal of this. Brought a whole crowd out here and announced that we'll be placing a dungeon here."

"Ha!" Redmane patted him on the back. "Ye can do that once the construction be done. We'll invite every citizen who wants to attend, some dignitaries like King Ironhand and the clan elders, the Archmagus, important merchants, mebbe even representatives from the Adventurer's Guild. We'll make a real celebration out of it."

"People who will spread the word that Stormhaven has a dungeon. And who might spend some money while they're here?" Max grinned at his chamberlain.

"Now yer gettin' it." Redmane grinned back up at him.

*****

It was three days before the new extension and outpost were fully constructed. Plenty of time for Redmane and the other councilors to arrange a full-blown state function in celebration of the new dungeon. The design had been drawn out, then modified half a dozen times as various dwarves gave their input. The earth mages had been brought in to construct the walls and buildings for the sake of speed, but the dwarven engineers made it clear they'd be making improvements soon after.

Lightsprocket had spent the time inspecting the core itself, asking Max more detailed questions about his vision and what the dungeon boss had told him. She made a quick trip back to the Mages' Guild to consult their archives, and returned the evening before along with the Archmagus and a few other mages who wished to observe.

Ironhand and Farstrider both accepted invitations, as did all the dwarven clan elders, including Stonebinder, which surprised Max. Apparently the birth of a new dungeon was interesting enough even for the grouchy old dwarf.

All three of the city's operating inns were packed with guests the night before the big day. Merchants, visiting dignitaries and their guards, curious mages. They booked all the available rooms and crowded the common room, celebrating well into the night. Those who couldn't get rooms, and weren't hosted in the palace, were allowed to camp in vacant buildings for the night.

In the morning the portal had been operating nonstop. Citizens from all of Stormhaven's properties came streaming in to witness the big event. A dozen tents were set up outside the new wall, some with bars set up inside them, others with camp kitchens preparing food.

Dozens of long tables with benches sat between them, ready for the feast to begin once the dungeon was born.

Max gave permission, for citizens who couldn't squeeze into the outpost to watch the dungeon creation, to climb atop the walls and observe from above alongside the guards.

Earlier that morning he'd given Ironhand, the elders, and Farstrider a private tour of the outpost. The dwarves had gone all out, and he was quite proud of their work. To begin with, the wall was the same height as the city walls, its outer surface completely blemish-free. No finger or toe holds for climbing. The main gate was ten feet tall, eight feet wide, a foot thick, and crafted of dwarven steel. Plenty secure as it was, the engineers had promised an even stronger one was forthcoming. Inside the wall was a wide open space large enough to park a dozen wagons. To the left of the gate as they entered was a two-story barracks that could comfortably sleep a hundred guards. It also featured a full mess hall and kitchen, restrooms, an armory, and common spaces where guards could entertain themselves. Attached to one end of the barracks was the healing station, this one only a single story. It contained two dozen beds for tending the wounded.

Directly across from those structures was a two-story inn and tavern. At the moment it was just a shell, with none of the interior framing done, but when it was completed it would feature twenty rooms as well as the tavern. Next to it was a squat single story structure meant to hold the general goods shop.

What most impressed Max, and what he didn't include in the tour, was that the dwarves and the mages had created lower levels to each of the structures, all of which had access to small tunnels that connected to a shelter and larger tunnel under the courtyard. Which in turn extended under the city wall to a building inside the city that Redmane had selected. The dwarven-crafted doors in each building were so well hidden that Max couldn't see them even knowing where they were. Redmane's clan were still working on the tunnels, installing mechanisms that would allow occupants to collapse the ceilings behind them as they retreated, in the event the walls were breached.

The thoughtful dwarves had even dug into the cliff face at the spot Max had chosen. Now there was a wide ramp leading down from the courtyard to a wide flat space that had been hollowed out as a staging area. Beyond that was a small guard house, and another gate. This one was much smaller, also crafted of dwarven steel. Past the gate was a small alcove, cut about six feet deep and eight feet wide, where Max could place the core. That way the guards could close the smaller gate right outside the entry portal if necessary. To keep people out, or monsters in.

By the time Max was ready to begin, thousands of his citizens were gathered around him. Morale was high, the mood festive. The folk of Stormhaven were proud of their king, who had already accomplished wondrous things, and was about to achieve another. Everywhere he looked Max saw smiling faces and laughter. He smiled himself as his ears picked up dozens of voices scattered through the crowd, loudly boasting how they'd be clearing the dungeon, slaying monsters single-handedly, or bringing out enough loot to retire on.

Hopping up on a cart that had been placed there for the ceremony, he waited for everyone to notice him and quiet down. When he had most everyone's attention, he raised his hands and shouted loudly enough for all to hear.

"Welcome, friends and fellow citizens! Allies, and honored guests! Seeing so many faces here today brings me great pleasure!" There was a muted round of applause, and he waited for it to end. Lowering his arms, he allowed his shoulders to slump slightly. "I'm sad to say, due to unforeseen circumstances, we won't actually be creating the dungeon today!" He slumped further as the crowd gasped and murmured in surprise. When the whispers died down a bit and people looked to him for an explanation, he took a deep breath.

"Just kidding! Of course we're creating the dungeon today!" He threw out his arms as he pulled the core from his inventory, the orb appearing in his right hand. He thrust it high into the air as the crowd first groaned, then cheered. "And when we're done, there's plenty of food and drink for everyone outside!" The cheering was much louder now. Everyone enjoyed a good feast. Especially the ogres, who roared so loudly several nearby citizens flinched in fear.

Bringing the core back down and holding it with both hands in front of his chest, he shook his head, still slightly amazed. "I've uh... never created a dungeon before. So forgive me if I'm a little nervous." The crowd laughed along with him. "But if this goes as expected, you will all witness something today that you can tell your great grandchildren about! Today is the day that Stormhaven created a dungeon!"

As he turned and hopped off the cart, the roar from the crowd behind him, and the equal number of celebrants atop the wall, echoed through the outpost like thunder. Feet began to stomp. Just a few at first, steel-shod dwarven boots. Then more joined in, until the thousands of stomping feet vibrated the ground beneath them. The dwarves in the crowd began a chant, a slow and steady melody carried by deep voices. The words were in dwarvish, but many of those who didn't understand simply hummed along, adding their voices. Deep drumbeats sounded from atop the walls as well as somewhere near the back of the crowd. Max felt the rhythm down to his soul as he carried the core down the ramp and into the alcove.

After placing it in a stone bowl atop a pedestal the dwarves had crafted for it, Max placed his right hand atop the orb. The surface was cool to the touch, and Max felt a slight tingle as text appeared in his vision.

You have placed a dungeon core in a
prime location above a mana spring.
Would you like to activate the core? Yes/No

Chapter 20

Despite Max's concerns, and the litany of questions he'd asked Lightsprocket, it turned out that activating the core was quite simple. Beyond making sure they picked the right location, most of her expertise and advice were centered around the care and feeding of the core once it was activated.

Still just a bit trepidatious despite the gnome's reassurances, Max selected *Yes*.

Within a few seconds of making that choice, the ground beneath his feet began to tremble. Behind him, the crowd gasped, grabbing hold of each other in an attempt to steady themselves as the trembling grew into violent tremors. Max had experienced his share of earthquakes as he served in various locales around the world, and if he had to guess, this one was about a 6.5 on the Richter scale. He reached out and braced himself against one wall of the portal alcove to keep from falling.

The back wall of the alcove began to glow a moment before the stone began to push itself outward toward him. It formed an arch about twelve feet tall and maybe half as wide. As Max watched, the stone face of the arch engraved itself, starting at the lower left and working up and over the top, then back down on the right side. It started with a scrollwork of leafy vines that swirled in a seeming random pattern. Then images formed in between the vines. Depictions of beasts and trees, for the most part.

Images that Max recognized.

"These are the same creatures from the book the dungeon boss gave me." He instantly had a suspicion of what the book was, and what the images meant.

The ground shook more violently, knocking most of the crowd off their feet, slamming Max's shoulder against the wall he was using for support. One of the onlookers, a female orc, fell screaming from atop the wall, then screamed again as she broke both legs and an arm when she landed atop the inn. Which was fortunate for her. Had she fallen all the way to the ground, the impact might have been fatal.

Another violent tremblor knocked Max to his butt, some of the crowd crying out in fear now. In the bar tents outside the wall, the neatly and carefully stacked kegs waiting to be tapped shook loose and began to roll away, nearly killing a dwarf bartender who barely managed to dive out of the way. In the kitchen tent, meat on spits fell from brackets into the flame, and boiling hot stew sloshed out of large cauldrons, burning two unfortunate goblins.

As Max got back to his feet, the tremors began to lessen a bit, fading into milder but near constant shaking that lasted another two minutes or so. The crowd got back to their feet, and Dalia ran into the inn, headed for the roof to heal the injured orc.

When the shaking finally came to a halt, a swirling, oval-shaped portal appeared just a few inches in front of the newly formed archway. Unlike the one he'd seen in Westreach, this one was mostly black, with streaks of neon purple and forest green swirling through it. Max was reaching out to touch it when another notification appeared.

Congratulations!
You have successfully activated a Level 1
Dungeon Core!
Current dungeon formation progress: 36%
Time to completion: 6.5 hours

Max pulled back his hand, unsure what would happen if he shoved it into a portal to an incomplete dungeon. Turning back to the crowd, he walked up the ramp and addressed them.

"Well, that was interesting!" He flashed them a smile, careful not to show his fangs. The flustered crowd was slow to respond, but after a moment there was laughter along with expressions of relief. "Is everyone alright? Anyone else injured?" He glanced up at the roof in time to see the orc getting to her feet. She and Dalia both returned a wave from Max. When no one else spoke up, he grabbed hold of the cart, which had been overturned in the quaking, and set it upright. Hopping up so that everyone could see him, he continued.

"So it looks like the core was successfully activated!" He pumped a fist into the air amid some ragged cheering. "The notification I got says that it's still forming down there, and will take another six hours or so to be complete." He waited for the murmurs of disappointment to die down. "Those of you who wish to stay and wait are welcome to do so. There's plenty of food and drink, so let's celebrate!"

This time the cheers were much louder as the crowd began to break up. Those on the walls headed for the nearest stairs. Those on the ground broke into two groups. The largest by far made their way out the gate toward the tents, while a smaller group drifted closer to the alcove, peering down the ramp at the darkened portal. As a precaution, Max reached out in party chat. "Master Redmane, please have the guards close and secure the portal gate. Can't have someone stumble drunk into the portal before it's ready." He gazed up at the walls for a second. "Also, please have someone start checking the walls and buildings for damage. That's not urgent, so don't pull anyone from the celebration."

He saw his chamberlain nod across the courtyard, then motion for the nearest guard that was on duty. Satisfied that the portal would be secured, Max rejoined Ironhand, Farstrider, and the other dignitaries that were still gathered near the cart.

"That was a bit more exciting than I expected." He grinned at his fellow sovereigns.

Ironhand snorted. "That be fer sure."

Behind the dwarf, Blake spun around in his sparkly mage robes, struck a pose, and sang, "You knock me off of my feet, now baby!" The two other corporals laughed as everyone else just looked at Blake like he was insane.

Max sought out Lightsprocket and motioned her closer, but spoke loud enough for everyone to hear. Removing the book he'd received in the Westreach dungeon, he held it up for a moment before handing it to the gnome. "That book was my reward from the final dungeon boss chest. Until now, I had no idea what it was for." He jerked a thumb over his shoulder toward the portal. "During all the shaking, an arch pushed out of the stone. Engravings appeared on the arch, with images of creatures that match the ones in that book. Images of the various monsters we faced inside Westreach dungeon."

The gnome gasped and opened the book even as she turned and sprinted toward the ramp. "Don't touch the portal!" He shouted after her, seeing that the gate wasn't yet secured. She waved a hand without turning or slowing down.

Addressing the rest of the group, he said, "My guess is that the core has already absorbed whatever knowledge it needs to create all the same creatures and resources that are in the Westreach dungeon." There were several murmurs, the loudest being exclamations of dismay from Smitty and Dylan, who were the most excited about customizing the dungeon. "Which makes that book some sort of... index? Guide? I'm not sure what you'd call it."

"It's the dungeon wiki!" Blake called out, still dancing and grinning like a maniac.

Ignoring him, Max waited for Ironhand or the others to say something. When no one did, he shrugged. "I suppose we'll find out soon enough. In the meantime, you're all welcome to stay and join in the celebration out there. Or we can retire to the palace for a more quiet meal if you prefer."

The dwarves, being dwarves, immediately opted for the rowdy celebration that was developing around the tents, even as the staff rushed to clean up the kitchens and recover the wayward kegs. Toppled tables and benches were set right, and runners were sent into the city for more food to replace what was lost or ruined in the flames. Farstrider and the Archmagus, along with the rest of the visitors, opted to join in as well.

Max was torn between accompanying them out to the party, or checking on Lightsprocket. Eventually he decided to leave her to her studying and get a report when she was through. Assuming she was through before the portal opened.

He exited through the gate and put a smile on his face as he approached the crowd. He greeted random citizens he encountered along the way to the food line, laughing at the various comments and bad jokes regarding the quakes. He deferred several requests from citizens who wanted to be the first into the dungeon, saying that privilege was already reserved for a select few, but that they would certainly get their turn.

It was a half hour before he actually made it to the chow line and was handed a plate already heaped with meat, vegetables, bread, and gravy. He grabbed a proffered mug of ale and took a seat at the long table designated for royals, clan leaders, and the Archmagus. A half dozen guards stood between that table and the others, keeping exuberant citizens from disturbing the VIPs while they ate.

Most of the others had reached the table well ahead of him, not having been distracted by the crowd. Ironhand had already cleaned his plate at least once, and was drinking directly from a pitcher of ale, which he raised in salute as Max took his seat. "Good party, Max!"

"Heh. Thank you. It started out a little shaky, but seems to be picking up." Max tipped over an empty mug in front of Ironhand, then set it upright again, grinning as nearly everyone at the table groaned.

"Boss gots dad jokes." Dylan observed from his bench at the end of the table.

"Really lame dad jokes." Smitty added.

"Yes, lame." Nessa agreed, both her tone and expression deadpan. After a moment of shock, the party members laughed heartily, raising their own mugs to the reserved panthera.

Max took a few bites of the delicious food as his guests bantered back and forth. He watched his people mingle at the various tables, Minotaurs next to kobolds, gnomes chatting with orcs. The ogres had mostly been assigned guard duty at other properties out of fear that if they all attended there wouldn't be enough food for everyone else. But all the other races were represented in the crowd, and were getting along extremely well. Max set his fork down and took a moment to soak it all in, letting a warm rush of pride flow through him.

Noticing the look on his face, Ironhand nodded once. "Aye, Max. Ye've done a good thing here. I thought ye daft when ye first demanded that Stormhaven be an open city. I'll admit I was wrong, and say that I'm proud of ye." Ironhand thumped his empty mug on the table several times, quickly joined by Farstrider and the dwarven clan leaders. Smiling even wider, Max raised his own mug in thanks.

"In fact, I discussed with me cousins, and we all be in agreement. We be rescinding yer probation, and acknowledgin' ye as the right n proper King o' Stormhaven!" This time the dwarves all raised their mugs and roared along with him. "To King Max!"

Max bowed his head briefly in thanks, then raised his mug and emptied it, slamming it down on the table. "To the alliance!" After the dwarves echoed his toast and quieted down, he put his right hand to his chest. "I sincerely thank you all for your faith in me. For your assistance, your friendship, and your understanding when it looked like I was trying to steal a city from you." He grinned as the dwarves laughed.

To everyone's utter surprise, Stonebinder got to his feet, still holding his mug. "Ye have accomplished much in a short time, King Max. Though I still don't much like ye, I can respect what ye've built here, and recognize the good intentions behind yer actions." He raised his mug, drank, and sat back down before Max had a chance to respond. The elders on either side of him clapped him on the back in approval.

"Not ta mention all the gold he's put in our pockets!" Ironhand shouted, getting grunts and shouts of agreement in return. The clans that had participated in the battle for Nogroz city were still collecting their percentage of everything Max and his kingdom earned. Max knew that it really didn't amount to all that much, but he appreciated the sentiment. His contribution of the party chat spell was more valuable by far. Add in access to Glitterspindle and his inventions, his newly formed dungeon, the new alliance with Westreach, and he felt he'd repaid their kindness pretty well.

Not that he minded the acknowledgement in the least. The warmth of pride grew inside him. It was definitely pride, and not the ale.

After finishing his meal and spending an hour or so at the head table, Max got up and began to circulate among the other tables. Each time he ran across children he produced treats from the bakeries, of which he had filled three whole slots in his inventory. He used the pastries, and a promise of a silver coin, to bribe the little ones into completing a quickly generated quest that involved running plates of food to the guards who were on duty, jealously eyeing the food and drink as they stood their posts. Soon enough there was a small army of children delivering plates to smiling guards before racing back to Max to claim their rewards.

Much to his delight, and that of the crowd, many of the little tykes leveled up after completing the quest. Max then offered them all a series of quests, some silly, like standing on their heads, others more useful, like running a stack of empty plates back to the kitchen tents to be washed. That last one had the unfortunate consequence of several citizens having their plates yanked from in front of them before they'd finished their meals.

Dylan predictably drifted over to one side of the dining area and began an exhibition of dance moves. As usual, a crowd of half-drunk citizens and kids gathered round, and eventually joined in with much stumbling and laughter. Teeglin, who had apparently been getting lessons, led a dozen children in her version of the electric slide, while a slightly plastered Blake began teaching some of them how to moonwalk, lifting his robes up around his hips so that they could watch his feet.

The celebration continued, some of the guards who'd been participating taking up duty posts so that the guards who'd been on duty could share in the fun. Max continued to circulate, meeting many of his citizens for the first time, giving out more simple quests for the smallest of them. He took special pleasure in one particular quest. A mother gnome sitting on a nearby bench had the most adorable baby gnome standing at her feet, dressed in a tiny version of her momma's mage robes, complete with a little knit pointy cap, holding on to both her hands. The baby was lifting one foot, then the other, clearly attempting to step forward, but hanging on to mom's hands for support. Max quickly generated a quest for the little one to take her first steps on her own, mostly as an experiment to see if it would work on one so young. To his surprise, it not only worked, but provided significant experience as a reward.

He then created one for the mom to encourage the little one to walk, and smiled when she glanced up at him, surprised.

Sitting cross-legged on the ground a few feet from the babe, he smiled and made cooing sounds at her, holding out his hands and asking her to walk to him. The tiny gnome baby, only about a foot tall, laughed and squealed at him, but held on to her mother's hands. On his shoulder, Red's voice whispered, "Alright, that's too stinkin' cute."

After another minute or so of encouragement from both Max and mom, the baby let go with one hand. She wobbled a bit, but stayed on her feet. Releasing the other hand, she stumbled forward unsteadily, looking a lot like Dylan after too many kegs of ale.

Leaning forward a bit too far, and with her tiny arms waving every which way, she half-stumbled, half-fell across the distance to Max, who scooped her up and held her high in the air with both hands. "You did it!" Nearby observers clapped and cheered.

There was a flash of light as both mother and child leveled up, and the little one giggled at Max even as a line of drool dripped off her chin onto his face. The momma gnome hopped up and rushed over to retrieve her, starting to reach a cloth toward Max's face to wipe it off, then hesitating. "I'm so sorry, King Max" she muttered as he just laughed it off, wiping the drool away with his sleeve.

"She is possibly the most adorable thing I've ever seen." Max gently poked the squirming infant in the belly, making her laugh again. "And she deserves a reward for her hard work!" He produced a gold coin and held it before the child's eyes. She quickly grabbed hold of it, her tiny hand barely strong enough to grip it, her eyes crossing slightly as she tried to focus on the shiny object. The moment Max let go, she shoved it into her mouth, causing everyone who'd been watching to laugh.

Chuckling to himself, he produced a piece of bacon from his inventory. "Let's test her barter skill." He smiled at the mom as he presented the bacon to the child. She initially showed no interest, until her nose twitched as she caught a whiff of the bacon. Half a second later she dropped the coin into mom's hand and reached with both hands, tiny fingers wiggling, for the bacon.

As with the coin, the moment she had the bacon tightly in her grip, it went straight to her mouth. Max and the others laughed with delight as her eyes lit up and she made little *nom nom* noises.

Max was distracted by a notification as he watched her jam more of the bacon into her mouth. His eyes widened when he saw what it was.

Dungeon formation complete!

Enter dungeon portal to complete dungeon core initialization.

Max jumped to his feet, startling mom and baby alike. He mumbled an apology and gave the little one a gentle kiss on the forehead. "Well done, little one." He whispered before smiling at the mother gnome and turning toward the outpost gate.

When he was far enough away not to startle the baby, he threw up his arms and roared, "It's time! The dungeon is complete!"

The slightly intoxicated crowd went silent for a moment as his words sunk in, then a cheer erupted. Everyone began to follow him in the direction of the portal. When he reached the cart near the ramp, he hopped up and waited for the crowd to gather and settle down. The portal behind him had changed from the dark swirling colors to a silvery mirror appearance featuring green and gold swirls. Max raised his arms until the crowd hushed.

"My notification says I need to go through the portal to finish the core initialization. You guys hang out here for a second, and I'll go take care of that real quick!" He grinned as half the crowd groaned with disappointment. Hopping down, his ears picked up several wagers being offered as to what was inside the dungeon. He walked quickly down the ramp, only to hear rapid footsteps coming up behind him. He turned to find Lightsprocket rushing to catch up, distractedly holding a mug of ale in one hand, a stick of meat in the other.

He paused at the portal gate, letting her catch up. "I'm supposed to step in and do something to finish the dungeon." He spoke quietly to her as the crowd inched closer. "Is it... would it be safe for you to go in too?"

She paused, finally noticing what she held in her hands and quickly depositing both food and drink into her storage. Looking thoughtful, she considered his question. "I don't know. This is a first, as far as our records go."

Looking disappointed as she came to a conclusion, she shook her head. "Better go in alone." She frowned and actually stomped a foot in frustration. Then she gave a little hop and clapped her hands. "But I want to go in next!"

Smiling at her excitement, and feeling more than a little of the same, Max turned and took a deep breath before stepping through the portal while many of the observers held their breath.

Max felt the expected momentary disorientation as his front foot struck the ground inside the dungeon and he had to catch his balance once he was fully through. He disliked stepping where he could not see, but it wasn't as bad as the first time he stepped into the Westreach dungeon portal.

Taking a moment, he glanced around. The portal had dropped him into a roughly circular stone chamber with half a dozen torches spaced evenly around the wall. The ceiling was low, barely high enough for him to stand upright without scraping his head. Floor, wall, and ceiling were all perfectly smooth, clearly formed with magic rather than cut with tools from the surrounding stone.

In the center of the room, just three paces from Max, stood the same pedestal he'd placed the core upon up above. The now brightly glowing core still sat atop it, pulsing regularly as if with a heartbeat. As Max's gaze took in the rest of the room, he found a single narrow exit in the wall behind him.

Turning back to the core, he stepped forward, holding out one hand, assuming he needed to touch the stone again to complete the activation. He froze in surprise when, after the first step, a voice sounded in his mind.

"Is that you, father?"

"Wha?" Max stammered as thoughts whirled through his head. Flashes of the visions he'd seen regarding the core. The orc boss lifting the newborn, then later placing it on a similar pedestal. "Father? Me?" He found himself wringing his hands nervously, unsure how to respond. The core was clearly intelligent, since it was speaking to him. Did it know the circumstances of its birth? Did it think he was its human father? Or the dungeon boss that had turned it into a core?

"I'm… not…" He began, but let his words fade away, still unsure what to say.

A moment later he heard bright, pealing laughter in his mind. "I am sorry, Maximilian Storm. I was just teasing you!"

Once again the only sound Max managed to eek out was "Wha?" Max cleared his throat and took a calming breath. "Teasing? You're… hmmm." Max paused again. "You are not what I expected."

"I am not?" The voice in his head sounded disappointed. "I am sorry, Maximilian Storm. I am but newly formed. I will grow and become stronger, just wait and see."

Realizing the core had misunderstood, Max stammered. "N-no. That's not what I meant. I just, I hadn't expected... you are much more than I had expected. I assumed you to be an infant, like the visions I saw of you when we first... met." He shook his head, having a hard time coming to terms with the situation. "I did not expect you to be so... I didn't expect you to be able to tease me." He smiled at the swirling gemstone on the pedestal in front of him.

"I see." The tone of the telepathic voice was understanding. "Though I was an infant when my mortal existence was converted to this one, I have spent nearly a thousand years inside my creator's dungeon. For much of that time I was as you no doubt expected I would be today. But I learned through observation. I watched the denizens of the dungeon battle and consume each other, drawing small bits of energy from each death. I listened to visitors speak amongst themselves, watched many of them perish as well. I tasted their blood, their emotions. I sampled the food and drink they carried, and studied the enchanted items they left behind."

Max let out a long, slow exhale. "Well, that is very good to hear!" He smiled at the core again. "We have been wondering if we would have to... teach you how to be a dungeon, I suppose?"

"Have you been a dungeon?" the inquiry was sincere, and Max resisted the urge to laugh.

"I have not. Which was cause for some concern. None of us, myself especially, have any experience with helping to create a dungeon. The fact that you seem to be very… advanced… is a nice surprise." He paused. "Uhm, what should I call you? Do you have a name?"

"My creator called me *Child*."

Max shook his head. "We can do better than that, Child. You are an amazing and potentially very powerful entity!" He raised a hand and scratched the back of his head, thinking. "How about this. You spend a little time thinking it over, decide what you'd like your name to be. If you don't come up with one you like, I'll give you some suggestions."

"That is acceptable, Maximilian Storm."

"Just call me Max. I think we're going to be very good friends, after all."

"I have never had a friend." The voice, which gave him a distinct feminine impression, took on a hopeful tone. "I would like to be your friend." After a short pause, it added, "But I must warn you, Max."

"Warn me?"

"I am a dungeon. I live to expand my domain, to grow stronger, to learn. I do this in part by killing and absorbing the energy, materials, and knowledge of those who venture inside my domain."

Max nodded, "That is my understanding of how things works, yes."

"As my master, you are safe within my walls. But all others, including those you may consider family, friends, or allies, are not safe. It is in my nature to challenge them."

Max's first thought was of Lightsprocket, who likely was dancing with impatience outside the portal. Then his mind turned to his plans to have Teeglin and other kids run the newly formed dungeon. In his mind he'd been picturing a dungeon full of fuzzy bunnies and maybe grumpy squirrels for the kids to put down and earn easy experience.

"By challenge, you mean it's in your nature to try to kill anyone else who comes in here." It wasn't really a question. "Is there no way I can designate others as... friendly?"

"There is not." The tone was flat, without a hint of regret. "Just as those who enter will strive to destroy my minions, my avatar, and even my core, I must defend myself and attempt to absorb them."

Max frowned, shaking his head. "No one who enters here will attempt to destroy you, Child. Not while I control access. Any who enter your domain will be warned that destroying your core will result in their immediate execution."

"That is good to hear. Thank you." The voice actually sounded pleased.

Still thinking of Teeglin, Max asked. "The notification I received said that you are level one. What does that mean in terms of the challenge you offer to visitors?"

There was a short pause before the voice in his head replied, "As I said, I am newly formed. While my knowledge of minion designs, traps, flora, fauna and loot items is considerable, my available resources are extremely limited. I am absorbing ambient mana at a significant rate, and have harvested local resources during my initial formation. But I have had little time to spawn minions to challenge visitors." This time the voice carried a definite flavor of disappointment.

"That is certainly understandable." Max grinned at the core. "When I was your age, all I could do was lay on my back, cry, and soil my diapers."

Clearly not understanding the humor, the core replied, "Yes, well. I will prepare for visitors as quickly as possible."

"What kind of minions have you created, if any?" Max looked around the chamber, eyeing the exit. "And how large is your structure?"

"At the moment, I have one upper level with six rooms and connecting corridors, and a lower level with one room, aside from this core chamber. As for minions, I have created twenty three level one goblins, and three level one orcs. The orcs are on the lower level, guarding this chamber."

Max nodded, thinking hard. Teeglin and the other dworc kids could handle such low level monsters with little trouble. And they certainly presented no danger to Lightsprocket. He began to wonder how quickly the dungeon would grow, which then got him wondering about what resources that would require. A couple of ideas came to mind immediately.

"Child, if I were to bring you the bodies of higher level beings, would they help you to grow more quickly?"

"I would benefit from absorbing the raw materials of their corpses, yes. But I would gain much more if their mana and life essence were dispersed within my domain. As well as potentially gaining knowledge from them."

"Alright, I think we can help you there." He paused before asking his next question, considering whether it might somehow offend or hurt Child.

"Child, before activating your core, my friends and I were discussing the possibility of … well, of designing the minions you create, and the loot you offer. I received the book that I believe outlines your currently available flora and fauna." He took a deep breath. "Are you… willing to work with me, to accept suggestions?"

"Certainly. You are my master." The voice sounded surprised at the question.

"Excellent. Then I will be bringing you some… resources to sample." He snapped his fingers, remembering Lightsprocket. "In a moment, a gnome mage named Lightsprocket is going to enter the portal. She is a friend of mine who is very interested in learning more about you. Be assured, she will not try to harm you in any way, other than eliminating any minions that attack her, I suppose."

"None but you may enter until my initialization is complete." The tone was back to flat again. Almost robotic.

"Fair enough. When we're done chatting here, I'll complete the initialization and depart to fetch the resources I mentioned. In the meantime, I have an idea for when Lightsprocket reaches you…" His grin turned wicked as he began to share his plan with his newly adopted dungeon core. When he was done, he placed his hand on the core and a notification popped up.

Do you wish to complete activation of a Level 1 Dungeon Core?

Max chose *Yes* to complete the initialization, and several more notifications flooded in.

Congratulations!
You have successfully constructed a Level 1 Dungeon!
Rewards; 100,000,000 exp; 100,000 gold; One Level 1 Dungeon

You have earned the Title: Dungeon Master!

Hidden Quest Completed: Dungeon Master!
Difficulty: Unique
You have obtained and successfully activated a dungeon core, designating yourself its master in the process. You will be able to communicate with the dungeon core, and walk its corridors without fear of harm. As a Dungeon Master, you will be able to share earned experience with

the dungeon core, and interact with it in other ways. See
your Dungeon tab for details.
Rewards: 25,000,000 exp; Dungeon Control Interface.
Max took the time to read through the notifications twice even as he felt the rush of leveling up twice. He brushed aside those notifications, focusing on the part of the description regarding shared experience. Quickly scanning his interface tabs, he found the new dungeon tab, which was handily glowing a bright silver, and opened it. After locating and reading the section on sharing experience, he blinked a few times, a wide smile growing on his face. He could indeed set it so that experience was shared between the dungeon and himself.

And it worked both ways.

He could designate a portion of his own personal earned experience from kills and quests to be assigned to Child, to help the dungeon level up a bit faster. On the other hand, he could set it so that a percentage of the dungeon's experience went to him, instead.

While Max had no interest in taking any of Child's experience at the moment, he could picture a time in the future when the experience requirements for him to level up would be impossibly high. When the dungeon might be killing off level one hundred adventurers, and sharing that experience with him on a regular basis.

For now, he made an adjustment to the setting to share ten percent of his experience with Child. "I've just set you up to receive some of my personal experience for a while, to help you grow." He informed the core, pulling his hand from the stone. "Welcome to Stormhaven!"

"Thank you, Max." the voice sounded pleased. "I look forward to growing more powerful with your assistance."

"I'm going to go fetch you a few things, Child. Think about a new name, and don't forget what we planned." He threw the core a wink before turning toward the exit.

"You need not walk through my levels, Max."

He turned back in time to see a portal form behind the pedestal. One that looked exactly like the entry portal in the alcove above. "Thank you, Child." Max gave the core a smile and a nod before stepping through the glowing oval. A moment later he was standing in front of Lightsprocket and the others, who cheered loudly enough to vibrate the stone when they saw him.

Chapter 21

"The dungeon is live!" Max shouted for the benefit of the crowd, causing the cheering to grow in volume. When it died down a bit, he added, "It's a level one dungeon, so I'm afraid those of you with dreams of heroic conquest will have to wait a bit!" He grinned as some in the crowd laughed, while others groaned or complained.

Behind him, one of the guards at the portal gate, a dwarf, cleared his throat loudly to get Max's attention. When he looked over his shoulder, the dwarf nodded toward Lightsprocket, whose gaze was laser focused on the portal, and who was fidgeting from one foot to the other as if doing some sort of pee pee dance. "Beggin' yer pardon, me king, but I'm thinkin if ye don't let this one through, she might burst."

The other guard, an orc, chuckled. "She threatened to turn us into mushrooms if we didn't let her in as soon as you came out. I assume that threat includes you, too, King Max."

The little gnome blinked a few times as she realized they were talking about her. "What? No. I said I'd turn your brains to mush." She scowled at the guards, then up at Max. "Level one shouldn't be a danger to me, majesty. May I enter?"

Max considered teasing her a bit more, making her wait. But the mage had been both helpful and patient, so he nodded. "Please, wait in the safe area when you get in there. I'll be sending a few adventurers in right behind you." The gnome smiled. They'd discussed Max's plans if the dungeon was low level, and she knew what to do. Max waved her toward the portal. Before his hand motion was even complete she shot through the gate and into the portal, leaving the two guards laughing quietly. Max looked at the guards. "Nobody else goes in without my permission. I'm going to round up a group." The guards both nodded, remaining at attention on either side of the gate.

Max walked up the ramp and addressed the crowd. "Thank you all again for coming to witness the birth of our dungeon! Enjoy what's left of the food and drink." He glanced through the gate to see a few folks already back by the tents continuing the revelry. "We'll post notices when there are slots available for dungeon excursions."

He watched for a moment as the crowd filed back out the gate. Some moved toward the tents, while others decided they'd had enough and headed into the city and the portal home. Ironhand approached Max with Farstrider at his side. "What're ye gonna do next, Max?"

Deep in thought and only half hearing the question, Max replied, "I'm going to send a group through." He was thinking of Teeglin and the lowest level dworclings. He sent out a message in party chat for his group to round them up.

"Ha! I meant in general, Max. Seems every time I turn me back ye come up with some new miracle or crazy adventure." Next to him Farstrider nodded.

Max blinked a few times, paying more attention. He took a moment to consider the long list of tasks he'd set for himself, or that his kingdom required him to accomplish. "Well, I've got the Shadow Walkers to deal with. The ones we captured, and the guild in general. I'm afraid I'm going to have to wipe them out, or at least kill so many of them that they agree to leave us alone." He paused again, mentally running through the list. "I still need to recruit several thousand new citizens to help fill our population needs. I'll be heading to the human queen's city soon to establish a formal embassy, and recruit as many of her people as I can." His wicked grin fully exposed his fangs, earning a snort from Farstrider. "There's still An'zalor to deal with to the south, and I should lead a group north to see if there are any of the red-eyed orcs left. I doubt The One brought every warrior he had south with him. Now that he's dead, whomever takes control of his people could continue to cause trouble."

Both kings nodded. Farstrider spoke first. "Now that hostilities with my neighbor have ceased, I offer you some of my men to assist."

"Aye, ye can have a hunnert o' me own warriors to hunt down them beasties." Ironhand agreed. "A hunnert from each o' the clans, as well."

Max offered a hand to each of them. "Thank you both. That is greatly appreciated. I'll let you know when we start out. Rather than move a large force through the mountains, I believe we'll do as we did before. A small scouting party will backtrack the army until we've found whatever's left, then I'll set up a portal and bring the troops through." He took a deep breath. "With their master dead, I'm hoping they'll go back to being normal orcs. Or, at least, more peaceful orcs. Maybe I can even convince them to join us."

Ironhand looked doubtful. "I know ye've a fondness fer orcs, Max. And me own opinion o' them in general be greatly altered since ye came along with yer aggravatin' peacemakin' n such." He winked at Max. "But the red-eyes be savage beasts. Their shaman did somethin' that changed 'em down to their souls." He shook his head, a solemn expression taking over his face. "I be thinkin' ye'll be forced to put em down. Every one o' them, down to the last babe."

Farstrider looked surprised at the last statement, but didn't argue. Before his agreement with Max, given the opportunity, he'd have ordered the slaughter of every orc in An'zalor's city himself. Centuries of war and ancient prejudices were hard to put aside.

Max let out a long, slow exhale. "You may be right. I may be forced to do just that, and I'll be prepared for it. But I'd like to try and make peace first. I'll take Or'gral and a few other respected orcs along in hopes that they can assist those efforts."

"Ye be sure n take them honkin' big ogres with ye too. Fer when it comes time to stomp em flat!" Ironhand patted Max's arm. "Just tell em there be juicy orc meat in their camp, and set 'em loose."

Teeglin and five other dworc orphans arrive as the sovereigns were concluding their discussion. Dalia and the corporals walked behind them. They'd been rounded up the previous morning after Dalia discussed with the dworc elders Max's plan. His party had then given them some pointers and a little training in group tactics. As Max's gaze took in each of them, he saw more than a little nervousness, but also determination. None of them was under level five, and each of them was armed. They all wore leather armor, and Dalia had gifted each of them a bandolier filled with health potions. With their small health pools, even medium grade potions would restore any of them to full health immediately.

Behind the group, a gathering of twenty or so dworcs, a significant portion of their remaining population after the losses from orc attacks on the village, gathered to wish the little ones good luck.

Taking a knee, Max looked at Teeglin first. "Princess Teeglin, I expect you to keep these others safe in there. Bring them back to us in one piece." The little dworc nodded solemnly, gripping the hilt of the short sword at her waist. He made a of show of addressing each one, inspecting their armor and weapons, expressing his approval. When he was done with that, he generated a quest for them to complete the dungeon.

"After you've killed all the beasts in there, and the dungeon boss, you collect your loot and leave. Do not harm the core in any way. Is that clear?" When they all nodded, he gestured toward the ramp. "Alright, time to head inside. Remember, if it starts to look like a fight is too hard for you to handle, there's no shame in retreating.

You stay alive, get stronger, and go back again later." He waited for another round of nods, then stepped aside.

The villagers called out encouragement, a few of them wiping tears from their eyes as the youngest dworcs walked down the ramp. The outpost guards and remaining citizens offered shouts of encouragement and applause, causing Teeglin to walk a little taller, her chest puffed out with pride as she led her party through the portal. To their credit, Max didn't see a single one of them pause or flinch before entering.

Turning to the villagers once the little tykes were gone, Max called out. "Mage Lightsprocket is in there, and she won't let any harm come to them."

Elder Pickstone laughed aloud. "Bah! It be only a level one dungeon, King Max. Any dworc babe old enough to walk be tough enough to handle them beasties!" The other dworcs nodded their agreement and smiled at Max. They truly did not seem worried.

*****

Lightsprocket was running her hand over the stone in the starting area of the dungeon when the dworclings stepped through. Turning to smile up at them, she put away the notebook she'd been scribbling in. "Well, hello there! Are you all ready to clear the dungeon?"

The others nodded as Teeglin stepped forward. In her most serious voice, she answered, "We will fight with honor and courage, and defeat the monsters with ease!"

Behind her, the others cheered softly, several of them flashing nervous glances toward the exit door.

"Very well then. I will not be assisting you with defeating the monsters. I am simply here to observe. The only time I may intervene is if one of you is mortally wounded. Be careful as you proceed, and don't forget to use your health potions if you need them. I have more, should you run out." She gave them one last warm smile before ushering them toward the exit.

Teeglin nodded toward a young boy who was a year older than her. He hefted a shield and a one-handed axe, rolled his shoulders a bit, then stepped forward. Behind him were a pair of twins a year younger than Teeglin. The boy gripped a two-handed axe tightly, while his sister hefted a spear that was longer than she was tall. Teeglin walked behind them, alongside another female dworc carrying a staff, a wand secured at her belt. She was their healer. Finally another boy with a shield and sword brought up the rear. Lightsprocket allowed them to get a good headstart, then followed behind. Smokeless torches placed in wall brackets every twenty feet or so along the way offered faint, flickering light, enough so that the young adventurers could see where they were going.

Max had not warned them regarding what they would face in the dungeon, so they proceeded with caution, maintaining a careful pace as they moved down a stone corridor. They might all be children, but they were born of two warrior races, and grew up amongst fighters. Most of them had lost their parents to battle in or around the village, and were no strangers to combat.

The end of the corridor opened into a wider chamber, maybe twenty paces across. The floor and walls were smooth stone, while the high ceiling featured several stalactites hanging down, occasionally dripping water onto the floor below. Toward the back of the chamber, not far from the exit, three goblins sat around a small campfire, roasting what appeared to be rats on sticks held over the flames. Each of them wore a simple loincloth, and nothing else.

The moment the lead dworc stepped into the room, the goblins abandoned their food, tossing the sticks to the floor, and grabbed weapons. One picked up a bow and nocked an arrow, while the other two grabbed spears and charged toward the party, their oversized feet slapping the stone floor.

Their tank took up position at the entry threshold, while the others spread out as best they could in the corridor behind him. An arrow bounced off the tank's shield as their mage raised her staff, mumbling a spell. A moment later a small fireball sped past the two charging goblins, striking the archer. The impact knocked the little goblin down, screaming as the skin on its chest and face was scorched. The string on its bow caught fire and quickly snapped in half, rendering the bow useless.

Three seconds later the two spear wielding goblins slammed into the tank, the stone points of their spears scraping across the metal shield. He clumsily deflected both blows before pushing back against them and stepping forward to chop at the right-hand goblin with his axe. The nimble creature hopped back out of range, causing him to miss, then stabbed at his face with its spear.

The motion was cut off as the twin dworcs attacked. The sister jammed her spear directly into the face of the right-hand goblin. Her spear being longer, her thrust pushed it backward even as the spearpoint penetrated deep into its head. Her brother dashed around the left side of the tank, swinging his axe over his crouched companion's head. The blow connected, the dworc's natural strength driving the blade cleanly through the goblin's neck.

From the back of the room the archer goblin screamed in rage and ran forward, a small stone dagger in hand. It didn't move as quickly as the others, being injured from the fireball attack. The tank, upset at missing his chance to finish the first goblin, shouted a challenge and stood upright, hurling his axe with an overhand throw. The goblin made it two more steps before the axe blade slammed into its chest, smashing through ribs and knocking it completely off its feet, dead before it hit the floor.

The group cheered their victory, enthusiastically thumping each other on the back. Teeglin gave them all a double thumbs-up, then had to explain to them what it meant. Behind them, Lightsprocket smiled fondly at the little ones, impressed by their performance.

After looting the bodies, from which they received a total of nineteen coppers and a stone dagger, the party resumed their formation and moved on. As they passed the campfire, the dworc at rearguard picked up one of the sticks, sniffed at the meat, then shrugged before stashing all three half-roasted rats in his bag. When times were tough in the village, all of them had eaten worse.

The exit led to another long corridor, and again they moved slowly, wary of traps. The flickering torchlight caused shadows to jump around, making it difficult to spot any potential tripwires or other triggers. Teeglin found herself sweating as they continued on, worried about traps, ambushes, or anything else that might hurt one of her comrades. She'd promised Max she would bring them out safe, and the responsibility weighed heavily on her shoulders.

Having traversed the second corridor without incident, they approached a second, larger chamber. This time the campfire near the back sat unattended, as the three goblin occupants were actively patrolling their post. Just as the party's tank neared the end of the corridor, the three goblins appeared, walking past the entry from left to right. Spotting the party instantly, they screeched a challenge and attacked.

The tank barely had time to raise his shield and block a spear thrust from the nearest goblin. The one right behind it cleverly stabbed downward, its spearpoint penetrating leather and slashing a deep cut across the tank's shin just below his knee. The third goblin ignored the tank completely, charging around his right side and leaping at the twin with the spear. That turned out to be a mistake, as she raised the tip of her spear, braced the butt end against her back foot, and held firm as the descending goblin skewered itself on her weapon. The point entered its gut just below the sternum, then burst from its back as its weight and momentum did her work for her.

This time Teeglin got into the action, drawing her sword and rushing up behind the tank, who was down on one knee, desperately trying to block the rapid spear thrusts from the two remaining goblins. The other twin saw Teeglin approach and motioned toward the right with one hand. When she nodded, he went left around the tank, and she went right. Shouting to distract her chosen goblin, she thrust her sword forward. The nimble goblin danced back, but not quite quickly enough, earning a shallow puncture wound between two of its ribs. Screaming in pain, it threw its spear at Teeglin, who dodged out of the way, slamming into the tank, causing both of them to fall on their backs.

The axe-bearing dworc was more successful, splitting his goblin's skull with an overhead chop. Struggling to remove the axe that was now lodged in the goblin's skull, he watched the last monster turn and run. "Don't let it get away! It'll warn the others!" He called out, giving the axe another yank. When it finally came free, he began to run after the goblin, but the little creature's short legs were practically a blur as it outpaced him across the cavern. An embarrassed Teeglin was still getting to her feet along with the tank, and his sister was struggling to push the goblin-kabob off her spear.

Just as it approached the campfire, a fireball struck it in the back. The force of the impact knocked it face-first into the campfire. Screaming, it rolled to one side, frantically trying to brush burning embers from its face. Stomping on its chest to hold it still, the twin chopped down at the goblin like it was firewood, removing its head from its shoulders.

As he looted its corpse, his companions did the same with the other two goblins. Teeglin called for a rest so that their mage could heal the tank and recover her mana. Again, from back at the chamber entry point, Lightsprocket nodded her approval. In her experience, too many young and enthusiastic adventurers failed to take the time needed between fights, simply charging forward into the next battle. Often they took serious injuries, or even perished, due to their lack of forethought.

After a short rest, during which their off-tank finished roasting the three skewered rats over the campfire, they moved on.

The next corridor curved toward the left, and was a bit longer than the first two. Just after the curve, the tank froze in his tracks, holding up a hand to keep the others back. When Teeglin approached him, he pointed at the floor. In the center of the corridor, about three paces in front of him, he'd noticed a section of floor that was slightly discolored. That in itself wasn't so unusual, except the discolored area was perfectly rectangle-shaped, stretching out about six feet front to back, and most of the way across the corridor from left to right, with only about a foot of normal colored stone along either wall.

"Likely a trap." He whispered to Teeglin, who nodded her agreement. Thinking quickly, she turned to their off-tank who waited patiently at the rear.

"Run back and fetch one o' those goblins. Hurry!" The dworc immediately complied, turning and sprinting back around the curve in the corridor. He was back in just a couple minutes with the headless goblin's body thrown over his shoulder. Pointing at the suspicious section of floor, she ordered, "Toss it there."

The dworc happily complied, heaving the corpse up into the air, its slight weight no challenge for his natural strength. It landed near the center of the discolored area of the floor, which promptly burst apart in two halves. Each half of the revealed trap door swung downward on unseen hinges, dumping the goblin corpse into an open pit. Several spikes at the bottom thrust up through it when it landed.

"That could have been us." The mages voice was barely a squeak as she peered down into the pit with the others. Looking up at the tank, she added, "Ye saved us from a nasty death."

The tank just shrugged, uncomfortable with the praise. Teeglin patted him on the shoulder. "She's right. Thank you." Turning so that her gaze took in the rest of the party, she said, "Everyone keep a close eye out for more traps."

The tank led the way forward, shuffling sideways along the narrow strip of solid ground left of the pit, his back against the wall, arms out to his sides for balance. The others followed behind just as carefully. When they'd moved on, Lightsprocket approached the pit and took a moment to examine the trap doors, drawing a quick sketch in her notebook before scribbling a few descriptive notes. When she was done, she backed up a few steps, then rushed forward, using her staff in a sort of pole vault maneuver that propelled her over the pit to safe ground on the other side. Suppressing a giggle, she continued on.

The next corridor was free of traps, and the chamber it led to contained another three goblins. However this time, all three were archers. The moment they spotted the dworcs, all three archers hopped up from around the campfire and began sending arrows across the chamber. The tank slammed his axe against his shield and shouted at them, but only one of the archers fired in his direction. Teeglin took an arrow to the shoulder, while the mage was hit in the gut.

"They be too far away! My taunt only works within twenty feet!" The tank, beginning to panic, abandoned the threshold where they normally fought, charging forward with his shield high. The twins dashed forward right behind him, and the off-tank moved forward to try and block the arrows that were still streaming toward Teeglin and their healer. She had dropped to her knees, clutching the arrow in her belly, moaning in pain. Teeglin gritted her teeth and ripped the arrow free of her shoulder, then dropped to her knees next to the healer. "I'm going to pull this out so ye can heal yerself."

"No! No! It'll rip my guts out!" The mage gasped, gripping the arrow more tightly to prevent Teeglin from pulling it out.

"We have to take it out, or you'll die!" Teeglin shouted directly into her companion's face. "We need ye to heal yerself, and us!" When the mage continued to shake her head and keep her grip tight on the arrow, Teeglin glanced over at the battle. One of the archers was down, missing an arm from an axe blow. The twins each sported an arrow, one in his leg, the other in her arm. "Please! We need you!" She took a moment to pull a health potion from her bandolier and pop it open, gulping down the healing liquid before yelling at the melee fighters. "Use your potions!"

She saw the twins each strike at an archer, taking them down. The moment the goblins were dead, they turned to each other and grinned. Taking turns, they ripped the arrows from each other's flesh, then gulped down healing potions before trotting back to Teeglin and the others.

"Please, ye have to let us take the arrow out. You can't stay here, and if you move with it in yer belly-"

She was interrupted by a scream from the healer. The tank had assessed the situation, and without hesitation or mercy, had gripped the fletched end of the arrow and ripped it free of the healer's belly. Her grip had been so tight that the stone arrowhead cut the palms of her hands as he tore it free.

Teeglin quickly poured a health potion down her throat, putting an end to her screaming. Tears rolled down the healer's cheeks as the potion repaired the damage to her flesh and innards. In less than thirty seconds she was fully healed, but unwilling to get back to her feet. It took half an hour of soft words and hugs from Teeglin before the mage calmed down enough to get to her feet.

"We should go back." She looked from the dead goblins to the corridor back the way they'd come in from.

"Why?" the off-tank moved in front of her, trying to make eye contact. "Because you took an arrow in yer belly? You're fine."

The healer snapped. "That arrow could just have easily hit me in the eye, and killed me. Or any o' you." She screamed at him, startling her comrades, as well as Lightsprocket, who was sitting against the wall a ways back in the corridor. The off-tank took a step back, anger clear on his face, about to retort. But Teeglin put a hand on his shoulder and pulled him back, taking his place.

"We knew before we came in here that there would be danger. Ye volunteered, just like the rest of us." Her thoughts raced as she tried to think of a way to calm her friend. "That arrow wasn't so bad. Ye got hurt worse falling from the brewery roof when we were little. Remember? Ye broke yer arm *and* your leg. And there was a knot on your head the size of an apple!" She grinned at the healer, poking her arm with one finger.

"I remember." The dworc scowled at her. "You and the others called me knothead for months."

"Oh, right. That wasn't very nice of us, was it." Teeglin blushed slightly at the reminder. "But today you have a chance to earn a new nickname. A much better one!" Teeglin locked onto an idea. "Like maybe… *Dungeon Killer*! Or… how bout *Goblin Slayer*!?"

The girl twin took a knee next to Teeglin. "Only a few o' the village elders have even seen a dungeon, let alone cleared one. Think about how much bragging ye can do? The others will be *so* jealous."

The healers tears subsided as she looked thoughtful. "I can pick me own nickname?"

"Sure!" Teeglin clapped her hands, getting to her feet and offering her friend a hand up. "I'll even ask King Max to declare it yer official nickname, so that everyone has to use it!"

The mage thought it over for a while, wiping the tears from her face, then nodded. "Alright, let's keep going. How many more will there be, do ye think?"

Teeglin shrugged. "I don't know. But if we stick together, we can beat them."

The next two rooms each held four goblins. They were a mixture of melee and archers, with two archers in the first room, only one in the second. To deal with the larger numbers, the off-tank abandoned his post at the rear of the group and took position up front beside their main tank. Between the two of them they managed to both hold the attention of the melee goblins, and block any arrows that might have hit their comrades. The healer gritted her teeth and lobbed fireballs at everything that moved, angry at being hurt, embarrassed at her reaction, and determined to kill every goblin living in the dungeon.

After killing the four goblins in the fifth chamber, Teeglin called for another rest. She pulled some meat on a stick and pastries from her storage ring, all of which had been gifts from Max. When the tank asked if she had ale in there too, a hopeful look on his face, she shook her head. "Only water, and melon juice."

"Me da used to let me drink ale. Why do so many other grownups act like it's a big deal." The tank shook his head and crossed his arms, pouting.

"Yer da didn't *let* ye drink ale." The healer scowled at him. "Ye steal'd it when he weren't lookin', or when he was asleep. The one time he caught ye, he whupped yer hide, and ye howled so loud the wolves in the forest answered ye!" She let out a short imitation howl, then pretended to rub her sore butt, and stuck her tongue out at him, making the others laugh.

She and the others went silent, though, when the boy looked down at his feet, and a look they all recognized spread across his face. His father had been killed in an attack by the red-eyed orcs. He'd rushed out the gate to defend the elders who'd accompanied Max back from Stormhaven. Each and every member of the party knew what he was thinking, and feeling, being orphans themselves.

Without speaking, the healer moved to sit next to him, leaning her head on his shoulder. The others stayed quiet, giving him the time he needed. Eventually, he looked up at Teeglin and spoke. "So, do we all get to pick our nicknames after this? I be thinkin' I want mine to be

Foe Smasher! Or mebbe *The Wall*! Get it? Cuz nothin' gets past me?" He gave them all a half smile, getting to his feet before helping the healer up as well.

Teeglin had to work hard not to scowl at his choices. Instead, she encouraged him, as she thought a princess would do. "Think on it some more. I'm sure the perfect name will come to ya."

There was another trap in the next corridor, this time a tripwire, that Teeglin spotted seconds before the tank would have triggered it. After carefully examining the floor on both sides, they decided not to risk cutting the wire, and simply stepped over it one at a time. Teeglin looked back to make sure that their gnome guardian had seen it, bit her finger and marked an x on the wall above it with her blood, then continued on.

The sixth room coincidentally held six goblins. This time there were three melee, two with spears and one with a sword. Behind them were two archers and a goblin wielding a staff with a crystal mounted at one end, marking it as a caster. Teeglin quickly assigned the mage to kill the goblin caster first. Followed by the archers. She and the others would deal with the three goblin fighters, then they could advance as a group and deal with the archers if they were still alive. The healer grunted her approval, already staring daggers at the goblin mage.

As soon as the two tanks stepped into the room with their shields raised, the goblin caster screeched out some kind of command and held up its staff, the crystal beginning to glow a sickly green color. The three warrior goblins rushed toward the dworcs, weapons raised, snarling. Teeglin moved up behind the tanks along with the twins, standing between them, ready to stab through the gap between their shields when a target presented itself. Their healer was already sending a fireball at the goblin caster.

The fight took a long while, and they suffered a few minor injuries, but they eventually prevailed. The goblin mage died after the third fireball hit it. At the same time, both archers had taken a little splash damage, one of their bows being disabled. Teeglin had been hit in the arm with an arrow, and the axe-wielding twin had a chunk of his ear ripped off by another. Both tanks had some minor stab wounds. By the time they finished off the melee goblins, only one of the archers was still shooting arrows at them. The other had drawn a dagger and charged, meeting its death when the twin sister hurled her spear at it. The heavy weapon punched through the goblin's chest, killing it instantly. The others quickly moved forward behind the two tanks' shields and finished off the final archer as their healer switched from fireballs to healing magic.

"That was great!" Teeglin beamed at her party members as they looted the corpses. The goblin mage actually awarded them a silver coin each, much to their surprise.

"Aye, that were fun." The main tank grinned back at her.

Once they'd rested, they found that the chamber's exit led to a stairway that descended around a curve.

"Looks like we've cleared the whole floor!" Teeglin pumped a fist in the air, a gesture she'd seen Dylan make quite often.

The tank visibly gulped, then coughed. "There be more than one floor?" He looked a little nervous. Everyone knew that each floor in a dungeon was slightly more difficult than the one before.

Understanding his fear, and feeling more than a little of it herself, Teeglin nevertheless tried to ease their minds. "We'll go down and see what's there. If there be monsters we can't defeat, we'll run away." The grin she flashed them as she said that last bit seemed to put them at ease.

After resting and recharging, they made their way downstairs in the usual formation. When they reached the bottom they found another straight corridor. As they slowly made their way through, searching for traps as they went, an orc stepped out of a door at the end of the hall. Spotting the dworcs, it roared a challenge and raised an oversized sword, charging at them.

Both tanks took up position in front of the group, sharing a look as they planted their shields and readied their weapons. Though it was only level one, the orc was still an orc. Nearly twice their height, and stronger than they were, it bore down on them with tusks bared and sword ready.

Two seconds later the monster barreled into the two tanks. Though they'd planted their feet and done their best to resist, the weight and momentum of the orc knocked them back. As it fell atop them, the twins immediately went to work. Chopping and stabbing at its back, they both scored critical hits before it managed to roll off the two tanks and regain its feet. With a defiant roar it took a swing at Teeglin, who'd leapt toward it hoping to stab it in the heart. It raised its sword arm, preparing to chop down at her, but froze as the twin's spear thrust up into its armpit. The arm went limp, the sword clanging on the floor, and the orc's roar turned into a wheeze. Blood sprayed from its lips when it coughed once, then fell facedown on the floor.

Before the party could celebrate, another orc charged through the door, having been alerted by the roar of the first one. This one carried a flail with a spiked ball at the end of the chain. The two tanks, just getting back on their feet, planted their shields again. Teeglin could tell from the looks on their faces that they didn't expect to be able to hold this one back any better than they had the last.

As it turned out, they managed. In part because the female twin executed a crow-hop and hurled her spear into the charging orc when it was too close to miss. The impact didn't stop it, but it slowed the orc's momentum enough that the tanks were able to hold when it crashed into them. Teeglin and the other twin hacked at it even as the tanks got in blows of their own. When the sister reclaimed her spear by yanking the haft sideways, the orc expired.

Before they even had time to loot the bodies of the two dead orcs, a third charged through the door. Still a level one, this one was slightly larger than the other two. It carried two hand axes, and spittle flew from its mouth as it roared a challenge after taking note of its dead comrades.

As it approached, the spear wielder stood between and just behind the two tanks, holding the point of the spear so that it hovered just above their shields. Her brother moved next to her, and they both gripped the haft, placing their feet behind the butt end to keep it from sliding on the stone floor. "When it hits, let it push ye back a pace." She whispered to the tanks, who both nodded. Giving way was better than being knocked over.

The mage hit the orc in the face with a fireball when it was still half a dozen paces away, forcing it to close its eyes as it continued to stumble forward. When it half fell into the two tanks, they allowed themselves to be pushed backward, their boots sliding on the stone. As the orc pushed into them, the point of the spear slid into its chest, splintering a rib as it penetrated deep. Both the twins were knocked backward by the force of the impact, but they quickly recovered as the two tanks hacked at the wounded orc. Teeglin leapt forward as well, driving her own blade deep into its shoulder near its neck. When she withdrew her sword, blood welled up from the wound, making it clear she'd hit an artery. A moment later the orc groaned, trying in vain to lift its arms and strike at the dworcs. The tanks slammed their shields into it, and it fell back. After a few seconds of struggle, it fell still.

All of the party members leveled up at the same time. A moment later they realized they'd cleared the dungeon when notifications filled their vision.

Congratulations!

You are the first to defeat the Level One Dungeon!

Reward: 50,000xp; 10 gold; rare item!

As the party began to cheer, a bronze chest large enough for Teeglin to crawl into rose up from the floor in front of them. The dworcs all gathered around as she stepped forward and opened the top. A soft light emanated from inside as they gasped in surprise. The healer was the first to have the guts to reach inside. When she did, her hand emerged holding a bright blue robe with silver and forest green embroidery. The two tanks each received shields, one with a mug engraved on its face, the other with an axe. The twins received a pair of matching crossbows, which they seemed extremely pleased with.

When Teeglin's turn came, she withdrew a headband that resembled a tiara. Squealing with delight, she immediately put it on her head. The others were confused by the seemingly useless item, until she clapped her hands and exclaimed, "It gives me a five percent boost to both *Strength* and *Intelligence*!"

"That is a great gift indeed." Lightsprocket congratulated her as she approached. "You all did very well, and I'm sure King Max will be quite proud." She beamed up at the dworcs, who were all taller than she was. "Now, it's time for you to return to the portal and share your adventure with him. Mind that you don't set off the tripwire on your way out." She pointed back up the corridor, indicating that they should get moving.

Teeglin and the others nodded and set off, anxious to show off their loot, tell their story, and choose their new nicknames. With one last smile at the retreating adventurers, Lightsprocket turned and headed for the door through which the orcs had emerged. She had a dungeon core to try and communicate with.

Chapter 22

Max and his party, along with Redmane and
Cavariel, accompanied the dworcs back to their village for
a celebration of the young ones' successful dungeon run.
The village residents hailed the adventurers as heroes,
providing a feast during which they were encouraged to tell
the tale of their trip through the dungeon.

Though it was the very lowest level of dungeons,
and the party had not been in serious danger, everyone
treated it as though it were an epic adventure, a great
accomplishment. Max was roped into making an official
declaration regarding the young dworcs' chosen
nicknames, a ceremony which he carried out as if it were a
solemn duty. He even stole a gimmick from some of the
old movies he saw, having the dworclings kneel, tapping
them on the shoulders, and calling them by their chosen
names. Smitty loved everything about it, even offering
some horrible name suggestions to the party members
before they chose. His suggestion for the tank was *Orc
Blocker*, which only earned him confused looks, though the
two other corporals snickered.

As the celebration died down and the heroes were
put to bed, Max asked Dalia where the new beehives were
located. She gladly escorted him outside the wall and
showed him around, giving him a light slap on the arm
when he braved the bees to steal a glob of honey on one
finger to taste it.

As they strolled back toward the gate, he asked, "How are the alchemy experiments going?"

"Well!" She beamed up at him, her teeth and eyes shining slightly in the moonlight. "Gonna be needin' more ingredients soon, though. We've been burnin' through 'em too fast."

Max had been thinking about going back to Brightwood himself, having a vague plan in his head to craft a few things with larger pieces of dragon bone. One of them being a throne crafted from a larger vertebrae than the one he carried around.

"Why don't we head out there tomorrow? Just you and me." He offered as they walked back through the gates, nodding to acknowledge the guards' quiet greeting.

"Aye, I'd like that. Ye can help me plant more o' the most useful shrubs. In a few years, when they've grown, we'll have a steady supply o' rare, exceptional quality ingredients."

"Planning for the future is almost always a good thing." Max agreed. He fell silent as he considered what challenges he had on his plate. His most immediate issue was surviving the next attack by the Shadow Walkers, and finding a way to scare them off, or eliminate them altogether. He was hoping that a rival guild would help him, and was awaiting a response to Redmane's inquiries.

As they reached the village tavern, they found Redmane and the others sitting at a long table outside the front door. Teeglin was curled up in Dylan's lap, snoring, as the others spoke quietly. Most of the villagers had already retired, so Max led his party, with Dylan gently carrying the dworc princess, back through the portal to Stormhaven.

The following morning Max and Dalia met up for an early breakfast before setting out to Brightwood. She handed him a storage ring filled with seedlings to be planted, and had more in her own inventory. They grabbed Pokey and her ja'kang from the stables, then portaled to the Outpost, which was the closest point to the ancient battleground.

The ride only took a few minutes, and they left their mounts to graze just outside the dangerous area while they got to work. Dalia stayed along the edge of the area of effect damage, planting her seedlings and cuttings in the mana dense, dragonblood enriched soil. Max ventured into the battlefield, ignoring the tiny amounts of damage that ticked off every second, and walked over to what was left of the dragon's corpse. After spending some time inspecting the ribs that jutted up from the earth, he took hold of one of the smaller ones near the back end of the rib cage. Small being relative, of course, as the rib bone stood nearly as tall as him. Grabbing hold of it with both arms, he rocked his body back and forth, using his weight as well as his strength to work the rib free of the dirt. After less than a minute it was loose enough that he was able to squat down and powerlift it out of the ground.

After dropping the rib into his inventory, he turned to the visible spinal column that ran through the center of the exposed rib cage. Choosing a vertebrae that was a good six feet high and almost nearly as wide, he put a shoulder against it and tried to shift it as he'd done with the rib. When it didn't budge even an inch, he shrugged and produced a shovel. After ten minutes of digging around the edges of the section, he tried again to move it. Frustrated when once again it didn't shift, he stepped back, growling. "How do I get you free?"

From where she was sitting at the nearby tree line, Dalia called out, "Did ye try n just put it in yer ring?"

Max looked up, eyebrows raised, and just stared across the field at her for moment. "That can't work, can it?" He muttered to himself as he stepped closer and put a hand on the bone. When he willed it into his inventory, it disappeared from under his hand, leaving a large gap in the spine. Behind him he heard Dalia giggling, and chose to ignore her. "I suppose I could have done that with the rib, as well." He shook his head. "I should have thought of that myself."

He took another half hour to search for more scales, planning to gift them to one or both of the Oakstones, depending on how many he found. He'd promised not to put any more up for auction for a while, but gifting them to his mentor wouldn't negatively impact their market value, he didn't think. At the end of the half hour he had another two dozen scales, as well as several more bone shards that might be shaped into decent dagger or short sword blades. He also grabbed a chunk of bone from near the end of the tail that was roughly the size of a bowling ball. The moment he'd seen it, he had a plan for it that made him grin like a kid who just successfully raided a cookie jar.

He was on his way back to join Dalia when a massive shadow passed over him. Looking up and expecting to see the Roc that had so terrorized him atop the ridge above the Outpost, he was shocked to see something much larger. Something that made a certain orifice pucker.

A dragon.

All he could see was a silhouette, as it was passing between him and the sun. A moment later it let out a roar that caused Max to duck down and cover his head. Out of the corner of his eye he saw Dalia retreat behind one of the massive trees nearby, and didn't blame her one bit.

He managed to raise his gaze after it passed, but to his horror, he saw that it was banking around toward him and descending. He got a glimpse of sunlight glinting off of black scales before he once again lowered his eyes. A moment later he felt the ground tremble, and a strong gust of air that would have knocked him over if he'd been standing upright. Terror gripped him. He couldn't move, could barely breathe. Just when he thought he might soil his shorts, the pressure eased, and a voice boomed through the field.

"My apologies, Maximilian. I have been hunting, and forgot to suppress my aura. Are you... damaged in any way?"

Max blinked a few times, then took a deep breath, coming to terms with the fact that he wasn't dragon food. When he raised his head and got a good look at the dragon standing in front of him, a wave of relief washed over him. He recognized this dragon.

It was Lysbane.

"G-greetings, mighty Lysbane." Max could barely get the words out, his heart still pumping adrenaline through him. He rose on unsteady legs even as the dragon lowered his head to be level with Max's. Which left his chin nearly touching the ground. "I am... uninjured. Thanks for asking."

"Tougher than you look." The dragon snorted, causing Max's hair to blow back like he was in a wind tunnel. "Most would have lost consciousness, at the least. That is in fact why I let loose my aura when hunting. Much easier to snatch up unconscious beasts than to chase terrified creatures." The dragon's mouth opened, its jaw widening into what Max guessed was a smile.

"I'm glad I didn't end up as a snack, once again." He tried to smile at the dragon. Taking a few more deep breaths, he focused on calming his heartbeat.

"Ha! I suppose in a way I was hunting you." Lysbane chuckled.

"Hunting me?"

"I decided to take you up on your offer to visit Stormhaven. Apparently I arrived just after you departed to come here. Your chamberlain, Redmane I believe, informed me that you had come here to do some gardening." His head shifted toward the tree line. "Lady Dalia, it is quite safe to come out, I assure you."

Max turned to look in Dalia's direction as well, but she didn't emerge. Lysbane sighed. "I feel I must apologize again. She has apparently lost consciousness." Max resisted the urge to run to her as the dragon continued speaking. "I decided to join you here and see the place where my cousin perished." He nodded toward the skeletal corpse. "So I teleported out here after getting rough directions from the dwarf. The moment I arrived, I spotted a tasty looking herd, and I'm afraid I was sidetracked by hunger."

Max looked nervous for a moment, and the dragon laughed. "My appetite is sated, for now." Realizing that his dragon form was making Max uncomfortable, Lysbane blinked once and shrank down to his more human form, the one he'd assumed while cooking with Max and his companions when they first met.

Red appeared on Max's shoulder and waved to Lysbane. "Good day to ya, dragon!"

"And to you, lady leprechaun." He smiled at her. After a moment of staring, he added, "You both seem to have grown significantly since last we met."

"Oh, aye! Max here has a knack for gettin' himself into trouble, and the luck to somehow get himself back out of it." She flashed him a wicked grin. "With my help and sage advice, o' course."

"Of course." The dragon returned the smile. "And what's this I see? You've become a dungeon master?" He raised one eyebrow, obviously curious.

"I have. I planted a dungeon core and created a new dungeon just yesterday." Max nodded, having calmed down enough to speak in full sentences.

"That is a tale worth hearing!" Lysbane turned and began to walk toward where Dalia had disappeared, Max quickly trotting after him. When they reached the dwarf, Lysbane cast a spell that immediately revived her, then helped her to her feet. "I am sorry, lady Dalia, for frightening you."

"L-Lysbane,?" Dalia looked around, confused. When her gaze found Max, he nodded in confirmation.

"Yes. I'm afraid I'm out of practice with regards to interacting with the younger races. I neglected to suppress my aura before approaching you. Again, my apologies." He bowed his head to the dwarf, who blushed furiously.

"No apology necessary." Her voice was barely more than a squeak. Max sympathized, having just experienced the same. "C-can we help ye with somethin'?"

"I have a few things to discuss, actually." Lysbane waved a hand and two comfortable looking sofas appeared. He took a seat in one, and motioned for Max and Dalia to use the other. As they settled, he asked, "Can I offer you a drink, first?"

When they both shook their heads, he said, "First, I want to congratulate you on your victory over the Battleborne!" His smile revealed sharp dragon's teeth inside his humanoid mouth.

"Ah, it wasn't much of a victory. I just convinced her to back off and leave Westreach alone."

Lysbane stared at him for a moment. "Her? Oh, you mean the human queen. Yes, that was an interesting interaction as well. Regin told me of your first interaction with her young noble, and the message you sent. Quite amusing." He smiled again. "But no, I was referring to the Battleborne you defeated at the ruined settlement in the valley north of my lair."

Max's mouth dropped open. "The red-eyed orc shaman? He was Battleborne?"

"You did not know?" Lysbane's expression clearly revealed his surprise.

"I did not. He was a threat to my people, so I went to confront him."

"Ah, well. It is still unsurprising that you met in battle. Throughout history, as long as Battleborne have been sent to this world, they have always seemed to find each other somehow. Usually resulting in the death of one or both."

Max found himself suspecting the gods of having something to do with that. Manipulating events so that Battleborne ended up confronting each other. *Has Regin been doing that with me?* He wondered briefly before the dragon interrupted his thoughts.

"In any case, my congratulations on your victory." Lysbane continued. "You were vastly outnumbered and out-leveled, but managed to prevail." He offered a nod of respect. "And while we're on the topic of that battle, there is something else I would like to address. After the battle, you claimed a significant section of the area for your kingdom."

"Yes, I did." Max shifted uncomfortably on the sofa as he realized that by claiming the land north of the dworcs' valley, he had probably also claimed the mountain in which the dragon's lair was located. He was opening his mouth and trying to find the proper words for an apology when Lysbane cut him off.

"I can see what you're thinking, Max. I don't mind that you claimed the land that includes my own mountain. Assuming you have no designs on my lair, or its contents?" He raised an eyebrow again, and Max immediately shook his head, raising his empty hands in a gesture of peace. "I didn't think so. However, the outpost that you constructed there was recently attacked by a mountain troll, which your people defeated."

Again Max nodded, his mind spinning, wondering where the dragon was headed.

"That troll was part of a small tribe that I seeded in those mountains a few millennia ago." He watched as Max and Dalia's eyes both widened, horrified at the thought that they'd somehow killed a friend or ally of the dragon. Lysbane raised a finger to stop them from speaking. "Your people were justified in killing it, as they were simply defending themselves. But I would ask that in the future you do not go hunting for the rest of its tribe."

Max shook his head emphatically. "I'm sorry, Lysbane. If they're friends of yours, we'll absolutely leave them in peace. I'll let my people know right away."

Lysbane chuckled, a deep rumbling sound that seemed to echo off the surrounding trees. "I would not call them friends, Max. Have you ever tried to converse with a mountain troll? They don't even have names, as far as I know." He shook his head. "You see, we dragons find mountain trolls to be quite tasty. I have several recipes that feature them as a main ingredient. Back then, so many of us were harvesting them that they nearly went extinct. So I rounded up a few dozen and transported them here to what was, at that time, my domain. I made it clear to my brethren that none were to hunt in my territory, giving them time to reproduce in peace."

Dalia's snort surprised Max. "Ye keep thirty foot tall giant trolls as farm animals!" She rolled her eyes at the dragon, causing Max to smile as well.

"That was one of the smaller ones. Not quite an adult." Lysbane replied. "A shame, too. It would have been tender and juicy…" He grinned as Dalia snorted again. "The fully mature adults can be fifty feet tall or more. I typically harvest one of those when I'm hosting three or four of my fellow dragons."

Max, remembering the portal Lysbane had opened after their first meeting, and the herd animals he'd seen on the other side, had an idea. "Lysbane, we will absolutely look out for your… herd? I'll make sure my people don't attack them in the wild. If another one should attack our outpost, we'll try to drive it away rather than kill it."

Lysbane shook his head. "Do not risk the lives of your warriors with such an effort. If one of the trolls attacks your outpost, defend yourself. But if you'd be so kind as to notify me afterwards, and leave its corpse for me to harvest, I would appreciate it."

"We can certainly do that." Max agreed. "And while we're on the topic of herds, can you tell me about the animals I saw when you opened that portal from your lair?"

Lysbane blinked, thinking back. "The auralos?"

Max nodded. "Big hairy creatures on four legs. They looked similar to what we called buffaloes on my world. Only several times larger."

"Yes. Migratory herd animals. Quite tasty. What would you like to know about them?"

"Well, you just answered my first and second questions. They're called auralos, and are tasty." Max grinned at the dragon. "I have a rapidly growing kingdom with thousands of citizens to feed, and purchasing supplies is sometimes difficult. So my third question is, might there be a way we could trade for a few of your auralos? If I could establish a herd here, it would go a long way toward solving our supply issues."

"Ha! They are not *my auralos*, Max. They roam free in a valley many months' travel from here on foot. But I would be happy to help you obtain a small herd for your kingdom. What would you offer in trade for my assistance?"

"What would you like? Gold? Diamonds?"

"Bah!" Lysbane waved a hand dismissively. "I am a dragon, Max. I have enough gold and gems to fill your palace to the rafters." He paused, thinking. "Have you run across any new recipes in your travels since we parted?"

"I have!" Max smiled. "And though we didn't think of them during our last cooking session, we have adapted several recipes from my old world. We've even opened a restaurant to serve them to the public!"

"Wonderful! Take me to this restaurant. I will sample your new recipes, maybe offer some suggestions to improve them. In return, you shall have your auralos." Lysbane clapped his hands, getting to his feet. Looking around, he asked, "Where would you like them?"

Max hesitated for a second, blinking in surprise. "You're going to get them right now?"

"Of course! It'll only take a moment." Lysbane grinned.

"Uh, here is fine, I guess." Max replied, then flinched as Dalia elbowed him in the ribs.

"Here is not fine. Them big beasties might eat all our ingredients!"

"Oh, right." Max grimaced over the huge mistake his almost made.

"Not to worry. I'll bring them through here, and drive them in whatever direction you choose." Lysbane raised an eyebrow, waiting.

Max pointed in the general direction of the Way Station. "We have a settlement about a day's ride that way. If you could just send them far enough that way that they won't return and munch on our valuable herbs here..."

"Say no more." Lysbane waved a hand and a massive portal opened in the middle of the battlefield. "The curse on this place should keep them away even if they were to turn back for some reason." He added before resuming his dragon form. He leapt into the air and flapped his wings once, propelling himself through the portal. On the other side Max saw the same grass-covered valley as before, and what looked like thousands of the buffalo creatures. Lysbane flapped his wings again, rising higher and disappearing from sight for a while. Max was tempted to step through the portal and look around, but just as he was about to move toward it, the dragon swooped back into sight in the distance. He roared, causing the auralos between him and the portal to flee in terror. The dragon cut left, then right, expertly herding the animals, bunching them together like cattle being pushed into a pen. Max grabbed Dalia and pulled her well to the side of the portal as the closest creatures to the portal fled through it.

Max's eyes widened as the first few rushed through. He'd thought they were large, but hadn't really had a proper perspective looking at them from a distance through the portal. The auralos were each nearly the size of an elephant! Taller than him at the shoulder, with stout legs and shaggy fur, each one must have weighed four or five tons each!

Max and Dalia drew back farther as Red giggled hysterically on his shoulder, pretending to fall and roll around with her arms wrapped around her belly as they watched dozens of the animals charge through.

"What are ye laughin' about?" Dalia asked before Max could.

"Well, first, the look on yer faces." The leprechaun paused her laughter to answer. "Also, ye just earned a ton o' sovereign points from makin' a bargain with a dragon, gettin' enough food to feed yer people for years to come, and all it cost ya was some recipes for what ya call junk food!" She paused, winking at Max. "See what I did there? A *ton* o' points? For *tons* o' meat on the hoof?"

"Very clever." Max deadpanned as they watched more of the creatures emerge. He didn't show it, but now that Red mentioned it, he was quite proud of himself.

By the time Lysbane himself emerged from the portal, more than a hundred of the auralos had passed through. He flapped his wings again, soaring higher before turning and driving the leaders of the stampede toward the Way Station. He then circled around behind the stragglers and roared, briefly unleashing the same aura that had incapacitated Max and Dalia earlier, sending the terrified beasts charging off into the distance.

Landing and reverting back to his humanoid form, he dismissed the portal. "I assume that will suffice?"

"More than suffice! I was hoping for maybe a dozen to use as breeding stock!" Max wanted to hug the dragon, but resisted the urge. "We can come back another time and plant the rest of the herbs." He looked at Dalia who nodded. "If you'd like to accompany us to Regin's outpost, we can take the portal back to Stormhaven, and we'll get you some tacos."

Lysbane shook his head. "I'm in no particular hurry. Let us plant your herbs first. It has been too long since I did any gardening. I quite enjoy it." When he saw Max's confused look, he added, "When one lives as long as I do, one learns to find joy in the simple things. Gardening is as good a way to pass the time as any. And when the plants have grown and blossomed, It gives me a sense of accomplishment."

Slightly stunned that an ancient and powerful being like a dragon would want to plant herbs with them, Max began to empty the storage ring that Dalia had given him. Lysbane promptly gathered up a dozen or so seedlings and, after looking around briefly, strolled over to his chosen spot and dropped to his knees. Using suddenly clawed fingers, he easily dug into the earth and began to gently place the plantings.

Max was standing still, staring, when Dalia slapped his butt. "Don't just stand there, get to work!"

When they were finished, Dalia went to retrieve their mounts while Max took a moment to use his communication rings. First he sent a message to Redmane, warning him that he was bringing a dragon back to the city, and asking him to have the cook at Eats N Treats prepare for a VIP visit. He also mentioned the new herd of edible giants. Then he used a different ring to contact Gro'nag and warn him about the approaching auralos. The very surprised mayor of the Way Station promised to send out some people to round them up.

"Just out of curiosity, have you heard of auralos before?" Max asked the elder orc.

"Heard of 'em, sure. Never seen one, or tasted one either. As far as I know, they were wiped out long ago. If you've found a whole herd, that'll be some valuable meat."

"Well, for now it's for our own use only. We need some people who can take care of them, raise them. When the herd gets large enough, we'll consider selling the meat."

"Aye, I'll take care of it, Max."

When Dalia returned with their mounts, Max pointed toward the Outpost. "It'll take us a little while to get there, but if you'd like to fly over, we'll catch up as quickly as we can."

"No need." Lysbane flicked his fingers and another portal opened. Through this one Max could see the front gate of Stormhaven. "That'll work, too. We can stop and see the dungeon on the way." He led Pokey toward the portal, following Lysbane through with Dalia walking alongside leading her mount.

*****

"Truly a remarkable circumstance!" Lysbane declared around a mouthful of burrito, after hearing Max's story of the dungeon core. "I've never heard of a dungeon creating a second core. Or of a humanoid's life force being converted into a core. I should like to visit it and take a look."

"You're welcome to do so, anytime. Right now a mage named Lightsprocket is in there studying the core, so you might have a hard time getting a word in edgewise." Max grinned across the table at the dragon.

They had once again shut down the restaurant in order to host Lysbane. Max had instructed the kitchen staff to bring out every dish on the menu, one every fifteen minutes or so. Lysbane had complimented each and every dish, and offered the cook tips on how they might improve the flavor, or the consistency, of most of them. He was particularly fond of the pizza with bacon and mushrooms, declaring it delicious just the way it was.

When Max had offered him the recipes, then asked him to keep them to himself until they'd opened several more restaurants, the dragon just laughed. "No need for the recipes, my friend. Remember, I am a master chef. I can tell you every ingredient and their quantities just from tasting and smelling each dish." He paused for a moment, recalling Max's words. "Did you say you're opening more restaurants?"

Smitty cut in, as the restaurant was mainly his baby. "We are. On our world we have what are called franchises.

466

An owner of a successful restaurant establishes a menu, a standard restaurant design, training plan for the staff, and so forth, then uses them to open several more restaurants in other neighborhoods, or other cities. Sometimes they license it, and sell the rights to other owners to open copies for themselves. The biggest franchises have thousands of locations."

"Other neighborhoods? How big are your cities?"

"Well, the largest spread out several miles in every directions, and are home to several million people each. Last I heard, New York City had something like ten million?"

Lysbane's eyes widened. "So many! How do you feed them all."

"We don't." Dylan mumbled, but the dragon had picked up his words, raising an eyebrow at him and motioning for him to elaborate. "A percentage of the humans back home are starving. Some because they live in areas where crops won't grow, or they're just too poor to afford food. As a nation, as well as individually." He sighed. "We have millions of people who work as farmers, raise livestock, etc. We even have massive machines that allow a single farm with half a dozen workers to produce more than all the farmers in Stormhaven currently can. But the food doesn't reach everyone." A scowl appeared as he looked down at his hands. "We have so much production capacity that governments pay some farmers not to grow food for a year or two, to let their soil recover and replenish itself."

Lysbane nodded, sensing the ogre's anguish. "It is ever the case, among the younger races, that the poor suffer and go without while the wealthy live in excess. The problem is not exclusive to your world." He motioned toward the door and the city beyond. "Though I have seen no orphans or beggars roaming the streets of your city, they can be found in almost any other on this continent."

Max cleared his throat. "We're a new kingdom, and we've been doing our best to make sure everyone is both employed, and fed. The herd you helped us with today will be a big help in that effort. So again, thank you."

"You have more than adequately repaid me for my effort with this wonderful evening." He smiled at Max and everyone else at the table. "That was a small fraction of the herd roaming that valley. If you need more, simply ask." He sat back in his chair, looking down at the last few bites of burrito and rubbing his belly. Max knew the dragon wasn't anywhere near full, that he was just being polite.

After a few moments of thought, he asked, "Would you mind if I remained here in the city for a short while? I find I'm quite enjoying having company again. The last time I mingled with the younger races for more than a short time, Regin had yet to ascend."

Dalia's eyes bulged at the reminder of how ancient the dragon was.

"You are our honored guest, and a friend of Stormhaven." Max declared, grinning as light swirled around the dragon, who grinned back. "You are welcome here anytime, and for as long as you want. We'll have a suite prepared for you in the palace." Max hesitated for a moment.

"I uh, feel I should warn you, though I'm sure they're no threat to you. Someone has put a contract on my head, hiring the Shadow Walkers guild to kill me. They've attacked the palace twice already, and we expect them to try again anytime now."

Lysbane growled slightly. "I have not heard of this Shadow Walkers guild. Are they dangerous?"

Redmane filled him in. "They be the largest and strongest o' the assassins' guilds on the continent. And they be especially interested in killin' me king here."

"Oh?" The dragon looked at Max, who shrugged and looked a bit sheepish.

"After their first attempt to kill me, I might have killed their grandmaster."

"Ha! It sounds like spending time here might be quite entertaining! Tell me." The dragon picked up the remains of his burrito and took a bite as Max began to tell the tale of the assassins.

Chapter 23

Max was working at his forge, chatting with Lysbane while he worked. The dragon hadn't been kidding when he expressed an interest in everyday activities. He sat on a stool across the anvil from Max, giving him occasional pointers. In turn, Max told the dragon bits of his story, hitting the highlights of his time on the new world. When Lysbane stopped him to ask a question, it was rarely about the big happenings, many of which he already seemed aware of. Rather, he asked about the panacea potion experiments, the efforts to create honey brandy, and the story behind the swamp hydra heads in the throne room.

To Max's great amusement, the dragon got excited when he mentioned he still had some of the swamp hydra meat in his inventory. Both uncooked, and the kabobs that his favorite meat vendor had prepared. Lysbane immediately demanded a taste of the kabobs, and after enjoying it, expressed a desire to meet the vendor. Then he turned his attention to the uncooked meat.

"What can I offer you in trade for whatever you have left?"

"No need for a trade. It's yours, my compliments." Max produced a pile of maybe ten pounds of the raw meat, setting it on the nearest work bench after making sure it was clean.

"I appreciate the thought, Max. But I must insist on a trade. Otherwise I'll feel as if I've intimidated you into presenting a valuable gift." The dragon's smile made it clear he was kidding about the intimidation bit. "Think it over, and let me know." He twitched a finger and the meat disappeared.

Before Max could reply, Master Oakstone entered the forge. "Max! I see ye be practicin! Glad to see it!" He paused midstep when he noticed Lysbane sitting nearby. "Ah, sorry, yer Majesty. I did not know ye had a customer. I'll leave ye be."

"Please stay, Master Oakstone. This is Lysbane. He's a friend, not a customer. He knows my secrets, so anything you wish to discuss can be said in front of him." The dwarf bobbed his head in greeting, receiving a smile in return from the dragon, then grabbed another stool and moved it closer. "Me grandsire said to tell ye he'll be finished with his commissions in a few more days. We're gatherin' the materials needed, and should be ready in a week, no more."

"Sooner than expected." Max stopped hammering on the sword he was forming, slipping the metal back into the forge to reheat.

"Aye, there was a wee delay in getting' the block o' dragonstone delivered. That'll be the final piece. The stone shaper will arrive along with it."

Lysbane perked up. "Did you say dragonstone?"

"Obsidian, not like the one I'm carrying." Max clarified, then felt stupid when he realized the dragon very likely knew what the dwarf meant.

Missing the context, the dwarf nodded. "Aye, we be planning to upgrade this smithy fer Max here. Me grandsire be a Grandmaster smith, and his home forge be built o' dragonstone. We'll be buildin' one here just like it."

"But there's a delay getting the stone delivered." Lysbane confirmed.

"It's not a big deal." Max replied. "The Grandmaster had some commissions to complete at home, anyway."

"Max, your metal is in danger of overheating. You might want to remove it." Lysbane gestured to the half-formed sword. Without even thinking, Max grabbed his tongs and removed it, only noticing as he set it down on the anvil that it wasn't actually fully heated. Confused, he looked up at Lysbane.

"Take a few steps back, both of you." He motioned Max and Oakstone toward the work bench that was a few paces behind the dwarf. When Oakstone looked at Max, he just shrugged and did as the dragon instructed.

As soon as he deemed them to be at a safe distance, Lysbane waved a hand toward the forge. In the blink of an eye, the entire metal structure disappeared. Oakstone gasped and started to take a step forward, his mouth open to question Lysbane, but Max put a restraining hand on his shoulder. When the dwarf looked up at him, he shook his head. Whatever Lysbane was doing, Max wasn't about to interfere.

"You know how we were just discussing payment for the swamp hydra meat?" Lysbane grinned at the two of them. "I've decided for you." With another wave of his hand the columns and roof of the smithy disappeared as well. He opened his mouth and breathed into the area where the forge had been, and a black mist poured out. An instant later the mist coalesced into a massive cube of obsidian, twelve feet tall and wide. As Oakstone's jaw dropped and his eyes widened, Lysbane looked from the two of them to the block, and back.

"On second thought, just go ahead and stand outside for a bit. This'll be much easier if you're completely out of the way."

Max had to take hold of the dwarf's arm and lead him out of the area, the dwarf stumbling slightly, not taking his eyes off Lysbane for a second. When they were once again standing still, he blinked several times, then looked up at Max.

"Yer doin it again, Max."

"Doing what?" Max took his gaze off the dragon and looked down at the dwarf.

"Doin things ye shouldn't be able to do." The dwarf shook his head as if waking from a dream. "I'll eat my own dirty shorts if that ain't a dragon." He paused, then added in a voice barely above a whisper. "He be the dragon ye told me about. I did not recognize the name."

Max nodded. "Lysbane came to pay us a visit. I think he's planning on staying for a while. Uh… do me a favor and keep his identity to yourself?"

Lysbane's voice drifted out of the smithy. "That's alright, Max. I have nothing to fear from anyone here in the city knowing my identity."

"Except the crowd of admirers that might start following you everywhere." Max thought of the flood of gnomes and dwarves that had inundated Glitterspindle's temple.

"I'm quite capable of discouraging any unwanted attention, Max." He could hear the grin in the dragon's voice.

"Just please don't make anyone piss themselves inside my palace." Max let it go. The dragon was correct, he could certainly take care of himself.

Silence reigned as Max and Oakstone observed Lysbane. The dragon had stepped up and put a hand on the massive block of obsidian, causing the stone to flow like a liquid at his touch. He then began shifting both hands, looking much like an orchestra conductor, guiding the stone as it separated and reshaped itself, moving some of it to the four corners of the structure, forming it into columns. From there, a sheet of it melted and spread across the floor, the dragon quickly lifting the anvil with one hand so that the flowing puddle of black stone could get underneath it.

Another large section of the block moved into the corner where the forge had been, changing its shape slowly as it moved. Lysbane hardened the floor and set the anvil back down, then began to move both hands and all his fingers as he willed the stone into the shape he wanted. When he was satisfied with that, he gestured at what remained of the original block, and it flowed up the columns to form a gravity-defying pool above his head. With another gesture it hardened just as the floor had, becoming the structure's ceiling.

"Alright, it is safe for you to return." He made a beckoning gesture with one hand. Max barely had time to take his first step before Oakstone sprinted the short distance into the structure, eliciting a chuckle from the dragon. Max hurried as well, not wanting to seem ungrateful.

When he caught up, he found his mentor staring wide-eyed at the new forge. Lysbane had created a sort of self-portrait in obsidian, shaping the forge into a likeness of himself, complete with half-spread wings, long neck, and a head with an open mouth from which blue flame flickered. The belly of the dragon was open, exposing a furnace with two levels of racks and the blue flame that was reflected in the mouth.

Oakstone shook his head again, then moved to find a stool and sat down. His gaze flicked to Lysbane, and he quickly stood and bowed at the waist. "Me apologies, Eldest. I dinna recognize ye."

"No apology necessary. And please just call me Lysbane." The dragon's grin was wide and friendly. "What do you think of the improvements."

"This... I do no' have the words, Eld... Lysbane." He shook his head again. "It be wondrous!" Shifting his gaze to Max, he continued. "Max, do ye know what the Eldest has give'd ye?" Not waiting for Max to respond, he answered his own question. "This be a true dragonforge!" He got up and stomped around a bit, looking at his reflection in the smooth obsidian floor. "Formed directly by the dragon's magic, from its own element! Heated with dragon fire!"

With a quick wink at Lysbane, and a respectful bow of his head, Max replied to the dwarf. "I'm guessing from your reaction that those are good things." He did his best to look innocent, but the dwarf wasn't buying it.

"Ye damned fool! Ye should be on yer knees, kissin' the Eldest's shoes, thankin' him fer the blessing he's give'd ye! Not that ye deserve it, if ye ask me!" Oakstone grumped at him, crossing his arms and glaring.

"I did give him some tasty swamp hydra meat." Max muttered to himself as he did his best not to smile back at the glaring dwarf. Turning to Lysbane, he bowed deeply and, with his most solemn expression, offered thanks. "Your wondrous gift is most sincerely appreciated, Eldest Lysbane. This is much too much compensation for a few pounds of meat."

Returning Max's previous wink with his head turned so that the dwarf couldn't see it, the dragon played along. "Ah, as you saw for yourself, it was only the work of a few moments. Less time, I'm sure, than it took you to defeat and harvest the hydra."

Oakstone huffed at Max again, but decided to let the matter of his disrespect go, turning his focus back to the forge. Stepping forward, he laid a hesitant hand atop the dragon's head, having to stand up on his toes to do so. "It be cool to the touch, despite the heat I feel in its breath."

"Obsidian is volcanic in origin. It takes a great deal of heat to warm the stone at all. Which is why it works so well for a dragon forge." With his back to Lysbane, Oakstone didn't see his patient smile. "If you keep your hand on the stone and focus your intent, you can increase or reduce the heat within the forge." They both watched as the dwarf did just that, causing the flames to burn higher, then reduce to barely a flicker.

Turning back to the dragon, Oakstone bowed deeply once again. "Thank ye fer lettin' me witness the creation o' this wonder, Eldest Lysbane. I be truly honored."

Lysbane nodded slightly in return, a gesture befitting his high station. "In that case, I'm sure Max wouldn't mind if you were the first to craft something in his new forge." He gave Max a sideways glance, and Max immediately agreed.

"Of course! Go right ahead." He chuckled as the dwarf immediately produced some metal from his inventory and charged toward the furnace, taking a moment to raise the temperature again before inserting it on to the lower rack. As the metal was heating, Lysbane looked down at the anvil, which now sat atop the obsidian floor.

"Hmm… this won't do." He lifted the anvil again, making it disappear, then waved his hand at the floor where it had just sat. A square block of obsidian raised up stopping at about knee height for Max. A moment later he placed an anvil atop the stone base, eyeing Max to measure the height. "This is about right for you, I think." Turning and clearing his throat to get Oakstone's attention, he added, "Just place your hand atop the anvil and exert your will the same as you did with the forge, and it will lower itself to a comfortable height for you to work."

The dwarf nodded and reached for the anvil, his hand pausing several inches above it. Looking up at Max, then at the dragon, he let out a sigh. "Ye gived him an orichalcum anvil."

Lysbane shrugged. "I assumed you wanted the dragonstone structure to assist with enchanting the items you craft. Orichalcum stores and conducts mana much better than iron, or even dwarven steel."

"Aye, that it does." Max saw the moment when the dwarf just gave up and decided to go with the flow. He turned back to the metal in the forge, using tongs to bring it out of the furnace and set it upon the new anvil. Producing a hammer from his inventory, he set to work pounding on the metal.

Lysbane and Max both took seats, content to watch the master smith at work. None of them spoke, other than the occasional muttering from Oakstone as he worked the metal. Max overheard the phrase "Wait'll me grandsire sees this." But for the most part tried not to eavesdrop. Max did note that the metal that his mentor had chosen was mithril. Not having seen it worked before, he paid careful attention to every detail he could take in. After fifteen minutes of close observation, a notification appeared.

Skill Level Up! Your Blacksmithing skill has increased by +1!

Max wanted to share his good fortune, but chose instead not to interrupt. He got a knowing look from Lysbane, and Max spent a moment wondering just how much of his information the dragon was able to see. Or whether Lysbane could just outright read his mind.

Half an hour later, Oakstone moved to the polishing wheel on a nearby workbench. He spent a few minutes there, humming to himself as he worked. When he was done, he picked up an engraving tool and spent another half hour working on the item, his back to his observers, blocking their view. Finally, he blew on the item a few times and rubbed it with a brush, then a cloth, to clear away any loose shavings. Turning to Lysbane, he held it out in the palm of both hands.

"I hope ye don't think it too presumptuous o' me, but I'd like ta offer ye this small token, in appreciation o' what ye've done here."

As he held it up, Max cast *Examine* on it.

Mithril Torq
Item Quality: Epic

Item Rarity: Unique
This torq was crafted by dwarven Master Smith
Oakstone for Eldest Lysbane.
Attributes: ??

Max was about to ask about the attributes that were hidden to him, when Oakstone explained. "I'd not presume to include spells or attribute bonuses fer one such as yerself. I doubt me ability be enough to make any difference anyway." He paused, taking a breath. "This'll tell any dwarf with the ability to see that ye be Revered by the Oakstone clan. Simply show it, and ye'll be welcomed as an honored guest in any Oakstone settlement or home." He smiled slightly before adding. "Or likely those o' any other clan as well. In case ye be hesitant to reveal yer identity as an Eldest."

Lysbane gently lifted the torq from the dwarf's trembling hands, making a show of inspecting it closely. Max wasn't sure, but he thought from the expression on the dragon's face, he was truly touched by the gift. A moment later, Lysbane confirmed it.

Reaching out with his free hand, he touched Oakstone's shoulder. "Bless you, Master Oakstone. This is among the most valuable of all treasures, a sincere gift from the heart. Thank you."

Max smiled as Oakstone's eyes went vacant, wondering if he'd received the same five point boost to his *Luck* stat that Lysbane's blessing had granted to Max and his party. When the dwarf blinked several times and refocused on the dragon, there were tears in his eyes. Max guessed that whatever the blessing was, it had been much more than a boost to *Luck*.

Overcome, the dwarf bowed again before retreating to his stool, wiping his eyes with his sleeve as he sat. When Max looked away from the dwarf, he found the dragon staring at him expectantly.

"Oh, my skill isn't nearly high enough to make proper use of all this." Max took a step back, then motioned toward the forge. "If you'd like to craft something yourself, I'm happy to watch. I gained a point in Blacksmithing watching Master Oakstone just now. I'm betting that watching you craft something will earn me several more."

"Ha! Well, if you insist, I don't mind if I do!"

Max watched as the dragon in human form turned the heat in the forge way up, then produced an ingot Max couldn't identify. When he tried to *Examine* it, he just got more question marks. By the look on Oakstone's face, he was having a similar issue.

Max moved to sit next to the dwarf, the two of them well out of the dragon's way as they observed. After a few minutes, while Lysbane was pounding on the heated ingot with what looked like a hammer made of glass, the dwarf elbowed him and whispered. "Ye know this all be fer show. The dragon could simply hold the metal in his hands n shape it the same as he did the forge."

"But what would be the fun in that?" Lysbane grinned over his shoulder without pausing the steady rhythmic hammering. "I quite enjoy the work. Making sure the metal reaches the proper heat, gauging the weight of the hammer and the perfect amount of force for each blow."

Both dwarf and chimera nodded at that, knowing the feeling, the dwarf's face reddening slightly at having interrupted the dragon while he was working.

It didn't take long for the dragon to finish. Turning to face his audience, he handed the item to Max. It was a smooth rod made of softly glowing metal with a dragon's head at one end. He and Oakstone *Examined* the item at the same time.

Rod of Recovery
Item Quality: Legendary
Item Rarity: Unique
Attributes: +10% Intelligence, Wisdom
Enchantments: Dimensional Pocket;
Translocation
This item was crafted by Grandmaster Lysbane for King Maximilian Storm.

Before he was even finished reading the description, Lysbane explained. "I've been thinking about the quest I gave you to return my cousin's head to his family. There are not many storage devices that will accept an item the size of my cousin's fat head." He pointed at the rod. "This creates a dimensional pocket large enough to carry it once you've retrieved it, saving you the trouble of loading it onto a cart and dragging it around. It will only carry a single item, so make sure it's empty before you try and stuff his head in there." He reached out and tapped the dragon's head at the end of the rod. "In case you're wondering, that's what he looked like."

Max nodded, taking in every detail of the likeness.

"As for the other enchantment, that's another time saver. Once you have recovered my cousin's head, activate the rod, and it will teleport you and your party, up to ten people, directly to his grave site. If I'm not there when you arrive, just wait. I'll be notified of your untimely intrusion when you activate the enchantment, and will join you at my earliest convenience." His smile made it clear he was teasing Max. "I'll bring his mate and offspring with me, so that you might return the skull to them directly."

"This is… amazing!" Max ran his fingers over the carved dragon head. "Thank you, Lysbane. I'll make good use of it, I promise."

"Oh, I'm certain you will, Max." The dragon placed a hand on his belly. "Now, I think I've had enough crafting for today. Do you suppose the kitchen at your restaurant is open? I've been curious about those things you mentioned. I believe you called them cheeseburgers?"

"They are open for you anytime!" Max grinned. "And if they're not, I'll cook you a cheeseburger myself! I'm pretty good on the grill, if I do say so myself."

*****

The kitchen was indeed open, and the trio took seats at the table reserved for Max and his party. There were a dozen or so other patrons already seated and enjoying the meal, speaking quietly amongst themselves. Max saw three gnomes at one table sharing a large pizza, while a quartet of dwarves were crunching through plates of tacos with gusto.

Birona, Smitty's wife and the woman running the restaurant, appeared almost immediately after having been notified of their arrival. She recognized both Lysbane and Oakstone from their previous visits, and greeted them just as warmly as she did Max, setting a pitcher and three mugs on the table. "Welcome back! What would you like me to bring you today?"

"We'll start with cheeseburgers all around." Max grinned at her. "Medium rare, with all the fixins. Oh! And a large order of onion rings. Or whatever you call them." The new world didn't have onions, but they'd found something similar that tasted nearly as good when deep fried in batter. Max could never remember the name of the vegetable they used. Smitty had even managed to create a delicious dipping sauce to go with them. To Max it tasted like a blending of thousand island and sweet barbecue sauce.

Cooking on this world being a much faster process than on Earth, Birona returned in just a few minutes with their meals. Max watched Lysbane's face as he took a hearty bite of the cheeseburger, allowing the grease to run down his chin as he chewed thoughtfully.

"I quite like this! And the presentation is… interesting." He peeked under the bun at the meat patty and condiments before taking a second bite.

"One of my all-time favorites." Max agreed. Oakstone simply grunted his approval, his mouth full of burger goodness.

They each wolfed down their burgers, and were partway through a second round, when Lysbane sat up straight, setting his burger back on his plate and staring at the door. In a quiet and calm voice, he said, "Max, there are a dozen stealthed individuals approaching this building." After a short paused, he added, "All of them dark elves."

"Shit. That'd be the Shadow Walkers." Max dropped his food and stood, drawing his sword even as he sent an alert to his party, and to Redmane. "How long till they get here?"

"They are moving cautiously. Half a minute." Lysbane got to his feet. "Each of them is level seventy or higher. No offense, Max, but you have little chance of surviving an encounter with them. Please, allow me."

Before Max could protest, Lysbane crossed the room and exited the restaurant, turning to face up the street. Max and Oakstone hurried behind him, but stayed inside when he motioned for them to stop at the doorway. The dragon scanned the street in front of him, then briefly looked up at a nearby rooftop. A second later he clapped this hands, sending a thunderous sound wave outward in a wide arc. The sound echoed off the nearby buildings and Max winced slightly, his elven ears complaining. In the blink of an eye twelve Shadow Walkers appeared as if out of nowhere, their stealth abilities having been canceled by the dragon's magic.

Just as surprised as Max was, the assassin's froze for a moment before tightening their grips on their weapons and rushing forward, all eyes on Max. Lysbane spoke a single word that froze them all in place.

"Stop!"

All eyes were now on Lysbane, including those of several score citizens who'd been minding their own business, then surprised by the thunderclap and sudden appearance of a dozen assassins, before being frozen in place along with the Shadow Walkers. Max could see from the expression on the dark elves' face that they were straining against whatever spell held them in place. He didn't think their odds of success were high.

Stepping up until he was just two paces from the nearest, and highest level, dark elf, Lysbane growled. "You are not welcome here." When the frozen lead elf tried unsuccessfully to reply, Lysbane made a gesture that freed up his head and neck, leaving the rest of him immobilized.

"We have a contract for the chimera king's life. Do not interfere with Shadow Walker business, mage, or you will find our displeasure focused on you, as well."

"Mage? You are mistaken, puny thing!" Lysbane roared, as he transformed back into his dragon form, accidently toppling a few bystanders who stood too close. "I am no simple mage!"

Max felt the familiar fear as the dragon unleashed a bit of his aura. The assassins all flinched, more then one of them wetting themselves, as did many of the nearby citizens. Guards, having been alerted by the noise, came rushing in from several directions, down the street and from connecting alleyways. Upon seeing the angry dragon snarling at the frozen assassin's they all came to a halt, looking to Max for direction. He held up a hand, signaling for them to hold.

Staring at the lead elf again, Lysbane growled as he motioned toward the others. "Take these into custody. This one will be returning to his nest of vipers." Not waiting for Max's approval, the guards rushed in and took hold of the other eleven elves, including two that were up on a roof. Rather than enter the building and climb up, the guards tossed grappling hooks and pulled them down, making no attempt to break their fall.

"I'm told your guild was hired to kill my friend Max." Lysbane pushed his massive head a bit closer to the lead elf, warm dragon breath blowing back his hair and drying out his eyes. "I'm also informed that the first two attempts failed miserably, resulting in the death of your Grandmaster. Is this true?"

Unable to find his voice in the face of the dragon's anger, the elf simply nodded.

"Then return from whence you came. Tell your new master that this attempt also failed. Your comrades' lives are forfeit, as I'm sure comes as no surprise to you. You only live to carry a warning to your guild. In fact… you don't need arms to speak." Lysbane reached out a single razor sharp claw and deftly removed the elf's right arm below the elbow, then cast a heal to prevent him from bleeding out. The wound was fully sealed before the severed limb struck the ground. Recalling the story Max had told him about questioning the grey dwarf captive, Lysbane grinned at the terrified elf.

"Master Oakstone, if you wouldn't mind, please retrieve that arm and take it to the kitchen for me? It has been many centuries since I prepared dark elf meat. Oh, and do be careful of the dagger. It is coated in a nasty poison." The elf's eyes widened even farther as he watched the dwarf dash forward and kick the dagger free of the lifeless hand before lifting the half limb and retreating back into the restaurant.

When Lysbane reached his claw toward the left arm, the elf wet himself. The dragon paused, then withdrew his claw. "I suppose you might need that hand, in case there are any doors to open before you report to your master." He chuckled as the elf whimpered.

"I'm going to be residing in Stormhaven for the foreseeable future, visiting with my friend Max and his companions. You have just interrupted me in the middle of a delicious meal. I do not take kindly to such interruptions." The elf nodded almost imperceptibly, then flinched when Lysbane shrank back into his human form and placed a hand on the elf's forehead. "Now, picture your home as clearly as you can. The front gate will do. Close your eyes and focus." When the elf complied, the dragon closed his own eyes for a moment. "That will do." Lysbane released the elf and flicked a hand, opening a portal in the middle of the street. On the other side Max could make out a black stone fortress. Without further comment, Lysbane took hold of the still immobilized elf with one hand and effortlessly hurled him through the portal. Max didn't even see the unfortunate assassin land before the portal closed.

Lysbane withdrew his aura and canceled the spell that had frozen everyone in sight. As several of Max's people fell to the ground with gasps of relief and more than a few whimpers, the dragon sighed. "My sincere apologies, good citizens of Stormhaven. I did not mean to cause such distress and discomfort."

After making sure that the guards had the Shadow Walkers well in hand, Lysbane turned and reentered the restaurant, taking his seat and lifting his burger as if nothing had happened.

Still holding the severed arm, Oakstone cleared this throat. When the dragon looked his way, he laughed. "Ha! Forgot about that. No, I don't really intend to eat it. But the elf clearly didn't know that. Neither will his master." The dragon snapped his fingers and the arm disappeared. When Max and Oakstone took their seats at the table, he grinned. "I don't suppose they'll be anxious to send more of their ilk in the near future, do you?"

"Aye, likely not." Oakstone shook his head.

"I wouldn't." Max agreed. "Thank you, Lysbane. You've lifted a great weight from my shoulders. At least, temporarily."

The dragon set the last quarter of his burger back down. "For the record, I did not forbid them from returning, suggest they cancel the contract for your life, or threaten retaliation should they succeed in killing you. I merely emphasized that interrupting my meal again would make me unhappy." He waited while both dwarf and chimera nodded. "Good. Beings such as myself have... guidelines for acceptable levels of interference in the events of the world. I would not want to be seen as violating them." Looking up briefly as if listening for a response, he nodded once and resumed his meal.

"Next I think I would like to try some of those tacos you mentioned."

Chapter 24

The following day was a busy one for Max. First on the agenda was dealing with the captured assassins. They were beginning to fill up his dungeon cells, and he wasn't inclined to keep feeding them. According to everyone he spoke to, there was no way of redeeming them. The oaths they'd already sworn to their guild meant that, should they get even the slightest chance, they'd try to kill him again.

They had to die.

Since he was going to kill them, he figured their deaths ought to serve a purpose. Most of them were a higher level than he was, and were worth some experience to him and his party. But they had another, more practical value as well.

Stripped down to their loincloths, having been carefully searched by Stormhaven guards, the Shadow Walkers were marched through the dungeon portal by Max, his three corporals, Nessa, and three guards who gave them liberal pokes with spear points to keep them moving.

Once inside, Max ushered them out of the safe zone and down the corridor toward the first chamber. As soon as they neared the first chamber, he called out to the core. "Child, please send all of your minions to the chamber near me."

A voice rang out through the corridor, startling the dark elves. "Of course, Master. It will be just a few moments.

Max had listened carefully to the descriptions Teeglin and her party had given of the low level monsters in the dungeon, and in particular their weapons. While they waited, he reached into his storage and produced twenty six common steel daggers, ten common spears with their shafts cut down to goblin size, three common swords sized for orcs, and half a dozen short recurve bows he'd had crafted for the occasion, tossing them all onto the floor in the first chamber.

He took a moment to invite the guards to his party along with the corporals and Nessa. "You all know the plan, yes?" When they each nodded, faces grim, he added, "You can still back out of this. No one will question you, or think less of you." He looked at the two dwarven guards in particular. "This isn't honorable combat. We'll be executing these assassins, plain and simple. I pronounce them all guilty of being murdering assholes who tried to kill me. The sentence is death." He looked at the row of dark elves standing against the wall. "It won't be a swift death."

One of the assassins, upon hearing this, decided to take his chances. He leapt up, snapping a kick at the face of one of the dwarves. The guard's nose shattered, and he was nocked back a few paces even as the dark elf tried to charge past him. Several of the others tried to make a break for it at the same time.

Dylan, who'd been standing at the back, hit the fleeing elf with a roundhouse punch that blasted it off its feet. He then drew his axe and roared at the rest. "The next one in reach loses a leg, or an arm!" Standing in the center of the corridor, the big ogre's reach included the entire width of the passage.

The rest of the party quickly got the dark elves back under control, wounding several of them in the process. Nessa hamstrung one of them, leaving him flopping on the ground, moaning in pain. The dwarf guard that had been kicked in the face recovered quickly and tackled the one that had kicked him, biting off one ear tip as they wrestled. The others mostly suffered bruises or minor cuts.

One had been smart enough to dash into the chamber and go for one of the daggers. Max saw this, and cast *Boom!* on the weapon. Just as the dark elf was about to take hold of it, the steel dagger exploded, shredding his hand, arm, and chest. He fell bleeding to the floor as the three goblins in the chamber noticed him and charged.

"I guess he's our first volunteer." Max growled, shaking his head. Calling out to the goblins, he ordered, "Pick up a dagger to use on the elf!"

The goblins, recognizing his authority as dungeon master, did as they were told. Barely pausing as they ran, they each scooped up a steel dagger, much better quality than the stone ones they held, and set to work on the badly injured dark elf.

When the elf fought back and critically injured one of the goblins with a kick, Nessa appeared behind him and slit his throat before stepping back and allowing the goblins to do their thing. They viciously stabbed and sliced the dark elf, doing minimal damage as he bled out on the floor. When he died, all three of the goblins leveled up.

Seeing their fate, a few of the assassins began to try to bargain for their lives. Max stared at each of them in turn. "If you can tell me who hired your guild to kill me, I'll give you a quick death."

When none of them spoke, which was no surprise, he offered, "If you can draw me a detailed map of your guild's keep, I'll grant you a quick death." Again, none of them moved, though it was clear that a few of them wanted to. Whatever oaths they'd sworn bound them tightly. Max shrugged and turned away as more goblins ran into the room. He waited until all twenty three goblins and the three orcs had arrived.

"Grab yourselves a weapon, and kill the elves." He ordered. All of them nodded and rushed forward, grabbing a weapon or two until all of them had one. Max nodded at his party, and they grabbed three of the dark elves. Each one was mortally wounded, their throat slit, a blade to the chest, a deep cut to the inner thigh, before being launched into the chamber with the dungeon minions. Goblins and orcs fell upon the dying assassins, finishing them off and leveling up several times as each one died. The process was repeated, three Shadow Walkers at a time, until they were all dead. The dungeon around them trembled, and a white glow emanated from the walls as the dungeon leveled up from the deaths of more than a dozen high level assassins.

"Thank you, Master." Child's voice echoed through the chamber. "That was a great deal of life energy."

"You're welcome, Child. I have something else for you as well." He began pulling the assassin's gear out of his ring and tossing it to the floor. Leather armor, poisoned daggers (the ones Nessa hadn't claimed for herself), health potions, everything they'd carried that wasn't of particularly high quality was donated to the dungeon. "Absorb these and use them for your minions, or as loot."

"I will do that, master." Child's voice replied. "I am sending Mage Lightsprocket directly to the exit. If you would be so kind as to retreat with your companions, I am going to use the energy you have gifted me and expand my domain."

Max did just that. Motioning for Dylan to lead the way, they walked back down the corridor and exited through the portal in the safe room. Max found the gnome mage waiting for him outside. "How goes your studying, Mage Lightsprocket?"

"Very well." Her response was subdued. "Child told me what you were doing, King Max. I understand ya had to do it, and I respect that you made use of the situation to help grow the dungeon."

"But it bothers you." Max concluded from her expression.

The little gnome surprised him when she snorted. "Me? Not at all. I've burned countless monsters, and more than a few sentient beings, to death with my magic. A much slower and more painful way to go than what the assassins got." She paused. "No, I was thinking more about the core witnessing such brutality. I spoke to her as it was happening, and she didn't seem greatly affected. But still, one has to wonder…"

"Child has witnessed much worse during her years in the other dungeon, I'm sure. The monsters in there killed brutally and messily. I doubt these executions had much impact."

The gnome just nodded, and flashed him a smile. "Speaking of the Westreach dungeon, if you'd be so kind as to send me to Westreach? Oh, and the Mages' Guild would like to commission some of your War Dogs to accompany me inside the dungeon so that I might try to speak to the core's avatar regarding this one."

Blake stepped forward. "You can speak to me about the War Dogs. We'd be happy to arrange an escort, for a steep fee, of course." He grinned at the gnome, who laughed. "Walk with me, I'll escort you to our guild headquarters, and then to the dungeon." He looked over his shoulder and paused for a moment. "Unless you need me for something else, boss?"

Max shook his head and motioned for the gnomes to move along.

From behind him, Dylan asked, "Who are you gonna let run this dungeon next, boss? The mobs are all over level fifteen after finishing all those elves. And thanks to you, they have decent weapons. Probably armor too, after the core absorbs all that gear."

Max looked at Smitty. "Did you hear that, Smitty? Corporal Dylan just volunteered to go through the list of applicants and figure out who's next to run the dungeon."

Smitty laughed as Dylan groaned. "I should have known better." He grumped. "At least tell me what you're thinkin', boss?"

"I'm thinking maybe we let a group of kobolds run through. But only if they bring us a couple live grey dwarves to toss in there. They can escort them in and execute them just as we did with the assassins. Tell them we'd also like some local underground monsters to send in there. Rock spiders, a stonetalon, spidorcs. But they need to be alive when they go in."

Dylan nodded, but had a question. "I thought we were going to try to customize the dungeon, boss. You know, feed it useful critters only."

"As dungeon master I can control what kind of monsters get created. This is about giving her patterns to use if we want them, but more about donating life energy to grow the dungeon."

"You're totally power leveling your dungeon core, boss!" Smitty offered him a fist bump. "If this were a VR game, that would be an epic cheat hack!"

"I've got an idea for another sort of cheat." Max grinned as he bumped fists. "I'll need you and Nessa to come with me, if you're not busy." Both of them nodded and followed Max out of the dungeon outpost and back through the city, making a stop at the bakery, of course.

When they got back to Max's study, he gave a waiting Redmane a nod. "It's done. The dungeon leveled up."

"A distasteful task, but well executed." Redmane offered.

"Badump bump!" Smitty muttered from over on a sofa. Though the executions had been distasteful to him, he knew they were necessary. And he'd gotten most of a level from it himself.

"Give me just a minute." Max sat at his desk, using his ring to contact Or'gral, Gr'tok, Ag'thorn, and Gro'nag, his highest ranked orc citizens, asking them all to report to his study as soon as possible.

Or'gral was the first to arrive, having been near the portal in the goblin city. When he was settled into one of the chairs in front of Max's desk, Max asked, "Or'gral, have you seen a dragon skull somewhere in An'zalor's city?"

The orc blinked at him for a second, then nodded. "Aye, did you not see it mounted above the arena entrance?"

Max grimaced. "We entered the arena through what I'm guessing was a back door, a ramp that led directly down to the cells we were held in."

"Ah, yes. Well it is there, mounted above the tunnel entrance. A trophy and an offering of respect to the gods of the arena."

"Alright, next question. You've seen the portal pedestals around Stormhaven. We're pretty sure there was a portal in that city before the orcs took it. Have you seen it?"

Or'gral nodded again. "In a courtyard just outside the keep, up against the wall. War chiefs have tried over the centuries to activate it, but failed. An'zalor has personally executed three shamans who swore they could open the portal, then couldn't. These days there are usually vendor stalls set up in front of it."

Max sat back in his chair, thinking. He left the others to make small talk while he formed a plan in his head. Leaving his study briefly, he went back out to the portal to see if he could access the portal in the orc city directly, but that wasn't an option, so he walked back to his study.

The other orc leaders began to arrive, Gro'nag being the last of them as he'd had to ride from the Way Station to the temple to use the portal there. When they had all settled, he asked, "I know orcs have been escaping from the city to join us here, or just to flee from An'zalor." He gaze swept between the orcs in the room. "Do any of you know a way we can sneak into the city?"

"Ha! You want to sneak in and take An'zalor's head!" Gro'nag looked pleased with the idea.

Chuckling, Max shook his own head. "Close, but not exactly…"

*****

Two days later Max rode pokey out of Glitterspindle's temple, headed south. With him rode Or'gral, Gr'tok, Ag'thorn, Nessa, Smitty, and Dalia. They rode past the mine, stopping briefly to check in to make sure everything was running smoothly. From there, Ag'thorn, the scout commander who had surrendered and joined Max after the battle at the mine, led them at a leisurely pace further south toward the orc city.

They camped at their usual spot late that night, enjoying a supper of warm meals from Eats N Treats and pastries from the bakery. In the morning they took their time again, not wanting to reach the city walls until well after dark.

They encountered two orc patrols along the way, dispatching one, and watching the other pass by from a distance. Or'gral had assured Max that by the time the dead patrol was missed, they'd have already accomplished their mission and left the city behind.

They arrived at the city walls just after midnight, having left their mounts behind with Dalia, Nessa, and Smitty, and approached the last half mile on foot. Ag'thorn quickly located the weak point that Gro'nag had described to them. A section of wall that had been damaged when the orcs took the city from the humans, then shoddily repaired. A few jabs with spearpoints and some levering of the shafts had the weak mortar crumbling. The group cleared the opening slowly and as quietly as possible, pausing when

Max heard the guard atop the wall approaching on his patrol.

In less than an hour the opening was large enough for Max and the wide-shouldered orcs to squeeze through. Once inside the wall, they wasted no time, following Or'gral through empty streets and alleys. The city was mostly quiet, except for a few pockets where orcs were celebrating in taverns or restaurants. Guard patrols were light, just as in dwarven cities, as few orcs would dare to steal from another. Murder was almost unheard of, and any serious arguments were settled in tavern fighting pits, or in the arena itself.

Fifteen minutes after entering the city, they stood against the outer wall of the arena. Or'gral pointed upward, and Max followed his gaze to find a massive dragon skull mounted above the fifteen-foot high entry arch.

"Alright, give me a boost." Max moved to stand under the skull. Gr'tok and Ag'thorn together lifted him up, allowing him to stand on their hands as he reached to touch the skull. As he'd hoped, the moment he touched it he was able to slip it into the special storage rod Lysbane had given him. He motioned for the orcs to let him down, all of them grinning over the blatant theft.

"An'zalor is going to lose his mind when this is reported to him." Gr'tok seemed especially pleased.

"I think he's going to be much angrier over this next part." Max clapped his friend on the shoulder. "Lead on."

Once again the former orc army commander led them on a winding path through the city. While his orc companions blended in just fine, especially wearing their old gear, Max wore a cloak with a hood covering his head, and kept his gaze low to hide his face.

Ten minutes later they entered a wide market square that Max recognized, having passed through it on his way to his first meeting with An'zalor. All around the outside of the square there were semi-permanent vendor stalls set up. Some were just tents, others were constructed of wood. Directly across the square from where he crouched in the shadow of a tent, four guards stood their post, two on either side of the closed gate leading into the inner keep. On the other side of that gate, Max knew, were hundreds of orc warriors sleeping in their barracks. Along with An'zalor, of course, who Max hoped was snoring in his own bed.

Or'gral motioned Max and the others to the right, sending them behind the row of tents and stalls, while he stood upright and strode openly into the center of the square. Max tensed as he watched. This was a make or break moment. If things went wrong here, the rest of the plan might fail catastrophically. Trusting in the commander, he followed Ag'thorn as they hurried to the end of the row of stalls, turned left, and continued behind the stalls on that side of the square.

Out in the courtyard, the four guards noticed Or'gral and became more alert. Tightening the grip on their weapons, all four were laser focused on him as he approached. Max did his best to catch glimpses in between tents as he rushed along.

Five feet from the gate guards, Or'gral came to a stop. Max's elven ears picked up a quietly growled phrase, and he paused at an opening to watch what came next, holding his breath. Gr'tok and Ag'thorn stopped as well.

As one, the four guards came to attention and slammed fists to chests, saluting their former commander. When they relaxed, Or'gral clapped each one on the shoulder, then motioned toward the gate before producing a length of heavy chain. The guards took the chain and quietly moved back to the gate. Within a minute they had wound it back and forth between the two huge iron rings that acted as each door's handle, then tied it off, sliding a spear haft through the rings at the center of the knot to keep it from unraveling.

Relieved, Max and the others quickly moved to the stall that was their destination. A large, forest green canvas tent with a wooden counter across the front. Moving past the woven tapestry hung behind the counter, then out a flap at the back of the tent, Max found the portal pedestal! Placed just as he'd been told, up against the outer wall of the keep. When the humans had controlled the city, it made sense for visiting merchants to arrive at the main market square, which could also be used as a staging area of troops, if necessary.

Taking hold of the portal key that Regin had gifted him, he placed his hand on the pedestal. "Yessss!" He smiled as a notification popped up asking if he wanted to take ownership of the portal. He selected yes, then selected Stormhaven as his destination, and opened the portal.

Thankfully, the portal made only a very slight sound when it opened, and the bulky tent obscured most of the light. Had a guard on the wall leaned over and looked directly down at them, he would have seen the portal. But from the ground level, it was well hidden.

Almost immediately after the portal opened, his companions began to whisper and wave. Orcs appeared from Max's left and right, moving quickly but quietly, many of them carrying packs, all of them carrying weapons. At first it was a few dozen, then scores, then Max lost count as orc men, women, and children hurried through the portal. Max saw Redmane and the general on the other side, directing traffic, looking quite pleased with themselves.

Max's heart continued to pound as his gaze swiveled left and right, then up at the wall. He was sure he'd hear pounding at the gate at any moment, a shift change looking to assume their posts, or a messenger sent on a late night mission. He moved to the front of the stall, crouching behind the counter to watch the square in case any guards or warriors who'd been out partying tried to return to the keep. Or'gral had assured him that the square was well guarded by their people, but Max couldn't help but check things out for himself.

The reason they'd set such a casual pace while traveling to the city was that Gr'tok and Or'gral had sent half a dozen of their most trusted underlings to the city ahead of them. They were tasked with discretely spreading the word amongst several hundred of his people's family members and trusted friends. Since An'zalor had locked down the city, many of those who'd wanted to escape had been trapped inside. The war chief's guilt and anger had him lashing out at his own citizens, and they were happy to leap at the chance Max offered.

For half an hour orc families streamed through the portal into Stormhaven. Max guessed there were at least five thousand of them by that point, and more were straggling in. Next half a dozen wagons, their wheels wrapped in thick canvas to silence them, emerged from an alley. Pushed by four orcs each, they moved slowly and quietly. The wagons were stacked with whatever food supplies the orcs could gather quietly, as well as family valuables and other items that couldn't fit in the several dozen storage rings Max had sent along with the infiltrators. He'd put Dylan, Erdun, and every enchanter among his citizens to work creating the rings the day after he'd conceived his plan. Most of the rings only had twenty five or fifty slots, but the ones made by Erdun were each one hundred slots.

Once the wagons were through, the orc warriors and infiltrators that had been escorting citizens and guarding the square, along with the four gate guards, converged on Max. He favored all of them with a wide smile, baring his fangs. "You have all done a great job. Now it's time for part three of the plan. All of you head on through, this next bit is all mine." He ushered them through, sending a thumb's up at Redmane on the other side, then closed the portal behind them, leaving just himself and the orc commanders who'd come with him, remaining in the city.

It was time for a little deception and chaos.

The three orc commanders gave him nods of respect before taking off back toward their entry point in the wall, with a couple of stops along the way. Max moved back into the tent, happy to be out of sight of any alert guard patrolling atop the wall. He forced himself to remain calm as he waited the agreed upon fifteen minutes. The moment Red appeared on his shoulder and told him it was time, he stepped back out next to the portal pedestal and cast *Levitate* on himself. Carefully controlling his progress, he lifted himself up the face of the wall, listening carefully for footsteps. He paused just below the top of the wall until he heard the single orc guard approach. As soon as the guard passed by him, he raised himself up behind the orc and grabbed him from behind, quickly snapping his neck and laying him as quietly as possible down on the stone parapet.

Activating his *Fade* and *Stealth* abilities, he moved quickly along the wall until he was as near as he could get to the small palace's front doors. Taking his time, he produced a dozen of the dworcs' clay pot grenades. Six of them were normal grenades. The other six, marked with a bright red x painted on the side, were his own special modifications.

Taking several deep breaths to calm himself, he tucked five of the standard grenades between his bent left arm and his chest, then lifted the sixth in his right hand. Standing upright, he hurled the grenades one after the other as rapidly as he could. The first two crashed against the palace entry doors. The next two crashed down in the doorway to the barracks. Taking a moment to cast Spark on the fuses of the last two, he tossed one at the palace doors, the other at the barracks. When those grenades hit, the contents of all the grenades burst into flame.

All of this had been accomplished in less than ten seconds. The first shattering pots had alerted the guards, who began to shout in alarm. The explosions created chaos as guards who were about to rush out of the barracks were pushed back by the flames. Max scooped up the special grenades and dashed back along the wall toward the gate. He lay flat on his back right above the gatehouse, listening and watching, smiling as roars of anger were peppered with cries of pain as a few unfortunate orcs managed to burn themselves.

A moment later, Max heard two more explosions. His attack had been a signal. Allied orcs at two of the city's gates were set to subdue or kill the guards stationed there, then open the gates and set fire to them using more of the clay pots. Other volunteers would then drive two or three wagons out each gate, making it look, at least superficially, like the thousands of missing orcs made a break through the gates. They'd ride the wagons deep into the forest before abandoning them and making their way north to the Way Station on their own, where they'd be welcomed as heroes. With the gates destroyed, any orcs who weren't among the trusted families he'd evacuated might take advantage and flee the city on their own, further reducing An'zalor's power, and giving his hunters that many more tracks to follow.

A third explosion in the direction of Max's infiltration point told him that his comrades had made it safely away. They would join Smitty and the others, making the best possible speed north, leaving a third trail for An'zalor's scouts to follow.

Max continued to wait, listening as more and more angry voices echoed up from the courtyard. He heard the burning palace doors burst open and loud curses as whomever opened them was greeted with a pool of flaming oil. Max sincerely hoped it was An'zalor himself.

Soon enough someone roared, "Open the gate!" A moment later there was the sound of someone pounding on the gate, and the rattling of the chains that were holding it closed. Max continued to wait, checking the special grenades sitting next to him. A guard approaching from further down the wall spotted him and roared, but the sound was drowned out by the furious uproar from below. Max wasted no time, focusing on the charging orc's face and whisper-shouting, "*Boom!*". The guard took one more step before his head exploded. His body took another step before tipping over and falling off the wall.

Max listened to the sound of more and more fists pounding on the gate. A rough voice called for something to use as a ram. Max rolled to his side, deeming it to be just about time for his next trick. When a commanding voice silenced all the others, Max rushed into action. Producing a candle from his storage, he cast spark to light the wick. Then he quickly lit the fuses of all six special grenades. The moment the last one was lit, he dropped the candle and lifted the grenades two at a time, gently tossing them over the edge of the wall to land right on the crowd of orcs pressing against the gate. The last two were already falling before the first two hit, and Max lay flat again.

The first two explosions were accompanied by screams of pain that only multiplied as two more grenades went off, then two more. Max couldn't resist rolling over and peeking over the edge. What he saw were dozens of burned and shredded dead orcs up against the gate, with scores more thrashing around as oil-soaked skin and armor burned, and still more struggling to move as they bled freely from multiple wounds. He couldn't immediately identify An'zalor in the crowd, and didn't watch long enough to keep trying before rolling back away from the edge.

His special grenades had each been filled with a vial of his blood to add some extra oomph to the explosion when they shattered. Around that vial he'd packed nails and sharp bits of scrap metal from his forge and others. Additionally, each and every bit of metal had been dunked in bowls of poison that caused excessive bleeding. Max noticed a slight fog of green smoke that was making many of the orcs cough. Best he could figure, the fire had burned some of the poison off the shrapnel to create the fumes.

As he lay atop the wall Max leveled up from the nearly one hundred deaths he'd just caused. With no more tricks up his sleeve, he took firm hold of the Rod of Recovery and got to his feet. Taking one last look down at the massacre in the courtyard, he called an audible.

Taking a deep breath, he cast *Intimidate*, followed by *Levitate* then *Molten Skin* in case he got hit with a lucky shot. Lifting himself high into the air so he could be seen in the flickering light of the flames, he roared down at the courtyard. "An'zalor! You honorless coward! If you've survived my little party tonight, know that I'll return soon enough for your head! The gods of your arena favor me! Do you have the courage to face the chimera king?!" He still couldn't locate the war chief, but he was sure An'zalor had heard him, if he wasn't killed in the explosions. Max was slightly disappointed at not finding his enemy. As part of his planning, he'd developed a vague fantasy in which he could *Jump* down behind An'zalor, grab him, and teleport away. Then he could deal with the orc chief alone, on his own terms, and possibly end the war right then and there.

He bared his fangs at the orcs below who were roaring in rage and pain. Just for fun he targeted a random orc holding a massive axe and cast *Boom!* again. The axe shattered, killing that orc and several others nearby, most of whom were already wounded. Targeting the burning palace doors, he roared *Boom!* again. That explosion took out a dozen or so more orcs, and sent flaming chunks hurtling inside the palace. To add to the chaos, he cast *Rot* on three of the largest orcs he spotted, assuming them to be officers, following up with three quick lightning bolts for visual effect. He wanted the survivors to fear the chimera king who could rain lightning and fire on them.

Max was tempted to explode the gates below him as well, since that was where most of the orcs were still clustered, but his plan for the allied orcs with the decoy wagons to escape required that most of the guards be trapped inside the keep for as long as possible.

An arrow slammed into his chest armor, the force of the impact pushing him backwards before the arrow skittered away. Another sliced open his cheek as it whistled past his head, and a third embedded itself in his thigh, barely missing his groin. Just as several more arrows were loosed at him, Max canceled his levitation spell and dropped like a stone even as he channeled mana into the rod. The arrows whistled by over his head. A moment later he disappeared, in mid-air, further enraging and intimidating the orcs below.

When Max hit the ground he was off balance and fell hard on his butt. His hands felt grass, and the familiar tick of damage from the Brightwood battleground curse made him laugh long and loud, sounding like a madman. He took a moment to pull the arrow from his leg and heal himself. Getting to his feet, he turned to find the stone dragon's ribs just behind him.

Taking a seat with his back against one of the ribs, he quickly used his rings to check in with his people. Smitty reported that his group was safely away and galloping home. Redmane informed him that eleven thousand grateful orcs had just sworn the oath and become Stormhaven citizens. Gro'nag confirmed that ten scouting parties, each with several spare mounts, were headed south to meet up with Smitty's party, as well as to locate and escort the wagon drivers, and to keep watch for a response from An'zalor.

Pleased with the night's outcome, Max relaxed against the rib at his back and waited for a visit from dragons.

Chapter 25

Max was surprised when a portal opened and five humanoids followed Lysbane onto the battleground. He hopped to his feet, suddenly feeling a bit guilty about lounging amongst the bones of the dragon's corpse with his family walking toward him.

Moving to greet them, he offered Lysbane a solemn nod. He wasn't sure how deeply the dragon family would be mourning their loss, and was determined to show some respect. While he was trying to find appropriate words, Lysbane spoke.

"King Maximilian Storm, this is my cousin's mate, and their offspring. Their names are much too complex for you to pronounce, so I'll save you the trouble."

Max bowed his head to the dragons. "I'm honored to meet you. My sincere condolences for your loss."

The stone dragon's mate offered him a small smile. "Thank you, King Storm. The loss happened long ago, and we have accepted it. Though seeing him like this does sadden me. I'm told he perished in a great battle." She looked around the mostly concealed battleground.

"I am told the same. Your mate, and father," He glanced at the younger ones, who had the appearance of being teens. "Slew thousands of orcs before he was overwhelmed by sheer numbers." He held up the rod, offering it to her with both hands. "They uhm… took his head as a trophy, and mounted it upon their arena, a place where they believe they commune with the gods through combat. Tonight we've managed to retrieve it."

She flashed a questioning glance at Lysbane, who nodded in confirmation. "I gave Max a quest to enter the city, one run by a war chief with whom he is currently at war, and retrieve my cousin's fat head." He winked at Max as she snorted. "I believe you'll find it stored in there." He nodded at the rod.

She made no move to take the rod from Max. Keeping her hands clasped in front of her, she smiled at Max. "Thank you, King Max. It must have been quite dangerous for you to retrieve his head. My offspring and I are grateful for your efforts, and I commend you for your courage."

Embarrassed now, and unsure what to do, Max bowed his head in return. "It was my pleasure, Eldest."

Without reaching for the rod, she and her children stepped past Max, walking over to stand among the exposed ribs, speaking softly between themselves. When Max saw that they were standing directly above the spot where he'd found the heart gem, he whispered to Lysbane. "Should I give them the dragon stone I found?"

Lysbane shook his head. "It's yours by right. They have no use for it, other than maybe to place it on a mantle, or something. Better you put it to good use." Max then offered the rod to him, and he again shook his head. A second later his quest completion notification appeared.

Quest Complete: Head Hunters!

You have infiltrated an enemy's city, retrieved the severed head of a stone dragon, and returned it to his family.
Rewards: 100,000,000xp; 10,000 gold; stone dragon's head; increased reputation with Lysbane; increased reputation with dragonkind.

Despite having just leveled up earlier that night, Max felt the rush of achieving another level.

"Thank you, Lysbane. That was quite generous of you."

The dragon kept his eyes on his family as he answered Max. "I observed your adventure in the city, and I must say it was very well done. You show great promise, Battleborne."

Max shook his head. "I just do what I can to deal with the problems that come along."

Still watching the other dragons, Lysbane nodded. "Keep doing what you're doing. I believe the Eternals who are observing you approve, so far. I know Regin does." He smiled and finally turned his gaze to Max. "She doesn't want the skull. I think you'll find that it now qualifies as a trophy for you, since you successfully raided an enemy city, liberated thousands of citizens being held hostage, killed more than a hundred warriors, and escaped in one piece with the skull." Max liked the way that sounded. "Mount it in your throne room, or above your inner gate, and I believe you'll find it provides a significant buff."

Max considered it for a moment, then gulped as a potential consequence occurred to him. "Won't uhm… other dragons be offended if I mount his head in my city?"

Lysbane shook his head. "Any dragon who sees it will be able to see its history. If anything, they will look more favorably upon you."

"I'll take your word for it." Max gave a slight bow of respect, depositing the rod with the skull inside back into his inventory. "That teleport spell worked extremely well."

Lysbane chuckled quietly. "I saw that! You took a big risk there, Max. I myself wasn't sure the spell would trigger before you hit the ground."

Max gulped, his mouth going slightly dry. He took a moment to produce some saliva and recover. "I had faith in your legendary dragon magic." The dragon just snorted. "Any chance you could teach me that spell? I've learned some portal magic, but your spell would be much more useful."

Lysbane shook his head. "I can, but not yet. You'd need many more points of *Intelligence*, and a much larger mana pool, to be able to cast the spell without it killing you."

"Then I have a goal to work toward." Max made a note to put all his currently earned points into *Intelligence* and *Wisdom*.

"Don't rush things, Max." Lysbane offered. "You're already growing at an incredible pace, and I expect you'll continue to do so. But take the time to do the important things, as well. Build your kingdom. Make your people stronger. Be sure that they can continue without you, should one of your stunts get you killed. Build a legacy that will endure. Because that's all that really matters in this world."

Not sure how to respond, Max simply nodded that he understood the dragon's words, then stood there in companionable silence for a while.

*****

The following day Max portaled from Stormhaven to the gnome's temple, then made the trip to the Way Station to meet up with his party. Dylan accompanied him, having worked out a schedule for the next week's dungeon runs. Blake had joined them as well, after making arrangements for a solid team of War Dogs to escort Lightsprocket into the Westreach dungeon. Behind them as they rode were a few thousand new orc citizens who had chosen to live in or around the Way Station.

His companions and commanders arrived around midday, tired after riding straight through from the orc city. Max welcomed them with applause, joined by all the town residents, to whom he'd told the tale of the raid. Having decided to stay in town and let them rest, they retired to the inn. The staff brought them all a hearty meal, which they ate as Max related the events of his attack on the keep.

Gro'nag especially was enthralled and amused by the details. "Ha! Ya trapped him in his own keep, killed maybe a quarter of the warriors in the barracks, maybe wounded the coward himself, stole the dragon's head, not to mention thousands of my people, right out from under his nose!" He got up and moved behind Max, laying a scarred hand on his shoulder. "If I didn't already respect you, Max, you'd have just earned my undying admiration!" The others laughed as the three corporals golf clapped, grinning as he rolled his eyes at them.

"Your ridiculously oversized beasties arrived, by the way. Our herders found them about halfway between the battleground and here, grazing in a meadow as calm as ya please. Took them a while to round them up and move them, but they're now living in a small valley just north of here. The minotaurs volunteered to watch over them. Apparently, back when their clan lived on the plains, they had their own herds of those monsters."

"Oversized beasts?" Or'gral asked, not having heard about the auralos where he'd been posted in the goblin city.

Gro'nag spread his arms out wide. "Herd animals. Picture one of them battle boars. Make it twenty times bigger, give it shaggy fur. Damned things can look a minotaur in the eye standing on all fours."

"They're called auralos." Max clarified. "Lysbane brought them to us from somewhere far away. We've got… how many did we end up with?" he looked at Gro'nag.

"One hundred thirty two." The orc reported. "Might be a few more runnin' around loose." He looked at

Or'gral. "Any single one of them could feed this entire town for a day." He pointed at the dishes on the table. "You've just tasted one. Broke its leg on the way here, so the herders harvested it. If you visit the tanner here in town, he's got the hide out back. Had to build three new racks just to hang it." He pointed at the floor. "If you made it into a rug, it'd cover this whole room."

Or'gral thumped the table. "I've heard of the beasts. They must have come from *very* far away, because they're supposed to be extinct."

Max nodded. "I heard the same. Apparently, they're not." He smiled. "We've got a large enough herd to reestablish them here. In a few years we'll have a thousand or more, if we limit how many of them we harvest. And protect them. They are a favorite snack of dragons." Max pictured one of the massive buffalo herds from Earth, wandering across a plain.

Max grinned to himself as he remembered something else. "Oh, and speaking of favorite dragon snacks, did you know that dragons consider mountain trolls a delicacy?" He watched as everyone's eyebrows rose. "It's true. Lysbane asked us not to hunt the tribe he seeded in the mountains around our new outpost up there."

"Ha! I'd like to meet this Lysbane who considers a fifty foot bundle o' muscle and hate to be a snack." Gro'nag thumped the table himself.

"He's currently hanging out in Stormhaven if you'd like to return with us and meet him."

*****

They held a feast that night in celebration of the raid, the liberation of so many orcs, and their immigration to town. Everyone got a taste of auralos meat, with which the cooks had managed to provide a four point boost to *Stamina* that lasted twelve hours. When Max asked about it, the head cook shrugged. "Most of it came from the critter itself. My guess is it could run all day if it wanted to."

Max took the opportunity to meet with the town council, getting updates on mine production, the town's growth, and their plans for further expansion. He warned them about poking An'zalor's metaphorical hornet's nest, and the likelihood that he would respond in the very near future.

"Ha!" Gro'nag sneered at Max, fully exposing his broken tusks. Max understood the expression was meant for An'zalor, not for him. "That coward will react, for sure. He'll choose the dumbest, most violent course of action. His pride was already wounded, his honor in question, and now you've bested him in his own home for a second time."

One of the dwarven engineers laughed. "Don't ye worry. We'll be ready fer him. He'll not get past our walls, and he'll likely waste half o' his army tryin'!" He smirked at Max. "Half o' whatever ye left him, I mean!"

The other councilor from the mine added, "We've pulled an entire shift from the mine to help finish the new outer wall. We'll be ready." He looked slightly nervous as he spoke, and Max realized he was concerned that reduced production at the mine would upset him.

"Our peoples' lives come first. Pull whomever you need to, from wherever you need them. Just keep in mind that he might attack the mine instead of the town. Or both."

The first dwarf's grin grew wide. "Either way, there be a thousand dwarven warriors from each o' the clans that can be ready in an hour to sneak through the portal in the temple n crush him against our walls!"

Max sincerely hoped it didn't come to that. While the defenders on the wall would be relatively safe, those who would be outside, the hammer against the anvil, would likely suffer heavy casualties. He was already considering another raid on the orc city, using the portal. A raid that would focus on killing An'zalor himself. Maybe once the dishonorable war leader was dead, his replacement would be willing to make peace.

*****

An'zalor growled in pain and frustration, snapping at the shaman next to him. "This is taking too long!"

"We are working as fast as we can, War Chief. The components are not easy to find. The shop where we would normally obtain them has been emptied out, the alchemist gone along with the others." The orc shaman gulped, nervous about An'zalor's reaction to the reminder of just how much he'd lost. He looked down at the bed where the injured orc lay, shaking his head. He had little faith that the healing ritual they were going to attempt would work.

An'zalor had been standing very near the locked gate when the first two shrapnel grenades had gone off. One landed almost at his feet, and the explosion set him sprawling. But not before shredding his right leg, and peppering the rest of his right side with deep puncture wounds. Fortunately for him, several of his warriors fell atop him before the subsequent grenades exploded, their bodies shielding him from most of the additional shrapnel. Unfortunately, the poison that the shrapnel injected into his body in dozens of places caused him to bleed more heavily than he normally would. Only his extraordinary regeneration and health pool kept him alive long enough for his lead shaman to reach him.

The shaman had been able to save him, barely. Most of his leg was gone below the knee, just a few ragged bits of flesh and muscle clinging to shattered bone. Orc shamans were not as skilled as dwarven healers, for example. Orc warriors tended to have a 'rub some dirt on it and shake it off' attitude toward injuries. Ghastly wounds left more impressive scars that they considered badges of honor. Most orc warriors would rather die with honor from their wounds than accept magical healing.

As a result, the shaman, the only one inside the locked keep at the time of the attack, wounded himself when burning oil set his robes afire, was unable to heal the mangled leg enough to even stop the bleeding. It was almost more than he could manage to overcome the heavy bleeding caused by the poison that riddled the war chief's body. He'd quickly made the harsh decision to remove the damaged part of the leg and cauterize the wound, thus saving An'zalor's life.

When he woke up many hours later, An'zalor was less than appreciative. He'd threatened to take the shaman's head if he did not restore his missing limb. The shaman had assured him that there was a ritual, one that required expensive components and the participation of at least three other shamans, that would enable him to regrow his severed leg. An'zalor had ordered it done with as much force as he could muster, still weak from blood loss and the effects of the poison.

Except they had no way to obtain more than half of the components they needed. The chimera king's raid had facilitated a mass exodus of families who were unwilling to tolerate An'zalor's rule any longer. Shaking his head, the shaman found himself wishing he'd been outside the gates during the raid, so that he might have departed as well. Though he enjoyed the power that came with his position of head shaman, there was no honor in serving a war chief that had no honor himself.

"Gone?!" An'zalor roared from his bed, attempting to prop himself up on his elbows, but still too weak to manage it. Which only increased his frustration. "Send more hunters! Bring back those components! I want the heads of every orc who fled the chimera king's attack like cowards in the night!" He pounded the bed frame with one heavy fist that normally might have shattered the wood. This time it just made a solid thump.

The shaman nodded while at the same time thinking that it wasn't King Storm that the city's citizens fled from. Not that he would ever point that out to An'zalor. He wasn't suicidal. He sat with his hands in his lap, tucked into the wide sleeves of his robes. His left hand gripped the hilt of a curved dagger he often used for dissection and harvesting ingredients from beasts. Not for the first time since the raid, he considered simply opening the war chief's throat. In his weakened condition, there would be no way An'zalor could stop him. Not that he had ambitions of ruling the tribes in his place. The shaman was no war chief. No, his urges toward murder were fueled purely by self-preservation. An'zalor had been growing more and more unstable before the raid. Now, embarrassed, further dishonored, and frustrated beyond reason by his injuries, the orc was as likely to order his execution as not. The shaman was absolutely sure that the hope An'zalor held of regaining his leg was the only thing keeping him alive. And he firmly believed that the moment the war chief was whole again, he'd be executed for some perceived failure to heal him more quickly.

His grip on the hilt tightened as An'zalor raged incoherently in his bed.

When he eventually wore himself out, the war chief asked, for at least the dozenth time, "How many did we lose?"

Keeping his tone calm and reserved, the shaman replied, "One hundred seventy three warriors died inside the keep. Another seventeen are still battling the poison, but are likely to survive. They should be fit to fight again in two or three days." The shamans had exhausted themselves healing the wounded after the gates had been forced open and help arrived. They'd burned through nearly their entire stock of healing potions, and the entire, very limited, supply of poison cures. Of those who'd died, only two thirds had perished directly from their wounds. The rest had slowly bled out as he and the other shamans tried to heal them.

"And the cowards that fled?"

"We are still counting, War Chief. Guards are searching the city and reporting in. So far, we have been able to identify a little over eight thousand missing." The shaman silently wished them luck.

"Where could they be hiding?" An'zalor growled, getting worked up again. "Wagons do not move so quickly that our hunters would not have caught them, even with a head start."

Shaking his head at having to repeat the report yet again, the shaman answered, "The wagons were found abandoned in the forest but a few hours outside the city. It looks as if those who fled have broken into smaller groups and dispersed through the forest in multiple directions. At least one large group headed north toward the chimera king's lands."

"The toy king!" An'zalor growled, clenching his fists so tightly that the recently healed stump of a severed pinky finger ruptured again and began to bleed. "I should have just taken his head with the sword when he handed it to me!

The shaman very wisely kept his opinion of that statement to himself. As far as he, and nearly every other orc in the city was concerned, the chimera and his comrades had fought valiantly, and with honor. The gods had rewarded them with victory in the arena, and over An'zalor himself. Had the chimera been an orc, he would probably be their new war chief.

"My army! They are to be prepared to march as soon as my leg is restored! I will look into the toy king's eyes as we slaughter the traitors who have joined him, burn his settlements to the ground! Then I will take his head with the dwarven sword, as I should have done before!"

The shaman did not point out that the army was greatly reduced. Between the loss of the previous forces the war chief had sent against the chimera, many of whom reportedly now served in his army, the losses from the raid, and the defections both before and after the raid, An'zalor was down to less than half of his previous standing army.

In fact, the shamans had been quietly wagering amongst themselves just how many of the hunters and warriors sent out after the raid would actually return. If he were among them, he would simply keep going. He unconsciously glanced at the amulet that hung from his neck. It contained the components for the regeneration ritual that they'd managed to gather. More importantly, it also contained all his worldly possessions. Just in case an opportunity to depart presented itself.

Toward that goal, the shaman placed a firm hand on the war chief's arm, attempting to calm him. "We can not assume that the alchemist will be caught, her wares recovered." He paused to make sure his semi-delirious patient had absorbed his words. "Allow me to take two of my fellow shamans, and a few warriors for protection, and go out to harvest what we need for your ritual."

An'zalor shook his head, his eyes widening. "You must stay here and heal me!"

"You are as whole as I can make you, War Chief. At least until we can perform the ritual. What you need now is rest, and food to replenish your inner resources. You lost much blood, and the toll that my healing took on your reserves was extreme. A lesser orc would certainly have perished." It never hurt to stroke the war leader's ego. "Your servants can feed and care for you. My time and skills are better used to gather what we need to restore your leg."

"NO!" An'zalor's roar was weaker than normal, but still loud enough to make nearby servants flinch. "Send the others, but you remain here. If the toy king attacks again, I will need you by my side."

Contempt flooded the shaman as he gazed down at his leader and saw fear in his eyes.

Contempt, and disappointment that his attempt to escape had failed. The orc motioned for one of his assistants to head out and try to find what they needed for the ritual. He had little faith that he'd live long enough for the other shamans to locate the components and return.

*****

Grandmaster Oakstone stood in the center of Max's new dragon forge, laughing.

It had started as a chuckle, quickly growing into a great belly laugh that echoed through the smithy. In part, he was laughing in pure joy and amazement at what he saw before him. But a good bit of his amusement was over the frustration his grandson seemed to get from witnessing Max's many accomplishments and apparent streak of good fortune.

"This be a thing o' true beauty, Max. A wonder." He stepped forward and stroked the top of the forge's dragon head.

"I wish I could take some credit for it." Max replied. "But Lysbane just sort of took it upon himself to create all this, without even being asked. Said he owed me a favor. I'm starting to get the impression that he doesn't like being in debt to anyone."

"Well, whatever ye did to deserve this, I'm damned glad ye did it!" The elder dwarf turned and grinned at Max. "Me own hands be sweatin', anxious to get to work!" He pulled a mithril ingot from his inventory and set it into the furnace. When he turned back to Max, though, his expression had become more thoughtful.

"Max, this forge be a great boon. Masters across the kingdom will want to come work in it. Even Grandmasters like meself." He shook his head. "The items we might forge in these flames could change the course o' battles." The dwarf glanced at the slowly heating metal for a moment, then looked at Max. "But this also be a danger to ye. I do no' say this lightly Max. When word o' this spreads, there will be more than one clan elder who'll covet yer forge."

Oakstone the younger grunted from the stool he was sitting on near the work bench.

"None o' me own king's elders, mind ye. They've all sworn to Ironhand's alliance with ye, and will not break their oaths. But there be other dwarven kingdoms, other unaligned clans. Not to mention the damned greys, who likely already have designs to retake their city." The dwarf gave Max a hard look, his gaze penetrating as he waited for Max to show he understood.

"So the target on my back just got a little bit bigger." Max sighed.

"More'n a little bit." Oakstone the younger added. "Not that ye need fear losin' this forge. Me king and those sworn to him, includin' our own clan, would destroy any who dared to assault this city."

"But there would be a cost in lives." Max finished for him. Just as it seemed there was for almost everything he did as a sovereign. His new forge, his claiming of Deepcrag and the goblin city, his raid on the orc city, the attack on The One's camp, his assassination of the Grandmaster of the Shadow Walkers. All had seemed like good ideas, even wise decisions, at the time. Yet every one of them were likely to cost lives among his people, or had already done so.

But to have made different decisions might have had similar costs.

For now, at least, there was nothing he could do to remove the target from his back. He could only hope he'd have time to grow stronger, to make his people stronger, to be able to deal with whatever comes next.

Shaking off the feeling of dread that threatened to overcome him, he looked over at the Grandmaster who was still staring expectantly at him. "I'll deal with any threats as they arise. Until then, I'll prepare the best I can." Both dwarves nodded, satisfied with his answer.

"In the meantime…" He crossed his arms and flashed a mischievous grin at the Grandmaster. "It seems to me that the honor and privilege of working in my shiny new dragon forge should come at a price. A *steep* price!"

"Bwahaha! Ye be learning, Max. Might be a slim hope that ye'll survive a bit longer after all!" The dwarf produced a gold coin and flipped it at Max, who caught it. "There! Paid in full!" the dwarf beamed at Max, who just laughed. "Feel free n charge me competitors so much they weep!"

Later that evening, as Max and Redmane were working through the usual stacks of paper on his desk, there was a hesitant knock on his door.

"Enter!" Max called out, expecting it to be Dalia with an update on the panacea potion experiments. Instead he was surprised when the door opened partway and a familiar goblin head appeared.

"Big King Max? Okay to talk?"

"Drig? Of course. Come on in." Max motioned toward the chair next to Redmane and waited while the little goblin scurried over and hopped up into the seat. "What can I do for you? Is something wrong with your family?"

Drig shook his head so violently that his oversize ears beat against his skull. "No, nothing wrong. Family good. Extra good now!" he beamed across the desk at Max. "Drig come to thank Big King! Give gift!"

"Thank me? For what?"

"Kobolds take Drig into baby dungeon. We fight! Kill many goblins, big orcs! Almost as big as Big King Max!" The goblin hopped up to stand on his chair, thumping his chest with one small fist. "Drig level ten!"

Max and Redmane both smiled with pride in the little goblin. "That's wonderful Drig!" He was about to say more, but the goblin held up a hand to interrupt him, earning an amused snort from Redmane.

"Drig have more to tell! Ugnok help Drig choose class. Drig goblin hunter now!"

Max paused for a second before asking. "A hunter? I thought you were working to become a butcher?"

This time the goblin's enthusiastic nod caused his ears to clap across his eyes. "Yes! Drig hunt, kill beasties! Bring back to shop, butcher meat, sell for many gold!"

"Ah, I see. That sounds like a very good plan, Drig. I'm proud of you!"

The goblin puffed out his chest and thumped it again. "Drig help protect Big King too, if bad people come. Drig kill many!" He took a moment to soak up the admiration of both Max and Redmane, then without warning hopped up onto Max's desk. Producing something from his inventory, he reached out and offered it to Max.

Carefully accepting the package, which was wrapped in wax paper that he likely got from the butcher's shop, Max held it for a moment, making a show of testing its weight.

"This for you, Big King! As thank you." Before Max could unwrap the package, the goblin shouted, "Is heart! Heart from first goblin Drig kill in dungeon. Big King eat heart, grow even stronger!"

Max was just opening his mouth to reply when Redmane chimed in. "Yes, Big King eat heart, grow stronger!" He reached over and patted the goblin on the back, grinning widely at Max the whole time. Both dwarf and goblin stared expectantly at Max as he unwrapped the package, understanding now why it was wrapped in butcher's paper.

Setting it down on his desk, he addressed the goblin. "Drig, thank you. This is a great honor."

"Go ahead, Big King! Eat heart!" Drig clearly expected Max to rip into it right there, goblin style.

"Drig, you remember when I taught Ugnok how to cook meat? How much better it tasted?"

"Drig remember!" Another ear-flapping nod followed.

"Well, I think I'll have this heart cooked. If that's okay with you."

"S'okay! Big King Max enjoy cooked heart!" The goblin launched himself off the desk and hurried out the door, his mission accomplished. The moment the door guard reached in to close the door behind the departed hunter, Redmane burst out laughing. Red appeared on the desk next to the package, rolling back and forth on her back, holding her belly with both arms.

Max waited patiently for the laughter to subside. When it did, Red got to her feet and peeked over the wrapping paper at the heart. "Yes, Big King Max, you go right ahead and enjoy that heart!" She snickered again.

"It be no joke, in truth." Redmane's amused expression had faded. "That be a sincere gift meant to honor ye. To reject it would dishonor ye, and the wee goblin."

Max looked up from Red's antics to raise an eyebrow at the dwarf. "You mean you expect me to actually eat this thing?" He felt a very slight urge to vomit.

"You'd likely lose sovereign points if you don't, Max." Red was still grinning, but now she had her arms crossed the way she often did when she lectured him.

"It be the heart o' a dungeon monster, Max. Not a natural born goblin." Red offered, as if that might help. And it actually did, if only a little. After some consideration, Max shrugged. He'd eaten worse in his life.

"Alright, I have an idea. Please call Teeglin in here, I need her to deliver a few messages for me." He grabbed some paper and began to write out a some instructions.

A few minutes later, alone in his study, Max took a moment to pull up his stat sheet and invest his available points. Between the dungeon creation, the raid, and the skull quest, he'd gained four levels in a short amount of time. He'd received the usual points for each level in *Strength* and *Constitution*, and had put his previous set of points into *Endurance*. Seeing as how his attacks in the successful orc raid were entirely magical, except for the grenades, he split his twelve available points between *Intelligence* and *Wisdom*, pushing them both over sixty before equipment boosts, increasing his mana pool and spell power. He hoped the extra smarts might help with his rune studies, as well.

Maximilian Storm	Health: 6,600/6,600
Race: Chimera; Level 47	Mana: 3,900/3,900
Battleborne, Sovereign	47,500,000/65,000,000
Endurance: 38 (48)	Intelligence: 65 (85)
Strength: 70	Wisdom: 65 (86)
Constitution: 76	Dexterity: 34 (35)
Agility: 35 (41)	Luck: 31 (43)

Chapter 26

Max sat at the head table, Redmane to his left, several empty seats on either side of them. In front of him a dozen more tables were arranged, most of them already fully occupied. There were palace staff, some residents of Stormhaven city, a small contingent of kobolds, an entire table of goblins, as well as the members of his party who were scattered amongst the others. He signaled with a nod of his head at one of the door sentries, who promptly saluted and exited the room.

"My fellow citizens of Stormhaven, I have brought you here today to witness a great honor!" Max got to his feet, which caused everyone else to do the same. The chatter in the room went silent as all eyes shifted to him. "First, if you haven't met him already, I'd like to introduce you to someone!" He gestured toward the door, which opened to reveal Drig and several other goblins who followed him into the room. Drig looked nervous, and slightly suspicious, this not being his first public audience with the king. The goblins behind him, his mate and their offspring, looked positively terrified.

"We welcome Drig the goblin hunter!" Max called out, causing the crowd to offer light applause, all of them wondering what was going on. "Drig, please bring your family up here to sit with me." He gestured to the empty chairs to his right as murmurs spread around the tables. The shy goblin led his family around to the indicated seats, reassuring them as they walked. Max did his best not to scare them, offering them a smile that was as wide as he could manage without baring his fangs. He wondered which of the children had drawn the picture mounted on the wall, and made a mental note to ask when things calmed down a bit.

As soon as they were seated, Teeglin came in bearing a platter with a covered dish. She set it in front of Max and took the seat on the other side of Redmane as a line of servers entered the hall, each of them carrying a dish for the head table. The other tables were already piled high with food, though none would dare touch it until the king said so.

When the servers retreated, Max cleared his throat. "Drig here recently entered our new dungeon with some comrades, including our esteemed kobold allies, whom I'd like to thank for all their efforts on our behalf." He paused to nod in the direction of the kobolds, who hissed with pleasure at the acknowledgement. "Drig's adventure resulted in him reaching level ten, and choosing the Class of Hunter!" Max paused while the goblin table went wild, and the rest of the gathered crowd applauded politely. Level ten wasn't a big deal for most, but it was the rare goblin who lived long enough to achieve it. At least, that was how it had been before Max came along.

"Drig came to me earlier today and offered me a precious gift, to thank me for allowing him into the dungeon." Max reached out and pulled the cover from his dish. "The heart of the first goblin he defeated inside the dungeon!" He lifted the plate and tilted it forward slightly so that all might see. The cheering from the non-goblins was a bit louder now. "Drig tells me his gift will make me stronger after I consume it, which it is now my honor to do!" He placed the plate back on the table, smiled at Drig and his family, and picked up his knife and fork. The cheering quickly subsided as people watched, not believing that their king would actually eat a goblin heart.

When Max had taken the heart to the kitchen, he'd carefully explained its significance to the head chef, as well as his plans. Then he'd all but begged her to find a way to make the blob of muscle edible. She'd laughed, patted him on the cheek, and said, "Aye, I'll fix it up right for ye, King Max. Ye have a good heart." Then she promptly kicked him out of her kitchen.

Now, facing the organ in question, Max kept the smile on his face as he took a deep breath. Despite being heavily tenderized, seasoned, slow roasted, and covered in what looked like mushroom gravy, it still looked like a heart. Determined to take one for the team, Max cut off a bite-sized section, surprised at how easily the blade sliced through the meat. Lifting it on his fork, he made a show of giving it a good sniff before waggling his eyebrows at Drig and shoving it into his mouth.

To his surprise, it tasted delicious! It was tender enough that it came apart after just a few chews, and when he'd swallowed that first bite, he received a buff of plus four to both *Strength* and *Agility*.

Looking over at Drig and his family, he grinned. "I feel stronger already!" There was much laughing and cheering from the other tables as the crowd caught on to what Max was doing. A few thought it was foolish, but most appreciated the effort that Max had clearly put into honoring a gift from Drig, who was arguably among the smallest and least important of his citizens.

"To thank you, Drig, for this delicious gift, I asked the chef to prepare something for you and your family. Special meat that will make you stronger, too!"

Drig's eyes widened as he looked down at his plate. Without hesitation he picked up a slice of the roasted meat with both tiny hands and raised it to his mouth, gnawing off a big chunk with his sharp goblin teeth. Much the same as Max had just experienced, the moment he swallowed the first bite he received a buff of plus five to *Strength* and plus ten to *Stamina*! Max had given the chef thirty pounds of auralos meat he'd swiped from the Way Station and asked her to prepare it for the evening's dinner. Everyone at all the tables received a small piece as part of their meal.

"Thank you, Big King!" Drig reached over with one greasy hand and patted Max on the arm. Max just smiled down at him, watching for a moment as his children took bites of the meat, their eyes widening at both the taste and the buffs. Turning to the crowd he saw similar reactions as they all had their first taste of roasted auralos.

Raising his glass, he called out. "To Drig the Hunter! One of Stormhaven's bravest, and most loyal!" The crowd raised their own cups and roared their approval, happily supporting Max's efforts. The corporals at their various tables began to shout, "Drig! Drig! Drig!" until the whole hall joined in. The little goblin puffed out his chest and waved at them all before downing his drink and returning his focus to gobbling down the meat on his plate.

*****

Trumpets blared and an honor guard rode out to greet Max as he approached the gates of the human queen's capitol city. The soldiers all rode jet black stallions, wearing gleaming plate armor with crimson capes. As they formed up and saluted, a familiar face called out, "Greetings, King Storm and honored guests. On behalf of Queen Anastasia, I bid you welcome to our city!"

"Lord Hastings. It is good to see you again. Thank you for the warm welcome." Max's smile for the human noble was sincere. The man had earned his respect when they met during the moot.

Hastings moved his mount up next to Max's and the two of them led the procession, the honor guard forming up in two rows on either side of Max's party. He'd brought along the corporals, Nessa, Dalia, Cavariel, Teeglin, and Josephine, who wanted to see about making some new business contacts in the city.

Hastings led the entire procession up the main boulevard of the city, passing hundreds of mostly quiet bystanders who were unsure of the multiracial party. Rumors had spread that Max had threatened to burn the entire kingdom, and had forced the queen to submit to his will. And while the vast majority of the populace were not fond of the usurper, she was still their queen, and Max was a potentially hostile monarch from a land of monsters. It wasn't long before they reached the inner wall that surrounded the palace, and were promptly ushered through. They dismounted, all but Dylan who'd unsummoned Princess outside the main gates and walked through the city. Hastings led them inside the oversized double doors of the palace proper, and soon enough they found themselves in the queen's throne room. Hundreds of courtiers, nearly all human, grew quiet and moved aside to create a path to the throne when Max was announced.

She sat atop an elevated throne made of gold-lacquered wood, wearing a shimmering emerald colored gown and a gem-encrusted crown atop her head. Flashing the same false smile she'd so often favored Max with, she called out. "Ah, King Max! Welcome to my home. I was wondering when you might honor us with a visit."

Max made the very slightest of bows in her direction. "Urgent matters required my attention, Majesty, but I thank you for the warm welcome. My compliments on your city. What I saw of it on my way here was quite lovely."

"Yes, even here we have heard rumors of your successful attack on the orc city. I'm told you killed more than a hundred orc warriors all by yourself." This statement caused a wave of murmurs and whispers to pass through the court.

Max shrugged. "I attempted to make peace with the War Chief, but was unsuccessful. He subsequently tried to kill my companions and I, caused the death of a dear friend, declared war on Stormhaven, and has attacked us several times. I thought it was time to send a message." He stared directly into the queen's eyes, making it clear the message was just as much for her as for An'zalor. Behind him, Hastings coughed into his hand to cover up a chuckle.

The queen's expression went stonily blank except for a slight narrowing of her eyes as she replied. "I hope you've not come to deliver a similar message to me." The entire court, suddenly nervous at being in an enclosed space with Max and his party, held their collective breath.

Max shook his head. "I don't think such a message is necessary here, your Majesty." He spread his arms out to his sides and spun around slowly, meeting the eyes of as many nobles as he could. "To my knowledge, other than my first encounter with a rash young noble, neither you nor your people have initiated any hostilities toward me or mine." His smile put his fangs on full display, causing another reaction amongst those gathered in the hall. He noticed that several gazes went to an angry looking older gentleman near the front on the left side of the room. Max assumed he was the father of the idiot he'd killed at the moot. He briefly wondered if that might be who hired the Shadow Stalkers to kill him.

"I've simply come to visit, and to establish an embassy, as promised. Maybe establish a few trade agreements with your esteemed merchants." He ended up facing the queen again, still showing his fangs.

"Well, I'm sure our city's leading merchants will be thrilled at the opportunity." Her lips barely twitched into a false smile. "You are welcome to stay here at the palace. Our best guest suites have been made ready for you." This time her smile was more enthusiastic. She knew full well he wouldn't be staying at the palace. Their visit had been planned and approved by both sides before he'd even left Stormhaven. The show was for the benefit of her court, forcing him to publicly decline her kind offer of hospitality.

"Thank you, Majesty, but I will only be staying this one night. I'm told my factors have secured a property to serve as our embassy, and I'd like to sample the accommodations they've arranged for me there. In addition, they've scheduled quite a few meetings for me, both this evening and through the morning tomorrow. Perhaps on my next visit?"

"Of course, *your majesty*. Whatever you wish." Her tone was so filled with malice that Max half expected her to spit on the floor at his feet. "I wish you good day, and the best of luck in your trade negotiations." The dismissal was clear. Max flashed her a smile and bared his fangs a final time.

"A good day to you as well." He purposely left off any honorific before turning his back on her and striding from the room, followed closely by Hastings. Behind him, the corporals smiled, waved, and Dylan even winked at a few attractive ladies as they departed. Just before stepping through the door, the ogre spoke loudly enough for the courtiers behind him to hear. "So, no fancy welcome feast like we got in Westreach, huh?" Max couldn't help but laugh as soon as the doors closed behind them. Surprisingly, Hastings laughed as well.

Escorting them out of the palace, he sounded amused as he spoke to Max. "I believe you'll find your new embassy quite comfortable. It belonged to a prominent merchant family until recently. The family's matron dared to suggest in public that our queen was less than worthy of her throne. She was executed, her family's trade contracts with the crown terminated. They thought it best to sell their assets within the city and retire to their manor in the country."

"I'm sorry to hear about their unfortunate circumstances." Max offered as their mounts were brought to them.

Hastings brought his own mount alongside Pokey and leaned close to Max, whispering, "Don't be sorry. They're friends of mine, and I assure you they are much better off out there."

Leaving the honor guard back at the palace, Hastings personally escorted Max to his new embassy. A huge compound with a three story manor house nearly the size of Max's palace at Stormhaven, enclosed by a twelve foot high stone wall with a sturdy looking iron gate. Seeing the expression on Max's face, Hastings smirked good naturedly. "I told you you'd like it."

They rode through the gate after it was opened by two soldiers in mismatched armor. When Max paused to inspect them, Hastings filled him in. "Mercenary guards from the local trade guild. They are bonded, and reliable enough. I recommended them to your factor. You can, of course, replace them with your own guards. This ground is now officially Stormhaven soil, and you can pretty well do as you please within its walls."

"Thank you for the information, and the assistance, Lord Hastings. It truly is a pleasure to see you again." Max thought for a few seconds before offering, "Would you accept my invitation to join us for dinner this evening?" When he saw the man glance over his shoulder at some passersby outside the gate, he added, "Assuming it would not cause you any... inconvenience, that is."

"I would be honored, King Storm." The man bowed in his saddle. Max noticed that the moment he accepted, a man loitering across the street turned and headed toward the palace.

"Then welcome to Stormhaven!" Max grinned at him. "Perhaps you're familiar enough with the manor to show me around a bit? And I could use any background information on the local merchants that you could provide, assuming you're willing."

"Of course." Lord Hastings dismounted along with the party, handing his reigns over to one of three stable hands who appeared to collect them. "First off, the stables are around back, next to the carriage house. You'll find the property is quite large, approximately three acres in total. There are extensive gardens all the way around." He motioned at the sculpted lawn and shrubbery on their side of the cobbled entry driveway that led up to a massive drive-through portico at the manor's main entry. In front of the portico an ornate fountain featuring what looked like a rearing centaur burbled quietly. "Out back the gardens are mostly filled with herbs and useful ingredients. A large part of the previous owner's business involved potions and alchemical components."

Hearing this, Dalia immediately headed around back, following the stable hands. "I'll find ye later, Max." She called over her shoulder. Max was half tempted to abandon the tour and go with her, but resisted the urge.

Hastings gestured to his left at a squat structure built up against the inside of the wall. "That is the guard barracks and armory. One of two armories, actually. The other, smaller one is inside the main house. The family kept a standing roster of thirty guards, most of whom accompanied them to the country. A few with families here in the city remained. I have absorbed them into my own house guard, but should you have need of them, I'm sure they'd be willing to serve here again. I can vouch for their loyalty."

Max nodded, always open to recruiting more fighters. "They'd need to become citizens of Stormhaven, and be willing to live and work alongside orcs, ogres, and such... but if they're willing, have them come see me in the morning."

They met Tomebinder, the dwarf that Goldentongue had assigned as Max's factor in the city, just outside the main doors. After introductions were made, and Max received a quick update on the status of the manor, Hastings began to show Max around. They were half an hour into the tour of the manor house, and had only covered three quarters of it, when Blake reported through party chat that their first appointment had arrived.

The visitor was a representative of the local Merchant's Guild. Greenleaf was an elderly man with white hair and a regal bearing. Hastings had informed Max during their tour that the extremely successful and wealthy man had recently purchased a noble title from the queen. He added that the merchant was honest enough in his business dealings, but firmly in the queen's pocket when it came to politics. His family had built a small empire growing and selling tea leaves, and had long desired a noble title denied to them for generations because of their humble beginnings. This Greenleaf had branched out into other enterprises as a young man, and single-handedly tripled his family's holdings in the years since.

"Merchant Greenleaf, welcome to this small slice of Stormhaven." Max greeted the man as he stepped into his new, plushly decorated, study. The man nearly leapt out of the chair he'd been waiting in, bowing deeply at the waist before replying.

"Thank you, King Storm, for the welcome and for agreeing to meet with me." Max motioned for Tomebinder, Hastings and Blake, who had accompanied him into the room, to take seats on either side of the merchant, while he lowered himself into the oversized, overstuffed leather chair that was obviously meant for him.

"Of course, of course." Max smiled at the man. "I'm told that if my merchants want to do business in the city, you're the man to talk to."

"Well, that may be a bit of an overstatement, Majesty. But I am certainly able to provide information, and act as a conduit between you and our most prominent merchant houses."

Max took a moment to consider his next words carefully. Taking a deep breath, he took a chance. "I appreciate that, truly. And I do not wish to sound ungrateful. But I'm less concerned with meeting the *most prominent* merchant houses than I am with finding honest and reliable people to do business with. I'm sure you're aware that those are not always the same people." He offered the now flustered man a fang-free smile.

Greenleaf quickly recovered his composure, and even managed a soft chuckle. "I am indeed, Majesty. It would help if you told me what types of goods you're interested in purchasing. Or in selling?"

Max shook his head. "I'll leave the specifics to Tomebinder and Councilor Goldentongue, as they know them much better than I do. I have many skills, but bartering is not one of them." He leaned forward in his chair, placing his elbows on his knees. "I want to be very clear about something, Lord Greenleaf. I have no interest in the politics of your city, or your kingdom. I don't wish to rub elbows with the elite. I will not pander to powerful nobles or merchant houses in an attempt to gain favor in any way. Nor will my representatives, if they wish to keep their positions. My relationship with the queen is cordial, at best. The rumors I'm sure you've heard that I threatened to burn her kingdom are true. There is no army marching outside your walls today because she agreed to play nice.

As long as she does, then we have no problems. In the meantime, I believe both our nations could benefit from a little free trade. My merchants will offer quality goods at fair prices, and expect the same in return. Nothing more, nothing less."

Max saw the disappointment in the merchant's eyes as he mentally calculated how much potential income he'd just lost from finders fees, bribes, and kickbacks. Not to mention the ability to steer Max's gold toward his allies. Still, the man maintained his regal mien and, to his credit, responded in a positive manner.

"That is refreshingly honest and direct, Majesty. I respect your position, and look forward to observing your interactions with my colleagues." He managed a crooked smile. "Should you ever be in need of tea leaves, or wish to ship goods up or down the river, I am at your service."

"I'll keep that in mind." Max got to his feet, the others rising as well. "Thank you for coming, Lord Greenleaf. It was a pleasure to meet you." Max sat back down as the man bowed before being led out by Tomebinder.

"I find I have to agree, King Storm. Refreshingly direct and honest." Hastings spoke as soon as the merchant had gone. "And while we're on the topic of honesty, I must inform you that the queen only tolerates my friendly attitude toward you because she believes I will be useful as a spy at some point in the future."

Max nodded. "I figured as much as soon as you agreed to stay for supper."

"Yet you still allowed me to sit in on this meeting."

Max chuckled. "In the first place, from even the limited interactions we've had, I believe you to be a man of honor. And to speak frankly, a man who's not inclined to go out of his way to serve his current queen." He held up a hand to stop Hastings from responding. "In the second place, nothing was going to be said here, or in any other meeting today, that I wouldn't want to get back to the queen. I'm not here to promote sedition." He grinned at the man. "Yet."

"Ha!" Lord Hastings slapped his leg. "I grow to like you more and more, King Storm."

*****

The rest of the day's meetings went quickly for Max. He smiled and greeted the various merchants when they arrived, then turned the meetings over to Tomebinder, who set each of them straight in much the same way Max had with Greenleaf, if in a less direct and more diplomatic manner. Max was amused to note that a few of the more prominent merchants, those he assumed received hurried warnings from Greenleaf, sent messengers with apologies for being unable to attend for one reason or another. Another sent a low level third cousin, rather than the house patriarch. Max didn't mind a bit. It just meant that his message to Greenleaf had been heard.

Dinner was a pleasant and relaxed affair, with good food and good company. Tomebinder had a naughty sense of humor that he didn't hesitate to share with his king, while Hastings proved both knowledgeable and helpful when it came to background information on the merchants. Everyone at the table, except Josephine, were combat veterans, and they shared a bond that none of them consciously considered, but that they all felt.

When Hastings departed, and the manor's staff went to their beds, Max stepped outside to explore the grounds. He poked around the armory, nodding at the guards on duty before moving on to sit on the edge of the fountain and enjoy the sounds it made, splashing water occasionally as he pondered the day's events. He checked in on Pokey in the stables, finding all the mounts well cared for and contentedly snoozing. After half an hour of exploring the gardens out back, he found what he was looking for. Up against the compound's side wall, between the stables and the carriage house, someone had planted several bushes with flowers that resembled roses enough that Max was going ahead and calling them rose bushes in his head. The thorny bushes had grown thick, and almost as tall as the wall. They were spaced about ten feet apart, which was perfect for Max's needs.

Carefully shouldering aside the one with bright yellow blooms, Max withdrew and placed a portal pedestal up against the wall, far enough behind the thick growth that it wouldn't be seen by anyone passing by. The portal, when activated, would appear to the left of the pedestal, in the open space between that bush and the next nearest. Anyone arriving through the portal, like an army, for example, would be a few steps from the cobblestone driveway that led from the carriage house, around the manor, to the front gate.

After completing the activation ritual, Max stepped free of the bush, allowing the branches he'd shoved aside to return to their normal position. After taking only two steps back, Max could no longer see the pedestal, despite knowing where it was. Satisfied that it wouldn't be accidentally discovered by prying eyes, he activated the portal to Stormhaven and gave a quick wave to the guards on duty before shutting it off again.

He authorized the usual people to access the portal, adding Tomebinder on the list. In the morning he'd inform the dwarf of the pedestal's location, along with instructions that it only be used in the most dire emergencies until Max instructed otherwise.

His true purpose for the trip accomplished, Max happily returned to his chambers on the top floor of the manor for a good night's sleep.

✶✶✶✶✶

The new Grandmaster of the Shadow Walkers remained seated at his desk when the one-armed journeyman assassin was escorted into his office. Grimacing at the elf's missing arm and bedraggled condition, he uttered just one word.

"Report."

"We failed, obviously." his subordinate had the stones to sneer at him, taking the liberty of sitting without permission. The two of them had been novices together, and had often worked together on contracts over the two centuries or so since, though they'd never been friends. "The others are dead, or soon will be. I was only allowed to live so that I could return and relay a message. A message you won't like." The sneer reappeared, causing a blood vessel at the Grandmaster's temple to throb slightly.

"What is this message." he growled across his desk, lifting a wicked looking dagger and thumbing the edge of the blade, a clear threat.

"First I must give you some details. We dared not use the portal after learning of the wards that the mages installed. Instead we crept through the front gate, scattered among the merchants and mushroom farmers as they entered. We met up at the designated abandoned building, then sent out scouts to locate the chimera. When we learned that he was taking a meal at a local restaurant outside the keep, we converged on that location." He paused, grimacing and rubbing at his stump with his other hand. The Grandmaster simply stared at him.

"We were steps from entering the restaurant when a being I initially took to be a human emerged and called out to us, already aware that we were there, despite our stealth abilities. His call broke our concealment, exposing us to everyone on the street."

"That is not possible. No human mage is that powerful."

The sneer reappeared, and the assassin leaned forward, thumping his shortened arm on the desk for emphasis. "I made that same mistaken assumption. He was no human. He was one of the Eldest. A dragon."

Finally the assassin saw emotion on his superior's face. Eyes widened, eyebrows raised, jaw dropped open in surprise. "Yes, you heard me correctly. The chimera currently enjoys the protection of a dragon."

"And it was the Eldest that sent you back with a message?"

"After removing my arm, then healing me, yes. He said to tell you that we disturbed his meal with his friend, the chimera, and that he did not appreciate being disturbed."

The other elf, after waiting several seconds, asked, "Is that all he said?"

Looking directly into his master's eyes, the assassin asked, "Isn't that enough?" He removed his stump from the desktop, leaning back in the chair. "I assume our client, in addition to failing to mention that the target was Battleborne, also neglected to disclose that he was under the protection of one of the Eldest." He waited for a nod from his superior. "As part of my official report, I strongly recommend we use that lack of disclosure as grounds to cancel the contract, and enforce the specified penalties against the client. Our losses have already been heavy." He gestured around the office to remind his new master of the assassination of the old master. "Guild reputation be damned. Our reputation means nothing if we're all dead. No one would fault us for refusing to take on a dragon."

When the Grandmaster didn't reply, the assassin shrugged. "Do as you like, *Grandmaster*." The sneer was back. "But know that I will not be returning to that kingdom, or pursuing that chimera, ever. I learned my lesson." He rubbed the stump again as he got up to leave.

Chapter 27

A full week passed without any assassination attempts. Max and his party were debating whether that was due to Lysbane's actions and the guild being afraid of him, or simply that it took that long for the next group to travel to Stormhaven from wherever their guild headquarters was. Since the assassins couldn't use the portal, they'd have to travel overland, as the last dozen had done. But since they were all dead, and hadn't talked, Max didn't know which way they'd traveled, from where, or for how long.

It was frustrating, not knowing if, or when, another attack might come. Max couldn't just hide in the castle for the rest of his life, relying on the wards and guards to protect him. He needed to be out hunting, fighting, completing quests in order to get stronger.

As it happened, he'd had plenty to do in Stormhaven to keep him occupied for the week. He'd been training under both of the Oakstones in the new forge several hours each day. He'd also spent time with Dalia and her father working on potions, conducting more experiments, and raising his *Alchemy* skill level quite a bit.

There was the usual kingdom business to discuss, the never-ending piles of paper on his desk. Goldentongue and Tomebinder had quickly negotiated several new trade agreements that were bringing in tremendous quantities of food, in return for gold, mithril, and in one case, a hundred of Dalia's high quality health potions. Max got some amusement out of watching his friend lose her mind, fussing and fuming when she learned from Goldentongue that the human alchemist that purchased those potions was selling them in his shop, and taking credit for creating them. Needless to say that contract was cancelled immediately, the alchemist blacklisted. He'd have to explain to his customers why he suddenly couldn't create any more.

Max laughed even harder when Dalia instructed Goldentongue to sell four dozen of the potions to that alchemist's main competitor at a significant discount, provided they credit her properly for their creation, and call out the first alchemist as a fraud to each customer who purchased a potion.

Now Max was free to spend a day at the Runemaster's outpost, studying the runes that were engraved on the various archways, structures, and even weapons found inside. Max had repeatedly read the three scrolls he'd received as quest rewards, but so far there was still no magical revelation or increase in knowledge, other than learning the names and potential uses of the rune pictured in each scroll. Today he'd get the opportunity to ask Funky about them.

The moment he arrived through the portal into his section of Dara Seans, the two guards snapped to attention and saluted. Recognizing them from a previous trip, he asked, "How are things going, now? Did the tavern open?"

"Aye, me king. It did! And a brewery to go with it." Both dwarves smiled widely. "Thank ye fer makin this place livable." Finding the dwarf who was interested in opening a tavern among the auction bidders had been pure serendipity, but Max was happy to take credit for it.

"You know me, always looking out for my guys!" He shot them a double thumbs-up as he turned to head for Enoch's office and the hidden outpost underneath. On the way he was happy to see people walking the street, several shops open, including a bakery, and hear the sounds of further construction somewhere nearby. Since the wall was completed, he hoped the construction was another shop getting ready to open, or some housing renovation for a new family. He knew that forty of the newly liberated orcs had been assigned to this settlement, along with their families. With the portals in place, the orcs, who would normally prefer to live on the surface, didn't mind being underground. If they began to miss the sun, it was easy enough to take a quick trip to visit friends and family at the Way Station, Northern Mine, or the Dworc village. A few of them had even taken a group trip to Westreach, causing a bit of a stir there when twenty orc men, women, and children strolled down the street.

Not finding Enoch in his office, he proceeded downstairs and activated the portal arch to the outpost. Max practically jogged down the ramp, his excitement building at the idea of questioning Funky about the scrolls.

The first person he encountered was a ragged looking Spellslinger. The dwarf was sitting on a bench outside one of the outpost buildings, elbows on his knees, head supported by his hands. When Max called out a greeting, the old dwarf barely bothered to look up.

"Welcome back, Max." His voice sounded rough, and tired.

"Long battle with a bottle of Firebelly's last night?" Max asked, taking a seat on the bench next to the dwarf and stretching his legs out in front of him.

Spellslinger shook his head. "I wish. Got caught up in studyin' a book we found, lost track o' time. That were three days ago."

Max whistled. "Must have been a good book. Did you learn anything useful?" The dwarf just shook his head in answer.

"Well, go get some sleep. I'm going to find Funky and see if I can get some answers." Max patted the dwarf on the shoulder and sprang back to his feet, setting off toward the area where the portal had opened and Funky had first walked through. He found the functionary golem there easily enough, standing still with his back against the wall. Max thought he was probably recharging, Borg style.

"Greetings, Funky! Did you miss me?" Max waved at the golem as he approached.

"Greetings, Novice Maximilian Storm. I... have anticipated your return." Max smiled at the golem. He supposed that was as close to emotion as Funky could get.

"I'm glad to be back. I have some questions for you regarding the scrolls you gave me, among other things."

"I will answer any questions that I am permitted to, Novice Maximilian Storm."

"Please, just call me Max. To save time, if nothing else." Max produced one of the three scrolls Funky had awarded him. "I read the primer, which taught me to read the old runes. And I can read the words on this scroll... but I'm not getting much from them. I can read the description that says this rune is called *Transfer*, but I get nothing from the rune itself. With other spell scrolls I've used, I open them, start to read them, and the knowledge of the spell is sort of implanted into my brain. Nothing like that happens with these scrolls."

Funky was silent for several seconds before asking. "Have your mana channels been damaged in some way?"

"What? No. Not that I'm aware of." Max quickly cast a light globe over their heads, and it appeared as normal. "Nope, I can cast spells just fine."

Funky held out a hand, palm up. "May I inspect the scroll in question?"

"Sure." Max placed the scroll on the open hand. Funky drew it closer to his face and his eyes lit up briefly before he extended his hand back toward Max. "I see no defects in the scroll. When you feed your mana into it, do you feel any resistance?"

"When I... what?" Max took the scroll and stared at it. "Is that it??" He nearly shouted at the golem, his heartrate picking up. "I need to feed mana into the scroll to use it?"

"Of course." Funky replied. "Any novice applicant knows... ah. My apologies, Max. I am aware that you have not followed the normal novice applicant procedures, and have none of the background knowledge an applicant would have. It simply did not occur to me that you would lack the most basic understanding of how rune magic works." The golem made a gesture that Max thought was supposed to represent a shrug. "Yes, with most tools used in rune magic, one must apply at least a small amount of mana to make proper use of the tool. This includes scrolls, engraving tools, engraved weapons, many containers and door locks, and much of the machinery one finds within guild structures."

Max thought about it for a moment. "What about the battle golems? I didn't push any mana into them."

"The battle golems have remained fully charged, and would have automatically drawn just enough mana from you upon contact to identify you and verify your access. Battle golems, and more advanced autonomous constructs such as myself, execute this procedure automatically upon first contact." He paused for a moment before adding, "Should I be deactivated for some reason, upon reactivation I would need to repeat the identification and authorization process with you and the others here in the outpost."

"Okay, that makes sense, actually." Max nodded. Having to use mana for everything runemaster related was yet another reason for him to put more points into his *Intelligence* and *Wisdom* attributes. Opening the scroll, he held it in both hands and focused on pushing just a little bit of mana into it. The moment he did, the rune on the scroll began to glow. The words on the page below it seemed to lift off the parchment and move directly into his eyes, like a weird 3D movie, except with blurry goggles. Max felt dizzy, and lost his balance, falling on his butt as the scroll evaporated in his hands.

"It is recommended that one be in a seated position, or laying down, when absorbing rune scrolls." Funky provided a bit too late. "Another bit of information a normal novice would already have."

Holding his head with one hand, Max continued to lay there, even as Enoch and several others who'd seen him fall came rushing over. "Thanks, Funky." Max would have rolled his eyes, but his head hurt too much.

When Enoch arrived, Max gave a half-hearted wave with his other hand. "Hey there, Enoch. Fancy meeting you here."

The dwarf looked both confused and concerned at the same time. "Be ye dyin', Max?"

"Nope. Just lost my balance…" He paused to grin up at the dwarf. *"Absorbing a rune scroll!"*

Enoch seemed to stop breathing, even as the others who'd gathered around gasped in surprise. Enoch's mouth moved a few times, but no words came out. Finally he gasped in a big breath and blurted out, "Ye did it, Max? Truly? Ye did it!" Max nodded as the others cheered.

Max had just taken the first real step toward recovering the runemaster's magic.

Enoch extended a hand and pulled Max to his feet, then steadied him when he threatened to fall again. "So, ye learned a rune! What's it do? Fire? Lightnin'?"

Max almost shook his head, but thought better of it at the last second. "Nothing like that. It's a transfer rune. Used to direct power from one rune sequence to another. You know, if you're engraving more than one rune onto a sword, for example."

Enoch and the others briefly looked disappointed, but the dwarf recovered quickly. "Still, ye learned a rune! And ye got two more to learn as well, yes?"

"Yes. But as Funky here somewhat belatedly pointed out, I should be sitting down when I learn them. How bout we retire to the conference room? I can recover before I try the next one, and Funky can fill me in on what I don't know that I don't know, but should know."

Not understanding in the least, Enoch agreed and guided Max in the general direction of the building that held the conference room, letting him walk on his own but staying close, just in case. When the others began to follow, he turned and shooed them away. "Bah! Ye see'd enough! Let our Max here study in peace!" The dwarves reluctantly dispersed, going back to whatever they'd been working on, but darting quick glances at Max every few seconds.

"Spellslinger's going to be mad he missed this, but I sent him off to bed." Max groaned as he sat down at the head of the conference table. Enoch took the seat to his right, folding his hands on the table to keep them from fidgeting. Funky took up a position standing near Max.

"Funky, still no word back from the guild on my comrades' applications?" Max asked as he regained his equilibrium. "These would all be much easier if we could undergo our novice training together, compare notes as we go."

"There has been no response as of yet, Max." Max smiled at the golem's use of his given name. "As I stated previously, the remaining guild officers are in isolation. They may choose not to respond to inquiries at all."

"Alright, then I suppose this is all on me, for now." Max produced the next scroll and, taking a deep breath, opened it. Just as before, he pushed a little mana into the item, and the words lifted off the scroll to invade his brain. This time, though, he was able to lean back in his chair, close his eyes, grip the table with both hands, and the dizziness was much less severe. He took some time to breathe steadily after it was over, and when he finally opened his eyes, he felt mostly normal.

"That one was *Light*." He smiled at Enoch. "Seems much more useful." He decided to try and experiment. Pulling a sheet of parchment from his inventory, he bit his finger and used the blood to draw the rune. His first two attempts failed, his still slightly unsteady hand causing him to make mistakes and start again. By the time he had the rune on paper matching the one in his head, he'd had to bite himself half a dozen times.

Holding the paper up to Funky, he asked, "Do you recognize this?"

"That is a basic light rune." the golem confirmed,

"Alright, let's see if it works. Enoch, you might want to step back. Maybe even wait outside, in case this explodes."

The dwarf, not wanting to miss out on witnessing the first casting of true rune magic, compromised. He went and stood outside the door, but leaned his head around the frame to peek.

Max took a deep breath and touched a corner of the parchment with one finger, then pushed the tiniest sliver of mana he could manage into it. Almost immediately the rune, and the parchment it was written on, began to glow with a crisp white light. Encouraged, Max pushed a bit more mana, and the glow increased.

"Well done, Max!" Enoch shouted from the doorway, moving back into the room. "That be a thing o' beauty!" Grinning at the dwarf's enthusiasm, and feeling a good bit of pride, Max pushed more mana into the parchment, then jerked his hand back as the glow brightened briefly before it burst into flame. Enoch paused mid-step near the far end of the table, eyes wide. "What happened?"

"I... don't know." Max admitted, staring at the pile of ash in front of him.

"You chose a medium with a limited capacity to actively channel mana." Funky replied. "When you exceeded the parchment's capacity, it was destroyed."

"Right. Mental note. No overcharging stuff with runes." Max wiped the ash off the table. Enoch nodded solemnly as he retook his seat. "I be thinkin' it'd be wise to study a bit more before ye try any other experiments."

"I agree." Max picked up the untied ribbon that had bound the scroll and examined it closely. He still didn't recognize any of the runes, so he held it up to Funky. "Can you tell us what this ribbon does?"

"That ribbon has multiple purposes, all centered around the concept of preservation. Attached to the preservation runescript are ones for protection from elements, and temporal stasis."

"So you can read and write runes?" Enoch asked.

The golem shook his head. "I can recognize a few simple runes that I have seen used and heard explained, like that basic light rune, which guild novices often inscribed on rocks and other items to light their way in dark places. However I am forbidden from writing runes, and do not possess the ability to channel mana into them. These restrictions were placed within my own core inscriptions to prevent my being used as a weapon in the event I am captured by non-guild entities. A safeguard I much prefer over the alternative, which would be self-destruction."

Max blinked for a second, the number of questions that information engendered forcing him to take a moment and prioritize. "Your core inscriptions? Does that mean you have a solid mana core that has runes inscribed on it? Or does core inscriptions mean like, your baseline programming, upon which your other inscriptions are based."

"If I understand the term programming correctly, the answer is yes to both. I have a rechargeable solid mana crystal core that is inscribed with the basic concepts that allow me to function. Those inscriptions feed into a multitude of secondary, tertiary, and so on inscriptions that increase my functionality considerably."

"How many is a multitude?" Max asked, curious about what it might take to create a golem.

"Three thousand eight hundred and seventy one separate inscriptions, not counting the transfer runes that connect them, or restriction runes that limit output."

Max whistled as Enoch's jaw dropped in silence. The two of them glanced at each other as Funky continued. "I am a master level creation. It took the runemaster who constructed me ten years just to properly form my perception, processing, and verbal response scripts."

"Durin's weighty stones!" Enoch let out an explosive exhale. "Ten years, just to make ye talk?"

"I believe the master was also experimenting with other facets of my creation at the same time, but yes, that is correct."

Max noticed the glum expression that appeared on the dwarf's face. "What?"

Enoch placed his hands flat upon the table, then clasped them together, staring down at them for a while before he spoke. When he did, his voice was quiet, his tone subdued. "Spellslinger and meself... we be too old fer this. Too old to be startin' out, I mean. If that be the sort o' time involved in masterin' the rune magic, we won't live to be more' n mebbe... apprentices?"

Max understood. Knowing ahead of time that you likely won't live long enough to accomplish some of your life goals was something he'd lived with himself.

Not willing to bullshit his comrade, or expecting that it would help in any way if he did, he chose to be frank. "So what if you die as an apprentice runecaster? You will still have been directly responsible for the restoration of the rune magic to your people. Hell, you're the one who found this place, and figured out what it was. You're already a hero! Everything you do from now on is just adding to your legend!" He waited to see signs that the dwarf was perking up a bit. When he did, he kept going.

"Of course, barring an unexpected death in battle, or a successful assassination attempt, I will outlive you by quite a bit. Which means I'll get to influence which legends get told, which songs get sung. I'm leaning toward songs about how you accidentally stumbled upon this place, pissed yourself when the first battle golem moved, and let Spellslinger outlearn you in rune magic studies. A mediocre hero, at best." He winked at the now wide-eyed dwarf.

Realizing that Max was kidding, Enoch snorted at him. "Ye better wait till I'm dead before ye spread such lies, or I'll be comin' fer ye meself!"

"Of course, you could always just give up right now, go back to negotiating trade agreements on behalf of the kingdom…"

"Ye couldn't drag me out o' this place with an army o' battle golems!" Enoch mock-growled at him. "Enough, Max. I get yer meanin'." He unclasped his hands and laid them flat on the table again, drumming his fingers. "I'll learn what I can, and make sure it be passed on to them that are young enough to complete the job."

"That's the spirit!" Max offered a fist to bump. He tilted his head, thinking. "I never asked, Enoch. Do you have kids? Someone you'd maybe like to name as your own apprentice to study here?"

"Aye, I've nine wee brats." The dwarf's pride was evident in his wide smile. "The youngest will be turnin' ninety this year." He didn't even need to consider the next bit, as he'd clearly put some thought into it already. "And aye, me second youngest be a cleric, and a bookworm. She'd rather bury her face in the dustiest o' the tomes in the archives than fight a proper battle." He shook his head as if unable to understand such an attitude. "She be good-hearted, with a level head."

Max thought she sounded perfect. "Then, *if* we get approval for more applicants from the guild officers, you should bring her in and get her started." Max grinned at him. "Unless, of course, you're worried she'll outlearn you."

"Bah! I'd be nothin' but proud if she did!"

Funky chose that moment to offer some advice. "Might I suggest that any future potential applicants be properly initiated per normal procedural guidelines? In order to prevent potential mishaps, and increase the efficiency of their studies."

"Instead of stumbling around and literally playing with fire, like I'm doing?" Max chuckled. "Good plan, Funky. Though we'll need your help with that, I'm sure."

"That is an effort for which I can provide extensive assistance, once the guild has approved the resumption of recruitment."

"Speaking of that, is there any way you might send a request for an update, or a follow-up of some kind?" Max asked.

"I can open the portal and transmit a status query, yes." Funky confirmed. "Though, such a thing may annoy guild officers who do not wish to be disturbed."

Max thought long and hard about that. The last thing he needed was an angry runemaster coming through the portal and commanding the battle golems to squash them all. Still, they were limited in what they could learn without permission to proceed properly with their studies. "Please do, Funky. But... be as gentle and considerate as possible?"

The golem turned without a word and headed out the door. Max looked at Enoch. "In the meantime, I want to practice this rune. Could you send someone out to grab me several dozen good rocks to engrave? Also... have you found anything like an engraving tool in this place? If not, I can run back to my smithy and grab one."

*****

Deep in the mountain ranges to the north of Max's territory, an ancient and withered face twitched, as if something had tickled its nose. A moment later, a hand twitched, calloused fingers curling up into a fist. Finally, eyes blinked open, and the dwarf, who had been enjoying a long nap frowned.

"What in the deepest chasm of the nine hells is this??" The dwarf growled, sitting up in his sleeping alcove. He tilted his head, listening to the annoying buzz that drifted across his sleeping chamber. Finally recognizing the sound as an alert from the guild communications system, he was tempted to lay back down. He had no interest in hearing from any of the other guild members. They hadn't spoken in a thousand years, at least, and he didn't see a need for them to start now.

Still, he knew that the insistent buzz would continue until he acknowledged it. Cursing quietly to himself, he set his feet on the floor and stomped across the room, stepping through the door into his lab. "I'll hear the message n shut the damned thing up. Nothin' says I have ta reply to whichever of those crusty old relics is blabbin' at me." He quickly checked the chronometer on his desk, which showed he'd been asleep for just over sixty years. "Mebbe I'll give 'em a piece o' me mind fer interruptin' me beauty sleep!"

He snorted to himself at that idea. The alcove he slept in was also a stasis chamber. So while no matter how long he slept he wouldn't age, he also wouldn't be getting any younger or prettier.

Taking a moment to grab a bottle of spirits from his desk as he passed, he made his way over to the communication terminal. He had amused himself by shaping his terminal into the form of a misshapen goblin's head that moved its lips and made googly-eyes when the person on the other end spoke. Mainly because he enjoyed watching it speak in his associates' voices, knowing they'd be offended if they could see it.

Touching a finger to the goblin's forehead, he activated the waiting message, surprised to see that there were in fact two messages. He was further surprised to find that the message was from one of the guild functionaries, rather than one of his colleagues, and that it originated from a long-abandoned outpost.

Taking a long swig from the bottle, followed by a second, he stared at the goblin's face for a while, debating whether to listen to the messages. On the one hand, he was curious. On the other, since it was a golem functionary sending the messages, it was likely something boring like a failure in a ward some place, or a malfunction in its own internal processing.

It also might be a prank. One of his former apprentices, now one of his few living guildmates, had once played a naming day prank by having a battle golem come to him directly to report a malfunction in its script that caused it to recite dirty jokes. Quite loudly.

"Bah! Whatever it be, it can wait." He took another swig from the bottle as he turned away from the goblin's head. The aged spirits went down smoothly, spreading a pleasurable burn through his belly. Stomping back into his sleeping chamber, he set the bottle down on a stand near the stone sleeping alcove before laying back down. He pulled up his interface and was about to reactivate the stasis spell when he noticed a tiny green light blinking in the bottom right corner. The light he'd designated to alert him when he had notifications. He'd long ago set his interface to automatically suppress them so as not to interrupt his work. Or his sleep.

Curious, he focused on bringing up his notifications.

A moment later he leapt from his bed and practically ran back to the goblin's head. What he was seeing in his notifications should not be possible! Yet the system didn't lie. If it was true, he needed to see for himself, and there was no time to waste!

His eyes widened as he quickly listened to the initial communication from functionary #213, then it's follow-up inquiry. He compared that to the notifications now displayed on his interface, and looked at the dates, grumbling, "Regin's hairy arse, why am I just seein' this now?" His eyebrows lifted, then dropped back into a frown. "And why have none o' the others responded?"

He looked away from the goblin's head to the personal portal arch on the wall across the room, considering. Should he reach out to the others using emergency protocols, or simply go and investigate on his own? If what he was being told was true, then there might be an advantage to being the first to arrive. On the other hand, disturbing his fellow guild officers, likely waking them from their own slumbers, would give him no little satisfaction.

Stroking his beard as he considered his options, he walked back toward the stand next to his alcove and retrieved the now half-empty bottle of spirits. A good drink always helped him think.

Chapter 28

Max was barely awake, having just gotten dressed and considering whether to stumble down to the dining hall for breakfast, or have some brought up to him, when Teeglin knocked on his door and called out, "King Max!"

"Come in, princess." He stepped into his sitting room and took a seat in the largest chair as she burst into the room. "Master Redmane said to come and wake you up! But you're already awake, so I guess I can just go ahead and tell you... you have a visitor." She paused, her eyes rolling up in her head as she thought, then added, "Actually it's three visitors. But they're all together."

"Interesting." Max wondered who might show up unannounced, other than Shadow Walkers. If it had been them, Max was sure Redmane wouldn't have so calmly sent Teeglin to let him know. The dwarf could always just notify Max of happenings via their rings, but he liked to give Teeglin the opportunity to hone her protocol skills, and as fast as the little scamp zoomed through the palace corridors, there wasn't all that much of a delay. "Do you know who they are?"

Teeglin shook her head, suddenly wondering if she was supposed to have found out first. "I can tell you they're dressed like warriors. Lots of armor, weapons, and scars."

Even more curious now, Max nodded. "Alright, where are they?"

"Small dining room. Master Redmane figured you'd want breakfast." Teeglin took the hint and led the way out the door. Rather than sprint ahead, she walked impatiently at his side, fidgeting as they went. Now she was just as curious about them as Max was.

A few minutes later she opened the door and loudly announced Max before moving aside. Redmane and the three others in the room, all humans, stood and bowed as he entered. "Good morning, Master Redmane. Who do we have here?" Max smiled to acknowledge the bows as he moved toward his spot at the head of the dining table. The others remained standing, waiting for him to sit.

"These be Master Steele o' the adventurers guild, and his companions, Stonehand and Blackwing."

"The adventurers' guild, eh? Welcome to Stormhaven." He motioned for them to sit as he checked them out. Steele seemed to be a frontline fighter, wearing nearly a full set of plate armor, mithril if Max wasn't mistaken. The hilt of a two-handed sword rose above his shoulder from a scabbard on his back. Stonehand was harder to place. He wore chainmail and an open helm, but carried no visible weapon. The third one, Blackwing, was an obvious rogue type. She wore dull black leather from neck to toe, and her hair was so black it shimmered slightly blue as the light shifted when she turned her head. As Teeglin had observed, they each bore several exposed scars on hands, necks, and faces. "To what do I owe the pleasure of your company this fine morning? Have you come hoping to establish a branch in Stormhaven?"

Steele cleared his throat, seeming slightly nervous in Max's company. Max was tempted to *Identify* the visitors, but held off, not wanting to be rude. Instead he sent a message through party chat for his corporals, Dalia, and Nessa to report for breakfast ASAP.

"No, King Storm, that's not why we're here, though we might discuss that if we can resolve our other business first."

"Well, that sounds ominous. What business would that be?" He gave them a friendly smile, with hardly any fang showing. There was a slight pause as platters of food were delivered to each of them, and they thanked the servers.

"It has come to our attention that you have established a guild by the name of War Dogs. One that recently cleared the Westreach dungeon, has been fighting monsters along one of Westreach's borders, and recently completed a mercenary quest at another border. Is that correct?"

Max shook his head, taking the time to chew some delicious sausage before answering. "Not quite. First, I did not establish the guild, though I am an officer. Second, when my companions and I cleared the dungeon in Westreach, we had not yet formed the guild. In fact, it was formed in order to resolve a sensitive situation regarding a deed to an estate that one of my corporals received as loot from the dungeon. The bits about clearing monsters around that estate, and the mercenary quest at the front lines are correct."

There was a long awkward silence as Steele took in that information, and was obviously having difficulty finding a way to proceed. Max, suspecting he now knew why they had come, took pity on him. "May I ask why the War Dogs' adventures are of interest to you?"

The man sighed, relaxing a little at being given an opening. "First, I should give you a bit of background, I think. We are aware that you are Battleborne, and recently arrived on our world, so you may not be aware of the Adventurers' Guild." Max held up a hand causing him to pause.

"King Farstrider told me of your guild. He mentioned that you'd sent a team that failed to clear the dungeon, and that he'd been expecting a stronger team to be sent. If you're here because you feel we somehow robbed you of the opportunity to clear the dungeon, I can only say that was not our intent."

Steele shook his head. "We do not feel that we were robbed by you and your team, King Storm. Though the team that arrived shortly after you cleared the dungeon was disappointed in the loss of time and potential loot. King Farstrider and commander Falcon explained the circumstances by which you were tasked with clearing the dungeon, as well as describing what you encountered inside, and the loot you received." There was clearly a twinge of jealousy over the loot on his face, but it passed quickly. "Because the Westreach portal was locked due to hostilities with another kingdom, our team had to travel by land. A trip of more than a week's time from our headquarters. King Farstrider had no way to know when to expect us."

Max nodded his understanding, wondering if he had members of that team sitting in front of him. "I'm glad to hear that you don't hold a grudge. But based on your questions, I must conclude that you have certain... concerns regarding the War Dogs?"

"Concerns would be an overstatement, Majesty." Steele looked uncomfortable again. "We are... curious regarding your plans for the guild. Specifically its future growth, and scope."

Blake and Dylan walked in just in time to hear this last query, and looked to Max as they moved to take seats themselves.

Guild Master Steele, I present to you Lord Blake, Guild Master of the War Dogs, and fellow guild officer Dylan." As he was speaking, the others streamed in through the door, and he made the rest of the introductions.

"Lord Guild Master Corporal Blake, would you like to answer Guild Master Steele's question?" He grinned widely as Blake rolled his eyes at the titles. The gnome turned to Steele.

"If you're asking if we plan to compete with your guild, the answer is no. We formed the guild as a way to accomplish the obligation of holding back beast attacks that came with the estate I received. We're focusing on that mission, and a few other local quests, using it as a way to make our people stronger. King Farstrider used us as mercenaries in his border conflict because we offered a way to bolster his forces without bringing in troops from Stormhaven or other allies, which would have been seen as an escalation on his part. Or so Falcon told us when he presented the quest."

Steele and the other two nodded, as Blake's response apparently corresponded with what they'd heard from Farstrider.

"We have our guild headquarters at my manor house, and currently have no plans, or inclination, to expand beyond that." He motioned toward Max. "King Storm here has extensive territories with more than enough monsters for us to take on without intruding upon your territory." He paused, thinking. "Though, if I recall correctly, your guild did not have a branch in Westreach."

"That is correct, we did not, at that time. I have recently been promoted to Guild Master and been sent to establish that branch. Hence my… curiosity regarding your plans."

Max blinked a couple times. He'd been thinking he was dealing with the master of the entire guild, not a newly promoted local guild master. That changed how he expected this meeting to go. From the look he received from Redmane, the dwarf was thinking the same.

Max stepped back into the conversation. "Master Steele, is it your guild's intention to limit my peoples' access to the Westreach dungeon? Either my guildmates, or my citizens, or those who happen to be both?" His tone was slightly less friendly than before.

Steele shook his head, raising his empty hands toward Max. "Not at all, Majesty. King Farstrider made it clear that your people are welcome to enter the dungeon. Our guild parties will do the same, both to help our adventurers advance, and to keep the dungeon monsters at acceptable strength. But that is a relatively minor function our guild will serve in Westreach. We'll be completing quests for local nobles and merchants, providing guards for trade caravans or hunting trips, gathering materials for crafters, offering training for locals who wish to learn how to fight, that sort of thing. The crown and its soldiers will continue to control access to the dungeon, as well as provide protection at the outpost."

"That is very good to hear." Max's tone returned to friendly. "Have we sufficiently satisfied your… curiosity regarding War Dogs future?"

"You have." All three adventurers nodded. "We thank you all for your understanding and forthrightness."

"In that case, please stay a while and enjoy your breakfast. I'd like to hear more about your guild and the services it offers. As I'm sure you're aware, my kingdom is still in its infancy. But as it grows, there may be room for your guild to have a presence here alongside the War Dogs."

Steele set down his fork, having been about to shovel some eggs into his mouth. "I must admit, my superiors in the guild have expressed interest in you, your kingdom, and most especially your newly activated dungeon core."

Max showed his fangs this time. "If your guild... I'm sorry, I don't know what your top person's title would be. Grandmaster?" He waited for Steele to nod. "If your Grandmaster would like to come and discuss it with me, maybe take a tour, I'd be happy to oblige."

"I'd be happy to pass along your gracious invitation." Steele gave a respectful nod. From his tone, Max didn't think the man expected his boss to bother coming to see a low level dungeon. No matter how unique. He decided to tweak the man just a bit.

"I'm sure our little dungeon is too low level to be of interest to folks of your level at this time. The monsters inside are currently between level ten and twenty, and that's only because I fed them a dozen or so high-leveled Shadow Walkers we captured when they attempted to assassinate me."

Max quite enjoyed the astonished looks on the three humans' faces.

"Y-you... did what?" Steel stammered.

"We captured a bunch of assassins who came for my head. Since they couldn't provide me any useful information, or forego their sworn oath to fulfill the contract and try to kill me, I had no choice but to execute them. I chose to do so by taking them into the dungeon, disabling them with not-quite-mortal wounds, and allowing the low level dungeon monsters to finish them off. They leveled up quite quickly. As did the dungeon core, which is now level two."

Max focused on his plate, grabbing a piece of bacon and popping it into his mouth, savoring the flavor as he waited for a response from the shocked adventurers. Finally, Blackwing spoke. "You realize that killing the Shadow Walkers in that manner will only anger the guild."

Max snorted as the others around the table laughed, confusing their visitors. Max took a moment to swallow his food before speaking. "I figured they're already pretty angry with me after I killed their Grandmaster."

"You... what?" Her expression turned from one of sympathy to a look of horror and disbelief. Her companions looked much the same.

Max shrugged. Getting to explain that particular decision never grew old. "After they tried and failed to kill me, and everyone I've grown to trust here on this world assured me they would keep trying, I decided to send them a message. In hopes that a show of my strength, and their weakness, might scare them off. I sent their assassins' bodies back in small pieces, along with a little surprise that successfully killed their Grandmaster." He paused, baring his fangs again as he shook his head. "It didn't work. Apparently they just chose a new master and tried again."

"The ones who survived were the ones we fed to the dungeon." Dylan clarified for them, a wide smile on his big ogre face. "It was that, or feed them to my ogre pals. Max figured the dungeon was a more efficient use of them as a resource."

"I... can see how that makes sense." Steele didn't sound at all sure of his words, but was making an effort to be polite. Blackwing actually put a hand over her mouth to try and stifle a laugh, then changed her mind and let loose a hearty belly laugh.

"Oh, I wish I could have seen their faces." Her eyes sparkled as she beamed at Max. "If you don't mind me saying so, I like your style, King Storm!"

"Not a big fan of the Shadow Walkers?"

"Quite the opposite. Besides them being strictly dark elf only, they have, in my humble opinion, a vastly overinflated opinion of themselves." She pressed her lips together. "They're the biggest, and most expensive, and their operatives are very well trained, I'll grant them that. But they're snooty, opinionated, and offer no respect to anyone not of their own ilk. I've had more than one run-in with them when they tried to steal a job from me. I survived, they did not."

Dylan let out a giggle that sounded distinctly odd coming from his large frame. "I like her, boss. Can we keep her?" He threw an exaggerated wink at the rogue, who threw one right back, much to the amusement of all three corporals.

The other two humans had been looking around the room as she spoke, as if suddenly wondering if it was wise for them to remain. Seeing this, Max reassured them. "Don't worry, there are wards throughout the palace. Wards set to kill, after they pushed through our previous stun wards and killed a few of my guards. You're quite safe here."

Max had briefly resisted the thought of disclosing the wards, then decided it wasn't a bad thing for word to spread that sneaking into his home was a bad idea.

"I see. That is very good to hear, Majesty." Steele acknowledged.

Max motioned toward a server and requested another platter of bacon after seeing that Dylan had hoarded most of it, having stacked it high on his plate, then covered the pile with scrambled eggs and sausage gravy. He waited patiently for the humans at the table to eat and think.

After half a minute or so of silence, Smitty changed the subject. "Hey, you guys have branches all over the place, right? Do you provide some kind of dining hall inside your branches?"

Stonehand spoke for the first time. "We do. The kitchens are open day and night, as we often keep odd schedules. The menu is limited, but the food tastes good, and provides excellent boosts."

"Then I have two very important questions for you." Smitty grinned. "First, would you consider allowing a restaurant to operate in place of your normal dining hall? And second, have any of you ever had a cheeseburger?"

*****

Max had planned to return to the outpost and check in with Enoch and Funky, but was further delayed by more unexpected visitors.

First, just minutes after the three humans departed, Lightsprocket returned from Westreach. She was excited to speak with Max, so he relented and invited her to his study. There she related to him and Redmane her adventure inside that dungeon. "The War Dogs team that escorted me successfully cleared all the monsters. We nearly lost one in the fight at the final boss's camp, but they were saved at the last instant by one of your amazing health potions. I managed to convince the final orc boss to speak with me after mentioning the infant core." She inhaled deeply, having said all that in one breath.

"He actually expressed an interest in her well-being, and asked me several questions about her activation and subsequent growth. When I told him how you fed her a bunch of high-level assassins, he roared with approval. Scared me a little bit." She shuddered. "He asked me to pass on his compliments, and that he's looking forward to facing you again."

Max shook his head. He had no interest in going back there, except maybe to harvest more of the tree-monster crystals for Dalia's potions. "What level was he when you saw him?'

"Level forty five. I found him quite reasonable, mostly. He allowed us to depart without a fight, which I did not expect. Even opened a portal back to the entrance for us. Oh!" She quickly produced a small bag and handed it to Max. "Your people asked me to deliver these, as agreed." Max opened it long enough to see a small quantity of the green crystals inside, then nodded his thanks.

When the gnome mage had hustled out, intending to go back into his dungeon to speak with Child and pass on a message to her as well, his next visitor arrived, stepping into his study alongside Redmane.

"Lord Hastings! Welcome. This is a pleasant surprise." Max motioned for the man to sit in one of the comfortable chairs near the fireplace. "What brings you here?"

"I apologize for the unannounced intrusion, Majesty." The man bowed before taking the indicated seat. "There has been a slight… wrinkle, at home."

"Wrinkle?"

"The queen forced my hand much sooner and more emphatically than I expected. Demanded that I offer whatever intelligence I have been able to glean from our interactions. When what I offered was all but useless to her, she threatened the lives of my heirs if I did not do better."

"I'm sorry to hear that. Are you here to ask me to kill her?" Max was already considering it, whether he was asked, or not. He had an extreme dislike for the woman, and had already been considering a raid similar to the one on the orc city, using his hidden pedestal.

Hastings chuckled at the offer. "Nothing so drastic, King Max. I have simply come to request asylum. If I move quickly enough, I may be able to secret my family and staff out of the city and get them to Westreach before her spies alert her. Failing that, I'd ask that you allow us to hide at your embassy until I can make other arrangements."

Max was ready to agree immediately, but a quick message via party chat from Redmane had him holding back.

"How many people are we talking about here, Lord Hastings? And would they all be willing to swear oaths and become Stormhaven citizens?"

"My immediate family and household staff number thirty or so. If I can gather my siblings, cousins, in-laws, personal guard, and most valued employees, another three hundred and fifty."

Max kept his face neutral. "Will the queen attack the embassy if she finds you're hiding in there?"

Hastings didn't hesitate. "She will not. Her likely anger and desire to take my head would be outweighed by her fear of you, and your allies. If it were solely up to her, she might order an attack in the heat of the moment. But her advisors would calm her before it was actually carried out." He grimaced at Max. "Even if I'm wrong, I have enough fighters among my retainers to hold that compound against a larger force for quite some time. We would not require your guards to risk themselves." Hastings mistook Max's questions and apparent hesitation as an expression of concern for his people. "We can, of course, compensate you for the risk, and inconvenience."

Max ignored the offer of payment for a moment. "The four hundred or so people you mentioned, they are all in the city?"

"Oh, yes. My house is one of the oldest and largest in the kingdom. All told, we number several thousand. Those who reside outside the capital will be in less danger, and will be warned. They'll have to choose for themselves whether to remain and take their chances with the queen, or flee. Obviously, I shall recommend that they flee. They'll also have time to consolidate resources sufficient to begin again elsewhere, if necessary."

Max's quick glance at Redmane got him a subtle nod of approval.

"Lord Hastings. One last question. Would it be easier, or safer, to sneak your people into my embassy, rather than out of the city and down the road to Westreach?"

"Considerably, Majesty. But negotiating with the queen for our release after that would be... costly."

"What if you didn't need to negotiate with her at all?" Max's grin made the human lord more than a little nervous.

*****

Max stood at the front door of his embassy, welcoming a group of twenty or so nervous humans and motioning them to step inside. As the last one passed through the door, he called out in party chat. "Report."

Nessa spoke first. "Three spies have been eliminated, and two others are currently… occupied by our guild friends." Max's elven hearing picked up the sounds of a loud argument taking place down the street. When he was formulating his plan, he'd reached out to Steele at the adventurer's guild to see about hiring some human guild members to do a job. They were currently executing their mission with impressive enthusiasm.

Nessa and Blackwing had scouted the area surrounding the embassy, spotting and identifying half a dozen people who were observing the comings and goings at his gate. It seemed the queen, or one of her advisors, were expecting Hastings and at least of few of his people to attempt to take shelter there. Those who were hidden atop roofs or inside buildings that weren't readily and believably accessible by other guild members were swiftly and quietly eliminated, their bodies stored in Nessa's inventory. The others were being loudly and rudely confronted by Blackwing's seemingly drunken and overly friendly guildmembers.

There was one final observer still to be taken care of. Blackwing had volunteered to take that one, as they were a high-level operative in the employ of The Ghost, much higher level than Nessa could handle.

They'd gone ahead and started moving people in, secure in the knowledge that the final observer would not survive to report what she saw.

A wagon filled with barrels of ale trundled down the street outside the gate, pausing as the driver cursed loudly and hopped down from the seat to check one of the horse's hooves, conveniently blocking the gate from the view of the beleaguered observers down the street, while another score of Hastings' people hustled out of an alley and through the gate. At the same time, nearly a hundred more were quietly slipping through the property's back gate. They were led by Blake to the nearby carriage house, rather than risk them being seen crossing the extensive gardens and entering the house by a curious neighbor who might peer over the walls. It was late at night, and Max expected the neighbors to be asleep, but one never knew.

"Dylan, how we doing?"

"Three ten by my count. Hastings himself is leading the last group. Mostly his fighters, who have been spread out making sure the others got here okay. Should be here any minute."

"Copy that." Max smiled as the group who'd just come through the front gate approached. He waved them inside with whispered welcomes just like the others. As soon as they were in, the wagon driver made a show of calling out. "Oy, you there at the gate? Is this the Stormhaven embassy? I've got an order of ale and spirits for a fella by the name of Tomebinder!"

When a laughing dwarf guard confirmed he was in the right place, the driver backed his wagon up far enough to turn his team into the gate. Before he passed through, he called out, again loudly enough for the observers to overhear, "There are two more wagons behind me. Is the king throwing a party, or something?"

Still laughing, the guard called back. "Have ye seen me king's big ogre friend? He drinks ale a barrel at a time! And once he gets to dancin', he drinks even faster!"

"Hey, I heard that." Dylan muttered into party chat. "He's not wrong, but I feel attacked."

"It be pure respect fer yer skills." Dalia assured him, the smile obvious in her tone.

"The final observer is dead." Nessa reported. "We're on our way back."

"Hastings and his guys are coming through the back now." Blake added. "Looks like they had a bit of a scuffle. They're moving fast, and a little bloody. Dalia, we could use a little help."

"Be there in a jiffy." The druid used a term that Smitty had taught her. She'd been a little confused when he told her it was also the name of his favorite brand of peanut butter, and he'd had to explain that as well. Red and Dalia had both immediately adopted the term.

"Alright Smitty, Cavariel, start moving everyone from the house to the barn. Blake, when you've got Hastings secure, move the folks from the carriage house into the barn as well." He watched as two more wagons trundled through the gate. As soon as the last one was through, the gates were closed and locked. A moment later the adventurers ceased harassing the queen's observers and faded away, the closed gate being their signal.

"Everyone's inside, we're good." Dylan reported. "Headed for the portal."

Taking his cue from the orc city raid, and in keeping with their cover story of preparing for a party on the embassy grounds, Max had erected a large, thick canvas tent in between the barn and the carriage house, right in front of the spot where the portal would open. Its sole purpose was to obscure the light from any unexpected observers in nearby homes. He'd taken the further precaution of setting up a mobile kitchen with a few tiki torches on the opposite side of the garden. The light, and the sounds of clanking pots and bustling cooks, should draw attention away from the area of the tent.

Max gave a wave to the amused dwarves at the gate, then strolled around the side of the house, hoping to draw the attention of any observers they missed. At this point, if there was one, the jig was already up. But by the time the queen's forces could react, it would be too late. If someone came looking for Hastings and company before sunrise, the guards had instructions to allow them in and let them look around. Everyone who wasn't supposed to be there would be long gone.

Stepping into the now very crowded barn, Max found Hastings waiting at the front of the group. As Blake had mentioned, his clothes were liberally splattered with blood. "Everything alright?" Max asked.

"We encountered a patrol who were unwilling to accept my assurances that my thirty guards and I were just out for a late night stroll." He looked down at his clothes. "None made enough noise to cause concern."

"Good enough." Max trusted the man to be honest in his explanation. It was, after all, his family whose lives were on the line. "Before we continue, I need two things." He held out his empty hand to Hastings, palm up, and raised an eyebrow.

After a moment of confusion, the man laughed and produced a single gold coin, placing it in Max's hand. "There we go, payment in full for services rendered." Max pocketed the coin before continuing. Placing it in an actual pocket rather than his inventory, where it would be mixed with others.

"Now, I'm going to need you all to listen carefully." He spoke loudly enough for all to hear. The barn doors were closed, and the cooks outside were happily clanking away.

"First, if there are any among you who are unwilling to swear the oath and become citizens of Stormhaven, now is the time to speak up. Raise your hand. We'll figure out some way to get you safely out of the city, then you're on your own." He waited for several breaths as the group turned and glanced at each other. When nobody took him up on the offer, he had just one more bit of business to take care of. "Before you take that oath, I'm going to ask that you each swear a separate oath never to reveal what you're about to witness here tonight. Breaking that oath may result in the deaths of many of my citizens, and the penalty from the gods will likely be severe. Again, anyone unwilling, raise your hand."

When not a single hand went up, Max nodded to Smitty who proceeded to administer both oaths. Once it was done, and Red confirmed that everyone inside the building had sworn in good faith, Max raised his arms.

"Welcome to Stormhaven! I know you have all prepared for a long and hazardous journey, but I think you'll find that your trip will be much shorter, and safer, than you'd hoped." He motioned for the doors to be opened, then led the procession out of the barn. His people were set up in two lines, funneling the visitors into the tent behind Max and Hastings.

When Max opened the flap at the back of the tent, and Hastings saw the open portal leading into Stormhaven's courtyard, he had to stifle a laugh. Turning to reassure his people and wave them through, he shook his head at a very pleased looking chimera who was doing the same on the other side of the column.

When they stepped through behind all of his people and Max's party, Hastings bowed low at the waist. His entire retinue, still surprised at being so suddenly and safely free of the city, immediately did the same. Straightening up, Hastings shook his head again in amazement. "I should have known, Majesty, that you would have arranged something like this as a contingency. I believe my former queen is badly outclassed in her conflict with you."

"Let's hope you're right." Max wholeheartedly agreed. "For now, let's get your people settled. You're welcome to reside in whichever of my properties you prefer. Redmane here will guide you all to the throne room, and inform you of what's available. There's space for you and your immediate family here in the palace, and there are enough rooms at the inns or the barracks for the rest, until you decide." He motioned toward the palace doors. "Oh, since the courtyard here was so crowded, the wagons with your supplies have been sent through another portal. They're safe where they are until you decide where you want them. Though, I'd make a decision soon. I can only keep a bunch of dwarves away from wagonloads of ale barrels for so long." His grin made it clear he was kidding.

Chapter 29

The ancient dwarf sat at a round table, glaring at the other dwarves in attendance. The table was surrounded by a dozen chairs, but only six in total were occupied. The six living Runemasters' Guild officers, rather than sit clustered at one side of the table, had elected to leave empty seats between each of them.

"Why have ye called us here, Runecarver?" The dwarf directly across the table from him growled. He looked nearly as ancient as Runecarver, as did the others. All of them were born several thousand years ago, and while they have been asleep for many of those years, they had each lived long and regrettably eventful lives. "What be important enough to risk us gatherin' in one place?"

"First, that be Grandmaster Runecarver, ye disrespectful whelp! Or simply Sage Runecarver, if the first be too much of a mouthful." His glare focused on the dwarf and intensified as he waited for the target of his ire to give a respectful bow of his head before continuing. "Have ye not read the messages from Functionary 213?"

Three of the other five shook their heads that they hadn't, having been roused from their stasis-induced slumber by loud and curse-filled demands from their master, and rushed to the meeting without checking their terminals. One nodded, but remained silent. The one who'd already spoken up replied, "Aye, I saw 'em. Some newborn king claimed a remote Guild outpost, and accidentally completed Quest 17 by killin' a lich. Good fer him. The other be a request fer a protocol exception fer some applicants." His tone made it clear he didn't think either message important enough to be awakened over, let alone so rudely summoned for an in-person meeting.

"Lazy git! Ye skimmed the messages!" Runecarver thumped the table, making everyone's mugs rattle, conveniently ignoring the fact that he'd initially done the same. "King Storm, the one who claimed the Outpost, our newest Novice, be a damned *Battleborne!*" He raised an eyebrow and watched the reactions around the table. The other five officers were definitely paying attention now.

"In addition, I have questioned the golem assigned to assist him due to the special circumstance o' his acceptance as a Novice. The three dwarven Masters that work fer him at the Outpost spoke o' him havin' *THREE* companions who *also be Battleborne*." Now the dwarves were leaning closer, hands or elbows on the table.

"They also spoke o' this Storm as bein' favored by Regin hisself, who has made at least one personal appearance at the Outpost, as well as the black dragon, Lysbane. He's earned his kingdom by right o' conquest, and declared it open to all races, except the damned greys he took it from."

Intrigued, but still annoyed at being awakened and summoned, the dwarf across the table from him turned his head and spat on the floor. "Great! Let him complete his studies and grow stronger, as any Novice would. It be yer turn to deal with this, as yer current agreed upon shift lasts fer another... eighty years?" He looked around the table and the others nodded that he was correct. When they'd voted to go into hibernation, they had allowed for the likelihood that issues would arise within the Guild that would require attention. They'd agreed that each of them would take shifts of responsibility lasting one hundred years. Runecarver was just a couple decades into his latest shift.

The Grandmaster growled in frustration. He'd hoped that by dangling those juicy bits of information, he'd fool one of the others into volunteering to teach the new novice, allowing him to return to his slumber. As the head of the guild, he could order one of them to do it, but the others would complain that he was shirking his duties, and he didn't want to hear their grumblings for another several thousand years.

He scowled across the table. "Bah! Go back to yer dreams o' drunken, overendowed troll women! Wouldn't want ye to strain the half-pickled, undersized, addlepated lump o' mush inside that skull o' yers! I'll handle this meself." He got up and stomped around a bit as each of the others gladly and hastily activated a rune on the table in front of them and were teleported back to their homes.

Sage Runecarver, third generation Grandmaster of the Runemasters' Guild, shook his head in disgust when he turned and noticed that he was alone. Producing a bottle from his inventory, he took a hefty swig. He had some decisions to make. The Guild had not accepted a new applicant in thousands of years. Those members who hadn't been seated at the table a few moments ago were all either long dead, or imprisoned in less comfortable stasis cells for the very war crimes that caused the Guild to retreat from the world, taking their secrets with them.

He and the others held out hope that one day the dwarven race would be worthy of the rune magic, and the terrible responsibility that came with it. Thus the alert system had been put in place, and the masters set to extend their lives indefinitely, prepared to take up the mantle of Guild trainers once again, should the proper opportunity arise.

Runecarver was inclined to simply open a portal to the Outpost in question, send an order for the golems to eliminate everyone they found there, including the new novice, Storm. He sat back in his seat and took another swig from the bottle. With a resigned sigh, he decided to visit the Outpost himself. It was, after all, his responsibility, if against all odds Storm and his companions were worthy, to teach them.

If he deemed them to be unworthy, well... he hadn't had a decent battle in millennia.

*****

The following morning Max accompanied Lord Hastings and most of his retinue to the Way Station, where they'd expressed an interest in settling. Most of them were not comfortable with the idea of living underground. A few were interested in the mine, and four adventurous soldiers with families asked to be stationed at the outpost north of the dworc valley. The town was expanding rapidly, the new wall completed in record time, and new structures already being built in between the two walls.

Max was just walking out of the combined tavern and town office building when he heard a shout of alarm. He and Hastings, whom he'd been introducing to the council and proposing as a new member, both spun toward the sound, swords already in hand. What they found caused the human to pause, and Max to growl as he took a threatening step forward.

Ten feet in front of him, both arms raised, one hand empty, the other missing, was the Shadow Walker that Lysbane had disarmed and sent back to deliver his non-message.

"Peace, King Storm!" The dark elf immediately called out, keeping his arms out to his sides. "I am not here for your life."

"I thought you were lying about the Shadow Walkers." Hastings whispered out of the side of his mouth. "A bold and harmless tale to add to your legend."

"Nope." Max shook his head, still laser focused on the assassin.

"Why are you here, then?" He growled at the elf, baring his fangs and putting as much menace into his tone as possible. Around them, most of his citizens were quickly taking shelter, while others were arming themselves and advancing to defend their king.

"As I said, peace. I bring a message from our new Grandmaster." He pointed toward his waist with his remaining hand. "If you'll allow me to retrieve it?"

By this time there were a dozen bows and crossbows pointed at the assassin at close range, making Max reasonably sure that if he made a move, he'd be dead before he could do any harm. He nodded at the dark elf, who instantly retrieved a scroll and held it out toward Max. When he saw Max wasn't making a move to take it, he got down onto his knees and held it out as far as he could.

"Open it and read it aloud." Max instructed. The elf shook his head.

"The contents of this message are not for the ears of everyone here, King Storm. My master was extremely insistent on that. If I am not able to deliver this to you alone, I am instructed to leave with it. We have a reputation to consider."

"You're not leaving here, with or without it." Max threatened, smiling as he heard bowstrings being drawn taught. "Lysbane gave you your life, and warned you about returning."

Max heard the elf mutter under his breath, "I should not have let him talk me into this…" before responding to Max in a louder voice. "This is not Stormhaven city, your Majesty, and I don't believe the dragon is here with you, or I would not have appeared." His smirk made Max want to explode his head. "There is no need for hostility. I have come with an opportunity. A *private* opportunity."

"No need for hostility?" Max roared, taking a step closer. "Your guild of assholesassins has tried to kill me three times! You've succeeded in killing some of my people as they fought to protect me, and I haven't had a decent night's sleep wondering when you'd be back! I'm feeling more than a little bit hostile!"

"I see your point." Still on his knees, the elf bowed low, his head nearly touching the ground while his arm still held out the scroll. "You have no reason to trust me, but I swear on my honor, on my own life, that I believe you'll want to read this message. The parchment is not poisoned, and presents no danger to you. Neither do I, at this time." He waved his stump around a bit as if to demonstrate that he wasn't a threat.

"King Max, please allow me." Hastings stepped toward the elf. "If it's poisoned, let it claim my life instead of yours." Even as Max ordered him to stop, the man reached out and snatched the scroll from the elf's fingers before stepping back. He didn't unroll it, simply held it in his hand and stared at it while Max cussed up a storm.

"Don't ever do that again." Max's growl caused Hastings to look up from the scroll he half expected would kill him. "I don't want any dead martyrs on my conscience. Understand me?"

"It doesn't appear to be poisoned, unless it's a very slow poison, Majesty. And yes, I understand." The man held the parchment out in one hand, sheathed his sword, then turned to face Max. Using both hands, he unrolled the scroll so that the writing was facing the ground at his feet.

When no spells or traps were set off, he offered, "I can hold it up so that you may read it without touching it."

Still angry, Max just nodded. Lord Hastings took a couple steps closer, then held up the unraveled scroll for him to read.

Max skimmed the words, then paused and went back to the beginning, reading the elegant script more carefully.

King Maximilian Storm,

The client who purchased the contract for your death has been found to have acted in bad faith, violating the terms of proper disclosure clearly outlined in our agreement. For this reason, the contract has been deemed null and void, and the client in default. Without the aforementioned contract, the Shadow Walkers' Guild has no further cause to pursue hostilities against you, barring further acts of aggression on your part.

It was unsigned, which came as no surprise to Max. He kept his expression under control, even as his thoughts raced. Was this an actual peace offering? He opened up party chat and called out to Redmane, giving a hasty update before reading the note to him. He waited for the dwarf to respond to his unvoiced question even as Smitty and the others who'd overheard began to cheer through the chat.

While he was waiting, he motioned for Hastings to close the scroll and looked at the assassin. "What happens to clients who default?"

"A wide range of penalties, depending on the severity of the offense, from a steep monetary penalty equal to double the contract fee, to more… permanent measures. In this case, their gross failure to disclose certain vital details has resulted in significant losses for the guild. I expect they were dead before I arrived here today."

"Details… like?" Max played for time. The elf just stared at him, face blank, clearly unwilling or unable to respond.

"And if another comes to you with a contract for my death?"

The elf considered his words carefully for a moment. "Few can afford the services of myself and my associates. Far, far fewer could afford, or would be willing to spend, the resources it would take for the Guild to undertake a contract that involves such… risk."

Now standing next to him, Hastings snorted as Max relayed the elf's exact words through party chat. A moment later Redmane responded.

"Aye, it sounds like they mean to leave ye alone, Max. Though I hesitate to say it, I think ye should let him go in peace. Takin' his head might be considered an act o' further aggression on yer part."

Max motioned for the dark elf to rise, then took a step closer and spoke quietly. "You may return to your new master. Tell him two things. First, I consider the hostilities between us to be concluded as suggested. Second, tell him I said he's welcome for the unexpected promotion."

The dark elf smirked at that, then nodded his head in agreement. "I shall relay your message. May you sleep well, live long, and prosper." He slowly turned his back on Max and walked toward the gate, passing through the ring of guards as Max waved for them to let him through. A dozen of them turned and followed him, weapons at the ready, until he exited the gate. At which point he dropped a smoke bomb and disappeared.

Still standing next to Max and holding the scroll, Hastings asked, "Would you mind if I…" He motioned toward the scroll with his free hand.

"Knock yourself out." Max replied, then clarified when the man looked confused. "Uh, that means go right ahead where I'm from."

Hastings quickly read the scroll, then laughed aloud. "Well, I must say that I'm certainly glad that I chose your side, sire." He handed the scroll to Max, who made it disappear into his inventory. Max briefly considered posting it in the throne room as another trophy, but decided it might annoy the guild enough to resume hostilities. "Any man… er… chimera who could force the Shadow Walkers to back down is not someone I would choose to confront."

"Next time you have tea with your former queen, maybe point that out to her." Max grinned at the man, trying to shake off the fear and adrenaline that had him trembling slightly. Hastings just snorted again.

*****

Six of the highest level orc shamans in the city gathered in a circle around An'zalor and the bed he reclined in. It had taken significant time, effort, and the life of one apprentice who hadn't taken a millipede viper seriously enough, but they'd managed to gather the components needed.

Impatient as ever, the war chief snarled at them as they placed items on the ground and arranged themselves around him at the proscribed distances. At a nod from the lead shaman, they all raised their staffs and began to chant. He began his own chant in counterpoint to theirs, concentrating on the rhythm and proper wording as he held his own staff aloft, while executing elaborate gestures with his free hand.

In the center of the circle, a green glow began to suffuse An'zalor's body. Clearly nervous, he examined his hands, then propped himself up to look down at his severed leg. A moment later, as the magic sank into his flesh, he grunted in pain. The grunt quickly evolved into a moan, then an outright roar of pain as he tried to sit up and grab the leg.

The shaman was tempted to shout at him to lay back, to keep from interfering in the ritual, but he couldn't stop his chant without breaking the ritual.

He wasn't about to risk the consequences of the failure.

An'zalor had been warned several times to hold still during the healing, no matter how much it hurt. The shaman had never had a limb regrown himself, but he imagined it did not feel good. Watching the orc chief struggle, while maintaining the rhythm of his chant, he half hoped An'zalor would roll off the narrow bed and out of the circle, a misstep that would likely end his life. That would solve a lot of problems for a lot of people.

Unfortunately, though the massive orc thrashed and wailed, he remained mostly in place atop the bed. All the shamans, and the warriors present as bodyguards to ensure their chief wasn't murdered, watched with fascination as the leg began to regrow. First the bone extended outward from the stump, then muscles and blood vessels began to wind around it. A couple of the warriors looked ill, and quickly stepped outside to empty their bellies. Three of the shamans didn't look much better, but they grimly held their places and maintained the ritual, knowing that failure meant death.

By the time the ankle was complete and the foot was starting to form, the shamans' legs were beginning to wobble from the strain of the mana drain. All but the leader had lowered the butts of their staffs to the ground and were using them as crutches to keep themselves on their feet. Still they chanted, and still they pushed mana through the focus of their staff to fuel the healing ritual.

The weakest among the shamans dropped to his knees as the toes were being regrown, stopping the chant momentarily as he gasped for air. The flow of mana from his staff ceased abruptly, increasing the strain on the others, who promptly collapsed as well, croaking out their chant as best they could. But the damage was done. The ritual halted.

Feeling the pain subside, An'zalor sat up, panting from the exertion, and stared down at his regrown limb. It was nearly perfect, with only his smallest toe incomplete. Instead of a fully formed toe, there was a white bone sticking out of flesh that only reached its base.

"Finish it!" He roared as he looked up from his foot to see the shamans were all prone on the floor, several of them unconscious. The lead shaman lifted his head and shook it. "We are spent, War Chief. There is nothing more we can do."

"No!" An'zalor leapt off the bed, ripping a sword from a sheath on one of the warrior's backs. "Finish the ritual!"

Again the shaman shook his head before allowing it to drop back to the floor with a thump. "We are spent, the components are used up. You will have to wait..." He never finished the sentence as An'zalor stepped toward the nearest collapsed shaman.

"No!" He stabbed downward, piercing the unconscious orc's heart. "You. Will. Continue!" With each word he executed another helpless shaman.

When he stood above the lead shaman and raised his sword, eyes wide and saliva drooling everywhere, the exhausted shaman raised his head in defiance. "May the gods turn from you for the dishonor and shame you have brought upon our people! May they strike you down, and leave your corpse for the worms!"

Furious, the war chief held back his blow, shifting to one side for a better angle before striking with a downward slash that decapitated the shaman. With a roar of frustration and rage, he stomped toward the door, limping slightly and staring down at his half-grown toe. "Ready the army! We march at sunrise!" He stormed through the door and down the hall, which is why he didn't hear one of this captains very quietly reply. "All hail An'zalor Nine-toes!"

The others snickered even more quietly.

*****

As An'zalor's army marched north the following morning, the war chief himself at the head of the column riding the largest and most vicious of ja'kangs, Max was getting up from an overnight study session in the conference room at Outpost 42. He and Redmane had been taking the opportunity to peruse the instruction manual while Enoch and Spellslinger slept.

Max felt the need to stretch his legs, had exited the building, and was wondering whether breakfast was being served yet, when one of the guards behind a nearby building let out a yelp of surprise.

Assuming that the assassins had been deceitful, and were attacking, Max drew his sword and charged around the corner. Instead of finding dark elves butchering a guard, he found the dwarf staring eyes wide, mouth agape, at the nearest wall.

Where the portal had just opened.

Max quickly sheathed his sword and stepped past the nervous dwarf guard even as he reached out to Spellslinger, Redmane, and Enoch via one of his rings. Ahead of him, the oldest looking dwarf Max had ever seen was striding with purpose through the portal.

He wore chainmail armor over a black robe embroidered with silver runes, and steel-clad boots, but no helm covered his head as he glared at Max, muttering something. The muttering quickly became shouting as the portal closed behind him. "Where in the deepest hells be Maximilian Storm?!" His gaze took in Max and his 'comfy clothes' for the briefest of instant's before dismissing him and turning to the dwarf guard, raising one impatient eyebrow.

"I'm Max." Max stated as he came to a halt since the dwarf was already advancing rapidly toward him. Or rather, toward the guard. His heart began pounding, since this visitor, coming through that particular portal, had to be a guild member. Which meant he was also a real live Runemaster.

At his words, though, the newcomer came to a stop. "Ye claim ta be the new novice? Bah! Ye ain't even a fickin' dwarf!"

"A condition I have often regretted." Max, despite his pounding pulse and sweaty palms, focused on acting calmer than he felt. "I am Maximilian Storm, King of Stormhaven, and recently accepted Novice of the Runemasters' Guild, at your service." He bowed his head to the dwarf, unsure of the proper protocol in the confusing situation.

The ancient dwarf stared at him for a moment, eyes unfocused and obviously reading the results of *Examining* him. When he'd apparently seen what he needed to, he shook his head.

"By Durin's hairy stones! The first new novice in an elf's age, and ye ain't even a damned dwarf! Ha! Big fella, ain't ya?" He tilted his head back, looking up at Max from just a step away. His next utterance was delayed as he was distracted by the three masters racing up behind Max, Spellslinger still struggling to fasten the buttons on his robe.

"Ah, and these would be the three that completed the lich quest with ye? The three wantin' to be novices?" He raised a judgmental eyebrow as the three elder dwarves came to a halt next to Max.

"Masters Enoch, Redmane, and Spellslinger." Max confirmed. "I'm sorry, I do not know your-"

"I be Sage Runecarver." the dwarf cut him off, once again ignoring him in favor of the three masters. "Grandmaster o' the Runemaster's Guild!" He thumped his chest with a scarred fist, glaring at the three dwarves who were suddenly on their knees with heads bowed. "Bah! Get to yer feet! I ain't no Eternal come to judge ye!" The three dwarves scrambled back to their feet. Spellslinger, obviously hung over, stumbled slightly as he stepped on the hem of his robe.

A rapid thumping of stone on stone preceded the appearance of Funky, who moved surprisingly quickly toward the group. Stopping a respectful distance from the angry dwarf, Funky bowed deeply at the waist. "Grandmaster! It is an honor to speak with you. Are you here regarding my queries?"

"Aye, the foolish shenanigans here, strangers claimin' this outpost, tryin' ta skip the normal process o' joinin' me guild, demandin' quest rewards…" He turned and scowled up at Max, taking a step back so he could stretch his neck a bit less. "Gimme two good reasons I shouldn't just tell the battle golems behind me to stomp the whole sorry lot o' ye flat fer wastin' me precious time, and go back to me nap?" He turned and stomped several steps away before turning back. "What makes any o' ye think yerselves worthy o' the rune magic?"

*** End Book Four ***

Acknowledgements

As always, a big thank you to my family for encouraging me when I'm in a slump, for forgiving the frustrated growls and snarls, and for offering their wisdom, typo-killing expertise, and just general support.

For semi-regular updates on books, art, and just stuff going on, check out my Greystone Guild fb page https://www.facebook.com/greystone.guild.7 or my website www.davewillmarth.com where you can subscribe for an eventual newsletter. Or you can follow me on that friggin Instagram thing at www.instagram.com/davewillmarth. For lots of LitRPG info, and to chat with other authors, join my new LitRPG and GameLit Readers Facebook group https://www.facebook.com/groups/940262549853662/

And don't forget to follow my author page on Amazon! **That way you'll get a nice friendly email when new books are released**. You can also find links to my Greystone Chronicles, Shadow Sun, and Dark Elf books there! https://www.amazon.com/Dave-Willmarth/e/B076G12KCL

PLEASE TAKE A MOMENT TO LEAVE A REVIEW!

Reviews on Amazon and Goodreads are vitally important to indie authors like me. Amazon won't help market the books until they reach a certain level of reviews. So please, take a few seconds, click on that (fifth!) star and type a few words about how much you liked the book! I would appreciate it very much. I do read the reviews, and a few of my favorites have led to friendships and even character cameos! There were several in this book.

Thanks to Gianpiero Mangliardi for the great cover art!